ACCLAIM FOR
MICHAEL CONNELLY'S
SIZZLING THRILLERS
FEATURING JACK McEVOY

THE SCARECROW

"A masterful narrative...Connelly has always been frank about his admiration for Raymond Chandler. It's a high bar to set for oneself, but he comes as close to clearing it as any mystery writer of his generation...One of the masters of contemporary crime fiction...His best work since *The Poet*."
—*Los Angeles Times*

"A return to form for Mr. Connelly...Pivots energetically among its subplots, often returning affectionately to the newspaper world."
—*New York Times*

"*The Scarecrow* is great Connelly...A page-turning thriller—cleverly plotted, fast-paced, and crisply written... surpassing *The Poet* as his finest."
—*Associated Press*

"Exquisitely plotted...With its ingenious story line and the twisted brilliance of the creeps involved, *The Scarecrow* holds its own with its predecessor."
—*Washington Post*

"A thriller, and a terrific one at that...Absorbing...An addictive read that, once it grabs you in those first few pages, won't let go of you."
—*Boston Globe*

"One of the best parts of *The Scarecrow* is the detailed, behind-the-scenes look at the newspaper business that the author provides. A former reporter for the *Los Angeles Times* (among other papers), Connelly is in a rare position to take readers into the newsroom, and the picture he paints is a bleak one, filled with compromises, uncertainty, and the erosion of a once-proud tradition of journalism."

—*Chicago Sun-Times*

"Swift and engrossing." —*Boston Phoenix*

"[Fans] should not miss *The Scarecrow*...Connelly makes timely, pertinent points about American society within a rousingly good crime yarn." —*Columbus Dispatch*

THE POET

"Infernally ingenious...An irresistibly readable thriller."
—*New York Times*

"Chilling...Connelly puts his foot on the gas and doesn't let up...The author roars through the final one hundred pages of the book delivering twists, turns, and thrills in every paragraph...This guy writes commercial fiction so well, he's going to end up on the 'literature' shelves along with Poe if he plays his cards right, and here's one reader who hopes he does."
—*Los Angeles Times*

"An intriguing new protagonist...Connelly doesn't just talk about poets, he writes like one, with a spare, elegiac tone that is the perfect voice for the haunting tale he has to tell."
—*People*

MICHAEL CONNELLY

THE SCARECROW

GRAND CENTRAL
PUBLISHING

NEW YORK   BOSTON

Grand Central Publishing
Hachette Book Group
1290 Avenue of the Americas, New York, NY 10104
grandcentralpublishing.com
twitter.com/grandcentralpub

Originally published in hardcover and ebook by Little, Brown and Company in May 2009
First trade paperback edition: September 2018

Grand Central Publishing is a division of Hachette Book Group, Inc. The Grand Central Publishing name and logo is a trademark of Hachette Book Group, Inc.

The publisher is not responsible for websites (or their content) that are not owned by the publisher.

The Hachette Speakers Bureau provides a wide range of authors for speaking events. To find out more, go to hachettespeakersbureau.com or call (866) 376-6591.

Library of Congress Control Number: 2009000855

ISBNs: 978-1-4789-4829-2 (trade paperback), 978-1-4789-4828-5 (oversize mass market reissue), 978-0-316-07345-5 (ebook)

Printed in the United States of America

LSC-H

10 9 8 7 6 5 4 3 2 1

To James Crumley,
for *The Last Good Kiss*

ONE: The Farm

C arver paced in the control room, watching over the front forty. The towers were spread out before him in perfect neat rows. They hummed quietly and efficiently and even with all he knew, Carver had to marvel at what technology had wrought. So much in so little space. Not a stream but a swift and torrid river of data flowing by him every day. Growing in front of him in tall steel stalks. All he needed to do was to reach in, to look and to choose. It was like panning for gold.

But it was easier.

He checked the overhead temperature gauges. All was perfect in the server room. He lowered his eyes to the screens on the workstations in front of him. His three engineers worked in concert on the current project. An attempted breach thwarted by Carver's skill and readiness. Now the reckoning.

The would-be intruder could not penetrate the walls of the farmhouse, but he had left his fingerprints all over it. Carver smiled as he watched his men retrieve the bread crumbs, tracing the IP address through the traffic nodes, a high-speed chase back to the source. Soon Carver would know who his opponent was, what firm he was with, what he had been looking for and the advantage he hoped to gain. And Carver would take a retaliatory action that would leave the hapless contender crumpled and destroyed. Carver showed no mercy. Ever.

The mantrap alert buzzed from overhead.

"Screens," Carver said.

The three young men at the workstations typed commands in unison, which hid their work from the visitors. The control room door opened and McGinnis stepped in with a man in a suit. Carver had never seen him before.

"This is our control room and through the windows there, you see what we call the 'front forty,'" McGinnis said. "All of our colocation services are centered here. This is primarily where your firm's material would be held. We have forty towers in here holding close to a thousand dedicated servers. And, of course, there's room for more. We'll never run out of room."

The man in the suit nodded thoughtfully.

"I'm not worried about room. Our concern is security."

"Yes, this is why we stepped in here. I wanted you to meet Wesley Carver. Wesley wears a number of hats around here. He is our chief technology officer as well as our top threat engineer and the designer of the data center. He can tell you all you need to know about colocation security."

Another dog and pony show. Carver shook the suit's hand. He was introduced as David Wyeth of the St. Louis law firm Mercer and Gissal. It sounded like crisp white shirts and tweed. Carver noticed that Wyeth had a barbecue stain on his tie. Whenever they came into town McGinnis took them to eat at Rosie's Barbecue.

Carver gave Wyeth the show by rote, covering everything and saying everything the silk-stocking lawyer wanted to hear. Wyeth was on a barbecue-and-due-diligence mission. He would go back to St. Louis and report on how impressed he had been. He would tell them that this was the way to go if the firm wanted to keep up with changing technologies and times.

And McGinnis would get another contract.

All the while he spoke, Carver was thinking about the intruder they had been chasing. Out there somewhere, not expecting the comeuppance that was speeding toward him. Carver and his young disciples would loot his personal bank accounts, take his identity and hide photos of men having sex with eight-year-old boys on his work computer. Then he would crash it with a replicating virus. When the intruder couldn't fix it he would call in an expert. The photos would be found and the police would be called.

The intruder would no longer be a concern. Another threat kept away by the Scarecrow.

"Wesley?" McGinnis said.

Carver came out of the reverie. The suit had asked a question. Carver had already forgotten his name.

"Excuse me?"

"Mr. Wyeth asked if the colocation center had ever been breached."

McGinnis was smiling, already knowing the answer.

"No, sir, we've never been breached. To be honest, there have been a few attempts. But they have failed, resulting in disastrous consequences for those who tried."

The suit nodded somberly.

"We represent the cream of the crop of St. Louis," he said. "The integrity of our files and our client list is paramount to all we do. That's why I came here personally."

That and the strip club McGinnis took you to, Carver thought but didn't say. He smiled instead but there was no warmth in it. He was glad McGinnis had reminded him of the suit's name.

"Don't worry, Mr. Wyeth," he said. "Your crops will be safe on this farm."

Wyeth smiled back.

"That's what I wanted to hear," he said.

TWO: The Velvet Coffin

Every eye in the newsroom followed me as I left Kramer's office and walked back to my pod. The long looks made it a long walk. The pink slips always came out on Fridays and they all knew I had just gotten *the word*. Except they weren't called pink slips anymore. Now it was an RIF form—as in Reduction in Force.

They all felt the slightest tingle of relief that it hadn't been them and the slightest tingle of anxiety because they still knew that no one was safe. Any one of them could be called in next.

I met no one's stare as I passed beneath the Metro sign and headed back into podland. I moved into my cubicle and slipped into my seat, dropping from sight like a soldier diving into a foxhole.

Immediately my phone buzzed. On the read-out I saw that it was my friend Larry Bernard calling. He was only two cubicles away but knew if he had come to me in person it would have been a clear signal for others in the newsroom to crowd around me and ask the obvious. Reporters work best in packs like that.

I put on my headset and picked up the call.

"Hey, Jack," he said.

"Hey, Larry," I said.

"So?"

"So what?"

"What did Kramer want?"

He pronounced the assistant managing editor's name *Crammer,* which was the nickname bestowed on Richard Kramer years earlier when he was an assignment editor more concerned with the quantity than the quality of news he got his reporters to produce for the paper. Other variations of his full or partial name evolved over time as well.

"You know what he wanted. He gave me notice. I'm out of here."

"Holy fucking shit, you got pinked!"

"That's right. But remember, we call it 'involuntary separation' now."

"Do you have to clear out right now? I'll help you."

"No, I've got two weeks. May twenty-second and I'm history."

"Two weeks? Why two weeks?"

Most RIF victims had to clear out immediately. This edict was instated after one of the first recipients of a layoff notice was allowed to stay through the pay period. Each of his last days, people saw him in the office carrying a tennis ball. Bouncing it, tossing it, squeezing it. They didn't realize that each day it was a different ball. And each day he flushed a ball down the toilet in the men's room. About a week after he was gone the pipes backed up, with devastating consequences.

"They gave me extra time if I agreed to train my replacement."

Larry was silent for a moment as he considered the humiliation of having to train one's own replacement. But to me two weeks' pay was two weeks' pay I wouldn't get if I didn't take the deal. And besides that, the two weeks would give me time to say proper good-byes to those in the newsroom and on the beat who deserved them. I considered the alternative of being walked out the door by security with a cardboard box of personal belongings even more humiliating. I was sure they would watch me to make sure I wasn't carrying tennis balls to work, but they didn't have to worry. That wasn't my style.

"So that's it? That's all he said? Two weeks and you're out?"

"He shook my hand and said I was a handsome guy, that I should try TV."

"Oh, man. We gotta get drunk tonight."

"I am, that's for sure."

"Man, this ain't right."

"The world ain't right, Larry."

"Who's your replacement? At least that's somebody who knows they're safe."

"Angela Cook."

"Figures. The cops are going to love her."

Larry was a friend but I didn't want to be talking about all of this with him right now. I needed to be thinking about my options. I straightened up in my seat and looked over the top of the four-foot walls of the cubicle. I saw no one still looking at me. I glanced toward the row of glass-walled editors' offices. Kramer's was a corner office and he was standing behind the glass, looking out at the newsroom. When his eyes came to mine he quickly kept them moving.

"What are you going to do?" Larry asked.

"I haven't thought about it but I'm about to right now. Where do you want to go, Big Wangs or the Short Stop?"

"Short Stop. I was at Wangs last night."

"See you there, then."

I was about to hang up when Larry blurted out a last question.

"One more thing. Did he say what number you were?"

Of course. He wanted to know what his own chances were of surviving this latest round of corporate blood-letting.

"When I went in he started talking about how I almost made it and how hard it was to make the last choices. He said I was ninety-nine."

Two months earlier the newspaper announced that one hundred employees would be eliminated from the editorial staff in order to cut costs and make our corporate gods happy. I let Larry think for a moment about who might be number one hundred while I glanced at Kramer's office again. He was still there behind the glass.

"So my coaching tip is to keep your head down, Larry. The axman's standing at the glass looking for number one hundred right now."

I hit the disconnect button but kept the headset on. This would hopefully discourage anybody in the newsroom from approaching me. I had no doubt that Larry Bernard would start telling other reporters that I had been involuntarily separated and they would come to commiserate. I had to concentrate on finishing a short on the arrest of a suspect in a murder-for-hire plot uncovered by the Los Angeles Police Department's Robbery-Homicide Division. Then I could disappear from the newsroom and head to the bar to toast the end of my career in daily journalism. Because that's what it was going to be. There was no newspaper out there in the market for an over-forty cop shop reporter. Not when they had an endless supply of cheap labor—baby reporters like Angela Cook minted fresh every year at USC and Medill and Columbia, all of them technologically savvy and willing to work for next to nothing. Like the paper and ink newspaper itself, my time was over. It was about the Internet now. It was about hourly uploads to online editions and blogs. It was about television tie-ins and Twitter updates. It was about filing stories *on* your phone instead of using it to call rewrite. The morning paper might as well be called the *Daily Afterthought*. Everything in it was posted on the web the night before.

My phone buzzed in my ear and I was about to guess it would be my ex-wife, having already heard the news in the Washington bureau, but the caller ID said VELVET COFFIN. I had to admit I was shocked. I knew Larry could not have gotten the word out that fast. Against my better judgment I took the call. As expected, the caller was Don Goodwin, self-appointed watchdog and chronicler of the inner workings of the *L.A. Times*.

"I just heard," he said.

"When?"

"Just now."

"How? I just found out myself less than five minutes ago."

"Come on, Jack, you know I can't reveal. But I've got the place wired. You just walked out of Kramer's office. You made the thirty list."

The "thirty list" was a reference to those who had been lost over the years in the downsizing of the paper. *Thirty* was old-time newspaper code for "end of story." Goodwin himself was on the list. He had worked at the *Times* and was on the fast track as an editor until a change of ownership brought a change in financial philosophy. When he objected to doing more with less he was cut down at the knees and ended up taking one of the first buyouts offered. That was back when they offered substantial payments to those who would voluntarily leave the company—before the media company that owned the *Times* filed for bankruptcy protection.

Goodwin took his payout and set up shop with a website and a blog that covered everything that moved inside the *Times*. He called it thevelvetcoffin.com as a grim reminder of what the paper used to be: a place to work so pleasurable that you would easily slip in and stay till you died. With the constant changes of ownership and management, the layoffs, and the ever-dwindling staff and budget, the place was now becoming more of a pine box. And Goodwin was there to chronicle every step and misstep of its fall.

His blog was updated almost daily and was avidly and

secretly read by everybody in the newsroom. I wasn't sure much of the world beyond the thick bomb-proof walls of the *Times* even cared. The *Times* was going the way of all journalism and that wasn't news. Even the *New York By God Times* was feeling the pinch caused by the shift of society to the Internet for news and advertising. The stuff Goodwin wrote about and was calling me about amounted to little more than rearranging deck chairs on the *Titanic*.

But in another two weeks it wouldn't matter to me. I was moving on and already thinking about the half-started, half-assed novel I had in my computer. I was going to pull that baby out as soon as I got home. I knew I could milk my savings for at least six months and after that I could live off the equity in my house—what was left of it after the recent slide—if I needed to. I could also downsize my car and save on gas by getting one of those hybrid tin cans everybody in town was driving.

I was already beginning to see my shove out the door as an opportunity. Deep down, every journalist wants to be a novelist. It's the difference between art and craft. Every writer wants to be considered an artist and I was now going to take my shot at it. The half novel I had sitting at home—the plot of which I couldn't even correctly remember—was my ticket.

"Are you out the door today?" Goodwin asked.

"No, I got a couple weeks if I agreed to train my replacement. I agreed."

"How fucking noble of them. Don't they allow anybody any dignity over there anymore?"

"Hey, it beats walking out with a cardboard box today. Two weeks' pay is two weeks' pay."

"But do you think that's fair? How long have you been there? Six, seven years, and they give you two weeks?"

He was trying to draw an angry quote from me. I was a reporter. I knew how it worked. He wanted something juicy he could put in the blog. But I wasn't biting. I told Goodwin I had no further comment for the Velvet Coffin, at least not until I was permanently out the door. He wasn't satisfied with that answer and kept trying to pry a comment out of me until I heard the call-on-hold beep in my ear. I looked at the caller ID and saw xxxxx on the screen. This told me the call had come through the switchboard rather than from a caller who had my direct number. Lorene, the newsroom operator I could see on duty in the booth, would have been able to tell I was on my line, so her decision to park a call on it rather than take the message could only mean the caller had convinced her that the call was important.

I cut Goodwin off.

"Look, Don, I've got no comment and I need to go. I've got another call."

I pushed the button before he could take a third swing at getting me to discuss my employment situation.

"This is Jack McEvoy," I said after switching over.

Silence.

"Hello, this is Jack McEvoy. How can I help you?"

Call me biased but I immediately identified the person who replied as female, black and uneducated.

"McEvoy? When you goin' to tell the truth, McEvoy?"

"Who is this?"

"You tellin' lies, McEvoy, in your paper."

I wished it *was* my paper.

"Ma'am, if you want to tell me who you are and what your complaint is about, I'll listen. Otherwise, I'm—"

"They now sayin' Mizo is'n adult and what kinda shit is that? He did'n kill no whore."

Immediately I knew it was one of those calls. Those calls on behalf of the "innocent." The mother or girlfriend who had to tell me how wrong my story was. I got them all the time but not for too much longer. I resigned myself to handling this call as quickly and politely as possible.

"Who is Mizo?"

"Zo. *My Zo.* My son, Alonzo. He ain' guilty a nothin' and he ain't no adult."

I knew that was what she was going to say. They are never guilty. No one calls you up to say you got it right or the police got it right and their son or their husband or their boyfriend is guilty of the charges. No one calls you from jail to tell you they did it. Everybody is innocent. The only thing I didn't understand about the call was the name. I hadn't written about anybody named Alonzo—I would have remembered.

"Ma'am, do you have the right person here? I don't think I wrote about Alonzo."

"Sure you did. I got your name right here. You said he stuffed her in the trunk and that's some motherfuckin' shit right there."

Then it came together. The trunk murder from last

week. It was a six-inch short because nobody on the desk was all that interested. Juvenile drug dealer strangles one of his customers and puts her body in the trunk of her own car. It was a black-on-white crime but still the desk didn't care, because the victim was a drug user. Both she and her killer were marginalized by the paper. You start cruising down to South L.A. to buy heroin or rock cocaine and what happens happens. You won't get any sympathy from the gray lady on Spring Street. There isn't much space in the paper for that. Six inches inside is all you're worth and all you get.

I realized I didn't know the name Alonzo because I had never been given it in the first place. The suspect was sixteen years old and the cops didn't give out the names of arrested juveniles.

I flipped through the stack of newspapers on the right side of my desk until I found the Metro section from two Tuesdays back. I opened it to page four and looked at the story. It wasn't long enough to carry a byline. But the desk had put my name as a tagline at the bottom. Otherwise I wouldn't have gotten the call. Lucky me.

"Alonzo is your son," I said. "And he was arrested two Sundays ago for the murder of Denise Babbit, is that correct?"

"I told you that is motherfucking bullshit."

"Yes, but that's the story we're talking about. Right?"

"That's right, and when are you goin' to write about the truth?"

"The truth being that your son is innocent."

"That's right. You got it wrong and now they say he's going to be tried as an adult and he only sixteen years old. How can they do that to a boy?"

"What is Alonzo's last name?"

"Winslow."

"Alonzo Winslow. And you are Mrs. Winslow?"

"No, I am not," she said indignantly. "You goin' put my name in the paper now with a mess a lies?"

"No, ma'am. I just want to know who I am talking to, that's all."

"Wanda Sessums. I don't want my name in no paper. I want you to write the truth is all. You ruin his reputation calling him a murderer like that."

Reputation was a hot-button word when it came to redressing wrongs committed by a newspaper, but I almost laughed as I scanned the story I had written.

"I said he was arrested for the murder, Mrs. Sessums. That is not a lie. That is accurate."

"He arrested but he didn' do it. The boy wouldn't hurt a fly."

"Police said he had an arrest record going back to twelve years old for selling drugs. Is that a lie, too?"

"He on the corners, yeah, but that don't mean he go an' kill nobody. They pinnin' a rap on him and you jes' along for the ride with your eyes closed nice and tight."

"The police said that he confessed to killing the woman and putting her body in the trunk."

"That's a damn lie! He did no such thing."

I didn't know if she was referring to the murder or the

confession but it didn't matter. I had to get off. I looked at my screen and saw I had six e-mails waiting. They had all come in since I had walked out of Kramer's office. The digital vultures were circling. I wanted to end this call and pass it and everything else off to Angela Cook. Let her deal with all the crazy and misinformed and ignorant callers. Let her have it all.

"Okay, Mrs. Winslow, I'll—"

"It's Sessums, I told you! You see how you gettin' things wrong all a time?"

She had me there. I paused for a moment before speaking.

"I'm sorry, Mrs. Sessums. I've taken some notes here and I will look into this and if there is something I can write about, then I will certainly call you. Meantime, best of luck to you and—"

"No, you won't."

"I won't what?"

"You won't call me."

"I said I would call you if I—"

"You didn't even ask me for my number! You don' care. You just a bullshit motherfucker like the rest a them and my boy goes to prison for somethin' he dint do."

She hung up on me. I sat motionless for a moment, thinking about what she had said about me, then tossed the Metro section back on the stack. I looked down at the notebook in front of my keyboard. I hadn't taken any notes and that supposedly ignorant woman had me pegged on that, too.

I leaned back in my chair and studied the contents of my cubicle. A desk, a computer, a phone and two shelves stacked with files, notebooks and newspapers. A red leather-bound dictionary so old and well used that the *Webster's* had been worn off its spine. My mother had given it to me when I told her I wanted to be a writer.

It was all I really had left after twenty years in journalism. All I would take with me at the end of the two weeks that had any meaning was that dictionary.

"Hi, Jack."

I turned from my reverie to look up at the lovely face of Angela Cook. I didn't know her but I knew her: a fresh hire from a top-flight school. She was what they call a *mojo*—a mobile journalist nimbly able to file from the field via any electronic means. She could file text and photos for the website or paper, or video and audio for television and radio partners. She was trained to do it all but in practice she was still as green as can be. She was probably being paid $500 a week less than me, and in today's newspaper economy that made her a greater value to the company. Never mind the stories that would be missed because she had no sources. Never mind how many times she would be set up and manipulated by the police brass, who knew an opportunity when they saw it.

She was probably a short-timer anyway. She'd get a few years' experience, get some decent bylines, and move on to bigger things, law school or politics, maybe a job in TV. But Larry Bernard was right. She was a beauty, with blond hair over green eyes and full lips. The cops were going to love seeing her around headquarters. It would take no more than a week before they forgot about me.

"Hi, Angela."

"Mr. Kramer said I should come over."

They were moving quickly. I had gotten pinked no more than fifteen minutes earlier and already my replacement had come knocking.

"Tell you what," I said. "It's Friday afternoon, Angela, and I just got laid off. So let's not start this now. Let's get together on Monday morning, okay? We can meet for coffee and then I'll take you around Parker Center to meet some people. Will that be okay?"

"Yeah, sure. And, um, sorry, you know?"

"Thank you, Angela, but it's okay. I think it'll end up being the best thing for me anyway. But if you're still feeling sorry for me you could come over to the Short Stop tonight and buy me a drink."

She smiled and got embarrassed because she and I both knew that wasn't going to happen. Inside the newsroom and out, the new generation didn't mix with the old. Especially not with me. I was history and she had no time or inclination to associate with the ranks of the fallen. Going to the Short Stop tonight would be like visiting a leper colony.

"Well, maybe some other time," I said quickly. "I'll see you Monday morning, okay?"

"Monday morning. And I'll buy the coffee."

She smiled and I realized that she was indeed the one who should take Kramer's advice and try TV.

She turned to go.

"Oh, and Angela?"

"What?"

"Don't call him Mr. Kramer. This is a newsroom, not

a law firm. And most of those guys in charge? They don't deserve to be called mister. Remember that and you'll do okay here."

She smiled again and left me alone. I pulled my chair in close to my computer and opened a new document. I had to crank out a murder story before I could get out of the newsroom and go drown my sorrows in red wine.

Only three other reporters showed up for my wake. Larry Bernard and two guys from the sports desk who might have gone to the Short Stop regardless of my being there. If Angela Cook had shown up it would have been embarrassing.

The Short Stop was on Sunset in Echo Park. That made it close to Dodger Stadium, so presumably it drew its name from the baseball position. It was also close to the Los Angeles Police Academy and that made it a cop bar in its early years. It was the kind of place you'd read about in Joseph Wambaugh novels, where cops came to be with their own kind and the groupies who didn't judge them. But those days were long past. Echo Park was changing. It was getting Hollywood hip and the cops were crowded out of the Short Stop by the young professionals moving into the neighborhood. The prices went up and the cops found other watering holes. Police paraphernalia still hung on the walls but any cop who stopped in nowadays was simply misinformed.

Still, I liked the place because it was close to downtown and on the way to my house in Hollywood.

It was early, so we had our pick of the stools at the bar.

We took the four directly in front of the TV; me, then Larry, and then Shelton and Romano, the two sports guys. I didn't know them that well, so it was just as well that Larry was between us. They spent most of the time talking about a rumor that all of the sports beats at the paper were going to be shuffled. They were hoping to get a piece of the Dodgers or the Lakers, the premier beats at the paper, with USC football and UCLA basketball close behind. They were good writers like most sports reporters have to be. The art of sports writing always amazed me. Nine out of ten times the reader already knows the outcome of your story before reading it. They know who won, they probably even watched the game. But they read about it anyway and you have to find a way to write with an insight and angle that makes it seem fresh.

I liked covering the cop shop because usually I was telling the reader a story they didn't know. I was writing about the bad things that can happen. Life in extremis. The underworld that people sitting at their breakfast table with their toast and coffee have never experienced but want to know about. It gave me a certain juice, made me feel like a prince of the city when I drove home at night.

And I knew as I sat there nursing a glass of cheap red wine that I would miss that most about the job.

"You know what I heard," Larry said to me, his head turned from the sports guys so he could be confidential.

"No, what?"

"That during one of the buyouts in Baltimore this one

guy took the check and on his last day he filed a story that turned out to be completely bogus. He just made the whole thing up."

"And they printed it?"

"Yeah, they didn't know until they started getting calls the next day."

"What was the story about?"

"I don't know but it was like a big 'fuck you' to management."

I sipped some wine and thought about that.

"Not really," I said.

"What do you mean? Of course it was."

"I mean the management probably sat around and nodded and said we got rid of the right guy. If you want to say 'fuck you,' then you do something that makes them think they messed up by letting you go. That tells them they should've picked somebody else."

"Yeah, is that what you're going to do?"

"No, man, I'm just going to go quietly into that good night. I'm going to get a novel published and that will be my fuck-you. In fact, that's the working title. *Fuck You, Kramer.*"

"Right!"

Bernard laughed and we changed the subject. But while I was talking about other things I was thinking about the big fuck-you. I was thinking about the novel I was going to restart and finally finish. I wanted to go home and start writing. I thought maybe it would help me get through the next two weeks if I had it to go home to each night.

My cell phone rang and I saw it was my ex-wife calling. I knew I had to get this one over with. I shoved off the bar stool and headed outside to the parking lot, where it would be quieter.

It was three hours ahead in Washington but the number on the caller ID was her desk phone.

"Keisha, what are you still doing at work?"

I checked my watch. It was almost seven here, almost ten there.

"I'm chasing the *Post* on a story, waiting for callbacks."

The beauty and bane of working for a West Coast paper was that the last deadline didn't come up until at least three hours after the *Washington Post* and *New York Times*—the major national competition—had gone to bed. This meant that the *L.A. Times* always had a shot at matching their scoops or pushing the lead on stories. Come morning, the *L.A. Times* could end up out front on a major story with the latest and best information. It also made the online edition must-reading in the halls of government three thousand miles from L.A.

And as one of the newest reporters in the Washington bureau, Keisha Russell was on the late shift. She was often tagged with chasing stories and pushing for the freshest details and developments.

"That sucks," I said.

"Not as bad as what I heard happened to you today."

I nodded.

"Yeah, I got downsized, Keish."

"I'm so sorry, Jack."

"Yeah, I know. Everybody is. Thanks."

It should've been clear I was in the gun sights when they didn't send me to D.C. with her two years earlier, but that was another story. A silence opened up between us and I tried to step on it.

"I'm going to pull out my novel and finish it," I said. "I've got some savings and there's got to be some equity in the house. I think I can go at least a year. I figure it's now or never."

"Yeah," Keisha said with feigned enthusiasm. "You can do it."

I knew she had found the manuscript one day when we were still together and had read it, never admitting it because if she did she would have to tell me what she thought. She wouldn't have been able to lie about it.

"Are you going to stay in L.A.?" she asked.

That was a good question. The novel was set in Colorado, where I had grown up, but I loved the energy of L.A. and didn't want to leave it.

"I haven't thought about it yet. I don't want to sell my place. The market's still so shitty. I'd rather just get an equity loan if I have to and stay put. Anyway, it's too much to think about right now. Right now I'm just celebrating the end."

"Are you at the Red Wind?"

"No, the Short Stop."

"Who's there?"

Now I was humiliated.

"Um, you know, the usual crew. Larry and some Metro types, a bunch of guys from Sports."

It was a split second before she said anything and in that hesitation she gave away that she knew I was exaggerating, if not outright lying.

"You going to be okay, Jack?"

"Yeah, sure. I just ... I just have to figure out what—"

"Jack, I'm sorry, I have one of my callbacks coming in."

Her voice was urgent. If she missed the call, there might not be another.

"Go!" I said quickly. "I'll talk to you later."

I clicked off the phone, thankful that some politician in Washington had saved me from the further embarrassment of discussing my life with my ex-wife, whose career was ascending day by day as mine sank like the sun over the smoggy landscape of Hollywood. As I shoved the phone back into my pocket I wondered if she had just made that up about getting the callback, attempting to end the embarrassment herself.

I went back into the bar and decided to get serious, ordering an Irish Car Bomb. I gulped it quickly and the Jameson's burned like hot grease going down. I grew morose watching the Dodgers start a game against the hated Giants and get shelled in the first inning.

Romano and Shelton were the first to bail and then by the third inning even Larry Bernard had drunk enough and been reminded enough of the dim future of the newspaper business. He slid off his stool and put his hand on my shoulder.

"There but for the grace of God go I," he said.

"What?" I said.

"It could've been me. It could've been anybody in that

newsroom. But they tagged you because you make the big bucks. You coming in here seven years ago, Mr. Bestseller and *Larry King* and all of that. They overpaid to get you then and that made you a target now. I'm surprised you lasted this long, to tell you the truth."

"Whatever. That doesn't make it any better."

"I know but I had to say it. I'm going to go now. You going home?"

"I'm going to have one more."

"Nah, man, you've had enough."

"One more. I'll be fine. If not, I'll take a cab."

"Don't get a DUI, man. That'd be all you need."

"Yeah, what are they going to do to me? Fire me?"

He nodded like I had made an impressive point, then slapped me on the back a little too hard and sauntered out of the bar. I sat alone and watched the game. For my next drink I skipped the Guinness and Baileys and went straight to Jameson's over ice. I then drank either two or three more instead of just the one. And I thought about how this was not the end to my career that I had envisioned. I thought by now I'd be writing ten-thousand-word takes for *Esquire* and *Vanity Fair*. That they'd be coming to me instead of me going to them. That I'd have my pick of what to write about.

I ordered one more and the bartender made a deal with me. He'd only splash whiskey on my ice if I gave him my car keys. That sounded like a good deal to me and I took it.

With the whiskey burning my scalp from underneath I thought about Larry Bernard's story about Baltimore and the ultimate fuck-you. I think I nodded to myself a couple times and held my glass up in toast to the lame-duck reporter who had done it.

And then another idea burned through and seared an imprint on my brain. A variation on the Baltimore fuck-you. One with some integrity and as indelible as the etching of a name on a glass trophy. Elbow on the bar top, I held the glass up again. But this time it was for myself.

"Death is my beat," I whispered to myself. "I make my living from it. I forge my professional reputation on it."

Words spoken before but not as my own eulogy. I nodded to myself and knew just how I was going to go out. I had written at least a thousand murder stories in my time. I was going to write one more. A story that would stand as the tombstone on my career. A story that would make them remember me after I was gone.

The weekend was a blur of alcohol, anger and humiliation as I grappled with a new future that was no future. After briefly sobering up on Saturday morning I opened the file that held my novel in progress and began reading. I soon saw what my ex-wife had seen long ago. What I should have seen long ago. It wasn't there and I was kidding myself if I thought it was.

The conclusion was that I would have to start from scratch if I was going to go this way, and the thought of that was debilitating. When I took a cab back to the Short Stop to get my car, I ended up staying and closing the place out early Sunday morning, watching the Dodgers lose again and drunkenly telling complete strangers about how fucked up the *Times* and the whole newspaper business was.

It took me all the way into Monday morning to get cleaned up. I rolled in forty-five minutes late to work after finally getting my car at the Short Stop and I could still smell the alcohol coming out of my pores.

Angela Cook was already sitting at my desk in a chair she had borrowed from one of the empty cubicles. There had been a lot of them since they'd started the buyouts and the layoffs.

"Sorry I'm late, Angela," I said. "It was kind of a lost weekend. Starting with the party on Friday. You should have come."

She smiled demurely, like she knew there had been no party, just a one-man wake.

"I got you some coffee but it's probably cold by now," she said.

"Thanks."

I picked up the cup she had gestured to and it had indeed cooled. But the good thing about the *Times* cafeteria was free refills—at least they hadn't changed that yet.

"Tell you what," I said. "Let me go check in with the desk and if nothing's happening we can go get refills and talk about how you're going to take over."

I left her there and walked out of podland and over toward the Metro desk. On the way I stopped at the switchboard. It sat like a lifeguard stand in the middle of the newsroom, built high so that the operators could look out across the vast newsroom and see who was in and able to receive calls. I stepped to the side of the station so one of the operators could look down and see me.

It was Lorene, who had been on duty the Friday before. She raised a finger to tell me to hold. She handled two quick transfers and then pulled one side of her headset off her left ear.

"I don't have anything for you, Jack," she said.

"I know. I want to ask about Friday. You transferred a call to me late in the afternoon from a lady named Wanda Sessums. Would there be any record of her phone number? I forgot to ask for it."

Lorene shoved her headset back in place and handled another call. Then without pulling her ear free she told me she didn't have the number. She had not written it down at the time and the system only kept an electronic list of the last five hundred calls to come in. It had been more than two days since Wanda Sessums had called for me and the switchboard got close to a thousand calls a day.

Lorene asked if I had called 411 to try to get the number. Sometimes the basic starting point was forgotten. I thanked her and headed on to the desk. I had called information at home and already knew there was no listing for Wanda Sessums.

The city editor at the moment was a woman named Dorothy Fowler. It was one of the most transient jobs at the paper, a position both political and practical and one that seemed to have a revolving door attached to it. Fowler had been a damn good government reporter and was only eight months into trying her hand at commanding the crew of city-side reporters. I wished her well but kind of knew it was impossible for her to succeed, given all the cutbacks on resources and the empty cubicles in the newsroom.

Fowler had a little office in the line of glass but she preferred to be an editor of the people. She was usually at a desk at the head of the formation of desks where all the aces—assistant city editors—sat. This was known as the raft because all the desks were pushed together as if in some sort of flotilla where there was strength in numbers against the sharks.

All city-side reporters were assigned to an ace as the first level of direction and management. My ace was Alan Prendergast, who handled all the cop and court reporters. As such, he had a later shift, usually coming in around noon, because news that came off the law enforcement and justice beats most of the time developed late in the day.

This meant my first check-in of the day was usually with Dorothy Fowler or the deputy city editor, Michael Warren. I always tried to make it Fowler because she ranked higher and Warren and I never got along. This might have had something to do with the fact that long before I had come to the *Times*, I had worked for the *Rocky Mountain News* out of Denver and had encountered Warren and competed with him on a major story. He had acted unethically and for that I could never trust him as an editor.

Dorothy had her eyes glued to a screen and I had to say her name to get her attention. We hadn't talked since I'd been pink-slipped so she immediately looked up at me with a sympathetic frown you might reserve for someone you just heard had been diagnosed with pancreatic cancer.

"Come inside, Jack," she said.

She stood up and left the raft and headed to her seldom-used office. She sat behind her desk but I stayed standing because I knew this would be quick.

"I just want to say we are really going to miss you around here, Jack."

I nodded my thanks.

"I am sure Angela will pick up without a blip."

"She's very good and she's hungry, but she doesn't have the chops. Not yet, at least, and that's the problem, isn't it? The newspaper is supposed to be the community's watchdog and we're turning it over to the puppies. Think of all the great journalism we've seen in our lifetimes. The corruption exposed, the public benefit. Where's that going to come from now with every paper in the country getting shredded? Our government? No way. TV, the blogs? Forget it. My friend who took the buyout in Florida says corruption will be the new growth industry without the papers watching."

She paused as if to ponder the sad state of things.

"Look, don't get me wrong. I'm just depressed. Angela is great. She'll do good work and in three or four years she'll own that beat the way you own it now. But the point is, between now and then, how many stories will she miss? And how many of them would have never gotten by you?"

I only shrugged. These were questions that mattered to her but no longer to me. In twelve days I was out.

"Well," she said after a delayed silence. "I'm sorry. I've always enjoyed working with you."

"Well, I still have some time. Maybe I'll find something really good to go out on."

She smiled brightly.

"That would be great!"

"Anything happening today that you know of?"

"Nothing big," Dorothy said. "I saw on the overnote

that the police chief is meeting with black leaders to talk about racially targeted crime again. But we've done that to death."

"I'm going to take Angela around Parker Center and I'll see if we can come up with something."

"Good."

A few minutes later Angela Cook and I refilled coffee cups and took a table in the cafeteria. It was on the first floor in the space where the old presses had turned for so many decades before they started printing the paper off-site. The conversation with Angela was stiff. I had met her briefly six months earlier when she was a new hire and Fowler had trotted her around the cubicles, making introductions. But since then I hadn't worked on a story with her, had lunch or coffee with her, or seen her at one of the watering holes favored by the older denizens of the newsroom.

"Where'd you come from, Angela?"

"Tampa. I went to the University of Florida."

"Good school. Journalism?"

"I got my master's there, yeah."

"Have you done any cop shop reporting?"

"Before I went back for my master's I worked two years in St. Pete. I spent a year on cops."

I drank some coffee and I needed it. My stomach was empty because I hadn't been able to keep anything down for twenty-four hours.

"St. Petersburg? What are you talking about there, a few dozen murders a year?"

"If we were lucky."

She smiled at the irony of it. A crime reporter always wants a good murder to write about. The reporter's good luck is somebody else's bad luck.

"Well," I said. "If we go below four hundred here we're having a good year. Real good. Los Angeles is the place to be if you want to work crime. If you want to tell murder stories. If you're just marking time until the next beat comes up, you're probably not going to like it."

She shook her head.

"I'm not worried about the next beat. This is what I want. I want to write murder stories. I want to write books about this stuff."

She sounded sincere. She sounded like me—from a long time ago.

"Good," I said. "I'm going to take you over to Parker Center to meet some people. Detectives mostly. They'll help you but only if they trust you. If they don't trust you, all you'll get are the press releases."

"How do I do that, Jack? Make them trust me."

"You know. Write stories. Be fair, be accurate. You know what to do. Trust is built on performance. The thing to remember is that the cops in this town have an amazing network. The word about a reporter gets around quickly. If you're fair, they'll all know it. If you fuck one of them over, they'll all know that too and they'll shut your access down everywhere."

She seemed embarrassed by my profanity. She would have to get used to it, dealing with cops.

"There's one other thing," I said. "They have a hidden nobility. The good ones, I mean. And if you can somehow get that into your stories, you will win them over every time. So look for the telling details, the little moments of nobility."

"Okay, Jack, I will."

"Then you'll do all right."

While we were making the rounds and the introductions in the police headquarters at Parker
Center we picked up a nice little murder story
in the Open-Unsolved Unit. A twenty-year-old rape and
murder of an elderly woman had been cleared when DNA
collected from the victim in 1989 was unearthed in case
archives and run through the state Department of Justice's
sex crimes data bank. The match was called a cold hit.
The DNA collected from the victim belonged to a man
currently doing time at Pelican Bay for an attempted rape.
The cold case investigators would put together a case
and indict the guy before he ever got a chance at parole
up there. It wasn't that flashy, because the bad guy was
already behind bars, but it was worth eight inches. People
like to read stories that reinforce the idea that bad people
don't always get away. Especially in an economic downturn, when it's so easy to be cynical.

When we got back to the newsroom I asked Angela to
write it up—her first story on the beat—while I tried to
run down Wanda Sessums, my angry caller from the Friday before.

Since there was no record of her call to the *Times*
switchboard and a quick check with directory assistance

had turned up no listing for Wanda Sessums in any of L.A.'s area codes, I next called Detective Gilbert Walker at the Santa Monica Police Department. He was the lead investigator on the case that resulted in Alonzo Winslow's arrest in the murder of Denise Babbit. I guess you could say it was a cold call. I had no relationship with Walker, as Santa Monica didn't come up very often on the news radar. It was a relatively safe beach town between Venice and Malibu that had a pressing homeless problem but not much of a murder problem. The police department investigated only a handful of homicides each year and most of these weren't newsworthy. More often than not they were body dump cases like Denise Babbit's. The murder occurs somewhere else— like the south end of L.A.—and the beach cops are left to clean up the mess.

My call found Walker at his desk. His voice seemed friendly enough until I identified myself as a reporter with the *Times*. Then it went cold. That happened often. I had spent seven years on the beat and had many cops in many departments that I counted as sources and even friends. In a jam, I could reach out. But sometimes you don't get to pick who you have to reach out to. The bottom line is you can never get them all in your corner. The media and the police have never been on comfortable terms. The media views itself as the public watchdog. And nobody, the police included, likes having somebody looking over their shoulder. There was a chasm between the two institutions into which trust had fallen long before I was ever around. Consequently, it made things tough for the lowly beat reporter who just needs a few facts to fill out a story.

"What can I do for you?" Walker said in a clipped tone.

"I'm trying to reach Alonzo Winslow's mother and I was wondering if you might be able to help."

"And who is Alonzo Winslow?"

I was about to say, *Come on, Detective,* when I realized I wasn't supposed to know the suspect's name. There were laws about releasing the names of juveniles charged with crimes.

"Your suspect in the Babbit case."

"How do you know that name? I'm not confirming that name."

"I understand that, Detective. I'm not asking you to confirm the name. I know the name. His mother called me on Friday and gave me the name. Trouble is, she didn't give me her phone number and I'm just trying to get back in—"

"Have a nice day," Walker said, interrupting and then hanging up the phone.

I leaned back in my desk chair, noting to myself that I needed to tell Angela Cook that the nobility I mentioned earlier did not reside in all cops.

"Asshole," I said out loud.

I drummed my fingers on the desk until I came up with a new plan—the one I should have employed in the first place.

I opened a line and called a detective who was a source in the South Bureau of the Los Angeles Police Department and who I knew had been involved in the

Winslow arrest. The case had originated in the city of Santa Monica because the victim had been found in the trunk of her car in a parking lot near the pier. But the LAPD became involved when evidence from the murder scene led to Alonzo Winslow, a resident of South L.A.

Following established protocol, Santa Monica contacted Los Angeles, and a team of South Bureau detectives intimately familiar with the turf were used to locate Winslow, take him into custody and then turn him over to Santa Monica. Napoleon Braselton was one of those South Bureau guys. I called him now and was flat-out honest with him. Well, almost.

"Remember the bust two weeks ago for the girl in the trunk?" I asked.

"Yeah, that's Santa Monica," he said. "We just helped out."

"Yeah, I know. You guys took Winslow down for them. That's what I'm calling about."

"It's still their case, man."

"I know but I can't get a hold of Walker over there and I don't know anybody else in that department. But I know you. And I want to ask about the arrest, not the case."

"What, is there a beef? We didn't touch that kid."

"No, Detective, no beef. Far as I know, it was a righteous bust. I'm just trying to find the kid's house. I want to go see where he was living, maybe talk to his mother."

"That's fine but he was living with his grandmother."

"You sure?"

"The information we got in the briefing was that he

was with the grandmother. We were the big bad wolves hitting grandma's house. There was no father in the picture and the mother was in and out, living on the street. Drugs."

"Okay, then I'll talk to the grandmother. Where's the place?"

"You're just cruising on down to say hello?"

He said it in a disbelieving tone and I knew that was because I was white and would likely be unwelcome in Alonzo Winslow's neighborhood.

"Don't worry, I'll take somebody with me. Strength in numbers."

"Good luck. Don't get your ass shot until after I go off watch at four."

"I'll do my best. What's the address, do you remember?"

"It's in Rodia Gardens. Hold on."

He put the phone down while he looked up the exact address. Rodia Gardens was a huge public housing complex in Watts that was like a city unto itself. A dangerous city. It was named after Simon Rodia, the artist who had created one of the wonders of the city. The Watts Towers. But there wasn't anything wonderful about Rodia Gardens. It was the kind of place where poverty, drugs and crime had cycled for decades. Multiple generations of families living there and unable to get out and break free. Many of them had grown up having never been to the beach or on an airplane or even to a movie in a theater.

Braselton came back on and gave me the full address

but said he had no phone number. I then asked if he had a name for the grandmother and he gave me the name I already had, Wanda Sessums.

Bingo. My caller. She had either lied about being the young suspect's mother or the police had their information wrong. Either way, I now had an address and would hopefully soon put a face with the voice that had berated me the Friday before.

After ending the call with Braselton I got up from my cubicle and wandered back into the photo department. I saw a photo editor named Bobby Azmitia at the assignment desk and asked if he had any floaters currently out and about. He looked down at his personnel log and named two photographers who were out in their cars looking for wild art—photographs unconnected to news events that could be used to splash color on a section front. I knew both of the floaters and one of them was black. I asked Azmitia if Sonny Lester could break free to take a ride with me down the 110 Freeway and he agreed to offer the photographer up. We made arrangements for me to be picked up outside the globe lobby in fifteen minutes.

Back in the newsroom I checked with Angela on the Open-Unsolved Unit story and then went over to the raft to talk to my ace. Prendergast was busy typing up the day's first story budget. Before I could say anything he said, "I already got a slug from Angela."

A slug and budget line were a one-word title for a story and a line of description that was put on the overall story budget so when editors gathered around the table in the daily news meeting they would know what was being produced for the web and print editions and could discuss what was an important story, what wasn't, and how it should all be played.

"Yeah, she's got a handle on that," I said. "I just wanted to let you know I'm going to take a ride down south with a photographer."

"What's up?"

"Nothing yet. But I may have something to tell you later on."

"Okay."

Prendo was always cool about giving me rope. Now it didn't matter anymore. But even before I got the Reduction in Force form, he had always exercised a hands-off approach to reporter management. We got along pretty well. He wasn't a pushover. I would have to account for my time and what I was pursuing. But he always gave me the chance to put it together before I had to bring him into the loop.

I headed away from the raft and over to the elevator alcove.

"Got dimes?" Prendergast called after me.

I waved a hand over my head without looking back. Prendergast always called that out to me when I left the city room to chase a story. It was a line from *Chinatown*. I didn't use pay phones anymore—no reporter did—but the sentiment was clear. Stay in touch.

The globe lobby was the formal entrance to the newspaper building at the corner of First and Spring. A brass globe the size of a Volkswagen rotated on a steel axis at the center of the room. The many international bureaus and outposts of the *Times* were permanently notched on the raised continents, despite the fact that many had been shuttered to save money. The marble walls were adorned with photos and plaques denoting the many milestones in the history of the paper, the Pulitzer Prizes won and the staffs that won them, and the correspondents killed in the line of duty. It was a proud museum, just as the whole paper would be before too long. The word was that the building was up for sale.

But I only cared about the next twelve days. I had one last deadline and one last murder story to write. I just needed that globe to keep turning until then.

Sonny Lester was waiting in a company car when I pushed through the heavy front door. I got in and told him where we were going. He made a bold U-turn to get over to Broadway and then took it to the freeway entrance just past the courthouse. Pretty soon we were on the 110 heading into South L.A.

"I take it that it's no coincidence that I'm on this assignment," he said after we cleared downtown.

I looked over at him and shrugged.

"I don't know," I said. "Ask Azmitia. I told him I needed somebody and he told me it was you."

Lester nodded like he didn't believe it and I didn't really care. Newspapers had a strong and proud tradition of standing up against segregation and racial profiling and things like that. But there was also a practical tradition of using newsroom diversity to its full advantage. If an earthquake shatters Tokyo, send a Japanese reporter. If a black actress wins the Oscar, send a black reporter to interview her. If the Border Patrol finds twenty-four dead illegals in the back of a truck in Calexico, send your best Spanish-speaking reporter. That's how you got the story. Lester was black and his presence might provide me safety as I entered the projects. That's all I cared about. I had a story to report and I wasn't worried about being politically correct about it.

Lester asked me questions about what we were doing and I told him as much as I could. But so far I didn't have a lot to go on. I told him that the woman we were going to see had complained about my story calling her grandson a murderer. I was hoping to find her and tell her that I would look into disproving the charges against him if she and her grandson agreed to cooperate with me. I didn't tell him the real plan. I figured he was smart enough to eventually put it together himself.

Lester nodded when I finished and we rode the rest of the way in silence. We rolled into Rodia Gardens about one o'clock and it was quiet in the projects. School wasn't out yet and the drug trade didn't really get going until dusk. The dealers, dopers and gangbangers were all still sleeping.

The complex was a maze of two-story buildings painted in two tones. Brown and beige on most of the buildings. Lime and beige on the rest. The structures were unadorned by any bushes or trees, for these could be used to hide drugs and weapons. Overall, the place had the look of a newly built community where the extras had not yet been put in place. Only on closer inspection, it was clear that it wasn't fresh paint on the walls and these weren't new buildings.

We found the address Braselton gave me without difficulty. It was a corner apartment on the second floor with the stairway on the right side of the building. Lester took a large, heavy camera bag out of the car and locked it.

"You won't need all of that if we get inside," I said. "If she lets you shoot her, you're gonna have to do it quick."

"I don't care if I don't shoot a frame. I'm not leaving my stuff in the car."

"Got it."

When we reached the second floor, I noticed that the front door to the apartment was open behind a screen door with bars on it. I approached it and looked around before knocking. I saw no one in any of the parking lots or yards of the complex. It was as though the place were completely empty.

I knocked.

"Mrs. Sessums?"

I waited and soon heard a voice come through the screen. I recognized it from the call on Friday.

"Who that?"

"It's Jack McEvoy. We talked on Friday. From the *Times*?"

The screen was dirty with years of grime and dust caked on it. I could not see into the apartment.

"What you doin' here, boy?"

"I came to talk to you, ma'am. Over the weekend I did a lot of thinking about what you said on the phone."

"How in hell you find me?"

I could tell by the closeness of her voice that she was on the other side of the screen now. I could only see her shape through the grit.

"Because I knew this is where Alonzo was arrested."

"Who dat wit' you?"

"This is Sonny Lester, who works at the newspaper with me. Mrs. Sessums, I'm here because I thought about what you said and I want to look into Alonzo's case. If he's innocent I want to help him get out."

Accent on *if*.

"A course, he's innocent. He didn't do nothin'."

"Can we come in and talk about it?" I said quickly. "I want to see what I can do."

"You can come in but don' be taking no pitchers. Uh-uh, no pitchers."

The screen door popped open a few inches and I grabbed the handle and pulled it wide. I immediately assessed the woman in the doorway as Alonzo Winslow's grandmother. She looked to be about sixty years old, with dyed black cornrows showing gray at the roots. She was as skinny as a broom and wore a sweater over blue jeans even though it wasn't sweater weather. Her calling herself his mother on the phone on Friday was a curiosity but not a big deal. I had a feeling I was about to find out that she had been both mother and grandmother to the boy.

She pointed to a little sitting area where there was a couch and a coffee table. There were stacks of folded clothes on almost all surfaces and many had torn pieces of paper on the top with names written on them. I could hear a washer or dryer somewhere in the apartment and knew that she had a little business running out of her government-provided home. Maybe that was why she wanted no photographs.

"Move some a that laun'ry and have a seat and tell me what you goin' to do for my Zo," she said.

I moved a folded stack of clothes off the couch onto a side table and sat down. I noticed there wasn't a single piece of clothing in any of the stacks that was red. The Rodia projects were controlled by a Crips street gang, and wearing red—the color of the rival Bloods—could draw harm to a person.

Lester sat next to me. He put the camera bag on the floor between his feet. I noticed he had a camera in his hand. He unzipped the bag and put it away. Wanda Sessums stayed standing in front of us. She lifted a laundry basket onto the coffee table and started taking out and folding clothes.

"Well, I want to look into Zo's case," I said. "If he's innocent like you said, then I'll be able to get him out."

I kept that *if* working. Kept selling the car. I made sure I didn't promise anything I wasn't going to deliver.

"Jus' like that you get him out, huh? When Mr. Meyer can't even get him his day in court?"

"Is Mr. Meyer his lawyer?"

"That's right. Public defender. He a Jew lawyer."

She said it without a trace of enmity or bias. It was said as almost a point of pride that her grandson had graduated to the level of having a Jewish lawyer.

"Well, I'll be talking to Mr. Meyer about all of this.

Sometimes, Mrs. Sessums, the newspaper can do what nobody else can do. If I tell the world that Alonzo Winslow is innocent, then the world pays attention. With lawyers that's not always the case, because they're always saying their clients are innocent—whether they really think it or not. Like the boy who cried wolf. They say it so much that when they actually do have a client who's innocent, nobody believes them."

She looked at me quizzically and I thought she either was confused or thought she was being conned. I tried to keep things moving so her mind wouldn't settle on any given thing I had said.

"Mrs. Sessums, if I'm going to investigate this I am going to need you to call Mr. Meyer and ask him to cooperate with me. I'll need to look at the court file and all the discovery."

"He ain't discovered nothin' so far. He just go roun' tellin' everybody to sit tight, is all."

"By 'discovery' I mean the legal term. The state—that's the prosecutor—has to turn all their paperwork and evidence over to the defense for viewing. I'll need to see it all if I'm going to work on getting Alonzo out."

Now she appeared not to be paying attention to what I had said. From the clothes basket she slowly raised her hand. She was holding a tiny pair of bright red panties. She held them away from her body like she was holding the tail of a dead rat.

"Look at this stupid girl. She don' know who she playin' with. Hidin' her red underneath. She a fool an' a half she think she get away wi' that."

She walked over to the corner of the room, used her foot to press a pedal that opened a trash can and dropped the dead rat inside. I nodded as though I approved and tried to get back on track.

"Mrs. Sessums, did you understand what I said about the discovery? I'm going to—"

"But how you going to say my Zo's innocent when all yo facts come from the po-po and they lie like the serpent in the tree?"

It took me a moment to respond as I considered her use of language and the juxtaposition of common street slang and religious reference.

"I'm going to gather all the facts for myself and make my own judgment," I said. "When I wrote that story last week, I was saying what the police said. Now I am going to find out for myself. If your Zo's innocent I will know it. And I'll write it. When I write it, the story will get him out."

"Okay, then. Good. The Lord will help you bring my boy home."

"But I'm going to need your help, too, Wanda."

I dropped into first-name mode now. It was time to let her think she was going to be part of this.

"When it comes to my Zo, I'm always ready to help," she said.

"Good," I said. "Let me tell you what I want you to do."

THREE: The Farm

Carver was in his office with the door closed. He was humming to himself and intently watching the cameras, his screens set in multiplex mode—thirty-six views on each. He was able to scan all of the cameras, even the angles nobody knew about. With a flick of his finger on the heat pad, he drew one camera angle into full screen on the middle plasma.

Geneva was behind the counter, reading a paperback novel. He tightened the focus, attempting to see what she was reading. He couldn't see the title but he could make out the author's name at the top of the page. Janet Evanovich. He knew she had read several books by this writer. He often saw her smiling to herself as she read.

This was good information to know. He would go to a bookstore and pick up a copy of an Evanovich book. He would make sure Geneva saw it in his bag when he walked through reception. It could be an icebreaker that could lead to conversation and maybe more.

He remotely moved the lens and saw that Geneva's purse was open on the floor next to her chair. He pulled in tight and saw cigarettes and gum and two tampons along with keys and matches and wallet. It was that time of the month. Maybe that was why Geneva had been so curt with him when he had come in. She had barely said hello.

Carver checked his watch. It was past time for her afternoon break. Yolanda Chavez from administration was due to walk through the door and let Geneva go. Fifteen minutes. Carver planned to follow her with the cameras. Out for a smoke, to the restroom for a squat, it didn't matter. He would be able to follow. He had cameras everywhere. He would see whatever she did.

Just as Yolanda walked through the door into reception, there was a knock on his own door. Carver immediately hit the escape command and the three screens returned to data flowcharts for three different server towers. He hadn't heard the mantrap buzzer out in the control room but he wasn't sure. Perhaps he had been concentrating so hard on Geneva that he had missed it.

"Yes?"

The door opened. It was only Stone. Carver became annoyed that he had killed his screens and that he was going to miss out on following Geneva.

"What is it, Freddy?" he asked impatiently.

"I wanted to ask you about vacation time," Stone said loudly.

He entered and closed the door. He moved to the chair on the other side of the worktable from Carver and sat down without permission.

"Actually, fuck vacation time," he said. "That was for the benefit of the guys out there. I want to talk about iron maidens. Over the weekend I think I found our next girl."

Freddy Stone was twenty years younger than Carver. Carver had first noticed him while lurking under a different identity in an iron maiden chat room. He tried to trail him but Stone was too good for that. He disappeared into the digital mist.

Undaunted and only more intrigued, Carver set up a catch site called www.motherinirons.com, and sure enough, Stone eventually came through. This time Carver made direct contact and the dance began. Shocked by his young age, Carver nevertheless recruited him, changed his looks and identity, and mentored him.

Carver had saved him, but after four years Stone was too close for comfort, and at times Carver could not stand him. Freddy assumed too much. Like just coming in and sitting down without permission.

"Really," Carver said, a note of disbelief placed intentionally in the word.

"You promised I could pick the next one, remember?" Stone responded.

Carver had made the promise, but it had come in the fervor of the moment. As they were on the 10 Freeway leaving the beach in Santa Monica, the windows open and the sea air blowing in their faces. He was still riding the high and he foolishly told his young disciple that he could pick the next one.

Now he would have to change that. He wished he could just go back to watching Geneva, maybe catch her changing that tampon in the restroom, and leave this inconvenience for later.

"Don't you ever get tired of that song?" Stone asked.

"What?"

Carver realized he had started to hum again while thinking about Geneva. Embarrassed, he tried to move on.

"Who did you find?" he asked.

Stone smiled broadly and shook his head like he could hardly believe his good luck.

"This girl who has her own porn site. I'll send you the link so you can check her out, but you're going to like her. I looked at her tax returns. Last year she cleared two hundred eighty K just from people signing up for twenty-five bucks a month to watch her fuck people."

"Where'd you find her?"

"Dewey and Bach, accountants. She got audited by something called the California Tax Franchise Board and they handled it. All her four-one-one is right there. Everything we need to set up. Then I went and checked her out on her website. Mandy For Ya dot com. She's a stone fox with long legs. Just our type."

Carver could feel the slight trill of anticipation in his dark fiber. But he wasn't going to make a mistake.

"Where exactly in California?" he asked.

"Manhattan Beach," Stone said.

Carver wanted to reach across the glass tabletop and whack Stone on the side of the head with one of the plasma screens.

"Do you know where Manhattan Beach is?" he asked instead.

"Isn't it down by Lo Jolla and San Diego? Down there?"

Carver shook his head.

"First of all, it's *La* Jolla. And no, Manhattan Beach

is not near it, anyway. It's by L.A. and not too far from Santa Monica. So forget her. We're not going back there for a good long time. You know the rules."

"But, Dub, she's perfect! Plus, I already pulled files on her. L.A.'s a big place. Nobody in Santa Monica is going to care about what happens in Manhattan Beach."

Carver shook his head emphatically.

"You can put the files right back. We just burned L.A. for at least three years. I don't care who you find or how safe you think it is. I am not deviating from the protocol. And another thing. My name is Wesley, not Wes, and certainly not Dub."

Stone looked down at the glass tabletop and seemed crushed.

"Tell you what," Carver said. "I'll go to work on it and I'll find us someone. You wait and see and you'll be very happy. I guarantee it."

"But it was going to be my turn."

Now Stone was pouting.

"You had your turn and you blew it," Carver said. "Now it goes to me. So why don't you go back out there and get to work. You still owe me status reports on towers eighty through eighty-five. I want them by the end of the day."

"Whatever."

"Go. And cheer up, Freddy. We'll be on the hunt again before the end of the week."

Stone stood up and turned toward the door. Carver watched him go, wondering how long it would be before he had to get rid of him. Permanently. Working with a partner was always preferable. But eventually all partners got too close and assumed too much. They started calling you by a name no one has ever used. They started thinking it was an equal partnership with equal voting rights. That was unacceptable and dangerous. One person called the shots. Himself.

"Close the door, please," Carver said.

Stone did as instructed. Carver went back to the cameras. He quickly pulled up the camera over the reception area and saw Yolanda sitting behind the counter. Geneva was gone. Jumping from camera to camera he started searching for her.

FOUR: The Big Three-oh

By the time Sonny Lester and I left the apartment where Wanda Sessums lived, the projects were alive and busy. School was out and the drug dealers and their customers were up. The parking lots, playgrounds and burned-out lawns between the apartment buildings were becoming crowded with children and adults. The drug business here was a drive-through operation with an elaborate setup involving lookouts and handlers of all ages who would direct buyers through the maze of streets in the projects to a buy location that was continuously changed throughout the day. The government planners who designed and built the place had no idea they were creating a perfect environment for the cancer that would in one way or another destroy most of its inhabitants.

I knew all of this because I had ridden with South Bureau narcotics teams on more than one occasion while writing my semiannual updates on the local drug war.

As we crossed a lawn and approached Lester's company car we moved with a heads-down-minding-our-own-business purpose. We just wanted to get out of Dodge. It wasn't until we were almost right to the car that I saw the young man leaning against the driver's door. He was wearing untied work boots, blue jeans dropped halfway down his blue-patterned boxer shorts and a spotless white T-shirt that almost glowed in the afternoon sun. It was the uniform of the Crips set, which ruled the projects. They were known as the BH set, which alternately meant Bounty Hunters or Blood Hunters, depending on who was spraying the paint.

"How y'all doin'?" he said.

"We're fine," Lester said. "Just going back to work."

"You the po-po now?"

Lester laughed like that was the biggest joke he'd heard in a week.

"Nah, man, we're with the paper."

Lester nonchalantly put his camera bag in the trunk and then came around to the door where the young man was leaning. He didn't move.

"Gotta go, bro. Can I get by you there?"

I was on the other side of the car by my door. I felt my insides tighten. If there was going to be a problem, it was going to happen right now. I could see others in the same gang uniform standing back on the shaded side of the parking lot, ready to be called in if needed. I had no doubt that they all had weapons either on their person or hidden nearby.

The young man leaning on our car didn't move. He folded his arms and looked at Lester.

"What you talking to moms about up there, *bro?*"

"Alonzo Winslow," I said from my side. "We don't think he killed anybody and we're looking into it."

The young man pushed off the car so he could turn and look at me.

"That right?"

I nodded.

"We're working on it. We just started and that's why we came to talk to Mrs. Sessums."

"Then she tell you about the tax."

"What tax?"

"Yeah, she pay a tax. Anybody in business 'round here payin' a tax."

"Really?"

"The street tax, man. See, any newspaper people that come 'round here to talk about Zo Slow has to pay the street tax. I can take it for you now."

I nodded.

"How much?"

"It be fitty dollah t'day."

I'd expense it and see if Dorothy Fowler raised hell. I reached into my pocket and pulled out my money. I had fifty-three dollars and quickly extracted two twenties and a ten.

"Here," I said.

I moved to the back of the car and the young man moved away from the driver's door. As I paid him Lester got in and started the car.

"We have to go," I said as I handed over the money.

"Yeah, you do. You come back and the tax is double, Paperboy."

"Fine."

I should have let it go at that but I couldn't leave without asking the obvious question.

"Doesn't it matter to you that I'm working on getting
Zo out?"

The young man raised his hand and rubbed his jaw as
though giving the question some serious thought. I saw
the letters F-U-C-K tattooed across his knuckles. My
eyes went to his other hand, hanging limp at his side. I
saw D-A-5-0 tattooed across the other ridge of knuckles
and I got my answer. Fuck the police. With sentiment
like that on his hands, it was no wonder he would extort
those trying to help a fellow member of the crew. It was
everybody for himself down here.

The kid laughed and turned away without answering.
He'd wanted me to see his hands.

I got into the car and Lester backed out of the space.
I turned around and saw the young man who had just
extorted fifty dollars from us doing the Crip walk. He
bent down and used the bills I had just given him to pan-
tomime a quick polish of his shoes, then straightened
up and did the heel-toe-heel-toe shuffle the Crips called
their own. His fellow bangers over in the shade whooped
it up as he approached.

I didn't feel the tension in my neck start to dissolve
until we got back to the 110 and headed north. Then I
put the fifty bucks out of my mind and started to feel
good as I reviewed what had been accomplished during
the trip. Wanda Sessums had agreed to cooperate fully
in the investigation of the Denise Babbit–Alonzo Winslow case. Using my cell phone, she had called Winslow's

public defender, Jacob Meyer, and told him that, as the defendant's guardian, she was authorizing my total access to all documents and evidence relating to the case. Meyer reluctantly agreed to meet with me the next morning between hearings in the downtown juvenile hall. He didn't really have a choice. I had told Wanda that if Meyer didn't cooperate, there were plenty of private attorneys who would handle the case for free once they knew there were headlines coming. Meyer's choice was either to work with me and get some media attention for himself or give the case up.

Wanda Sessums had also agreed to get me into Sylmar Juvenile Hall so that I could interview her grandson. My plan was to use the public defender's case file to become familiar with the case before I sat down to talk to Winslow. It would be the key interview of the piece I would write. I wanted to know all there was to know before I talked to him.

All in all, it had been a good trip—the fifty-dollar tariff notwithstanding—and I was thinking about how I was going to present my plan to Prendergast. Then Lester interrupted my thoughts.

"I know what you're doing," he said.

"What am I doing?" I said.

"That washerwoman might be too dumb and the lawyer too worried about headlines to see it but I'm not."

"What are you talking about?"

"You're comin' on like you're the white knight that's gonna prove the kid innocent and set him free. But you're going to do the exact opposite of that, man. You're going to use them to get inside the case to get all the juicy details, then you're going to write a story about how a sixteen-year-old kid becomes a stone-cold killer. Hell, getting an innocent man free is a damn newspaper cliché nowadays. But gettin' inside the mind of a young killer like that? Tellin' how society lets that kind of thing happen? That's Pulitzer territory, bro."

I didn't say anything at first. Lester had me cold. I put together a defense and then responded.

"All I promised her was that I would investigate the case. Where it goes it goes, that's all."

"Bullshit. You're using her because she's too ignorant to know it. The kid will probably be just as stupid and go along, too. And we all know the lawyer will trade the kid for headlines. You really think you're going to win the big one with this, don't you?"

I shook my head and didn't respond. I could feel my face getting red and I turned to look out the window.

"Hey, but it's okay," Lester said.

I turned and looked back at him and I read his face.

"What do you want, Sonny?"

"A piece, that's all. We work it as a team. I go with you up to Sylmar and to court and I do all the photo work. You fill out a photo request, you put my name on it. Makes it a better package anyway. Especially for submissions."

Meaning submissions to Pulitzer and other prize judges.

"Look," I said, "I haven't even told my editor about this yet. You are jumping way ahead. I don't even know if they'll—"

"They'll love it and you know it. They're going to cut you loose to work it and they might as well cut me loose too. Who knows, maybe we both get a prize. They can't lay you off if you bring home a Pulitzer."

"You're talking about the ultimate long shot, Sonny. You're crazy. Besides that, I already got laid off. I've got twelve days and then I could give a shit about the Pulitzer Prize. I'm out of here."

I saw his eyes register surprise at the news of my layoff. Then he nodded as he factored the new information into his ongoing scenario.

"Then this is the ultimate adios," he said. "I get it. You leave 'em with a fuck-you—a story so good they gotta enter it in contests even though you're long out the door."

I didn't respond. I hadn't thought I was so easy to read. I turned back to the window. The freeway was elevated here and I could see block after block of houses crowded together. Many had blue tarps tied over their old, leaky roofs. The farther south you went in the city, the more of those tarps you saw.

"I still want in," Lester said.

With complete access to Alonzo Winslow and his case now established, I was ready to discuss the story with my editor. By that I meant that I would officially say I was working it and my ace could put it on his futures budget. When I got back to the newsroom, I went directly over to the raft and found Prendergast at his desk. He was busily typing into his computer.

"Prendo, you got a minute?"

He didn't even look up.

"Not right now, Jack. I got tagged with putting together the budget for the four o'clock. You got something for tomorrow besides Angela's story?"

"No, I'm talking more long-range."

He stopped typing and looked up at me and I realized he was confused. How long-range could a guy with twelve days left go?

"Not that long-range. We can talk later or tomorrow. Did Angela turn in the story?"

"Not yet. I think she was waiting for you to look it over. Can you go do that now and get it in? I want to get it out on the web as soon as we can."

"I'm on it."

"Okay, Jack. We'll talk later or send me a quick e-mail."

I turned and my eyes swept the newsroom. It was as long as a football field. I didn't know where Angela Cook's cubicle was located but I knew it would be close. The newer you were, the closer they kept you to the raft. The far reaches of the newsroom were for the veterans who supposedly needed less supervision. The south side was called Baja Metro and was inhabited by veteran reporters who still produced. The north side was the Deadwood Forest. This was where the reporters who did little reporting and even less writing were located. Some of them had sacrosanct positions by virtue of political connections or Pulitzer Prizes, and others were just incredibly skilled at keeping their heads down so they wouldn't draw the attention of the assignment editors or the corporate cutters.

Over the top edge of one of the nearby pods I saw Angela's blond hair. I went over.

"Howzit going?"

She jumped, startled.

"Sorry. Didn't mean to scare you."

"That's okay. I was just so absorbed in reading this."

I pointed to her computer screen.

"Is that the story?"

Her face colored. I noticed she had tied her hair behind her head and stuck an editing pencil through the knot. It made her look even sexier than usual.

"No, actually, it's from archives. It's the story about you and that killer they called the Poet. That was creepy as hell."

I checked the screen more closely. She had pulled out of archives a story from twelve years before. From when I was with the *Rocky Mountain News* and in competition with the *Times* on a story that had stretched from Denver to the East Coast and then all the way back to L.A. It was the biggest story I had ever chased. It had been the high point of my journalistic life—no, check that, it had been the apex of my entire life—and I didn't want to be reminded that I had crossed that point so long ago.

"Yeah, it was pretty creepy. Are you finished with today's story?"

"What happened to that FBI agent you teamed up with? Rachel Walling. One of the other stories said she was disciplined for crossing ethical lines with you."

"She's still around. Here in L.A., in fact. Can we look at today's story? Prendo wants us to get it in so he can put it on the web."

"Sure. I have it done. I was just waiting for you to see it before I sent it to the desk."

"Let me get a chair."

I pulled a chair away from an empty cubicle. Angela made room for me next to her and I read the twelve-inch story she had written. The news budget had slugged it in at ten inches, which meant it would likely be cut to eight, but you could always write long for the web edition because there were no space restrictions. Any reporter worth his or her salt would naturally go over budget. Your ego dictated that your story and your skill in telling it would make the ladder of editors who read it realize it was too good to be anything less than what you had turned in, no matter what edition it was written for.

The first edit I made was to take my name off the byline.

"Why, Jack?" Angela protested. "We reported this together."

"Yeah, but you wrote it. You get the byline."

She reached over to the keyboard and put her hand on top of my right hand.

"Please, I would like to have a byline with you. It would mean a lot to me."

I looked at her quizzically.

"Angela, this is a twelve-inch story they're probably going to cut to eight and bury inside. It's just another murder story and it doesn't need a double byline."

"But it's my first murder story here at the *Times* and I want your name on it."

She still had her hand on mine. I shrugged and nodded.

"Suit yourself."

She let go of my hand and I typed my name back into the byline. She then reached over again and held my right hand once more.

"Is this the one that got hurt?"

"Uh..."

"Can I see?"

I turned my hand over, exposing the starburst scar in the webbing between my thumb and forefinger. It was the place the bullet had passed through before hitting the killer they called the Poet in the face.

"I saw that you don't use your thumb when you type," she said.

"The bullet severed a tendon and I had surgery to re-attach it but my thumb's never really worked right."

"What's it feel like?"

"It feels normal. It just doesn't do what I want it to do."

She laughed politely.

"What?"

"I meant, what's it feel like to kill somebody like that?"

The conversation was getting weird. What was the fascination this woman—this girl—had with killing?

"Uh, I don't really like to talk about that, Angela. It was a long time ago and it wasn't like I killed the guy. He kind of brought it on himself. He wanted to die, I think. He fired the gun."

"I love serial killer stories but I had never heard about the Poet until some people said something about it today at lunch and then I Googled it. I'm going to get the book you wrote. I heard it was a bestseller."

"Good luck. It was a bestseller ten years ago. It's now been out of print at least five years."

I realized that if she had heard about the book at lunch, then people were talking about me. Talking about the former bestseller, now overpaid cop shop reporter, getting the pink slip.

"Well, I bet you have a copy I could borrow," Angela said.

She gave me a pouting look. I studied her for a long moment before responding. In that moment I knew she was some sort of death freak. She wanted to write murder stories because she wanted the details they don't put in the articles and the TV reports. The cops were going to love her, and not just because she was a looker. She would fawn over them as they parceled out the gritty and grim descriptions of the crime scenes they worked. They would mistake her worship of the dark details for worship of them.

"I'll see if I can find a copy at home tonight. Let's get back to this story and get it in. Prendo is going to want to see it in the basket as soon as he's out of the four o'clock meeting."

"Okay, Jack."

She raised her hands in mock surrender. I went back to the story and got through the rest of it in ten minutes, making only one change in the copy. Angela had tracked down the son of the elderly woman who had been raped and then stabbed to death in 1989. He was grateful that the police had not given up on the case and said so. I moved his sincerely laudatory quote up into the top third of the story.

"I'm moving this up so it won't get cut by the desk," I explained. "A quote like that will score you some points with the cops. It's the kind of sentiment from the public that they live for and don't often get. Putting it up high will start building the trust I was telling you about."

"Okay, good."

I then made one final addition, typing –30– at the bottom of the copy.

"What does that mean?" Angela asked. "I've seen that on other stories in the city desk basket."

"It's just an old-school thing. When I first came up in

journalism you typed that at the bottom of your stories. It's a code—I think it's even a holdover from telegraph days. It just means end of story. It's not necessary anymore but—"

"Oh, God, that's why they call the list of everybody who gets laid off the 'thirty list.' "

I looked at her and nodded, surprised that she didn't already know what I was telling her.

"That's right. And it's something I always used, and since my byline's on the story..."

"Sure, Jack, that's okay. I think it's kind of cool. Maybe I'll start doing it."

"Continue the tradition, Angela."

I smiled and stood up.

"You think you are okay to make the round of police checks in the morning and swing by Parker Center?"

She frowned.

"You mean without you?"

"Yeah, I'm going to be tied up in court on something I'm working on. But I'll probably be back before lunch. You think you can handle it?"

"If you think so. What are you working on?"

I told her briefly about my visit to the Rodia Gardens projects and the direction I was going. I then assured her that she wouldn't have a problem going to Parker Center on her own after only one day's training with me.

"You'll be fine. And with that story in the paper tomorrow, you'll have more friends over there than you'll know what to do with."

"If you say so."

"I do. Just call me on my cell if you need anything."

I then pointed at the story on her computer screen, made a fist and banged it lightly on her desk.

"Run that baby," I said.

It was a line from *All the President's Men*, one of the greatest reporter stories ever told, and I immediately realized she didn't recognize it. Oh, well, I thought, there is old school and then there is new school.

I headed back to my cubicle and saw the message light on my phone flashing at a fast interval, meaning I had multiple messages. I quickly pushed the strange but intriguing encounter with Angela Cook from my mind and picked up the receiver.

The first message was from Jacob Meyer. He said he had been assigned a new case with an arraignment scheduled for the next day. It meant he had to push back our meeting a half hour to 9:30 the next morning. That was fine with me. It would give me more time to either sleep in or prepare for the interview.

The second message was a voice from the past. Van Jackson was a rookie reporter I had trained on the cop beat at the *Rocky Mountain News* about fifteen years before. He rose through the ranks and got all the way up to the post of city editor before the paper shuttered its doors a few months earlier. That was the end of a 150-year publishing run in Colorado and the biggest sign yet of the crashing newspaper economy. Jackson still hadn't found a job in the business he had dedicated his professional life to.

"Jack, it's Van. I heard the news. Not a good thing,

man. I'm so sorry. Give me a call and we can commiserate. I'm still here in Denver freelancing and looking for work."

There was a long silence and I guess Jackson was looking for words that would prepare me for what was ahead.

"I've gotta tell you the truth, man. There's nothing out there. I'm just about ready to start selling cars, but all the car dealers are in the toilet, too. Anyway, give me a call. Maybe we can watch out for each other, trade tips or something."

I played the message again and then erased it. I would take my time about calling Jackson back. I didn't want to be dragged down further than I already was. I was hitting the big three-oh but I still had options. I wanted to keep my momentum. I had a novel to write.

Jacob Meyer was late to our meeting on Tuesday morning. For nearly a half hour I sat in the waiting room of the Public Defender's Office surrounded by clients of the state-funded agency. People too poor to afford their own legal defense and reliant on the government that was prosecuting them to also defend them. It was right there in the constitutionally guaranteed rights—*If you cannot afford an attorney, one will be appointed for you*—but it always seemed to be a contradiction to me. Like it was all some kind of racket with the government controlling both supply and demand.

Meyer was a young man who I guessed was no more than five years out of law school. Yet here he was, defending a younger man—no, a child—accused of murder. He came back from court, carrying a leather briefcase so fat with files it was too awkward and heavy to carry by the handle. He had it under his arm. He asked the receptionist for messages and was pointed to me. He switched his heavy briefcase to his left arm and offered to shake my hand. I took it and introduced myself.

"Come on back," he said. "I don't have a lot of time."

"That's fine. I don't need a lot of your time at this point."

We walked single file down a hall that had been narrowed because of a row of file cabinets pushed against the right wall and extending its entire length. I was sure it was a fire code violation. This was the kind of detail I would normally put in my back pocket for a rainy day. *Public Defenders Work in Fire Trap.* But I was no longer worried about headlines or coming up with stories for the slow days. I had one last story to write and that was it.

"In here," Meyer said.

I followed him into a communal office, a twenty-by-twelve room with desks in every corner and sound partitions between them.

"Home sweet home," he said. "Pull over one of those chairs."

There was another lawyer, sitting at the desk catty-corner to Meyer's. I pulled the chair over from the empty desk next to his and we sat down.

"Alonzo Winslow," Meyer said. "His grandmother is an interesting lady, isn't she?"

"Especially in her own environment."

"Did she tell you how proud she was to have a Jew lawyer?"

"Yeah, actually she did."

"Turns out I'm Irish, but I didn't want to spoil it for her. What are you looking to do for Alonzo?"

I pulled a microrecorder out of my pocket and turned it on. It was about the size of a disposable cigarette lighter. I reached over and placed it on his desk between us.

"You mind if I record this?"

"Not at all. I would like there to be a record myself."

"Well, like I told you on the phone, Zo's grandmother is pretty convinced the cops picked up the wrong guy. I said I would look into it because I wrote the story in which the cops said he did it. Mrs. Sessums, who is Zo's legal guardian, has given me full access to him and his case."

"She might be his legal guardian, and I would have to check on that, but her granting you full access means nothing in legal terms and therefore means nothing to me. You understand that, right?"

This was not what he had said on the phone when I'd had Wanda Sessums speak to him. I was about to call him on that and his promise of cooperation when I saw him throw a quick glance over his shoulder and realized he might be talking for the benefit of the other lawyer in the room.

"Sure," I said instead. "And I know you have rules in regard to what you can tell me."

"As long as we understand that, I can try to work with you. I can answer your questions to a point but I am not at liberty at this stage of the case to turn over any of the discovery to you."

As he said this he swiveled in his seat to check that the other lawyer's back was still to us and then quickly handed me a flash drive, a data-storage stick with a USB-port connection.

"You will have to get that sort of stuff from the prosecutor or the police," he said.

"Who is the prosecutor assigned to the case?"

"Well, it has been Rosa Fernandez but she handles

juvenile cases. They're saying they want to try this kid as an adult, so that will probably mean a change in prosecutors."

"Are you objecting to them moving this out of juvenile court?"

"Of course. My client is sixteen and hasn't been going to school with any kind of regularity since he was ten or twelve. Not only is he not an adult by any legal standards but his mental capacity and acuity is not even that of a sixteen-year-old."

"But the police said this crime had a degree of sophistication and a sexual component. The victim had been raped and sodomized with foreign objects. Tortured."

"You are assuming my client committed the crime."

"The police said he confessed."

Meyer pointed to the flash drive in my hand.

"Exactly," he said. "The *police* said he confessed. I have two things to say about that. My experience is that if you put a sixteen-year-old kid in a closet for nine hours, don't feed or hydrate him properly, lie to him about evidence that does not exist and refuse to let him talk to anybody—no grandmother, no lawyer, nobody—well, then, eventually he's going to give you what you want if he thinks it will finally get him out of the closet. And secondly, it's a question of what exactly he confessed to that concerns me. The police point of view is definitely different from mine on that."

I stared at him a moment. The conversation was intriguing but too cryptic. I needed to get Meyer to a place where he could speak freely.

"Do you want to go get a cup of coffee?"

"No, I don't have time. And as I said, I can't get into specifics of the case. We have our rules here and we are dealing with a juvenile—despite the state's efforts to the contrary. And, ironically, the same District Attorney's Office that wants to prosecute this child as an adult will happily come down on me and on my boss if I give you any case documents relating to a juvenile. This is not in adult court yet, so rules of privacy designed to protect the juvenile are still in place. But I'm sure you have sources in the police department who can give you what you need."

"I do."

"Good. Then, if you want a statement from me, I would say that I believe that my client—and, by the way, I am not at liberty to identify him by name—is almost as much a victim here as Denise Babbit. It is true that she is the ultimate victim because she lost her life in a horrible manner. But my client's freedom has been taken from him and he is not guilty of this crime. I will be able to prove that once we get into court. Whether that will be in adult or juvenile court doesn't really matter. I will vigorously defend my client because he is not guilty of this crime."

It had been a carefully worded statement and nothing short of what I expected. But, still, it gave me pause. Meyer was crossing a line in giving me the flash drive and I had to ask myself why. I didn't know Meyer. I had never written a story involving him and there was none of the trust that builds between reporter and source as stories are written and published. So if Meyer wasn't crossing the line for me, who was he doing it for? Alonzo Winslow? Could this public defender with the briefcase bursting with his guilty clients' files actually believe his own statement? Did he really think Alonzo was a victim here, that he was actually innocent?

It dawned on me that I was wasting time. I had to get back to the office and see what was on the stick. From the digital information I held hidden in my hand I would find my direction.

I reached over and turned my digital recorder off.

"Thanks for your help."

I said it sarcastically for the benefit of the other lawyer in the room. I nodded and winked at Meyer, then I left.

As soon as I got to the newsroom I went to my cubicle without checking in at the raft or with Angela Cook. I plugged the data stick into the slot on my laptop computer and opened its contents. There were three files on it. They were labeled SUMMARY.DOC, ARREST.DOC and CONFESS.DOC. The third file was largest by far. I briefly opened it to find that the transcript of Alonzo Winslow's confession was 928 pages long. I closed it, saving it for last, and suspected that because it was labeled CONFESS instead of, say, INTERROGATION, it was a file that had been transmitted to Meyer from the prosecutor. It was a digital world and it was not surprising to me that the transcript from nine hours of questioning a murder suspect would be transmitted from police to prosecutor and from prosecutor to defense in electronic format. With a page count of 928 the costs of printing and reprinting such a document would be high, especially considering it was the product of just one case in a system that carries thousands of cases on any given day. If Meyer wanted to print it out on the public defender's budget, then that was up to him.

After loading the files onto my computer, I e-mailed them to the in-house copy center so that I would have hard copies of everything. Just as I prefer a newspaper you can hold in your hand to a digital version, I like hard copies of the materials I base my stories on.

I decided to take the documents in order even though I was familiar with the charges and the arrest of Alonzo Winslow. The first two documents would set the stage for the confession that followed. The confession would then set the stage for my story.

I opened the summary report on my screen. I assumed this would be a minimalist account of the movements of the investigation leading to the arrest of Winslow. The author of the document was my pal Gilbert Walker, who had so kindly hung up on me the day before. I was not expecting much. The summary was four pages long and had been typed on specific forms and then scanned into a computer to create the digital document I now had. Walker knew as he typed it that his document would be studied for weaknesses and procedural mistakes by lawyers on both sides of the case. The best defense against that was to make the target smaller—to put as little into the report as possible—and from the looks of it Walker had succeeded.

The surprise in the file, however, was not the short summary but the complete autopsy and crime scene reports as well as a set of crime scene photographs. These would be hugely helpful to me when I wrote the description of the crime in my story.

Every reporter has at least a splice of the voyeur gene. Before going to the words I went to the photos. There were forty-eight color photographs taken at the crime scene that depicted the body of Denise Babbit as it had been found in the trunk of her 1999 Mazda Millenia and as it was removed, examined on scene and then finally bagged before being taken away. There were also photographs that showed the interior of the car and the trunk after the removal of the body.

One photo showed her face behind a clear plastic bag pulled over her head and tied tightly around her neck with what looked like common clothesline. Denise Babbit had died with her eyes open in a look of fear. I had seen a fair number of dead people in my time, both in person and in photographs like these. I never got used to the eyes. I had known a homicide detective—my brother, in fact—who told me not to spend too much time with the eyes because they stayed with you long after you turned yours away.

Denise had that kind of eyes. The kind that made you think about her last moments, about what she saw and thought and felt.

I went back to the investigative summary and read it through, highlighting the paragraphs with information I thought was important and useful and moving them onto a new document I had created. I called this file POLICE STORY.DOC and I took each paragraph I had moved from the official report and rewrote it. The language of the police report was stilted and overloaded with abbreviations and acronyms. I wanted to make the story my own.

When I was finished I reviewed my work, looking to make sure it was accurate but still had narrative momentum. I knew that when I finally wrote the story for publication, many of these paragraphs and nuggets of information would be included. If I made a mistake at this early stage it could very well be carried wrong into publication.

Denise Babbit was found in the trunk of her 1999 Mazda Millenia at 9:45 A.M. on Saturday, April 25, 2009, by SMPD patrol officers Richard Cleady and Roberto Jiminez. Detectives Gilbert Walker and William Grady responded as lead investigators of the crime.

The patrol officers had been called by Santa Monica parking enforcement, who found the car in the public beach lot next to the Casa Del Mar hotel. While access to the lot is open overnight, it becomes a pay lot from 9 to 5 every day and any cars still remaining are ticketed if a parking pass is not purchased and displayed on the dashboard. When parking enforcement officer Willy Cortez approached the Mazda to check for a pass he found the car's windows open and the key in the ignition. A woman's purse was in plain view on the passenger seat and its contents were dumped beside it. Sensing that something wasn't right, he called the SMPD and officers Cleady and Jiminez arrived. In the course of checking the license plate in order to determine ownership of the car they noticed that the trunk had been closed on what appeared to be part of a woman's silk-patterned dress. They reached into the car and popped the trunk.

The body of a woman later identified as Denise Babbit, owner of the car, was in the trunk. She was naked
and her clothing—undergarments, dress and shoes—
were found on top of the body.

Denise Babbit was 23 years old. She worked as a
dancer at a Hollywood strip bar called Club Snake Pit.
She lived in an apartment on Orchid Street in Hollywood. She had an arrest record for possession of heroin
dating back to a year before. The case was still pending, the conclusion delayed because of a pretrial intervention program that placed her in an outpatient drug
treatment program. She had been arrested during an
LAPD sting operation in Rodia Gardens in which suspects were observed by undercover police making drug
buys and then stopped after leaving the drive-through
drug market.

Hair and fiber evidence collected from inside the car
included multiple exemplars of canine hair from an
unknown but short-haired dog breed. Denise Babbit did
not own a dog.

The victim had been asphyxiated with a length of
commonly purchased clothesline used to tie the plastic
bag around her neck. There were also ligature marks
on her wrists and legs from when she had been bound
during her abduction. Autopsy would show that she
had been repeatedly raped with a foreign object. Minute splinters found in the vagina and anus indicated this
object was possibly a wooden broom or tool handle. No
semen or hair evidence was collected from the body.

Time of death was set at 12 to 18 hours before the discovery of the body.

The victim had worked her normally scheduled night shift at the Snake Pit, leaving work at 2:15 A.M. on Friday, April 24. Her roommate, Lori Rodgers, 27, a fellow dancer at the Snake Pit, told police that Babbit did not come home after work and never returned to the Orchid Street apartment during the day on Friday. She did not show up for her shift at the Snake Pit that evening and her car and body were found the following morning.

It was estimated that during the previous evening the victim made in excess of $300 in tips while dancing at the Snake Pit. No cash was found in her purse, which had been dumped out in her car.

Crime scene investigators found that the person who abandoned the victim's car with the body in the trunk had unsuccessfully attempted to remove evidence from the car by wiping down all surfaces that potentially held fingerprints. The door handles, steering wheel and shift lever were all wiped clean inside. On the outside, the trunk lid and outside door handles were also wiped clean. However, the investigators found a clear thumbprint on the interior rearview mirror, presumably left when someone driving the car adjusted it.

The thumbprint was matched by computer as well as physical comparison by a latent prints specialist to Alonzo Winslow, 16, who carried a juvenile arrest record for sale of narcotics in the same projects where Denise Babbit had bought heroin and been arrested the year before.

An investigative theory emerged: After leaving her job
in the early morning hours of April 24 the victim drove
to the Rodia Gardens projects in order to buy heroin
or other drugs. Despite her being white and Rodia Gardens' being 98 percent black in population, Denise Babbit was familiar and comfortable going to the projects
to make her purchase because she had purchased drugs
there many times before. She may have even personally known dealers in Rodia Gardens, including Alonzo
Winslow. She may have also had a past history of trading sex for drugs.

However, this time she was forcefully abducted by
Alonzo Winslow and possibly other unknown individ-
uals. She was held in an unknown location and sexually tortured for six to eighteen hours. Because of the
high levels of petechial hemorrhaging around the eyes,
she also appeared to have been repeatedly choked into
unconsciousness and then revived before final asphyxiation occurred. Her body was then stuffed in the trunk
of her car and driven almost twenty miles to Santa
Monica, where the car was abandoned in the ocean-side
parking lot.

With the fingerprint as a solid piece of evidence sup-
porting the theory and linking Babbit to a known drug
dealer in Rodia Gardens, detectives Walker and Grady
obtained an arrest warrant for Alonzo Winslow. The
detectives contacted the LAPD in order to elicit cooperation in locating and arresting the suspect. He was
taken into custody without incident on Sunday morning,

April 26, and after a lengthy interrogation confessed to the murder. The following morning police announced the arrest.

I closed out the summary file and thought about how quickly the investigation had led to Winslow, all because he had missed one fingerprint. He had probably thought that the twenty miles between Watts and Santa Monica was a distance no murder charge could leap. Now he sat in a juvy cell up in Sylmar, wishing he had never turned that rearview mirror to make sure he wasn't being followed by the police.

My desk phone rang and I looked over to see Angela Cook's name on the caller ID screen. I was tempted to let it go, to maintain focus on my story, but I knew it would ring through to the switchboard and whoever answered would tell Angela that I was at my desk but apparently too busy to take her call.

I didn't want that, so I picked up.

"Angela, what's happening?"

"I'm over here at Parker and I think something is going on but nobody's telling me shit."

"Why do you think something's going on?"

"Because there's all kinds of reporters and cameras coming in."

"Where are you?"

"I'm in the lobby. I was leaving when I saw a bunch of these guys coming in."

"And you checked with the press office?"

"Of course I did. But nobody's answering."

"Sorry, that was a stupid question. Um, I can make some calls. Stay there in case you need to go back up. I'll call you right back. Were they only TV guys?"

"Looked like it."

"You know what Patrick Denison looks like?"

Denison was the main cops and crime reporter for the *Daily News*, the only real print competition the *Times* faced on a local level. He was good and every now and then broke an exclusive I would have to chase. It was a reporter's worst embarrassment to have to follow a competitor's scoop. But I wasn't worried about getting scooped here, not if the TV media was already in the building. When you saw TV reporters on a story, that usually meant that they were following yesterday's news or were headed to a press conference. The TV news in this town hadn't had a legitimate scoop since Channel 5 came up with the Rodney King beating tape back in 1991.

After hanging up with Angela I called a lieutenant in Major Crimes to see what was shaking. If he didn't know, then I would try Robbery-Homicide Division and then Narcs. I was confident I would soon know why the media was storming Parker Center, and the *L.A. Times* was the last to know about it.

I talked my way through the city secretary who answers phones in Major Crimes and got to Lieutenant Hardy without much of a wait. Hardy was less than a year in the job and I was still doing the dance with him, slowly procuring him as a trusted source. After I identified myself, I asked what the Hardy Boys were up to. I had taken to calling the detectives in his command the Hardy Boys because I knew giving the lieutenant ownership of the squad played to his ego. The truth was, he was simply a manager of people, and the investigators in his command worked pretty autonomously. But it was part of the dance and so far it had worked.

"We're laying low today, Jack," Hardy said. "Nothing to report."

"You sure? I heard from somebody else in the building that the place is crawling with TV people."

"Yeah, that's for that other thing. We've got nothing to do with that."

At least we weren't behind the curve on a Major Crimes story. That was good.

"What other thing?" I asked.

"You need to talk to either Grossman or the chief's office. They're having the press conference."

I started to get concerned. The chief of police didn't usually hold press conferences to discuss things already in the newspaper. He usually broke things out himself—so he could control information and get credit if credit was due him.

The other reference Hardy had made was to Captain Art Grossman, who was in charge of major narcotics investigations. Somehow we had missed an invitation to a press conference.

I quickly thanked Hardy for the help and told him I would check with him later. I called Angela back and she answered right away.

"Go back in and head up to the sixth floor. There is

some sort of narcotics press conference with the chief and Art Grossman, who is the head narc."

"Okay, what time?"

"I don't know yet. Just get up there in case it's happening right now. You didn't hear about this?"

"No!" she said defensively.

"How long have you been over there?"

"All morning. I've been trying to meet people."

"Okay, get up there and I'll call you back."

After hanging up I started multitasking. While putting in a call to Grossman's office I went online and checked the CNS wire. The City News Service operated a digital newswire that was updated by the minute with breaking news from the city of angels. It was heavy with crime and police news and was primarily a tip service that provided press conference schedules and limited details of crime reports and investigations. As a police reporter I checked it continuously through the day like a stock market analyst keeps his eye on the Dow crawl at the bottom of the screen on the Bloomberg channel.

I could have stayed further connected to CNS by signing up for e-mail and cell phone text alerts, but that wasn't the way I operated. I wasn't a mojo. I was an *oldjo* and didn't want the constant bells and whistles of connectivity.

However, I had neglected to tell Angela about these options. And with her spending the morning at Parker Center and my spending it chasing the Babbit case, nobody had gotten any bells or whistles, and nobody had made the old-fashioned manual checks.

I started scrolling backward on the CNS screen, looking for anything about a police press conference or any other breaking crime news. My call to Grossman was answered by a secretary but she told me the captain was already upstairs—meaning the sixth floor—at a press conference.

Just as I hung up, I found a short blurb on CNS announcing the eleven A.M. press conference in the sixth-floor media room at Parker Center. There was little information other than to say it was to announce the results of a major drug sweep conducted through the night in the Rodia Gardens housing complex.

Bang. Just like that, my long-term story was hooking nicely into a breaking story. The adrenaline kicked in. It often happened this way. The daily grind of the news gave you the opening to say something bigger.

I called Angela back.

"Are you on six?"

"Yeah, and they haven't started. What's this about? I don't want to ask any of these TV people, because then I'll come off as stupid."

"Right. It's about a drug sweep overnight in Rodia Gardens."

"That's it?"

"Yeah, but it could go big because it's probably in response to the murder I told you about yesterday. The woman in the trunk was traced back to that place, remember?"

"Oh, right, right."

"Angela, it connects with what I'm working on, so I

want to try to sell it to Prendo. I want to write it because it will help set up my story."

"Well, maybe we can work on it together. I'll get as much as I can here."

I paused but not too long. I had to be delicate but decisive.

"No, I'm going to come over for the conference. If it starts before I get there, take notes for me. And you can feed them to Prendo for the web. But I want this story, Angela, because it's part of my larger story."

"That's cool, Jack," she said without hesitation. "I'm not trying to bogart the beat. It's still your baby and the story is yours. But if you need anything from me, just ask."

I now thought I had overreacted and was embarrassed at having acted like a selfish prick.

"Thanks, Angela. We'll figure it out. I'm going to give Prendo a heads-up on this for the daily budget and then I'll be over."

Parker Center was in its last months of life. The crumbling building had been the command center for police operations for nearly five decades and was at least one decade past obsolescence. Yet it had served the city well, seen it through two riots, countless civil protests and major crimes, and had been the location of thousands of press conferences like the one I was going to attend right now. But as a working headquarters it was long outdated. It was overcrowded. Its plumbing was shot and its heating-and-air-conditioning system almost useless. There weren't enough parking spots, office space or jail cells. There were known areas in hallways and offices where the air was tainted and sour. There were buckles in the vinyl flooring, and the structure's prospects of surviving a major earthquake were questionable. In fact, many detectives tirelessly worked cases on the street, pursuing clues and suspects to extraordinary lengths, just so they wouldn't be in the office when the big one hit.

A beautiful replacement was weeks from completion on Spring Street, right next to the *Times*. It would be state of the art and spacious and technologically savvy. Hopefully, it would serve the department and the city for another five decades. But I would not be there when it was time to move in. My beautiful replacement would be the one, and as I rode the rickety elevator up to the sixth floor I decided that this was how it was meant to be. I would miss Parker Center precisely because I was like Parker Center. Antiquated and obsolete.

The press conference was in full swing when I got to the big media room next to the chief's office. I pushed past a uniformed officer in the doorway, grabbed a copy of the handout from him and ducked under the line of cameras—a reluctant courtesy—along the back wall and took an open seat. I had been in this room when it was standing room only. Today, with the bottom line being that the PC was about a drug raid, the attendance was perfunctory. I counted representatives from five of the nine local TV channels, two radio reporters, and a handful of print people. I saw Angela in the second row. She had her laptop open and was typing. I assumed she was online and filing for the web edition even as the press conference was still under way. She was a mojo tried-and-true.

I read the handout to get up to speed. It was one long paragraph, designed to set forward the facts, which the police chief and his top narc could elucidate further during the press conference.

In the wake of the murder of Denise Babbit, presumed to have occurred somewhere in the Rodia Gardens Housing Project, the LAPD's South Bureau Narcotics Unit conducted one week of high-intensity surveillance of drug activities in the housing project and arrested sixteen suspected drug dealers in an early morning sweep. The suspects included eleven adult gang members and five juveniles. Undisclosed amounts of heroin, crack cocaine and methamphetamine were seized during raids on twelve different apartments in the housing project. Additionally, Santa Monica police and investigators with the District Attorney's Office executed three search warrants in regard to the murder investigation. The warrants sought additional evidence against the 16-year-old charged with the murder as well as others who may have been involved.

Having read thousands of press releases over the years, I was pretty good at reading between the lines. I knew that when they didn't disclose the amounts of drugs seized it was because the amounts were so low as to probably be embarrassing. And I knew that when the press release said the warrants *sought* additional evidence, then the likelihood was that none had been found. Otherwise, they would have trumpeted the fact that more evidence was gathered in the execution of the warrants.

All of this was of mild interest to me. What had my adrenaline moving was the fact that the drug sweep was in response to the murder and it was an action that was sure to instigate racial controversy. That controversy would help me sell my long-term story to my own command staff.

I looked up at the podium just as the chief was passing the lead to Grossman. The captain stepped up to the microphone and started the narration that went along with a PowerPoint presentation of the sweep. On the screen to the left of the podium, mug shots of the arrested adults started flashing, along with listings of the charges against each individual.

Grossman got into the specifics of the operation, describing how twelve teams of six officers each simultaneously raided twelve different apartments at six-fifty in the morning. He said there was only one injury and that was to an officer who was hurt in a bizarre case of being in the wrong place at the wrong time. The officer was hurrying down the side of one of the project buildings to cover the rear, when the suspect inside was awakened by pounding on his front door. The suspect threw a sawed-off shotgun out the window so as not to be in possession of the illegal weapon. It struck the passing officer in the head, knocking him unconscious. He was treated by paramedics and would be held overnight for observation in an undisclosed hospital.

The mug shot of the gangbanger who had extorted fifty dollars from me the day before flashed on the screen. Grossman identified him as twenty-year-old Darnell Hicks and described him as a "street boss" who had several younger men and boys working for him selling drugs. I felt a small amount of joy seeing his face up there on the big screen and knew I would put his name first among the arrested when I wrote the story for tomorrow's paper. That would be my way of doing the Crip walk right back at him.

Grossman took another ten minutes to finish giving

out the details the department was willing to part with and then opened it up to questions. A couple of the television reporters threw him softballs, which he easily hit over the wall. No one asked him the tough question until I raised my hand. Grossman was scanning the room when he saw my hand. He knew me and where I worked. He knew he wasn't going to get a softball from me. He kept scanning the room, probably hoping that another dimwit TV guy would put up a hand. But he didn't get lucky and had no choice but to bring it back to me.

"Mr. McEvoy, do you have a question?"

"Yes, Captain. I was wondering if you can tell me whether you are expecting any backlash from the community?"

"Backlash from the community? No. Who complains about getting drug dealers and gangbangers off the street? Besides that, we had enormous support and cooperation from the community in regard to this operation. I don't know where the backlash would be in that."

I put the line about support and cooperation from the community into my back pocket for later and stayed on point with my response.

"Well, it's pretty well documented that the drug and gang problems in the Rodia projects have been there for a long time. But the department only mounted this large-scale operation after a white woman from Hollywood got abducted and murdered going down there. I was wondering if the department considered what the community reaction to that would be when it went ahead with this operation."

Grossman's face got pink. He took a quick glance at the chief but the chief made no move to take the question or even help Grossman out. He was on his own.

"We don't...uh, view it that way," he began. "The murder of Denise Babbit only served to focus attention on the problems down there. Our actions today—and the arrests—will help make that community a better place to live. There's no backlash in that. And it's not the first time we have conducted sweep operations in that area."

"Is it the first time you called a press conference about it?" I asked, just to twist him a little.

"I wouldn't know," Grossman said.

His eyes scanned the room for another hand from a reporter but nobody bailed him out.

"I have another question," I said. "In regard to the search warrants evolving from the murder of Denise Babbit, did you find the location where she was allegedly held and murdered after her abduction?"

Grossman was ready for that with a pass-the-buck answer.

"That's not our case. You will have to speak to Santa Monica police or the District Attorney's Office about that."

He seemed pleased with his answer and with stiffing me. I had no further questions and Grossman scanned the room one last time and ended the news conference. I stood near my seat, waiting for Angela Cook to work her way back from the front of the room. I was going to tell her that all I would need from her were her notes on the police chief's comments. I had everything else covered.

The uniformed officer who had given me the handout at the door made his way to me first and signaled me to the door on the other side of the room. I knew it led to a side room where some of the equipment used in presenting the graphics during press conferences was housed.

"Lieutenant Minter wants to show you something," the officer said.

"Good," I said. "I wanted to ask him something."

We went through the door and Minter was there waiting for me, sitting on the corner of a desk, his posture ramrod straight. A handsome man with a trim body, smooth coffee skin, perfect diction and a ready smile, Minter was in charge of the Media Relations Office. It was an important job in the LAPD but one that always confounded me. Why would any cop—after getting the training and the gun and the badge—want to work in media relations, where zero police work was ever done? I knew the job put you on TV almost every night and got your name in the paper all the time, but it wasn't cop work.

"Hey, Jack," Minter said to me in a friendly manner as we shook hands.

I immediately acted like I had called for the meeting.

"Hey, Lieutenant. Thanks for seeing me. I was wondering if I could get a mug shot of the suspect named Hicks for my story."

Minter nodded.

"No problem, he's an adult. You want any others?"

"No, probably just him. They don't like running mug shots, so I probably will only be able to use one, if I'm lucky."

"It's funny that you want a photo of Hicks."

"Why?"

He reached behind his back to the desk and brought around a file. He opened it and handed me an 8 × 10 photo. It was a surveillance shot with police codes in the lower right frame. It was of me handing Darnell Hicks the fifty dollars he had charged me in street tax the day before. I immediately noted how grainy the shot was and knew it had been taken from a distance and at a low angle. Remembering the parking lot where the pay-off had taken place, I knew I had been in the heart of the Rodia projects and the only way the shot could have been taken was if it had been taken from inside one of the surrounding apartment buildings. I now knew what Grossman had meant by community support and cooperation. At least one resident in Rodia had allowed them to use an apartment as a surveillance post.

I held the photo up.

"Are you giving me this for my scrapbook?"

"No, I was just wondering if you can tell me about it. If you have a problem, Jack, I can help."

He had a phony smile on his face. And I was smart enough to know what was happening. He was trying to squeeze me. A photo out of context like this could certainly send the wrong message if leaked to a boss or competitor. But I smiled right back.

"What do you want, Lieutenant?"

"We don't want to stir up controversy where there isn't any needed, Jack. Like with this photo. It could have several different meanings. Why go there?"

The point was clear. Lay off the community backlash angle. Minter and the command staff above him knew that the *Times* set the table as far as what was news in this town. The TV channels and everybody else followed its lead. If it could be controlled or at least contained, then the rest of the local media would fall in line.

"I guess you didn't get the memo," I said. "I'm out. I got a pink slip on Friday, Lieutenant, so there isn't anything you can do to me. I'm down to my last two weeks. So if you want to send this picture to somebody at the paper, I would send it to Dorothy Fowler, the city editor. But it's not going to change who I talk to on this story or what I write. Besides that, do the narcs down in South Bureau know you're showing their surveillance shots around like this? I mean, this is dangerous, Lieutenant."

I held the photo up so he could see it now.

"More than what it says about me, it says your drug team had a setup inside somebody's apartment in Rodia. If that gets out, those Crips down there will probably go on a witch hunt. You remember what happened up on Blythe Street a couple years ago, don't you?"

Minter's smile froze on his face as I watched his eyes go over the memory. Three years earlier the police had conducted a similar peep-and-sweep operation at a Latino gang–operated drive-through drug market on Blythe Street in Van Nuys. When surveillance photos of drug deals were turned over to lawyers defending those arrested, the gang soon figured out what apartment the shots had been taken from. One night the apartment was firebombed and a sixty-year-old woman was burned to death in her bed. The police department didn't get much positive media attention out of it and I thought Minter was suddenly reliving the fiasco.

"I gotta go write," I said. "I'll go down to media relations and pick up the mug shot on my way out. Thanks, Lieutenant."

"Okay, Jack," he said routinely, as if the subterranean context of our conversation had not existed. "Hope to see you again before you go."

I stepped through the door back into the press conference room. Some of the cameramen were still there, packing up their equipment. I looked around for Angela Cook but she hadn't waited for me.

After picking up the mug shot of Darnell Hicks I walked back to the *Times* building and up to the third-floor newsroom. I didn't bother checking in because I had already sent my editor a budget line on the drug sweep story. I planned to make some calls and flesh it out before I went back to Prendo and tried to convince him it was a story that ought to go out front on the home page as well as the print edition.

The 928-page printout of the Winslow confession as well as the other documents I'd sent to the copy shop were waiting for me on my desk. I sat down and had to resist the urge to immediately dive into the confession. But I pushed the six-inch stack to the side and went to the computer. I opened my address book on the screen and looked up the number for the Reverend William Treacher. He was the head of a South L.A. association of ministers and was always good for a viewpoint contrary to that of the LAPD.

I had just picked up the phone to call Preacher Treacher, as he was informally known by his flock as well as the local media, when I felt a presence hovering over me and looked up to see Alan Prendergast.

"Didn't you get my message?" he asked.

"No, I just got back and wanted to call Preacher Treacher before everybody else did. What's up?"

"I wanted to talk about your story."

"Didn't you get the budget line I sent? Let me make this call real quick and then I might have more to add to it."

"Not today's story, Jack. Cook's already putting it together. I want to hear about your long-term story. We have the futures meeting in ten minutes."

"Wait a minute. What do you mean Cook's already putting today's story together?"

"She's writing it up. She came back from the press conference and said you were working together on it. She already called Treacher, too. Got good stuff."

I held back on telling him that Cook and I weren't supposed to be working together on it. It was my story and I'd told her so.

"So whadaya got, Jack? It's related to today's thing, right?"

"Sort of, yeah."

I was still stunned by Cook's move. Competition within the newsroom is common. I just hadn't expected her to be so bold as to lie her way onto a story.

"Jack? I don't have much time."

"Uh, right. Yeah, it's about the murder of Denise Babbit—but from the killer's angle. It's about how sixteen-year-old Alonzo Winslow came to be charged with murder."

Prendo nodded.

"You have the goods?"

By "the goods," I knew he was asking if I had direct access. He wouldn't be interested in a story with *police said* used as attribution everywhere. He wouldn't want to see the word *allegedly* anywhere near this piece if he was going to try to give it a good ride on the futures budget. He wanted a crime feature, a story that went behind the basic news everybody already had and rocked the reader's world with gritty reality. He wanted breadth and depth, the hallmark features of any *Times* story.

"I have a direct line in. I've got the kid's grandmother and his lawyer, and I'm probably going to see the kid tomorrow."

I pointed to the freshly printed stack of documents on my desk.

"And that's the pot of gold. His nine-hundred-page confession. I shouldn't have it but I do. And nobody else will get it."

Prendo nodded with approval and I could tell he was thinking, trying to come up with a way to sell the story in the meeting or make it better. He backed out of the cubicle, grabbed a nearby chair and pulled it over.

"I've got an idea, Jack," he said as he sat down and leaned toward me.

He was using my name too much and the leaning into my personal space was uncomfortable and seemed completely phony, since he had never done it with me before. I didn't like the way this was going.

"What is it, Alan?"

"What if it wasn't just about how a boy became a

murderer? What if it was also about how a girl became a murder victim?"

I thought about it for a moment and slowly nodded. And that was my mistake, because when you start by saying yes, it becomes hard to put the brakes on and say no.

"It's just going to take me more time when I split the focus of the story like that."

"No, it won't because you won't have to split your focus. You stay with that kid and give us a kick-ass story. We'll put Cook on the vic and she'll cover that angle. Then you, Jack, weave both strands together and we've got a column-one story."

Column one on the front page was reserved each day for the signature story of the paper. The best-written piece, the one with the most impact, the long-term project—if the story was good enough, it went out front, above the fold and in column one. I wondered if Prendergast knew he was taunting me. In seven years with the *Times* I had never had a column-one story. In more than two thousand days on the beat, I had never come up with the best piece of the day. He was waving the possibility of going out the door with a column-one at me like a big fat carrot.

"Did she give you this idea?"

"Who?"

"Who do you think? Cook."

"No, man, I just thought of it. Right now. What do you think?"

"I'm wondering who's going to cover the cop shop while we're both running with this."

"Well, you both can trade off on it. Like you've been doing. And I can probably get some help from time to time from the GA group. Even if it was just you on this, I couldn't cut you loose completely, anyway."

Whenever general assignment reporters were pulled in to work the crime beat, the resulting stories were usually superficial and by the numbers. It wasn't the way to cover the beat, but what did I care anymore? I had eleven days left and that was it.

I didn't believe Prendergast for a moment and was not swayed by his column-one overture. But I was smart enough to know that his suggestion—whether truly his or Angela Cook's—could lead to a better story. And it had a better chance of doing what I wanted it to do.

"We could call it 'The Collision,'" I said. "The point where these two—killer and victim—came together and how they got there."

"Perfect!" Prendergast exclaimed.

He stood up, smiling.

"I'll wing it in the meeting, but why don't you and Cook put your heads together and give me something for the budget by the end of the day? I'm going to tell them you'll turn the story in by the end of the week."

I thought about that. It was not a lot of time but it was doable, and I knew I could get more days if needed.

"Fine," I said.

"Good," he said. "I gotta go."

He headed on to his meeting. In a carefully worded e-mail I invited Angela to meet me in the cafeteria to get a cup of coffee. I gave no indication that I was upset with or suspicious of her. She responded immediately, saying she would meet me there in fifteen minutes.

Now that I was free of the daily story and had fifteen minutes to fill, I pulled the stack back over to the center of the desk and started reading the confession of Alonzo Winslow.

The interview was conducted by the lead detectives Gilbert Walker and William Grady at the Santa Monica Police Department beginning at eleven A.M., Sunday, April 26, about three hours after Winslow had been taken into custody. The transcript was in Q&A format with very little description added. It was easy and fast to read, the questions and answers mostly short at first. Back and forth like Ping-Pong.

They began by reading Winslow his rights and having the sixteen-year-old acknowledge that he understood them. Then they went through a series of questions employed at the start of interviews with juveniles. These were designed to elicit his knowledge of right and wrong. Once that was established, Winslow became fair game.

For his part, Winslow fell victim to ego and the oldest flaw in the human book. He thought he could outsmart them. He thought he could talk his way out of it and maybe pick up some inside information about their investigation. So he readily agreed to talk to them—what innocent kid wouldn't?—and they played him like a three-string bass guitar. *Dum-de-dum-de-dumb*. Getting every implausible explanation and outright lie on record.

I breezed through the first two hundred pages, skipping page after page of Winslow's denials of knowing anything or seeing anything pertaining to Denise Babbit's murder. Then, in very casual conversation, the detectives turned the questions toward Winslow's whereabouts on the night in question, obviously trying to get either facts or lies on the record, because either way they would be helpful to the case—a fact was a marker that could help them navigate through the interview; a lie could be used like a club on Winslow when revealed.

Winslow told them that he was at home sleeping and his "moms"—Wanda Sessums—could vouch for him. He continually denied any knowledge of Denise Babbit, repeatedly rejected knowing her or anything about her abduction and murder. He held up like a rock, but then on page 305 the detectives started lying to him and setting traps.

WALKER: That's not going to work, Alonzo. You gotta give us something here. You can't just sit there and say no, no, no, I don't know anything, and expect to walk out of here. We know you know something. I mean, we know it, son.

WINSLOW: You don't know shit. I ain't ever seen that girl you been talking about.

WALKER: Really? Then how come we got you on tape dropping her car in that parking lot by the beach?

WINSLOW: What tape you got?

WALKER: The one of the parking lot. We got you getting out of that car and nobody else goes near it until
they find the body in it. That puts this whole thing on
you, man.
WINSLOW: Nah, it ain't me. I didn't do this.

As far as I knew from the discovery documents the
defense lawyer had given me, there was no video that
showed the victim's Mazda being left in the parking lot.
But I also knew that the U.S. Supreme Court had upheld
the legality of the police's lying to a suspect if the lie
would reasonably be seen as such by an innocent person. By spinning everything off the one piece of evidence
they did have—Winslow's fingerprint on the rearview
mirror—they were within bounds of this guideline and
they were leading Winslow down the path.

I once wrote a story about an interrogation where the
detectives showed the suspect an evidence bag containing the gun used in the murder. It wasn't the real murder
weapon. It was an exact duplicate. But when the suspect saw it, he copped to the crime because he figured
the police had found all the evidence. A murderer was
caught but I didn't feel too good about it. It never seemed
right or fair to me that the representatives of our government were allowed to employ lies and tricks—just like
the bad guys—with full approval of the Supreme Court.

I read on, skimming another hundred or so pages,
until my cell phone rang. I looked at the screen and realized I had read right through my coffee meeting with
Angela.

"Angela? Sorry, I got tied up. I'm coming right down."

"Please hurry. I need to finish today's story."

I hustled down the steps to the first-floor cafeteria and joined her at a table without getting any coffee. I was twenty minutes late and I saw her cup was empty. On the table next to it was a stack of paper turned print-side down.

"You want another latte?"

"No, I'm fine."

"Okay."

I looked around. It was midafternoon and the cafeteria was almost empty.

"Jack, what's up? I need to get back upstairs."

I looked directly at her.

"I just wanted to tell you face-to-face that I didn't appreciate you guzzling today's story. The beat is technically still mine, and I told you I wanted this story because it set up the bigger one I'm working on."

"I'm sorry. I got excited when you asked all the right questions in the press conference and I got back to the newsroom and sort of exaggerated things. I said we were working on it together. Prendo told me to start writing."

"Is that when you suggested to Prendo that we work together on my other story, too?"

"I didn't. I don't know what you're talking about."

"When I got back, he told me we were on it together. I take the killer and you take the victim. He also told me it was your idea."

Her face colored red and she shook her head in embar-

rassment. I had now outed two liars. Angela I could deal
with because there was something honest about her lying.
She was boldly going for what she wanted. Prendo was
the one that hurt. We had worked together for a long
time and I had never seen him as a liar or manipulator.
I guessed he was just choosing sides. I was out the door
soon and Angela was staying. It didn't take a genius to
see that he was picking her over me. The future was with
Angela.

"I can't believe he ratted me out," Angela said.

"Yeah, well, I guess you have to be careful who you
trust in a newsroom," I said. "Even your own editor."

"I guess so."

She picked up her cup and looked to see if there was
anything left, even though she knew there wasn't. Anything to avoid looking at me.

"Look, Angela, I don't like how you did this but I
admire how you just go after what you want. All the best
reporters I have known are that way. And I have to say
your idea of doing the double-profile of both killer and
victim is the better way to go."

Now she looked at me. Her face brightened.

"Jack, I'm really looking forward to working with you
on it."

"The one thing I want to get straight right now is that
this started with me and it ends with me. When the reporting is all done, I'm the one who is going to write this.
Okay?"

"Oh, absolutely. After you told me what you were

working on, I just wanted to be a part of it. So I came up with the victim angle. But it's your story, Jack. You get to write it and your name goes first on the byline."

I studied her closely for any sign that she was dissembling. But she'd looked me sincerely in the eye as she had spoken.

"All right. Well, that's all I had to say."

"Good."

"You need any help with today's story?"

"No, I think I'm all set. And I'm getting great stuff from the community off that angle you brought up at the press conference. Reverend Treacher called it one more symptom of racism in the department. They create a task force when a white woman who takes her clothes off for a living and puts drugs in her body gets killed, but do nothing whenever one of the eight hundred innocent residents in those projects gets killed by the gangbangers."

It sounded like a good quote but it came from the wrong voice. The reality was that Treacher was an opportunistic weasel. I never bought that he was standing up for the community. I thought he was usually just standing up for himself, getting on TV and in the papers to further serve his celebrity and the benefits it brought. I had once suggested to an editor that we do an investigation of Treacher but was immediately shot down. The editor said, "No, Jack, we need him."

And that was true. The paper needed people like Treacher to voice the contrarian view, to give the incendiary remark and get the fire burning.

"Sounds good," I said to Angela. "I'll let you get back to it and I'll go up and write up a budget line for the other story."

"Here," she said.

She slid the short stack of papers across the table to me.

"What's this?"

"Nothing, really, but it might save you some time. Last night before I went home I was thinking about the story after you told me what you were working on. I almost called you to talk more about it and suggest we work together. But I chickened out and went on Google instead. I checked out 'trunk murder' and found there is a long history of people ending up in the trunks of cars. A lot of women, Jack. And a lot of mob guys, too."

I turned the pages over and looked at the top sheet. It was a printout of a *Las Vegas Review-Journal* story from almost a year earlier. The first paragraph told me it was about the conviction of a man charged with murdering his ex-wife, putting her body into the trunk of his car, and then parking it in his own garage.

"That's just a story that sounded a little like yours," she said. "There's some others in there about historical cases. There's a local one from the nineties where this movie guy was found in the trunk of his Rolls-Royce, which was parked on the hill above the Hollywood Bowl. And I even found a website called trunk murder dot com, but it's still under construction."

I nodded hesitantly.

"Uh, thanks. I'm not sure where all this might fit in but it's good to be thorough, I guess."

"Yeah, that's what I was thinking."

She pushed her chair back and picked up her empty cup.

"Well, okay, then. I'll e-mail you a copy of today's story as soon as I have it ready to send in."

"You don't have to do that. It's your story now."

"No, your name is going on it, too. You asked the questions that gave it good ol' B and D."

Breadth and depth. What the editors want. What the reputation of the *Times* was built on. Drilled into you from day one, when you came to the velvet coffin. Give your stories breadth and depth. Don't just tell what happened. Tell what it means and how it fits into the life of the city and the reader.

"Okay, well, thanks," I said. "Just let me know and I'll give it a quick read."

"You want to walk up together?"

"Uh, no, I'm going to get a coffee and maybe look through all this stuff you came up with."

"Suit yourself."

She gave me a pouty smile like I was missing something really good and then walked away. I watched her dump her coffee cup into a trash can and head out of the cafeteria. I wasn't sure what was happening. I didn't know if I was her partner or mentor, whether I was training her to take over or she already had. My instinct told me that I might only have eleven days left on the job but I would have to watch my back with her during every one of them.

After writing up a budget line and e-mailing it to Prendergast, and then signing off on Angela's story for the print edition, I found an unoccupied pod in the far corner of the newsroom where I could concentrate on the Alonzo Winslow transcript and not be intruded on by phone calls, e-mail or other reporters. The transcript had my full attention now and as I read, I marked with yellow Post-its pages where there were significant quotes.

The reading went fast except in places where there was more than the back and forth of ping-pong dialogue. At one point the detectives scammed Winslow into a damaging admission and I had to read the passage twice to understand what they did. Grady apparently pulled out a tape measure. He explained to Winslow that they wanted to take a measurement of the line that ran from the tip of his thumb to the tip of his first index finger on each hand.

Winslow cooperated and then the detectives announced that the measurements matched to within a quarter inch the strangulation marks left on Denise Babbit's neck. Winslow responded with a vigorous denial of involvement in the murder and then made a big mistake.

WINSLOW: Beside that, the bitch wasn't even strangled with anybody's hands. Motherfucker tied a plastic bag over her head.
WALKER: And how do you know that, Alonzo?

I could almost see Walker smiling when he asked it. Winslow had slipped up in a huge way.

WINSLOW: I don't know, man. It must've been on TV or something. I heard it somewhere.
WALKER: No, son, you didn't, because we never put that out. The only person who knew that was the person who killed her. Now, do you want to tell us about it while we can still help you, or do you want to play it dumb and go down hard for it?
WINSLOW: I'm telling you motherfuckers, I didn't kill her like that.
GRADY: Then tell us what you did do to her.
WINSLOW: Nothing, man. Nothing!

The damage was done and the slide had begun. You don't have to be an interrogator at Abu Ghraib to know that time never favors the suspect. Walker and Grady were patient, and as the minutes and hours ticked by, Alonzo Winslow's will finally began to erode. It was too much to go up alone against two veteran cops who knew things about the case that he didn't. By page 830 of the manuscript he began to crack.

WINSLOW: I want to go home. I want to see my moms. Please, let me go talk to her and I'll come back tomorrow to be with you fellas.

WALKER: That's not happening, Alonzo. We can't let you go until we know the truth. If you want to finally start telling us the truth, then we can talk about getting you home to Moms.

WINSLOW: I didn't do this shit. I never met that bitch.

GRADY: Then how did your fingerprints get all over that car, and how come you know how she was strangled?

WINSLOW: I don't know. That can't be true about my prints. You fuckers lying to me.

WALKER: Yeah, you think we're lying because you wiped that car down real good, didn't you? But you forgot something, Alonzo. You forgot the rearview mirror! Remember how you turned it to make sure nobody was following you? Yeah, that was it. That was the mistake that's going to put you in a cell the rest of your life unless you own up to things and be a man and tell us what happened.

GRADY: Hey, we can understand. Pretty white girl like that. Maybe she mouthed off to you or maybe she wanted to trade, a little poon for a spoon. We know how it works. But something happened and she got killed. If you can tell us, then we can work with you, maybe even get you home to Moms.

Winslow: Nah, man, you got it all wrong.

Walker: Alonzo, I'm tired of all your bullshit. I want to get home myself. We've been going at this for too long trying to help you out. I want to get home to my dinner. So you either come clean right now, son, or you're going into a cell. I'll call your moms and tell her you ain't never coming back.

Winslow: Why you want to do this to me? I'm nobody, man. Why you setting me up for this shit?

Grady: You set yourself up, kid, when you strangled the girl.

Winslow: I didn't!

Walker: Whatever. You can tell that to your moms through the glass when she comes visit you. Stand up. You're going to a cell and I'm going home.

Grady: He said, Stand up!

Winslow: Okay, okay. I'll tell you. I'll tell you what I know and then you let me go.

Grady: You tell us what really happened.

Walker: And then we talk about it. You got ten seconds and then this is over.

Winslow: Okay, okay, this is the shit. I was walking Fuckface and I saw her car over by the towers and when I look inside I saw the keys and I saw her purse just sitting there.

Walker: Wait a minute. Who's Fuckface?

Winslow: My dog.

Walker: You have a dog? What kind of dog?

Winslow: Yeah, for like protection. She a pit.

Walker: Is that a short-hair dog?

WINSLOW: Yeah, she short.

WALKER: I mean her fur. It's not long hair.

WINSLOW: No, she short-hair, yeah.

WALKER: Okay, where was the girl?

WINSLOW: Nowhere, man. Like I told you, I never saw her—when she was alive, I mean.

WALKER: Uh-huh, so this is just a boy and his dog story, huh? Then what?

WINSLOW: So then I jump in the ride and take off.

WALKER: With the dog?

WINSLOW: Yeah, with my dog.

WALKER: Where did you go?

WINSLOW: Just for a ride, man. Get some fuckin' air.

WALKER: All right, that's it. I'm tired of your bullshit. This time we go.

WINSLOW: Wait, wait. I took it over by the Dumpsters, okay? Back in Rodia. I wanted to see what I got in the car, okay? So I pull in and I check out her purse and it's got like two hundred fifty dollars and I check the glove box and everything and then I popped the trunk, and there she was. Plain as motherfuckin' day and already dead, man. She was naked but I didn't touch her. And that's the shit.

GRADY: So you are now telling us and you want us to believe that you stole the car and it already had the dead girl in the trunk.

WINSLOW: That's right, man. You ain't pinning nothing else on me. When I saw her in there, that was fucked up. I closed that lid faster than you can say mother-fucker. I drove that car outta there and I was thinking

I'd just put it back where I found it, but then I knew it would bring all kinda pressure down on my boys, so I drove it on up to the beach. I figure she a white girl, I put her in the white 'hood. So that's what I did and that's all I did.

WALKER: When did you wipe the car down?

WINSLOW: Right there, man. Like you said, I missed the mirror. Fuck it.

WALKER: Who helped you dump the car?

WINSLOW: Nobody helped me. I was on my own.

WALKER: Who wiped the car down?

WINSLOW: Me.

WALKER: Where and when?

WINSLOW: At the parking lot, when I got up there.

GRADY: How'd you get back to the 'hood?

WINSLOW: I walked mostly. Walked all fucking night down to Oakwood and then I got a bus.

WALKER: You still had your dog with you?

WINSLOW: No, man, I dropped her with my girlfriend. That's where she stay 'cause my moms don't want no dog in the house on account of all the people's laundry and shit.

WALKER: So who killed the girl?

WINSLOW: How would I know? She dead when I found her.

WALKER: You just stole her car and robbed her money.

WINSLOW: That's it, man. That's all you got me on. I give you that.

WALKER: Well, Alonzo, that doesn't add up to the evidence we've got. We got your DNA on her.

WINSLOW: No, you don't. That a lie!

WALKER: Yes, we do. You killed her, kid, and you're
    going down for it.
WINSLOW: No! I didn't kill nobody!

And so it went for another hundred pages. The cops
threw lies and accusations at Winslow and he denied
them. But as I read those last pages, I quickly came to
realize something that stood out like a 72-point headline. Alonzo Winslow never said he did it. He never said
he strangled Denise Babbit. If anything, he denied it dozens of times. The only confession in his so-called confession was his acknowledgment that he had taken her
money and then dumped the car with her body inside it.
But that was a long way from him taking credit for her
murder.

I got up and quickly walked back over to my pod and
dug through the stack of papers in my outbox, looking
for the press release distributed by the SMPD after Winslow was arrested for the murder. I finally found it and
sat down to reread its four paragraphs. Knowing what I
knew now from the transcript, I realized how the police
had manipulated the media into reporting something
that was not, indeed, true.

The Santa Monica Police announced today that a 16-
year-old gang member from South Los Angeles has been
taken into custody in the death of Denise Babbit. The
youth, whose name will not be released because of his
age, was being held by juvenile authorities at a detention
center in Sylmar.

Police spokesmen said identification of fingerprints collected from the victim's car after her body was found in the trunk Saturday morning led detectives to the suspect. He was taken in for questioning Sunday from the Rodia Gardens housing project in Watts, where it was believed the abduction and murder took place.

The suspect faces charges of murder, abduction, rape and robbery. During a confession to investigators, the suspect said he moved the car with the body in the trunk to a beach parking lot in Santa Monica so as to throw off suspicions that Babbit had been killed in Watts.

The SMPD wishes to acknowledge the help of the Los Angeles Police Department in bringing the suspect into custody.

The press release was not inaccurate. But I now viewed it very cynically and thought it had been carefully crafted to convey something that was not accurate, that there had been a full confession to the murder when there had not been anything close to that. Winslow's lawyer was right. The confession would not hold up, and there was a solid chance that his client was innocent.

In the field of investigative journalism, the Holy Grail might be the taking down of a president, but when it came to the lowly crime beat, proving a guilty man innocent was as good as it gets. It didn't matter how Sonny Lester had tried to play it down the day we went to Rodia Gardens. Springing an innocent kid trumped all. Alonzo

Winslow may not have been judged guilty of anything yet, but in the media he had been condemned.

I had been part of that lynching and I now saw that I might have a shot at changing all of that and doing the right thing. I might be able to rescue him.

I thought of something and looked around on my desk for the printouts Angela had produced from her research on trunk murders. I then remembered I had thrown them out. I got up and quickly left the newsroom, going down the stairs to the cafeteria. I went directly to the trash receptacle I had used after looking over the printouts Angela had pushed across the table to me as a peace offering. I had scanned and dismissed them, thinking at the time that there was no way stories about other trunk murders could have any bearing on a story about the collision between a sixteen-year-old admitted killer and his victim.

Now I wasn't so sure. I remembered things about the stories from Las Vegas that no longer seemed distant in light of my conclusions from Alonzo's so-called confession.

It was a large commercial trash can. I took the top off it and found that I was in luck. The printouts were on top of the day's detritus and were no worse for wear.

It dawned on me that I could have simply gone on Google and conducted the same search as Angela instead of rooting through a trash can, but I was elbows deep now and this would be quicker. I took the printouts over to a table to reread them.

"Hey!"

I turned and saw a double-wide woman with her hair in a net staring at me with her fists balled tightly on her ample hips.

"You just going to leave that there?"

I looked behind me and saw I had left the top of the trash receptacle on the floor.

"Sorry."

I went back and returned the top to its rightful place, then decided it would be best to review the printouts back in the newsroom. At least the editors weren't wearing hairnets.

Back at my desk I looked through the stack. Angela had found several news stories about bodies being found in trunks. Most were quite old and seemed irrelevant. But a series of stories in the *Las Vegas Review-Journal* did not. There were five of them and they mostly repeated the same information. They were reports on the arrest and trial of a man charged with killing his ex-wife and stuffing her body into the trunk of his car.

Ironically, the stories had been written by a reporter I knew. Rick Heikes had worked for the *Los Angeles Times* until he took one of the early buyouts. He banked the check from the *Times* and promptly took the job with the *Review-Journal* and had been there ever since. He had made it over the wall and by all accounts was the better for it. The *Times* was the loser because it had let another fine reporter go to another newspaper.

I quickly scanned the stories until I found the one I remembered. It was a report on the trial testimony given by the Clark County coroner.

Coroner: Ex-Wife Held, Tortured for Hours

BY RICK HEIKES,
Review-Journal Staff Writer

Autopsy results showed that Sharon Oglevy was strangled more than 12 hours after her abduction, the Clark County coroner testified Wednesday in the murder trial of the victim's ex-husband.

Gary Shaw testified for the prosecution and revealed new details of the abduction, rape and murder. He said the time of death was determined during autopsy to be approximately 12 to 18 hours after a witness saw Oglevy forced into a van in a parking garage behind the Cleopatra Casino and Resort, where she worked as a dancer in the exotic Femmes Fatales show.

"For at least twelve hours she was with her abductor and many horrible things were done to her before she was finally killed," Shaw testified under questioning from the prosecutor.

A day later her body was found in the trunk of her ex-husband's car by police officers who had gone to his home in Summerland to ask if he knew his ex-wife's whereabouts. He allowed the police to search the premises and the body was found in the car parked in the home's garage. The couple's marriage had dissolved eight months earlier in an acrimonious divorce. Sharon Oglevy had sought a restraining order prohibiting her ex-husband, a blackjack dealer, from coming within 100 feet of her. In her petition she said her husband had threatened to kill her and bury her in the desert.

Brian Oglevy was charged with first degree murder, kidnapping and rape with a foreign object. Investigators said they believed he had placed the victim's body in the trunk of his car with the intention of burying it later in the desert. He has denied killing his ex-wife and said he was set up as a fall guy for her murder. He has been held without bail since his arrest.

Shaw provided jurors with several lurid and ghastly details of the murder. He said Sharon Oglevy was raped and sodomized repeatedly with an unknown foreign object that left significant internal injuries. He said histamine levels in the body were unusually high, indicating that the injuries that caused her body to manufacture the chemical had occurred well before her death by asphyxiation.

Shaw testified that Oglevy had been asphyxiated with a plastic bag that had been pulled over her head and tied closed around her neck. He said several cord markings or furrows on the victim's neck and a high level of hemorrhaging around her eyes indicated she had been asphyxiated slowly and may have been allowed to lose and regain consciousness several times.

While Shaw's testimony illuminated much of the prosecution's theory of how the murder took place, there are still blanks to fill in. Las Vegas Metro Police have never been able to determine where Brian Oglevy allegedly held and then murdered his ex-wife. Crime scene technicians spent three days examining his home after his arrest and determined that it was unlikely that the murder occurred there. The defendant has also not been linked by evidence to a van, which witnesses said Sharon Oglevy was abducted in.

Brian Oglevy's attorney, William Schifino, objected several times during the coroner's testimony, asking the judge to stop Shaw from editorializing and putting his personal view of the details into his testimony. Schifino was successful at times, but for the most part the judge allowed Shaw to speak his mind.

The trial continues today. Schifino is expected to mount his defense sometime next week. Brian Oglevy has denied killing his wife since the crime occurred but has not publicly offered a theory on who killed her and set him up to take the fall.

I studied the *Review-Journal*'s trial stories that came before and after the one I had just read, and none gripped me like the report on the autopsy. The missing hours and the plastic bag and slow asphyxiation were descriptions that matched the murder of Denise Babbit. And, of course, the car trunk was the strongest match of all.

I pushed back from the desk but stayed in my seat, thinking. Could there be a connection here or was I engaged in a reporter's fantasy, seeing innocent people accused of crimes they did not commit? Had Angela, in her industrious but naive manner, stumbled onto something that was under the radar of all of law enforcement?

I didn't know—yet. But there was one way to find out. I had to go to Las Vegas.

I stood up and headed toward the raft. I had to inform Prendo and get a travel authorization. But when I got there his seat was empty.

"Anybody seen Prendo?" I asked the other aces on the raft.

"He took early dinner," said one. "He should be back in an hour."

I checked my watch. It was after four and I needed to get moving, first home to pack a bag, and then to the airport. If I couldn't get a flight on short notice, I'd drive to Vegas. I glanced over at Angela Cook's cubicle and saw it was empty, too. I walked over to the switchboard and looked up at Lorene. She pulled one earphone back.

"Did Angela Cook check out?"

"She said she was going out for a bite to eat with her editor but that she'd be back after. You want her cell number?"

"No, thanks, I've got it."

I headed back to my desk with suspicion and anger growing inside in equal parts. My ace and my replacement had gone off together to break bread and I was not informed or invited. To me it only meant one thing. They were planning their next assault on my story.

That was okay, I decided. I was a giant step ahead of them and planned to stay that way. While they were off scheming I would be off chasing the real story. And I would get there first.

FIVE: The Farm

Carver had been busy all day routing and opening the final gateways that would allow for a test run of data transmission from Mercer and Gissal in St. Louis. It had consumed him and he had not made his appointed rounds until late in the day. He checked his traps and a charge shot through his chest when he saw he had caught something in one of his cages. The screen avatar displayed it as a fat gray rat running on a wheel inside the cage labeled TRUNK MURDER.

Using his mouse, Carver opened the cage and took out the rat. Its eyes were ruby red and its sharp teeth gleamed with ice-blue saliva. The animal wore a collar with a silver identity tag on it. He clicked on the tag and brought up the rat's information. The date and time of the visit had occurred the night before, just after he had last checked his traps. A ten-digit Internet protocol address had been captured. The visit to his www.trunkmurder.com site had lasted only twelve seconds. But it was enough. It meant someone out there had plugged the words *trunk murder* into a search engine. Now he would try to find out who and why.

Two minutes later Carver's breath caught in his throat

as he followed the IP—a basic computer address—back to an Internet service provider. There was good and bad news. The good news: it wasn't a huge provider like Yahoo, which had traffic gateways all over the world and was time-consuming as hell to trace. The bad news: it was a small private provider with the domain name of LATimes.com.

The *Los Angeles Times,* he thought as something inside clutched his chest. A reporter from Los Angeles had gone to his trunk murder website. Carver leaned back in his chair and thought about how he should approach this. He had the IP address but no name to go with it. He couldn't even be sure it was a reporter who had made the visit. A lot of non-reporters work at newspapers.

He rolled his chair down to the next workstation. He logged on as McGinnis, having broken his codes long ago. He went to the *Los Angeles Times* website and in the search window of the online archive typed *trunk murder.*

He got three hits on stories containing the phrase in the last three weeks, including one published on the website just that evening and due to go into the next morning's paper. He pulled the latest story up on screen first and read it.

• • •

LAPD Drug Crackdown Draws Community Fire

BY ANGELA COOK and JACK MCEVOY
Times Staff Writers

A drug crackdown at a housing project in Watts has drawn fire from local activists who complained Tuesday that the LAPD only paid attention to the problem in the minority-populated complex when a white woman was allegedly murdered there.

Police announced the arrest of 16 residents of Rodia Gardens on drug charges and the seizure of a small amount of drugs following a one-week investigation. Police spokesmen said the "peep and sweep" operation was in response to the murder of Denise Babbit, 23, of Hollywood.

A 16-year-old alleged gang member who is a resident of Rodia Gardens was arrested in the slaying. Babbit's body was found two weeks ago in the trunk of her car at a beachside parking lot in Santa Monica. The investigation traced the crime back to Rodia Gardens, where Santa Monica police believe Babbit, an exotic dancer, went to buy drugs. Instead, she was abducted, held for several hours and repeatedly sexually assaulted before being strangled.

Several community activists questioned why efforts to stem the tide of drug dealing and related crime in the projects did not come before the murder. They were quick to point out that the victim of the trunk murder was white while the members of the community are almost 100 percent African American.

"Look, let's face it," said Rev. William Treacher, head of a group called South Los Angeles Ministers, also known as SLAM, "this is just another form of police racism. They ignore Rodia Gardens and let it become a stew of drugs and gang crime. Then this white woman who puts drugs in her body and takes her clothes off for a living goes down and gets herself killed there and what do you get? A task force. Where were the police before this? Where was the task force? Why does it take a crime against a white person to draw attention to problems in the black community?"

A police spokesman denied that race had anything to do with the anti-drug operation and said similar operations have occurred in Rodia Gardens numerous times before.

"Who complains about getting drug dealers and gangbangers off the street?" asked Capt. Art Grossman, who directed the operation.

Carver stopped reading the story. He didn't sense any threat to him. Still, it didn't explain why someone from the *Times*—presumably Cook or McEvoy—had put *trunk murder* into a search engine. Were they just being thorough, covering all the bases? Or was there something else? He looked at the two previous stories in the archives that mentioned trunk murder and found they had been written by McEvoy. They were straight news stories about the

Denise Babbit case, one about the discovery of her body, and the second—a day later—about the arrest of the young gangbanger in her murder.

Carver couldn't help but smile to himself as he read about the kid getting tagged for the murder. But his humor didn't let him drop his caution. He plugged McEvoy into the archive search and soon found hundreds of stories, all related to crime in Los Angeles. He was the crime beat reporter. At the bottom of each of his stories was his e-mail address: JackMcEvoy@LATimes.com.

Carver then put Angela Cook into the search engine and got far fewer stories. She had been writing for the *Times* for less than six months and only in the past week had she written any crime stories. Before that, she wrote a variety of stories on events ranging from a garbage strike to a competitive eating contest. She seemed to have no specific beat until this week when she shared two bylines with McEvoy.

"He's teaching her the ropes," Carver said out loud.

He guessed that Cook was young and McEvoy was old. That would make her the easier mark. He took a chance and went onto Facebook, using a phony ID he had concocted long ago, and sure enough she had a page. The contents weren't for public consumption but her photo was there. She was a beauty with shoulder-length blond hair. Green eyes and a trained pout to her lips. That pout, Carver thought. He could change that.

The photo was a portrait shot. He was disappointed that he could not see all of her. Especially the length and shape of her legs.

He started humming. It always calmed him. Songs he remembered from the sixties and seventies, when he was a boy. Hard rockers a woman could dance and show her body off to.

He kept searching, finding that Angela Cook had abandoned a MySpace page a few years earlier but had not deleted it. He also found a professional profile on LinkedIn and that led to the mother lode—a blog page called www.CityofAngela.com in which she kept an ongoing diary of her life and work in Los Angeles.

The latest entry in the blog brimmed with Cook's excitement over being assigned to the police and crime beat, and being trained for the position by the veteran Jack McEvoy.

It was always amazing to Carver how trusting or naive young people were. They didn't believe that anybody could connect the dots. They believed that they could bare their souls on the Internet, post photos and information at will, and not expect any consequences. From her blog he was able to glean all the information he needed about Angela Cook. Her hometown, her college sorority, even her dog's name. He knew Death Cab for Cutie was her favorite band and pizza at a place called Mozza was her favorite food. In between the meaningless data, he learned her birthday and that she only had to walk two blocks from her apartment to get her favorite pizza at her favorite restaurant. He was circling her and she didn't even know it. But each time around he got closer.

He paused when he found a blog post from nine months earlier with the heading *My Top 10 Serial Killers*. Below it she listed ten killers that were household names because of their cross-country rampages of murder. Number one on her list was Ted Bundy—*Because I'm from Florida and that's where he ended up.*

Carver's lip twitched. He liked this girl.

The mantrap alert sounded and Carver immediately killed the Internet connection. He switched screens and on the camera saw McGinnis coming through. Carver swiveled around and was facing McGinnis as he opened the final door to the control room. He had his key card on a retractable cord that was clipped to his belt. It made him look like a dork.

"What are you doing out here?" he asked.

Carver stood up and rolled the chair back into place at the empty workstation.

"I'm running a program in my office and just wanted to check something on Mercer and Gissal."

McGinnis didn't seem to care. He looked through the main window into the server room, the heart and soul of the business.

"How's that going?" he asked.

"A few routing hiccups," Carver reported. "But we'll work it out and we'll be up and running before the target date. I may have to go back out there but it will be a quick trip."

"Good. Where is everybody? You alone?"

"Stone and Early are in the back, building a tower. I'm watching things up here until my night shift comes in."

McGinnis nodded approvingly. Building another tower meant more business.

"Anything else happening?"

"We have an issue in tower thirty-seven. I moved things off it until I can figure it out. It's temporary."

"We lose anything?"

"Not that I can tell."

"Whose blade?"

"Belongs to a private nursing facility in Stockton, California. Not a big one."

McGinnis nodded. It wasn't a client he needed to worry about.

"What about last week's intrusion?" he asked.

"Taken care of. The target was Guthrie, Jones. They're in tobacco litigation with a firm called Biggs, Barlow and Cowdry. In Raleigh-Durham. Somebody at Biggs—a low-ranking genius—thought Guthrie was holding back on discovery and tried to take a look for himself."

"And?"

"The FBI has opened a child porn investigation and the genius is the primary target. I don't think he'll be around to bother us very much longer."

McGinnis nodded his approval and smiled.

"That's my scarecrow," he said. "You're the best."

Carver didn't need McGinnis to say it to know it. But he was the boss. And Carver owed the older man for giving him the chance to create his own lab and data center. McGinnis had put him on the map. A month didn't go by that Carver wasn't wooed by a competitor.

"Thanks."

McGinnis moved back to the mantrap door.

"I'm going to the airport later. We've got somebody

coming in from San Diego and they'll take the tour tomorrow."

"Where are you taking him?"

"Tonight? Probably Rosie's for barbecue."

"The usual. And then the Highlighter?"

"If I have to. You want to come out? You could impress these people, you know, help me out."

"Only thing they'll be impressed by will be the naked women. Not my scene."

"Yeah, well, it's a tough job but somebody's gotta do it. I'll leave you to it, then."

McGinnis left the control room. His office was up on the surface in the front of the building. It was private and he stayed there most of the time to greet prospective clients and probably to keep clear of Carver. Their conversations in the bunker always seemed a bit strained. McGinnis seemed to know to keep those times to a minimum.

The bunker belonged to Carver. The business was set up with McGinnis and the administrative staff up top at the entry point. The web hosting center with all the designers and operators was on the surface as well. The high-security colocation farm was below surface in the so-called bunker. Few employees had subterranean access and Carver liked it that way.

Carver sat down again at the workstation and went back online. He pulled up Angela Cook's photo once more and studied it for a few minutes, then switched over to Google. It was now time to go to work on Jack McEvoy and to see if he had been smarter than Angela Cook in protecting himself.

He put the name into the search engine and soon a new thrill blasted through him. Jack McEvoy had no blog or any profile on Facebook or anywhere else that Carver could find. But his name scored numerous hits on Google. Carver had initially thought the name was familiar and now he knew why. A dozen years earlier McEvoy had written the definitive book on the killer known as the Poet, and Carver had read that book—repeatedly. Check that, McEvoy had done more than simply write the book about the killer. He had been the journalist who had revealed the Poet to the world. He had gotten close enough to breathe in the Poet's last breath.

Jack McEvoy was a giant slayer.

Carver slowly nodded as he studied McEvoy's book jacket photo on an old Amazon page.

"Well, Jack," he said out loud. "I'm honored."

ngela Cook's dog did her in. The dog's name was Arfy—according to a five-month-old entry in her blog. From there it took Carver only two variations—for fitting it into the six-character password requirement—to come up with Arphie and to successfully log on to her LATimes.com account.

There was always something oddly tantalizing about being inside another person's computer. The mercurial addiction of invasion. It gave him a deep tug in the guts. It was like he was inside another's mind and body. He was them.

His first stop was her e-mail. He opened it up and found that she kept a clean board. There were only two unread messages and a few others that had been read and saved. He saw none from Jack McEvoy. The new messages were a how-are-you-doing-out-there-in-L.A. from a friend in Florida—he knew this because the server was Road Runner in Tampa Bay—and an internal *Times* message that appeared to be a terse back-and-forth with a supervisor or an editor.

From: Alan Prendergast <AlanPrendergast@LATimes.com>
Subject: Re: collision

Date: May 12, 2009 2:11 PM PDT
To: AngelaCook@LATimes.com

Hold tight. A lot can happen in two weeks.

From: Angela Cook <AngelaCook@LATimes.com>
Subject: collision
Date: May 12, 2009 1:59 PM PDT
To: AlanPrendergast@LATimes.com

You told me I WOULD write it! ☹

It looked like Angela was upset. But Carver didn't know enough about the situation to understand it, so he moved on, opening up her old mail folder and getting lucky. She had not cleared her old mail list in several days. Carver scrolled through hundreds of messages and saw several from her colleague and cowriter Jack McEvoy. Carver began with the earliest one and started working his way forward to the most recent messages.

Soon he realized it was all innocuous, just basic communication between colleagues about stories and meetings in the cafeteria for coffee. Nothing salacious. Carver guessed from what he read that Cook and McEvoy were strangers until quite recently. There was a stiffness or formality to the e-mails. No shorthand or slang employed by either. It appeared that Jack didn't know Angela until she had been assigned to the crime beat and he was assigned to train her.

In the last message, sent just a few hours before, Jack had sent Angela an e-mail with a proposed summary for a story they were working on together. Carver eagerly read it and felt his concerns about detection ease with every word.

From: Jack McEvoy <JackMcEvoy@LATimes.com>
Subject: collision slug
Date: May 12, 2009 2:23 PM PDT
To: AngelaCook@LATimes.com

Angela, this is what I sent Prendo for the futures budget. Let me know if you want any changes.

Jack

COLLISION—On April 25th the body of Denise Babbit was found in the trunk of her own car in a beachside parking lot in Santa Monica. She had been sexually assaulted and asphyxiated when a plastic bag was pulled over her head and secured with clothesline. The exotic dancer with a history of drug problems died with her eyes wide open. It wasn't long before police traced a lone fingerprint left on her car's rearview mirror to a 16-year-old drug dealer and gangbanger from a South L.A. housing project. Alonzo Winslow, who grew up fast in the projects, not knowing his father and rarely seeing his mother, was arrested and

charged as a juvenile with the crime. He confessed his role
to the police and now awaits efforts by the state to prosecute
him as an adult. We talk to the suspect and his family as
well as those who knew the victim, and trace this fatal
collision back to its origins. 90 inches—McEvoy and Cook,
w/art by Lester

Carver read it again. He felt the muscles in his neck
start to relax. McEvoy and Cook didn't know anything.
Jack the giant slayer was climbing the wrong bean stalk.

Just as he had planned it. Carver made a mental note
to check back to read the story when it was published.
He would be one of only three people on the planet
to know how wrong it was—including that poor soul
Alonzo Winslow.

He killed the list and brought up Cook's sent messages. There was just the overlap of the back-and-forth
with McEvoy and the missive to Prendergast. It was all
pretty dry and useless to Carver.

He closed the e-mail and went to the browser. He
scrolled down, seeing all the websites Cook had visited in
recent days. He saw trunkmurder.com as well as several
visits to Google and the websites of other newspapers.
He then saw a website that intrigued him. He opened
up DanikasDungeon.com and was treated to a visit to
a Dutch bondage-and-domination site replete with photos of women controlling, taunting and torturing men.
Carver smiled. He doubted there was a journalistic reason for Cook's visit. He believed he was getting a glimpse
of Angela Cook's private interests. Her own dark journey.

Carver didn't linger. He put the information aside, knowing it might be useful at a later time. He tried Prendergast next, since it appeared his password was obvious. He went with Prendo and was in on his first attempt. People were so stupid and obvious sometimes. He went to the mailbox, and there at the top of the list was a message from McEvoy that had been sent only two minutes earlier.

"What are you up to, Jack?"

Carver opened the message.

From: Jack McEvoy <JackMcEvoy@LATimes.com>
Subject: collision
Date: May 12, 2009 4:33 PM PDT
To: AlanPrendergast@LATimes.com
Cc: AngelaCook@LATimes.com

Prendo, I was looking for you but you were at dinner. The story is changing. Alonzo *didn't* confess to the killing and I don't even think he did it. I'm heading to Vegas tonight to pursue things further tomorrow. Will fill you in then. Angela can handle the beat. I've got dimes.

—Jack

Carver felt his gorge rise in his throat. His neck muscles tightened sharply and he pushed back from the table in case he had to vomit. He pulled the trash can out from underneath so he could use it if necessary. His vision momentarily darkened at the edges but then the darkness passed and he cleared.

He kicked the trash can back into place and leaned forward to study the message again.

McEvoy had made the connection to Las Vegas. Carver now knew that he had only himself to blame. He had repeated his modus operandi too soon. He had left himself open and now Jack the giant slayer was on his trail. A critical mistake. McEvoy would get to Las Vegas and with even minimal luck he would put things together.

Carver had to stop that. A critical mistake didn't have to be a fatal mistake, he told himself. He closed his eyes and thought for a long moment. It brought his confidence back. Some of it. He knew he was prepared for all eventualities. The beginning tendrils of a plan were reaching to him and the first order of business was to delete the message on the screen in front of him, and then go back into Angela Cook's account and delete it from her mailbox as well. Prendergast and Cook would never see it and, with any luck, they'd never know what Jack McEvoy knew.

Carver deleted the message but before signing off uploaded a spyware program that would allow him to track all of Prendergast's Internet activities in real time. He would know who Prendergast e-mailed, who contacted him and what websites he viewed. Carver then returned to Cook's account and quickly took the same actions.

McEvoy was next but Carver decided that could come later—after Jack got to Vegas and was operating out there alone. First things first. He got up and put his hand on the reader next to the glass door to the server room.

Once the scan was completed and approved, the door unlocked and he slid it open. It was cold in the server room, always kept at a brisk sixty-two degrees. His steps echoed on the raised metal flooring as he walked down the third row to the sixth tower. He unlocked the front of the refrigerator-size server with a key, bent down and pulled two of the data blades out a quarter inch. He then closed and relocked the door and headed back to his workstation.

Within a few seconds a screen alarm buzzed from the workstations. He typed in commands that would bring up the response protocol. He then waited a few more seconds and reached over to the phone. He pushed the intercom button and typed in McGinnis's extension.

"Hey, boss, you still there?"

"What is it, Wesley? I'm about to head out."

"We've got a code three problem. You better come look."

Code 3 meant drop everything and move.

"I'll be right there."

Carver tried to suppress a smile. He wouldn't want McGinnis to see it. Three minutes later McGinnis came through the door, his key card snapping back to his belt. He was out of breath from taking the stairs down.

"What's wrong?" he demanded.

"Dewey and Bach in L.A. just got data-bombed. The whole route collapsed."

"Jesus, how?"

"You got me."

"Who did it?"

Carver shrugged.

"Can't tell from this end. It might've been internal."

"You call them yet?"

"No, I was waiting to tell you first."

McGinnis stood behind Carver, shifting his weight from foot to foot and looking through the glass at the servers, as if the answer was in there.

"What do you think?" he asked.

"The problem's not here—I've checked everything. It's on their end. I think I need to send somebody out there to fix it and reopen the traffic. I think Stone is up. I'll send him. Then we see where it came from and make sure it won't happen again. If it's a hack, then we burn the fuckers in their beds."

"How long will it take?"

"They have flights to L.A. almost every hour. I'll put Stone on a plane and he'll hit it first thing tomorrow."

"Why don't you go? I want this taken care of."

Carver hesitated. He wanted McGinnis to keep thinking it was his idea.

"I think Freddy Stone can handle it."

"But you're the best. I want Dewey and Bach to see that we don't fuck around. We get things done. You got a problem, we send our best man. Not some kid. Take Stone or whoever you need, but I want you to go."

"I'll leave right now."

"Just keep me informed."

"Will do."

"I gotta get to the airport myself to make that pickup."

"Yeah, you've got the tough job."

"Don't rub it in."

He clapped Carver on the shoulder and went back out through the door. Carver sat there motionless for a few moments, feeling the residual compression on his shoulder. He hated to be touched.

Finally, he moved. He leaned toward his screen and entered the alarm disengagement code. He confirmed the protocol and then deleted it.

Carver pulled his cell phone and hit a speed dial number.

"What's up?" Stone said.

"Are you still with Early?"

"Yeah, we're building the tower."

"Come back to the control room. We have a problem. Actually, two problems. And we need to take care of them. I'm working on a plan."

"On my way."

Carver closed the phone with a snap.

SIX: The Loneliest Road in America

At nine A.M. Wednesday I was waiting outside the locked door of the offices of Schifino & Associates on the fourth floor of an office building on Charleston near downtown Las Vegas. I was tired and slid down the wall to sit on the nicely carpeted floor. I was feeling particularly unlucky in a town that was supposed to inspire luck.

The early morning had started out well enough. After checking into the Mandalay Bay at midnight, I found myself too keyed up to sleep. I went down to the casino and turned the two hundred dollars I had brought with me into three times that amount at the roulette and blackjack tables.

The growth of my cash portfolio along with the free booze I'd drunk while gambling made sleep come easier when I returned to my room. Things took a dramatic downturn after my wake-up call came. The problem was I wasn't supposed to have a wake-up call. The front desk was calling to tell me my *Times*-issued American Express card had been rejected.

"That doesn't make sense," I said. "I bought an airline ticket with it last night, I rented a car at McCarran and it was fine when I checked in here. Somebody ran the card."

"Yes, sir, that is just an authorizing process. The card is not charged until six A.M. on the morning of checkout. We ran the card and it was rejected. Could you please come down and give us another card?"

"No problem. I wanted to get up now anyway so I could win some more of your money."

Only there *was* a problem, because my three other credit cards didn't work either. All were rejected and I was forced to chip back half of my winnings to get out of the hotel. Once I got to my rental car I pulled out my cell to start calling the credit-card companies one by one. Only I couldn't make the calls because my phone was dead, and it wasn't a matter of being in a bad cell zone. The phone was *dead*, service disconnected.

Annoyed and confused but undaunted, I headed to the address I had looked up for William Schifino. I still had a story to pursue.

A few minutes after nine, a woman stepped off the elevator and headed down the hallway toward me. I noticed the slight hesitation in her step when she saw me on the floor leaning against Schifino's door. I stood up and nodded as she got closer.

"Do you work with William Schifino?" I said with a smile.

"Yes, I'm his receptionist. What can I do for you?"

"I need to speak to Mr. Schifino. I came from Los Angeles. I—"

"Do you have an appointment? Mr. Schifino sees potential clients by appointment only."

"I don't have an appointment but I'm not a potential

client. I'm a reporter. I want to talk to Mr. Schifino about Brian Oglevy. He was convicted last year of—"

"I know who Brian Oglevy is. That case is on appeal."

"Right, I know, I know. I have new information. I think Mr. Schifino will want to speak to me."

She paused with her key a few inches from the lock and turned her eyes as if to size me up for the first time.

"I know he will," I said.

"You can come in and wait. I don't know when he'll be in. He doesn't have court until this afternoon."

"Maybe you could call him."

"Maybe."

We entered the office and she directed me to a couch in a small waiting area. The furnishings were comfortable and seemed relatively new. I got the feeling that Schifino was an accomplished lawyer. The receptionist went behind her desk, turned on her computer and began her routine of preparing for the day.

"Are you going to call him?" I asked.

"When I get a moment. Just make yourself comfortable."

I tried to but I didn't like waiting around. I pulled my laptop out of my bag and turned it on.

"Do you have WiFi here?" I asked.

"We do."

"Could I borrow it to check my e-mail? I'll only be on a few minutes."

"No, I'm afraid not."

I studied her for a moment.

"Excuse me?"

"I said no. It's a secured system and you will have to ask Mr. Schifino about that."

"Well, could you ask him for me when you call him to tell him I am waiting here?"

"As soon as possible."

She gave me an efficient smile and went back to her busywork. The phone buzzed and she opened an appointment book and started scheduling a meeting for a client and telling him about the credit cards they accepted for legal services rendered. It reminded me of my own current credit-card situation and I grabbed one of the magazines off the coffee table to try to avoid thinking about it.

It was called the *Nevada Legal Review* and it was chock-full of ads for lawyers and legal services like transcription and data storage. There were also articles about legal cases, most of them dealing with casino licensing or crimes against casinos. I was twenty minutes into a story about a legal attack on the law that kept brothels from operating in Las Vegas and Clark County when the office door opened and a man stepped in. He nodded to me and looked at the receptionist, who was still on the phone.

"Hold, please," the receptionist said.

She pointed to me.

"Mr. Schifino, this man has no appointment. He says he's a reporter from Los Angeles. He—"

"Brian Oglevy is innocent," I said, cutting her off. "And I think I can prove it."

Schifino studied me for a long moment. He had dark hair and a handsome face with an uneven tan from wearing a baseball cap. He was either a golfer or a coach. Or maybe both. His eyes were sharp and he quickly came to a decision about me.

"Then I guess you better come on back to the office," he said.

I followed him to his office and he sat down behind a large desk while signaling me to the seat on the other side.

"You work for the *Times?*" he asked.

"Yes."

"Good paper but in a lot of trouble these days. Financially."

"Yeah, they all are."

"So how did you come to the conclusion in L.A. that my guy over here is an innocent man?"

I gave him my best scoundrel's smile.

"Well, I don't know that for sure, but I had to get in to see you. But this is what I've got. I've got a kid over there, sitting in jail for a murder I am thinking he didn't commit, and it seems to me that the details are a lot like the details in your Oglevy case—what details I know. Only, my case happened two weeks ago."

"So if they are the same, my client has an obvious alibi and there might be a third party here at work."

"Exactly."

"All right, well, let's see what you've got."

"Well, I was hoping I could see what you've got too."

"Fair enough. My client is in prison and I don't think he's too worried about attorney-client privilege at this point, not if my trading information might help his cause. Besides, most of what I tell you is available in court records."

Schifino pulled his files and we began a show-me-yours-show-you-mine session. I told him what I knew about Winslow and maintained a reserved excitement as we went through the crime reports. But when we moved into side-by-side comparisons of the crime scene photos, the adrenaline kicked in and it became difficult to contain myself. Not only did the Oglevy photos completely match those from the Babbit case, but the victims looked stunningly alike.

"This is amazing!" I said. "It's almost like the same woman."

Both were tall brunettes with large brown eyes, bobbed noses and long-legged dancer's bodies. Immediately I was hit with the profound sense that these women had not been selected randomly by their killer. They had been chosen. They fit some kind of mold that had made them targets.

Schifino was riding the same wave. He pointed from photo to photo, accenting the similarities in the crime scenes. Both women were suffocated with a plastic bag that was tied around the neck with a thin white cord. Each was placed naked and facing inward in the trunk of the car, and their clothes were simply dropped on top of them.

"My God...look at this," he said. "These crimes are absolutely the same and it doesn't take an expert to see that. I have to tell you something, Jack. When you came in here, I thought you were going to be this morning's entertainment. A diversion. Some wild-ass reporter who shows up chasing a pipe dream. But this…"

He gestured to the side-by-side sets of photos we had laid out across the desk.

"This is my client's freedom right here. He's getting out!"

He was standing behind his desk, too excited to sit down.

"How did this happen?" I asked. "How did this slip through?"

"Because they were solved quickly," Schifino said. "In each case the police were led to an obvious suspect and looked no further. They didn't look for similars because they didn't need to. They had their suspects and were off to the races."

"But how did the killer know to put Sharon Oglevy's body in her ex-husband's trunk? How would he even know where to find the car?"

"I don't know, but that is off point. The point here is that these two killings are of such a strikingly similar pattern that there is just no way that either Brian Oglevy or Alonzo Winslow could be responsible. The other details will fall into place when the real investigation is begun. But for now, there is no doubt in my mind that you're exposing something huge here. I mean, how do you know that these are the only two? There could be others."

I nodded. I hadn't thought about that possibility. Angela Cook's online search had only come up with the

Oglevy case. But two cases make a pattern. There still could be more.

"What will you do now?" I asked.

Schifino finally sat down. He rotated back and forth in his chair while considering the question.

"I'm going to draw up and file a petition for a writ of habeas corpus. This is new information that is exculpatory and we're going to put it into open court."

"But I'm not supposed to have those files. You can't cite them."

"Sure I can. What I don't have to do is say where I got them."

I frowned. I would be the obvious source once my story was published.

"How long will it take for you to get this into court?"

"I have to do some research but I'll file it by the end of the week."

"That's going to blow this up. I don't know if I can be ready to publish my story by then."

Schifino held his hands out wide and shook his head.

"My client's been up at Ely for more than a year. Do you know that the conditions are so bad at that prison that on frequent occasion death row inmates drop their appeals and volunteer to be executed, just to get out of there? Every day he is up there is a day too long."

"I know, I know. It's just that..."

I stopped to think about things and there was no way I could justify keeping Brian Oglevy in prison even a day longer just so I could have time to plan and write the story. Schifino was right.

"Okay, then I want to know the minute you file it," I said. "And I want to talk to your client."

"No problem. You get the exclusive as soon as he walks."

"No, not then. Now. I am going to write the story that springs him and Alonzo Winslow. I want to talk to him today. How do I do it?"

"He's in maximum security and unless you're on the list, you won't get in to see him."

"You can get me in, can't you?"

Schifino was sitting behind the aircraft carrier he called a desk. He brought a hand up to his chin, thought about the question and then nodded.

"I can get you in. I need to fax a letter up to the prison that says you are an investigator working for me and that you are entitled access to Brian. I then give you a to-whom-it-may-concern letter that you carry with you, and that identifies you as working for me. If you work for an attorney, you don't need a state license. You carry the letter with you and show it at the gate. It will get you in."

"Technically, I don't work for you. My paper has rules about reporters misrepresenting themselves."

Schifino reached into his pocket and pulled out his cash. He handed a dollar across the desk to me. I reached across the murder scene photos to take it.

"There," he said. "I just paid you a dollar. You work for me."

That didn't really cut it but I wasn't too worried about it, considering my employment situation.

"I guess that will work," I said. "How far is Ely?"

"Depending on your driving, it's three to four hours north of here. It's in the middle of nowhere and they call the road going up there the loneliest road in America. I don't know if it's because it leads to the prison or if it's the landscape you cross, but it's not called that without good reason. They have an airport. You could take a sand jumper up there."

I assumed that a sand jumper was the same as a puddle jumper, a small prop plane. I shook my head. I had written too many stories about little planes going down. I didn't fly in them unless I absolutely had to.

"I'll drive. Write the letters. And I'm going to need copies of everything in your files."

"I'll work on the letters and get Agnes to start making copies. I'll need copies of what you have for the habeas petition. We can say that's what my dollar bought."

I nodded and thought, Yeah, put officious Agnes to work for me. I would like that.

"Let me ask you something," I said.

"Shoot."

"Before I came in here and showed you all of this, did you think Brian Oglevy was guilty?"

Schifino cocked his head back as he thought it over.

"Not for publication?"

I shrugged. It wasn't what I wanted but it was what I'd take.

"If that's the only way you'll answer."

"Okay, for publication I can tell you that I knew Brian

was innocent from day one. There was just no way he could've committed this horrible crime."

"And not for publication?"

"I thought he was guilty as sin. It was the only way I could live with losing the case."

After stopping at a 7-Eleven and buying a throw-away phone with a hundred minutes of call time on it, I headed north through the desert on Highway 93 toward Ely State Prison.

Highway 93 took me past Nellis Air Force Base and then connected with 50 North. It wasn't too long before I began to see why it was known as the loneliest road in America. The empty desert ruled the horizon in every direction. Hard, chiseled mountain ranges, barren of any vegetation, rose and fell away as I drove. The only signs of civilization were the two-lane blacktop and the power lines carried over the ranges by iron stick figures that looked like they were giants from another planet.

The first calls I made with my new phone were to the credit-card companies, demanding to know why my cards were not working. With each call I got the same answer: I had reported the card stolen the night before, thereby temporarily canceling use of the account. I had gone online, answered all security questions correctly and reported the card stolen.

It didn't matter that I told them I hadn't reported the cards stolen. Someone else had, and that someone had known my account numbers as well as my home address, birth date, mother's maiden name and Social Security number. I demanded that the accounts be reopened and the service reps gladly complied. The only catch was that new credit cards with new numbers had to be issued and sent to my home. That would take days and in the meantime I had no credit. I was being fucked with on a level I had never experienced before.

I next called my bank in Los Angeles and found a variation on the same scheme, but with a deeper impact. The good news was that my debit card still worked. The bad news was that there was no money in my savings and checking account to draw from. The night before, I had used the online banking service to combine all my money in the checking account and then did a debit transfer of the full amount to the Make-A-Wish Foundation in the form of a general donation. I was now broke. But the Make-A-Wish Foundation sure liked me.

I disconnected the call and screamed as loud as I could in the car. What was happening? There were stories in the paper all the time about stolen identities. But this time the victim was me and I was having trouble believing it.

At eleven I called the city desk and learned that the intrusion and destruction had moved up yet another notch. I got hold of Alan Prendergast and his voice was tight with nervous energy. I knew from experience that this made him repeat things.

"Where are you, where are you? We've got the ministers' thing and I can't find anybody."

"I told you, I'm in Vegas. Where's—"

"Vegas! Vegas? What are you doing in Vegas?"

"Didn't you get my message? I sent you an e-mail yesterday before I left."

"Didn't get it. Yesterday you just disappeared, but I don't care. I care about today. I care about right now. Tell me you are at the airport, Jack, and that you'll be back in L.A. in an hour."

"Actually, I'm not at the airport and I'm technically not in Vegas anymore. I'm on the loneliest road in America heading to the middle of nowhere. What are the ministers doing?"

"What else? They're staging a big fucking rally in Rodia Gardens to protest the LAPD and the story is about to go national. But I've got you in Vegas and I haven't heard from Cook. What are you doing there, Jack? What are you doing?"

"I told you in the e-mail you haven't read. The story is—"

"I check e-mail regularly," Prendergast said curtly. "I've got no e-mail from you. No e-mail."

I was about to tell him he was wrong but thought about my credit cards. If somebody was able to crash my credit and wipe out my bank accounts, then maybe they crashed my e-mail as well.

"Listen, Prendo, something is going on. My credit cards are dead, my phone's dead and now you're telling me my e-mail never made it. Something is not right here. I—"

"For the last time, Jack. What are you doing in Nevada?"

I blew out my breath and looked out the side window. I saw the hardscrabble landscape that hadn't changed in all the time mankind had ruled the planet, and which would remain unchanged long after mankind was gone.

"The story on Alonzo Winslow has changed," I said. "I found out he didn't do it."

"He didn't do it? He didn't *do* it? You mean the murder of that girl? What are you talking about, Jack?"

"Yeah, the girl. He didn't do it. He's innocent, Alan, and I can prove it."

"He confessed, Jack. I read it in *your* story."

"Yeah, because that's what the cops said. But I read the so-called confession and all he confessed to was stealing her car and her money. He didn't know her body was in the trunk when he stole it."

"Jack..."

"Listen, Prendo, I connected the murder to another murder in Vegas. It was the same thing. A woman strangled and put in a trunk. She was a dancer, too. There's a guy in prison here for that one and he didn't do it either. I'm heading up to see him right now. I'm going to have to report and write this all by Thursday. We have to go with it on Friday because that's when it's going to come out of the bag."

There was a long silence.

"Prendo? You there?"

"I'm here, Jack. We need to talk about this."

"I thought we were. Where is Angela? She should handle the ministers. She's on the beat today."

"If I knew where Angela was, I would have her going with a photographer to Rodia Gardens. She hasn't come in yet. She told me last night before she went home that she would stop by Parker Center and make the morning rounds before coming in. Only, she hasn't come in."

"She's probably out running down Denise Babbit. Did you call her?"

"Of course I called her. I *called* her. I've left messages but she hasn't called in. She probably thinks you are here and is ignoring my calls."

"Well, look, Prendo, this is bigger than Preacher Treacher's rally, okay? Put a GA on that. This is huge. There's a killer out there who has flown completely below the radar of the cops and the FBI and everybody else. There's a lawyer here in Vegas who is going to file a motion by Friday that exposes the whole thing. We've got to beat him and everybody else to the punch. I'm going to go talk to this guy in prison and then head back. I don't know when I'll get in. It'll be a long drive back to Vegas before I can catch the plane. Luckily, I think my return is still good. I bought it before somebody canceled my credit cards."

Again I was met with silence.

"Prendo?"

"Look, Jack," he said, a calmness in his voice for the first time in the conversation. "We both know the situation and what is going on here. You're not going to be able to change anything."

"What are you talking about?"

"About the layoff. If you think you can come up with a story that's going to save your job, I don't think that's going to work."

Now I was silent as the anger welled up in my throat.

"Jack, you there? You there?"

"Yeah, I'm here, Prendo, and my only response is, Fuck you. I'm not concocting this story, man. This is happening! And I'm out here in the middle of nowhere and am not sure who is screwing with me or why."

"Okay, okay, Jack. Calm down. Just calm it down, okay? I am not suggesting that you—"

"The fuck you're not! You more than suggested it. You just said it."

"Look, I'm not going to respond if you are going to direct that sort of language at me. Can we talk in a civil manner, please? A civil manner."

"You know, Prendo, I've got other calls to make. If you don't want the story or you think this is a made-up story, then I'll find somebody who will print it, okay? The last thing I expected was for my own ace to try to cut me off at the knees while I'm out here with my ass in the wind."

"No, Jack, it's not like that."

"I think it is, Prendo. So fuck you, man. I'll talk to you later."

I hung up the phone and nearly threw it out the window. But then I remembered I didn't have the replacement cash to spare. I drove in silence for a few minutes so I could compose myself. I had one more call to make and I wanted to sound cool and calm when I made it.

I looked out the windows and studied the bluish gray mountains. I found them to be beautiful in a primitive and stark way. They had been stepped and broken by glaciers ten million years before but they had survived and would reach forever toward the sun.

I pulled my inoperable phone from my pocket and opened up the contacts list. I got the number for the FBI in Los Angeles and punched it into the throwaway. When the main operator answered I asked to speak to Agent Rachel Walling. I was transferred and it took a while to go through, but once it rang it was answered immediately.

"Intelligence," a male voice said.

"Let me speak to Rachel."

I said it as calmly as possible. I didn't ask for Agent Rachel Walling this time, because I didn't want to be asked who I was and possibly give her the opportunity to deflect my call. My hope was that I sounded like an agent and my call would be put through.

"Agent Walling."

It was her. It had been a few years since I had heard her voice over the phone but there was no doubt.

"Hello? This is Walling, can I help you?"

"Rachel, it's me. Jack."

Now it was her turn to be caught in silence.

"How are you doing?"

"Why are you calling me, Jack? We agreed that it would be better that we not talk."

"I know...but I need your help. I'm in trouble, Rachel."

"And you're expecting me to help you? What kind of trouble?"

A passing car blew past me going a hundred, at least, and making me feel like I was standing still.

"It's sort of a long story. I'm in Nevada. In the desert. I'm chasing a story and there's a killer out there nobody knows about. I need somebody to believe me and to help me."

"Jack, I'm the wrong person and you know it. I can't help you. And I'm in the middle of something here. I have to go."

"Rachel, don't hang up! Please..."

She didn't answer at first, but she didn't hang up. I waited.

"Jack...you sound frazzled. What is going on with you?"

"I don't know. Somebody's messing with me. My phone, my e-mail, my bank accounts—I'm driving through the middle of the desert and I don't even have a credit card that works."

"Where are you going?"

"To Ely, to talk to somebody."

"The prison?"

"That's right."

"What, somebody called you up and said he was innocent and you come running, hoping to prove the real cops are wrong again?"

"No, nothing like that. Look, Rachel, this guy is strangling women and stuffing them into the trunks of cars. He does horrible things to them and he's been getting away with it for at least two years."

"Jack, I've read your stories about the girl in the trunk. It was a gangbanger and he confessed."

I got an unexpected thrill from knowing she was reading my stories. But it wasn't helping me to convince her.

"Don't believe everything you read in the paper, Rachel. I'm getting to the truth now and I need someone—somebody in authority—to step in and—"

"You know I'm not in Behavioral anymore. Why call me?"

"Because I can trust you."

That brought a long moment of silence. I refused to break first.

"How can you say that?" she finally said. "We haven't seen each other in a long, long time."

"Doesn't matter. After what we went through back then, I'll always trust you, Rachel. And I know you could help me now...and maybe make up for some things yourself."

She scoffed at that.

"What are you talking about? No—wait, don't answer that. It doesn't matter. Please don't call me again, Jack. The bottom line is, I can't help you. So good luck and be careful. Be safe."

She hung up the phone.

I held it to my ear for nearly a minute after she was gone. I guess I was hoping that she'd change her mind, pick up the phone and call me back. But that didn't happen and after a while I dropped the phone into the cup holder between the seats. I had no more calls to make.

Up ahead the car that had passed me disappeared over the next ridgeline. I felt like I had been left all alone on the surface of the moon.

As with most people who pass through the gates of Ely State Prison, my luck did not change for the better upon arrival at my destination. I was allowed in through the attorney/investigator entrance. I clutched the introduction letter William Schifino had written for me and showed it to the watch captain. I was placed in a holding room and waited for twenty minutes for Brian Oglevy to be delivered to me. But when the door opened, it was the watch captain who entered. No Brian Oglevy.

"Mr. McEvoy," the captain said, pronouncing my name wrong. "I'm afraid we're not going to be able to do this today."

I suddenly thought that I had been exposed as a fraud. That they knew I was a reporter working on a story and not an investigator for a defense attorney.

"What do you mean? It was all set up. I have the letter from the lawyer. You saw it. He also faxed you a letter saying I was coming."

"Yeah, we got the fax and I was prepared to carry through but the man you want to see is unavailable at this time. You come back tomorrow and you can have your visit."

I shook my head angrily. All of the problems of the day were about to boil over and this prison captain was going to get burned.

"Look, I just drove four hours from Vegas to do this interview. You're telling me to turn around and go back and then do the whole thing again tomorrow? I'm not go—"

"I'm not telling you to go back to Vegas. I was you, I'd just go into town and stay at the Hotel Nevada. It ain't a bad place. They got a gaming hall and a hoppin' bar on most nights. You put up there and get back in here tomorrow morning and I'll have your man all ready for you. I can promise you that."

I shook my head, feeling impotent about everything. I had no choice here.

"Nine o'clock," I said. "And you'll be here?"

"I'll be here to personally set it up."

"Can you tell me why I can't see him today?"

"No, I can't. It's a security issue."

I shook my head in frustration one final time.

"Thank you, Captain. I guess I'll see you tomorrow."

"We'll be here."

After getting back to my rental, I plugged the Hotel Nevada in Ely into the GPS and followed instructions until I got there in thirty minutes. I pulled the car into the parking lot and emptied my pockets before deciding to go in. I had $248 in cash. I knew I had to budget at least $75 for gas to get back to the airport in Vegas. I could eat cheap until I got home but would need another $40 for the cab ride from the airport to my house. So I calculated I had about a hundred bucks for the hotel. Looking up at its tired six floors, I figured that wasn't going to be a problem. I got out, grabbed my carry-on bag and went inside.

I took a forty-five-dollar-a-night room on the fourth floor. The room was neat and clean and the bed was reasonably comfortable. It was only four P.M., too early to put the remainder of my fortune toward alcohol. So I pulled out my throwaway phone and started eating into my minutes. I first called Angela Cook, trying both her cell and desk line and getting no answer on either. I left the same message twice, then swallowed my pride and called Alan Prendergast back. I apologized for my outburst earlier and my use of foul language. I tried to calmly explain what was happening and the pressure I was feeling. He responded monosyllabically and said he had a meeting to go to. I told him I would get him a budget line for the revised story if I could get online and he told me not to rush.

"Prendo, we've got to get this into Friday's paper or everybody else will have it."

"Look, I talked about this in the news meeting. We want to move cautiously. We've got you running around in the desert. We haven't even heard from Angela and, frankly, we're getting worried. She should have checked in. So what I want you to do is get back here as soon as you can and then we will all sit down and see what we've got."

I could have gotten angry all over again about the way I was being treated but something more pressing had come through from him. Angela.

"You've gotten no message from her all day?"

"Not a one. I sent a reporter to her apartment to see if she was there but there was no answer. We don't know where she is."

"This ever happen with her before?"

"She's called in sick a few times very late in the day. Probably hungover or something. But at least she called in. Not this time, though."

"Well, listen. If anybody hears from her, let me know, okay?"

"You got it, Jack."

"Okay, Prendo. We'll talk when I get back."

"Got dimes?" Prendergast asked by way of a peace offering.

"A few," I said. "I'll see you when I see you."

I closed the phone and thought about Angela being missing in action. I started wondering if everything was connected. My credit cards, nobody hearing from Angela. It seemed like a stretch because I couldn't see where anything linked up.

I looked around my forty-five-dollar room. There was a little pamphlet on the side table that said the hotel was more than seventy-five years old and at one time was the tallest building in all of Nevada. That was back when copper mining had made Ely a boomtown and nobody had ever heard of Las Vegas. Those days were long past.

I booted up my laptop and used the hotel's free WiFi to try to sign into my e-mail account. But my password was not accepted after three tries and I was locked out.

No doubt whoever had canceled my credit cards and my cellular phone service had also changed my password.

"This is crazy," I said out loud.

Unable to make outside contact, I concentrated on the internal. I opened a file on the laptop and pulled out my hard-copy notes. I started writing a narrative summarizing the moves of the day. It took me well over an hour to complete the project but when I was done I had thirty solid inches of story. And it was good story. Maybe my best in years.

After reading it over and making some editing improvements, I realized that the work had made me hungry. So I counted my money once again and left the room, making sure the door was locked behind me. I walked through the gaming hall and into a bar by the dollar slots. I ordered a beer and a steak sandwich and sat at a corner table with an open view of the mechanical money takers.

Looking around, I saw that the place had an aura of second-rate desperation, and the idea of another twelve hours there depressed me. But I wasn't looking at a lot of choices. I was stuck and was going to stay stuck until the morning.

I checked my cash stash again and decided I had enough for another beer and a roll of quarters for the cheap slots. I set up in a row near the lobby entrance and started feeding my money into an electronic poker machine. I lost my first seven hands before hitting on a full house. I followed that with a flush and a straight. Pretty soon I was thinking about being able to afford a third beer.

Another gambler took a seat two machines over from me. I barely noticed him until he decided he liked the comfort of conversation while he lost his money.

"You here for the pussy?" he asked cheerily.

I looked over at him. He was about thirty and had large muttonchop sideburns. He wore a dusty cowboy hat over dirty blond hair, leather driving gloves and mirrored sunglasses, even though we were inside.

"Excuse me?"

"Supposed to be a couple brothels outside of town. I was wondering which one's got the best-looking pussy. I just blew in on a stretch from Salt Lake."

"I wouldn't know, man."

I went back to my machine and tried to concentrate on what to hold and what to drop. I had the ace, three, four and nine of spades along with the ace of hearts. Do I go for the flush or stay conservative, take the pair and hope for a third ace or another pair?

"Birds in hand, man," said Sideburns.

I looked over at him and he nodded as if to say no charge for the sage advice. I could see the reflection of my screen in his mirrored glasses. All I needed was somebody coaching me on quarter poker. I held the spades, dropped the ace of hearts and hit the draw button. The machine god delivered. I got the jack of spades and a seven-to-one payoff on the flush. Too bad I was only betting quarters.

I hit the cash-out button and listened as a whopping fourteen dollars in quarters dropped into the tin tray. I scooped it into a plastic change cup and got up, leaving Sideburns behind.

I took my quarters to the cage and asked to cash out. I no longer had an appetite for gambling with small change. I was going to invest my winnings in two more beers and take them back to my room. There was more writing I could be doing, as well as preparing for the next morning's interview. I was going to talk to a man who'd been in prison for more than a year for a murder I was convinced he hadn't committed. It was going to be a wonderful day, the goddamn start of every journalist's dream to free an innocent man from an unjust imprisonment.

While waiting for the elevator in the lobby I carried the bottles down by my side in case I was breaking some sort of house rule. I stepped in, pushed the button and moved to the back corner. The doors started to come together but then a gloved hand poked in and hit the infrared beam and the doors reopened.

My pal Sideburns stepped in. He raised a finger to push a button but then pulled it back.

"Hey, we've got the same floor," he said.

"Wonderful," I said.

He went to the opposite corner. I knew he was going to say something and there was no place for me to go. I just waited for it and I wasn't disappointed.

"Hey, buddy, I didn't mean to mess up your mojo down there. My ex-wife used to say I talked too much. Maybe that's why she's my ex-wife."

"Don't worry about it," I said. "I have to get some work done anyway."

"So you're here on work, huh? What kind of business would take you to this godforsaken part of the world?"

Here we go again, I thought. The elevator was moving so slowly that it would've been faster taking the stairs.

"I have an appointment tomorrow at the prison."

"Gotcha. You a lawyer for one of them guys?"

"No. Journalist."

"Hmm, a writer, huh? Well, good luck. At least you'll get to go home after, not like them other fellas in there."

"Yeah, lucky me."

I moved toward the door as we reached the fourth floor, a clear signal that I was finished with the conversation and wanted to get to my room. The elevator stopped moving and it seemed an interminable amount of time before the doors finally began to open.

"Have a good night," I said.

I stepped quickly out of the elevator and to the left. My room was the third door down.

"You, too, partner," Sideburns called after me.

I had to switch the two beer bottles to my other hand to get my room key out. As I stood in front of the door, pulling it out of my pocket, I saw Sideburns coming down the hallway toward me. I turned and looked to my right. There were only three more rooms going down and then the exit to the stairwell. I had a bad feeling that this guy would eventually come knocking on my door during the night, wanting to go down for a beer or out to get some pussy. The first thing I planned to do was pack up, call the desk and change my room. He didn't know my name and wouldn't be able to find me.

I finally got the key into the lock and pushed the door

open. I looked back at Sideburns and gave him a final nod. His face broke into a strange smile as he got closer.

"Hi, Jack," a voice said from inside my room.

I abruptly turned to see a woman getting up from the chair by the window in my room. And I immediately recognized her as Rachel Walling. She had an all-business look on her face. I felt the presence of Sideburns go by my back on his way to his room.

"Rachel?" I said. "What are you doing here?"

"Why don't you come in and close the door?"

Still stunned by the surprise, I did as instructed. I closed the door behind me. From out in the hallway I heard another door close loudly. Sideburns had entered his room.

Cautiously, I stepped farther into my room.

"How'd you get in here?"

"Just sit down and I'll tell you all about it."

Twelve years earlier I'd had a short, intense and, some would say, improper relationship with Rachel Walling. While I had seen photos of her in the papers a few years ago when she helped the LAPD run down and kill a wanted man in Echo Park, I had not been in her presence since we had sat in a hearing room nearly a decade earlier. Still, not many days went by in those ten years that I didn't think about her. She was one reason—perhaps the biggest reason—that I have always considered that time the high point of my life.

She showed little wear and tear from the years that had passed, even though I knew it had been a tough time. She paid for her relationship with me with a five-year stint in a one-person office in South Dakota. She went from profiling and chasing serial killers to investigating bar stabbings on Indian reservations.

But she had climbed out of that pit and had been posted in L.A. for the past five years, working for some sort of a secretive intelligence unit. I had called her when I'd found out, gotten through to her but been rebuffed. Since then I had kept tabs on her, when I could, from afar. And now she was standing in front of me in my hotel room in the middle of nowhere. It was strange, sometimes, how life worked out.

My surprise over her appearance aside, I couldn't stop staring and smiling at her. She maintained the professional front, but I could see her eyes holding on me. It wasn't very often you got to be this close to a former lover of so long ago.

"Who was that you were with?" she asked. "Are you with a photographer on this story?"

I turned and looked back at the doorway.

"No, I'm by myself. And I don't know who that was. Just some guy who'd been talking to me downstairs in the gambling hall. He went to his room."

She abruptly walked past me, opened the door and looked both ways in the hall before coming back into the room and closing the door.

"What was his name?"

"I don't know. I wasn't really talking to him."

"Which room is he in?"

"I don't know that either. What's going on? How come you're in my room?"

I pointed to the bed. My laptop was open and my printouts of notes, the copies of the case files I had gotten from Schifino and Meyer as well as the printouts from Angela Cook's online search were fanned across it. The only thing missing from the spread was the transcript of the Winslow interrogation, and that was only because it had been too heavy to take with me.

I hadn't left it all on the bed like that.

"And were you going through my stuff? Rachel, I asked you for help. I didn't ask you to break into my room and—"

"Look, just sit down, would you?"

The room had only one chair, the one she had been waiting in. I sat on the bed, closing my laptop sullenly and gathering the paperwork into one stack. She remained standing.

"Okay, I showed my creds and asked the manager to let me in. I told him your safety might be in jeopardy."

I shook my head in confusion.

"What are you talking about? Nobody even knows I'm here."

"I wouldn't be so sure about that. You told me you were going to the prison up here. Who else did you tell? Who else knows?"

"I don't know. I told my editor and there's a lawyer down in Vegas who knows. That's it."

She nodded.

"William Schifino. Yes, I talked to him."

"You talked to him? Why? What is going on here, Rachel?"

She nodded again, but this time not in agreement. She nodded because she knew she had to tell me what was going on, even if it was against the FBI creed. She pulled the chair over to the middle of the room and sat down facing me.

"Okay, when you called me today, you weren't making the most sense, Jack. I guess you are a better writer than a teller of stories. Anyway, of all that you told me, the part that stuck with me was what you said about your credit cards and bank accounts and your phone and e-mail. I know I told you I couldn't help you but after I hung up, I started thinking about that and I got concerned."

"Why?"

"Because you were looking at all of that like it was an inconvenience. Like a big coincidence, that it just happened to be going on while you were on the road working on this unrelated story about this supposed killer."

"There's nothing supposed about this guy. But are you saying it could be related? I thought about this but there's no way. The guy I am trying to chase down would have no idea that I'm even out here and on to him."

"Don't be so sure about that, Jack. It is a classic hunting tactic. Separate and isolate your target and then move in for the kill. In today's society, separating and isolating someone would entail getting them away from their comfort zone—the environment they know—and then eliminating their ability to connect. Cell phone, Internet, credit cards, money."

She ticked them off on her fingers.

"But how could this guy know about me? I didn't even know about him until last night. Look, Rachel, it's great to see you and I hope you stick around tonight. I want you to be here, but I'm not getting this. I mean, don't get me wrong. I appreciate the concern—in fact, how did you get here so damn quick?"

"I took an FBI jet to Nellis and had them jump me up here in a chopper."

"Jesus! Why didn't you just call me back?"

"Because I couldn't. When you called me, it was trans-ferred to the off-site location where I work. There's no caller ID on those transfers. I didn't have your number and I knew you were probably on a throwaway line."

"So what's the bureau brass going to say when they find out you dropped everything and hopped on a plane to save me? Didn't you learn anything in South Dakota?"

She waved the concern away. Something about the gesture reminded me of our first meeting. It happened to have also been in a hotel room. She had driven my face down hard into the bed and then handcuffed and arrested me. It wasn't love at first sight.

"There's an inmate in Ely that has been on my inter-view list for four months," she said. "Officially, I came to interview him."

"You mean like he's a terrorist? Is that what your unit does?"

"Jack, I can't talk to you about that side of my work. But I can tell you how easy it was to find you and why I know I wasn't the only one tracking you."

She froze me with that word. *Tracking.* It conjured bad things in my imagination.

"Okay," I said. "Tell me."

"When you called me today you told me you were going to Ely and I knew that had to be to interview a prisoner. So when I got concerned and decided to do something about it, I called Ely and asked if you were there and I was told you just left. I spoke to a Captain Henry there and he said your interview was put off until tomorrow morning. He said he recommended you go into town and stay at the Nevada."

"Yeah, Captain Henry. I was dealing with him."

"Yeah, well, I asked him why your interview was postponed and he told me that your guy, Brian Oglevy, was in lockdown because there was a threat against him."

"What threat?"

"Hold on, I'm getting to it. The warden got an e-mail today with a message that said the AB was planning to hit Oglevy today. So as a precaution they put him in lockdown."

"Oh, come on, they took that seriously? The Aryan Brotherhood? Don't they threaten everybody who isn't a member? Isn't Oglevy a Jewish name, too?"

"They took it seriously because the e-mail came from the warden's own secretary. Only she didn't write it. It was written anonymously by someone who had gained access to her state prison systems account. A hacker. It could have been someone inside or someone from the outside. It didn't matter. They took it as a legitimate warning because of the way it was delivered. They put Oglevy in lockdown, you didn't get to see him and you were sent to spend the night here. Alone, in unfamiliar surroundings."

"Okay, what else? This is still a stretch."

She was beginning to convince me but I was acting skeptical to get her to tell me more.

"I asked Captain Henry if anybody else had called and asked about you. He said the lawyer you were working for, William Schifino, called to check on you and he was told the same thing, that the interview was delayed and you were probably spending the night at the Nevada."

"Okay."

"I called William Schifino. He said he never made that call."

I stared at her for a long moment as a cold finger went down my spine.

"I asked Schifino if anyone besides me had called about you and he told me he had gotten one call earlier. It was from someone who said he was your editor—used the name Prendergast—and that he was worried about you and wanted to know if you had come to see Schifino. Schifino said you had come by and that you were on your way up to the prison in Ely."

I knew my editor could not have made that call because when I had called Prendergast, he had not gotten my e-mail and had no idea I had gone to Las Vegas. Rachel was right. Someone had been tracking me and doing a good job of it.

My mind flashed on thoughts of Sideburns and riding up in the elevator with him, then of him following me down the hallway to my room.

What if he hadn't heard Rachel's voice? Would he have walked on by or would he have pushed in behind me?

Rachel got up and walked over to the room's phone. She dialed the operator and asked for the manager. She was on hold for a few moments before her call was taken.

"Yes, it's Agent Walling. I'm still in room four ten and I've located Mr. McEvoy and he's safe. I am now wondering if you can tell me if there are any guests in the next three rooms going down the hall. I think that would be four eleven, twelve and thirteen."

She waited and listened and then thanked the manager.

"One last question," she said. "There is a door marked EXIT at the end of the hall. I'm assuming those are stairs. Where do they go?"

She listened, thanked him again and then hung up.

"There's nobody registered in those rooms. The stairs go down to the parking lot."

"You think that guy with the sideburns was him?"

She sat back down.

"Possibly."

I thought about his wraparound sunglasses, the driving gloves and the cowboy hat. The bushy sideburns covered most of the rest of his face and drew the eye away from any other distinguishing features. I realized that if I had to describe the man who had followed me, I would only be able to remember the hat, hair, gloves, sunglasses and sideburns—the throwaway or changeable features of a disguise.

"Jesus! I can't believe how stupid I was. How? How did this guy find out about me and then actually find me? We're talking about less than twenty-four hours and he's sitting next to me at the slots."

"Let's go down and you show me what machine he was at. We might be able to pull prints."

I shook my head.

"Forget it. He was wearing driving gloves. In fact,

even the ceiling cameras down there won't help you. He was wearing a cowboy hat, sunglasses—his whole getup was a disguise."

"We'll pull the video anyway. Maybe there will be something that will help us."

"I doubt it."

I shook my head again, more to myself than to Rachel.

"He got right next to me."

"That trick with the prison secretary's e-mail shows he has a certain skill set. I think it would be wise to consider your e-mail accounts to be breached at this point."

"But that doesn't explain how he knew about me in the first place. In order for him to breach my e-mail, he had to know about me."

I slapped the bed in annoyance and nodded my head.

"Okay, I don't know how he knew about me, but I did send e-mails last night. To both my editor and my partner on the story, telling them that the story was changing and that I was following a lead to Vegas. I talked to my editor today and he said he never got it."

Rachel nodded knowingly.

"Destroying outgoing communications. That would fall under isolation of the target. Did your partner get his?"

"It's a her and I don't know if she got it because she's not answering her phone or her e-mail and she didn't—"

I stopped in my verbal tracks and looked at Rachel.

"What?"

"She didn't show up for work today. She didn't call in and nobody could reach her. They even sent somebody to her apartment but they got no answer."

Rachel abruptly stood up.

"We've got to go back to L.A., Jack. The chopper's waiting."

"What about my interview? And you said you were going to pull the video from downstairs."

"What about your partner? The interview and video can wait till later."

Embarrassed, I nodded and got off the bed. It was time to go.

had no idea where Angela Cook lived. I told Rachel what I did know about her, including her odd fixation with the Poet case, and that I'd heard she had a blog but had never read it. Rachel transmitted all the information to an agent in L.A. before we boarded the military chopper and headed south toward Nellis Air Force Base.

On the flight there we wore headsets, which cut down on the engine noise but didn't allow for conversation that wasn't in sign language. Rachel took my files and spent the hour with them. I watched her making comparisons between the crime scene and autopsy reports of Denise Babbit and Sharon Oglevy. She worked with a look of complete concentration on her face and took notes on a legal pad she'd pulled out of her own bag. She spent a lot of time looking at the horrible photos of the dead women, taken both at the crime scene and on the autopsy table.

For the most part I sat in my straight-back seat and racked my brain, trying to put together an explanation for how all of this could have happened so fast. More specifically, how this killer could have started hunting me when I had barely started hunting him. By the time we landed at Nellis, I thought I had something and was waiting for the opportunity to tell Rachel.

We immediately transferred to a waiting jet on which we were the only passengers. We sat across from each other, and the pilot informed Rachel that there was a call holding for her on the onboard telephone. We strapped in, she picked up the phone and the jet immediately started taxiing out to the runway. On the overhead the pilot told us we would be on the ground in L.A. in an hour. Nothing like the power and might of the federal government, I thought. This was the way to travel—except for one thing. It was a small plane and I didn't fly small planes.

Rachel mostly listened to her caller, then asked a few questions and finally hung up.

"Angela Cook was not at her home," she said. "They can't find her."

I didn't respond. A sharp stab of fear and dread for Angela worked its way up under my ribs. This didn't ease any as the jet took off, rising at a steeper angle than I was used to with commercial airliners. I almost tore the armrest off with my fingernails. After we were safely up I finally spoke.

"Rachel, I think I know how this guy could've found us so quickly—Angela, at least."

"Tell me."

"No, you first. Tell me what you found in the files."

"Jack, don't be so petty. This has become a little bit larger than a newspaper story."

"That doesn't mean you can't go first. It's also larger

than the FBI's penchant for taking information but not giving anything back in return."

She shook off the barb.

"Fine, I'll start. But first let me commend you, Jack. From what I have read about these cases, I would say there is absolutely no doubt that they are connected by a single killer. The same man is responsible for both. But he escaped notice because in each case an alternate suspect came to light quickly and the local authorities proceeded with blinders on. In each case, they had their man from the beginning and didn't look into other possibilities. Except of course in the Babbit case, their man was a boy."

I leaned forward, beaming with confidence after her compliment.

"And he never confessed like they put out to the press," I said. "I have the transcript back at my office. Nine-hour interrogation and the kid never confessed. He said he stole her car and her money, but the body was already in the trunk. He never said he killed her."

Rachel nodded.

"I assumed that. So what I was doing with the material you have here was profiling the two killings. Looking for a signature."

"The signature's obvious. He likes strangling women with plastic bags."

"Technically they weren't strangled. They were asphyxiated. Suffocated. There's a difference."

"Okay."

"There is something very familiar about the use of

the plastic bag and the cord around the neck, but I was actually looking for something a little less obvious than the surface signature. I was also looking for connections or similarities between the women. If we find what connects them we'll find the killer."

"They were both strippers."

"That's part of it but a little broad. And, technically, one was a stripper and one was an exotic performer. There is a slight difference."

"Whatever. They both showed their naked bodies off for a living. Is that the only connection you found?"

"Well, as you must have noticed, they were very similar in physical makeup. In fact, the difference in weight was only three pounds and the difference in height was half an inch. Facial structure and hair was also alike. A victim's body type is a key component in terms of what makes them chosen. An opportunistic killer takes what comes along. But when you see two victims like this with exactly the same body type, it tells us this is a predator who is patient, who chooses."

It looked like she had more to say but stopped. I waited but she didn't continue.

"What?" I said. "You know more than you're saying."

She dropped the hesitation.

"When I was in Behavioral it was in the early days. The profilers often sat around and talked about the correlation between the predators we hunted and the predators in the wild. You'd be surprised how similar a serial killer can be to a leopard or a jackal. And the same could be said for victims. In fact, when it came to body types we often assigned victims animal types. These two women we would have called giraffes. They were tall and long-legged. Our predator has a taste for giraffes."

I wanted to write some of this down to use later but I was afraid that any obvious recording of her interpretation of the files would cause her to shut down the exposition. So I tried not to even move.

"There's something else," she said. "At this point this is purely conjecture on my part. But both autopsies ascribe marks on each of the victims' legs to ligature. I think that might be wrong."

"Why?"

"Let me show you something."

I finally moved. We were in seats that faced each other. I unbuckled and moved to the seat next to her. She went through the files and pulled several of the copies of photos from the crime scenes and the autopsies.

"Okay, you see the marks left above and below the knees here and here and here?"

"Yeah, like they were tied up."

"Not quite."

She used a clear polished fingernail to trace the markings on the victims as she explained.

"The marks are too symmetrical to be from traditional bindings. Plus, if these were ligature marks we would see them around the ankles. If you were going to tie someone up to control them or to prevent escape, you would tie their ankles. Yet we have no ligature marks in these areas. The wrists, yes, but not on the ankles."

She was right. I just hadn't seen it until she explained it.

"So what made those marks on the legs?"

"Well, I can't say for sure, but when I was in Behavioral, we came upon new paraphilias on almost every case. We started categorizing them."

"You're talking about sexual perversions?"

"Well, we didn't call them that."

"Why, you had to be politically correct around serial killers?"

"It may be very nuanced, but there is a difference between being perverted and abnormal. We call the behaviors paraphilias."

"Okay, and these marks, they're part of a paraphilia?"

"They could be. I think they are marks left by straps."

"Straps from what?"

"Leg braces."

I almost laughed.

"You've got to be kidding. People get off on leg braces?"

Rachel nodded.

"It even has a name. It's called abasiophilia. A psychosexual fascination with leg braces. Yes, people get off on it. There are even websites and chat rooms dedicated to it. They call them irons and calipers. Women who wear braces are sometimes called iron maidens."

I was reminded how thoroughly intoxicating Rachel's skill as a profiler had been when we were chasing the Poet. She had been dead-on about the case in many ways. Damn near prescient. And I had been captivated by her ability to take small pieces of information and obscure details and then draw telling conclusions. She was doing it again and I was along for the ride.

"And you had a case with this?"

"Yes, we had a case in Louisiana. A man abducted a woman off a bus bench and held her for a week in a fishing shack out in a bayou. She managed to escape and make her way through the swamp. She was lucky because the four women he grabbed before her didn't escape. We found their partial remains in the swamp."

"And it was a basophilia case?"

"Abasiophilia," she corrected. "Yes, the woman who escaped told us the subject made her wear leg braces that strapped around the legs and had side irons and joints running from her ankles to her hips and several leather straps."

"This is so creepy," I said. "Not that there is anything like a normal serial killer, but leg braces? Where does an addiction like this come from?"

"It's unknown. But most paraphilias are embedded in early childhood. A paraphilia is like a recipe for an individual's sexual fulfillment. It's what they need to get off. Why someone would need to wear leg braces or have their partner wear them is anybody's guess, but it starts young. That is a given."

"Do you think the guy from your case back then could be—"

"No, the man who committed those murders in Louisiana was put to death. I witnessed it. And right up to the end, he never spoke a word to us about any of it."

"Well, I guess that gives him a perfect alibi for this."

I smiled but she didn't smile back. I moved on.

"These braces, are they hard to find?"

"They are bought and sold over the Internet every day. They can be expensive, with all kinds of gadgetry and straps. Next time you're on Google, plug in *abasiophilia* and see what you get. We're talking about the dark side of the Internet, Jack. It's the great meeting house, where people of like interests come together. You may think your secret desires make you a freak, and then you get on the Internet and find community and acceptance."

As she said it I realized there was a story in this. Something separate from the trunk murders case. Maybe even a book. I put the idea aside for later and went back to the case at hand.

"So what do you think the killer does? He makes them put on leg braces and then he rapes them? Does the suffocation mean anything?"

"Every detail means something, Jack. You just need to know how to read it. The scene he creates reflects his paraphilia. More than likely this is not about killing the women. It's about creating a psychosexual scene that fulfills a fantasy. The women are killed afterward because he is simply finished with them and he can't have the threat of them living to tell about him. My guess is that he may even apologize to them when he pulls the bag over their head."

"They both were dancers. Do you think he made them dance or something?"

"Again, it's all conjecture at this point, but that could be part of it, yes. But my guess is that it's about body type. Giraffes. Dancers by trade have thin muscular legs. If that is what he wanted, then he would look at dancers."

I thought about the hours the two women spent with their killer. The stretch of hours between abduction and time of death. What happened during those hours? No matter what the answer, it added up to a horrible and terrifying end.

"You said something before about the bag being familiar somehow. Do you remember how?"

Rachel thought for a moment before answering.

"No, there's just something about it. Some familiarity. Probably from another case but I can't place it yet."

"Will you put all of this through ViCAP?"

"As soon as I get the chance."

The FBI's Violent Criminal Apprehension Program was a computer data bank of the details of thousands of crimes. It could be used to find crimes of similar nature when the details of a new crime were entered.

"There's something else that should be noted about the killer's program," Rachel said. "In both cases he left the bag and neck ligature in place on the victims but the limb constraints—whether braces or not—were removed."

"Right. What does that mean?"

"I don't know but it could mean a number of things. The women are obviously constrained in some way during their captivity. Whether it is through braces or otherwise, those are removed but the bag stays in place. This could be part of a statement, part of his signature. It might have a meaning we are not aware of yet."

I nodded. I was impressed by her take.

"How long has it been since you worked in Behavioral Sciences?"

Rachel smiled but then I saw that what I had meant to be a compliment had made her wistful.

"A long time," she said.

"Typical bureau politics and bullshit," I said. "Take someone who is damn good at something and put them somewhere else."

I needed to get her back on focus and away from the memory that her relationship with me had cost her the position she was best suited for.

"You think if we ever capture this guy we'll be able to figure him out?"

"You never figure any of them out, Jack. You get hints, that's all. The guy in Louisiana was raised in an orphanage in the fifties. There were a lot of kids in there who had contracted polio. A lot of them wore leg braces. Why that became the thing that got him off as an adult and led him down the road to serial murder is anybody's guess. A lot of other boys were raised in that orphanage, and they didn't become serial killers. Why one does is ultimately just guesswork."

I turned and looked out the window. We were over the desert between L.A. and Vegas. There was only darkness out there.

"I guess it's a sick world down there," I said.

"It can be," Rachel said.

We flew in silence for a few moments before I turned back to her.

"Are there any other connections between them?"

"I made a list of similarities as well as a list of dissimilar aspects of the cases. I want to study everything further, but for now the leg braces are the most significant to me. After that, you have the physical pattern of the women and the means of death. But there's got to be a connection somewhere. A link between these two women."

"We find it and we find him."

"That's right. And now it's your turn, Jack. What did you put together?"

I nodded and quickly composed my thoughts.

"Well, there was something that wasn't in the stuff Angela had found on the Internet. She only told me about it because there wasn't anything to print out. She said that she found the Las Vegas stories and some of the old L.A. stories when she did an online search with the phrase *trunk murder,* okay?"

"Okay."

"Well, she told me that she also got a hit on a website called trunk murder dot com, but that when she went to it, there was nothing there. She clicked a button to enter and there was a sign that said it was under construction. So I was thinking, because you said this guy's skill set included being able to do things on the Internet, that maybe—"

"Of course! It could have been an IP trap. He would be alert for anybody fishing around on the Internet for intel on trunk murders. He could then trace the IP back and find out who was looking. That would have led him to Angela and then to you."

The jet started its descent, again at an angle that was much steeper than anything I had experienced on a commercial flight. I realized I was digging my fingernails into the armrest again.

"And he probably got a big thrill when he saw your name," Rachel said.

I looked at her.

"What are you talking about?"

"Your pedigree, Jack. You were the reporter who chased down the Poet. You wrote the book on it. Mr. Big Bestseller. You were on *Larry King*. These serial guys pay attention to all of that. They read these books. No, actually, they study these books."

"That's great to know. Maybe I can sign a copy of the book to him."

"I'll make a bet with you. When we get this guy, we'll find a copy of your book in his possessions somewhere."

"I hope not."

"And I'll make you another bet. Before we get this guy, he will make direct contact with you. He'll call or e-mail or get to you in some way."

"Why? Why would he risk it?"

"Because once it's clear to him that he's in the open— that we know about him—he will reach out for attention. They always do. They always make that mistake."

"No bets, Rachel."

The idea that I had or would somehow feed the warped psychology of this guy or anyone else wasn't what I wanted to be thinking about.

"I guess I don't blame you," Rachel said, picking up on my discomfort.

"But I appreciate that you said 'when we get this guy' instead of 'if we get this guy.'"

She nodded.

"Oh, don't worry, Jack. We're going to get this guy."

I turned and looked back out the window. I could see the carpet of lights as we crossed from the desert into civilization again. Civilization as we know it. There were a billion lights out there on the horizon and I knew that all of them put together weren't enough to light the darkness in the hearts of some men.

W e landed at Van Nuys Airport and got into the car Rachel had left there earlier. She checked in by phone to see if there was anything new on Angela Cook and was told there wasn't. She hung up and looked over at me.

"Where's your car? At LAX?"

"No, I took a cab. It's at home. In the garage."

I don't think any line so basic could have sounded so ominous. *In the garage.* I gave Rachel my address and we headed off.

It was almost midnight and traffic on the freeway was light. We took the 101 across the bottom of the San Fernando Valley and then down through the Cahuenga Pass. Rachel exited on Sunset Boulevard in Hollywood and headed west.

My house was on Curson a block south of Sunset. It was a nice neighborhood full of mostly small houses built for middle-class families that had long since been priced out of the neighborhood. I had a two-bedroom Craftsman with a separate single-car garage in the back. The backyard was so small, even a Chihuahua would have felt cramped. I had bought the place twelve years earlier with money from the sale of my book on the Poet. I split every check I got from the deal with my brother's widow to help her raise and educate their daughter. It had been a while since I had seen a royalty check and even longer since I had seen my niece, but I had the house and the kid's education to show for that time in my life. When I had gotten divorced, my wife made no claim on the house, since I had already owned it, and now I had only three years of mortgage payments before it was mine free and clear.

Rachel pulled in and drove down the driveway to the rear of the property. She parked but left the car's lights on. They shone brightly on the closed garage door. We got out and approached slowly, like bomb techs moving toward a man in a dynamite vest.

"I never lock it," I said. "I never keep anything in it worth stealing except for the car itself."

"Then, do you lock the car?"

"No. Most of the time I forget."

"What about this time?"

"I think I forgot."

It was a pull-up garage door. I reached down and raised it and we stepped in. An automatic light went on above and we stared at the trunk of my BMW. I already had the key ready. I pushed the button and we heard the *fump* of the trunk lock releasing.

Rachel stepped forward without hesitation and raised the trunk lid.

Except for a bag of clothes I'd been meaning to drop at the Salvation Army, the trunk was empty.

Rachel had been holding her breath. I heard her slowly releasing it.

"Yeah," I said. "I thought for sure..."

She slammed the trunk closed angrily.

"What, you're upset that she's not in there?" I asked.

"No, Jack, I'm upset because I'm being manipulated. He had me thinking in a certain way and that was my mistake. It won't happen again. Come on, let's check the house to be sure."

Rachel went back and turned her lights off and then we went through the back door and into the kitchen. The house smelled musty but it always did when it was closed up. It didn't help that there were overly ripe bananas in the fruit bowl on the counter. I led the way through, turning lights on as we went. The place looked unchanged from the way I had left it. Reasonably neat but with too many stacks of newspapers on tables and the floor next to the living room couch.

"Nice place," Rachel said.

We checked the guest room, which I used as an office, and found nothing unusual. While Rachel moved on to the master bedroom I swung behind the desk and booted up my desktop computer. I had Internet access but still couldn't get into my *Times* e-mail account. My password was rejected. I angrily shut down the computer and left the office, catching up to Rachel in my bedroom. The bed had been left unmade because I wasn't expecting visitors. It was stuffy and I went to open a window while Rachel checked the closet.

"Why don't you have this on a wall somewhere, Jack?" she asked.

I turned. She had discovered the framed print of the

full-page ad that had run for my book in the *New York Times*. It had been in the closet for two years.

"It used to be in the office, but after ten years with nothing else to follow, it sort of started mocking me. So I put it in there."

She nodded and stepped into the bathroom. I held my breath, not knowing what kind of sanitary condition it was in. I heard the shower curtain being slid open, then Rachel stepped back out into the bedroom.

"You ought to clean your bathtub, Jack. Who are all the women?"

"What?"

She pointed to the bureau, where there was a row of framed photos on little easels. I pointed as I went down the line.

"Niece, sister-in-law, mother, ex-wife."

Rachel raised her eyebrows.

"Ex-wife? You were able to get over me, then."

She smiled and I smiled back.

"It didn't last long. She was a reporter. When I first came to the *Times* we shared the cop beat. One thing led to another and we got married. Then it sort of went away. It had been a mistake. She works in the Washington bureau now and we're still friends."

I wanted to say more but something made me resist. Rachel turned and headed back to the hallway. I followed her into the living room. We stood there, looking at each other.

"What now?" I asked.

"I'm not sure. I'll have to think on it. I should probably let you get some sleep. Are you going to be all right here?"

"Sure, why not? Besides, I've got a gun."

"You have a gun? Jack, what are you doing with a gun?"

"How come the people with guns always question why citizens have guns? I got it after the Poet, you know?"

She nodded. She understood.

"Well, then, if you're okay, I'll leave you here with your gun and call you in the morning. Maybe one of us will have a new idea about Angela by then."

I nodded and knew that, Angela aside, it was one of those moments. I could reach out for what I wanted or I could let it go like I had a long time before.

"What if I don't want you to leave?" I asked.

She looked at me without speaking.

"What if I've never gotten over you?" I asked.

Her eyes dropped to the floor.

"Jack...ten years is a lifetime. We're different people now."

"Are we?"

She looked back at me and we held each other's eyes for a long moment. I then stepped in close, put my hand on the back of her neck and pulled her into a long, hard kiss that she did not fight or push away from.

Her phone dropped out of her hand and clunked to the floor. We grabbed at each other in some sort of emotional desperation. There was nothing gentle about it. It was about wanting, craving. Nothing loving, yet it was all about love and the reckless willingness to cross the line for the sake of intimacy with another human being.

"Let's go back to the bedroom," I whispered against her cheek.

She smiled into my next kiss, then we somehow managed to get to my bedroom without taking our hands off one another. We urgently pulled our clothes off and made love on the bed. It was over before I could think about what we were doing and what it might mean. We then lay side by side on our backs, the knuckles of my left hand gently caressing her breast. Both of us breathing in long, deep strides.

"Uh-oh," she finally said.

I smiled.

"You are so fired," I said.

And she smiled, too.

"What about you? The *Times* has to have some kind of rule about sleeping with the enemy, doesn't it?"

"What are you talking about, 'the enemy'? Besides, they laid me off last week. I've got one more week there and then I'm history."

She suddenly was up on her side and looking down at me with concerned eyes.

"*What?*"

"Yeah, I'm a victim of the Internet. I got downsized and they gave me two weeks to train Angela and clear out."

"Oh, my God, that's awful. Why didn't you tell me?"

"I don't know. It just didn't come up."

"Why you?"

"Because I have a big salary and Angela doesn't."

"That's so stupid."

"You don't have to convince me. But that's how the newspaper business is run these days. It's the same everywhere."

"What are you going to do?"

"I don't know, probably sit in that office and write the novel I've been talking about for fifteen years. I think the bigger question is what are we going to do now, Rachel?"

She averted her eyes and started rubbing my chest.

"I hope this wasn't a onetime thing," I said. "I don't want it to be."

She didn't respond for a long time.

"Me, neither," she finally said.

But that was all.

"What are you thinking?" I asked. "You always seem to go off to dwell on something."

She looked at me with a half smile.

"What, you're the profiler now?"

"No, I just want to know what you're thinking about."

"To be honest, I was thinking about something a man I was with a couple years ago said. We'd, uh, had a relationship and it wasn't going to...work. I had my own hang-ups and I knew he was still holding out for his ex-wife, even though she was ten thousand miles away. When we talked about it, he told me about the 'single-bullet theory.' You know what that is?"

"You mean like with the assassination of Kennedy?"

She mock-punched me in the chest with a fist.

"No, I mean like with the love of your life. Everybody's got one person out there. One bullet. And if you're lucky in life, you get to meet that person. And once you do, once you're shot through the heart, then there's nobody else. No matter what happens—death, divorce, infidelity, whatever—nobody else can ever come close. That's the single-bullet theory."

She nodded. She believed it.

"What are you saying, that he was your bullet?"

She shook her head.

"No, I'm saying he wasn't. He was too late. You see, I'd already been shot by someone else. Someone before him."

I looked at her for a long moment, then pulled her down into a kiss. After a few moments she pulled back.

"But I should go. We should think about this and everything else."

"Just stay here. Sleep with me. We'll get up early tomorrow and both get to work on time."

"No, I have to go home now or my husband will worry."

I sat up like a bolt. She started laughing and slipped off the bed. She began getting dressed.

"That wasn't funny," I said.

"I think it was," she insisted.

I climbed off the bed and started getting dressed, too. She kept laughing in a punch-drunk sort of way. Eventually, I was laughing too. I pulled my pants and shirt on first and then started hunting around the bed for my shoes and socks. I found them all except for one sock. I finally got down on my knees and looked for it under the end of the bed.

And that was when the laughter stopped.

Angela Cook's dead eyes stared at me from under the bed. I involuntarily propelled myself back on the carpet, smashing my back into the bureau and making the lamp on it wobble and then fall to the floor with a crash.

"Jack?" Rachel yelled.

I pointed.

"Angela's under the bed!"

Rachel came quickly around to me. She was only wearing her black panties and white blouse. She got down to look.

"Oh, my God!"

"I thought you checked under the bed!" I said excitedly. "When I came in the room I thought you'd already looked."

"I thought you did while I was checking out the closet."

She got on her hands and knees and looked up and down the underside of the bed for a long moment before turning to look back at me.

"She looks like she's been dead about a day. Suffocation with a plastic bag. She's naked and completely wrapped in a clear plastic sheet. Like she's ready to be transported. Or maybe it was to contain the smell of decay. The scene is quite diff—"

"Rachel, please, I knew her. Can you please not analyze everything right now?"

I leaned my head back against the bureau and looked up at the ceiling.

"I'm sorry, Jack. For her and you."

"Can you tell, did he torture her or just...?"

"I can't tell. But we need to call the LAPD."

"I know."

"This is what we'll say. We'll say I brought you home, we searched the place and we found her. The rest we leave out. Okay?"

"Fine. Okay. Whatever you say."

"I have to get dressed."

She stood up and I realized the woman I had just made love to had completely disappeared. She was all bureau now. She finished getting dressed, then bent over to study the top of the bed at a side angle. I watched her start to pick hairs off the pillows so they couldn't be collected by the crime scene team that would soon descend on my house. The whole time I didn't move. I could still see Angela's face from where I sat and I had to adjust myself to the reality of the situation.

I barely knew Angela and probably didn't even like her too much but she was far too young and had far too much life ahead to suddenly be dead. I had seen a lot of dead bodies in my time and I had written about a lot of murders, including the killing of my own brother. But I don't think anything I had ever seen or written about before affected me like seeing Angela Cook's face behind that plastic bag. Her head was tilted back, so that if she'd been standing she would've been looking upward at me. Her eyes were open and frightened, almost glowing at me from the darkness under the bed. It seemed as though she were disappearing into that darkness, being pulled down into it and looking up at the last light. And it was then that she had made one last desperate push for life. Her mouth was open in a final, terrible scream.

I felt like I was somehow intruding on something sacred by even looking at her.

"This isn't going to work," Rachel said. "We have to get rid of the sheets and pillows."

I looked up at her. She started pulling the sheets off the bed and gathering them into a ball.

"Can't we just tell them what happened? That we didn't find her until after we—"

"Think, Jack. I admit something like that and I am the butt of every joke in the squad room for the next ten years. Not only that, I lose my job. I'm sorry but I don't want that. We do it this way and they'll just think the killer took the sheets."

She balled everything up together.

"Well, maybe there's evidence from the guy on the sheets."

"That's unlikely. He's too careful and he's never left anything before. If there was any evidence on these sheets he would have taken them himself. I doubt she was even killed on this bed. She was just wrapped up and hidden underneath it—for you to find."

She said it so matter-of-factly. There was probably nothing in this world that surprised her or horrified her any longer.

"Come on, Jack. We have to move."

She left the room, carrying the bedsheets and the pillows. I slowly got up then, found my missing sock behind a chair and carried my socks and shoes out to the living room. I was putting them on when I heard the back door close. Rachel came in empty-handed and I assumed she had stashed the pillows and sheets in the trunk of her car.

She picked her phone up off the floor. But instead of making a call she started pacing, head down and deep in thought.

"What are you doing?" I finally said. "Are you going to call?"

"Yes, I'm going to call. But before it turns crazy, I'm trying to figure out what he was doing. What was this guy's plan here?"

"It's obvious. He was going to pin Angela's murder on me, but it was a stupid plan because it wasn't going to work. I went to Vegas and I can prove it. The time of death will show I couldn't have done this to Angela and that I was set up."

Rachel shook her head.

"With suffocation it is very difficult to pinpoint exact time of death. Narrowing it to even a two-hour window could still put you in the picture."

"So you're saying my being on a plane or in Vegas is no alibi?"

"Not if they can't pinpoint time of death to exactly

when you were on that plane or already in Vegas. I think our guy is smart enough to realize that. It was part of his plan."

I slowly nodded and felt a terrible fear start to rise in me. I realized I could end up like Alonzo Winslow and Brian Oglevy.

"But don't worry, Jack. I won't let them put you in jail."

She finally raised her phone and made a call. I listened to her speak briefly to someone who was probably a supervisor. She didn't say anything about me or the case or Nevada. She just said she had been involved in the discovery of a homicide and would shortly be interacting with the LAPD.

Next she called the LAPD, identified herself, gave my address and asked for a homicide team. She then gave her cell phone number and ended the call. She looked at me.

"What about you? If you need to call someone you better do it now. Once the detectives arrive they're probably not going to let you use your phone."

"Right."

I pulled out my throwaway and called the city desk at the *Times*. I checked my watch and saw it was well past one. The paper had long been put to bed but I needed to inform someone of what was happening.

The night editor was an old veteran named Esteban Samuel. He was a survivor, having worked for the *Times* for nearly forty years and having avoided all the shake-ups and purges and changes of regime. He did it largely by keeping his head down and staying out of the way. He didn't come to work until six P.M. each day and that was usually after the corporate cutters and editorial axmen like Kramer had gone home. Out of sight, out of mind. It worked.

"Sam, it's Jack McEvoy."

"Jack Mack! How you doing?"

"Not so well. I've got some bad news. Angela Cook has been murdered. An FBI agent and I just found her. I know the morning edition is closed but you might want to call whoever needs to be called or at least leave it on the overnote."

The overnote was a list of notes, ideas and incomplete stories that Samuel put together at the end of his shift and then left for the morning editor.

"Oh, my God! How terrible! That poor, poor girl."

"Yes, it's awful."

"What happened?"

"It's related to the story we were working on. But I don't know a whole lot. We're waiting on the LAPD to show up now."

"Where are you? Where did this happen?"

I knew he would get around to asking that.

"My house, Sam. I don't know how much you know, but I went to Las Vegas last night and Angela went missing today. I came back tonight and an FBI agent escorted me home and we searched the house. We found her body under the bed."

The whole thing sounded insane as I said it.

"Are you under arrest, Jack?" Samuel asked, his confusion clear in his voice.

"No, no. The killer is trying to set me up but the FBI

knows what's going on. Angela and I were onto this guy and somehow he found out. He killed Angela and then he tried to get me in Nevada but the FBI was there. Anyway, all of this will be in the story I write tomorrow. I'll be in as soon as I clear this scene and I will write it for Friday's paper. Okay? Make sure they know that."

"Got it, Jack. I'll make some calls and you stay in touch."

If I can, I thought. I gave him the number of my throwaway and ended the call. Rachel was still pacing.

"That didn't sound very convincing," she said.

I shook my head.

"I know. I realized I sounded like a nut job as I was saying it. I've got a bad feeling about this, Rachel. Nobody's going to believe me."

"They will, Jack. And I think I know what he was trying to do. It's all coming together now."

"Then, tell me. The cops will be here any second."

Rachel finally sat down, taking the chair across the coffee table from me. She leaned forward to tell her story.

"You have to look at it from his point of view and then make some assumptions about his skills and location."

"Okay."

"First of all, he's close. Our first two known victims were in L.A. and Las Vegas. Angela's murder and his attempt to get to you were in L.A. and a remote part of Nevada. So my guess is that he lives in or is close to one of these places. He was able to react quickly and in a matter of hours get to both you and Angela."

I nodded. It sounded right to me.

"Next, his technical skill. We know from his e-mail to

the prison warden and from how he was able to attack you on multiple levels that his tech skill is quite high. So if we assume that he was able to breach your e-mail account, then we can also assume that he breached the entire *L.A. Times* data system. If he had free rein inside, then he would have been able to access home addresses for both you and Angela, right?"

"Sure. That information has got to be in there."

"What about you being laid off? Would there be any e-mail or a data trail involving that?"

I nodded.

"I got a ton of e-mails about it. From friends, people at other papers, everywhere. I told a few people by e-mail, too. But what would it have to do with any of this?"

She nodded as though she was way ahead of me and my answer fit perfectly with what she already knew.

"Okay, so then what do we know? We know that somehow Angela or possibly you hit a trip wire and alerted him to your investigation."

"Trunk murder dot com."

"I will have it checked out as soon as I can. Maybe that was it and maybe it wasn't. But somehow our guy was alerted. His response was to invade the *Los Angeles Times* and try to find out what you two were up to. We don't know what Angela put in her e-mails but we know that you put your plan to go to Las Vegas last night into an e-mail. I am betting that our guy read it and a lot of your other e-mails and keyed his plan off of it."

"We keep saying 'our guy.' We need a name for him."

"In the bureau we would call him an unknown subject

until we knew exactly who we were dealing with. An Unsub."

I got up and looked through the curtains on the front window. The street was dark out there. No cops yet. I walked over to a wall switch and turned on the outside lights.

"Okay, Unsub, then," I said. "What do you mean he keyed his plan off of my plan?"

"He needed to neutralize the threat. He knew that there was a good chance you had not confirmed your suspicions or talked to the authorities yet. Being a reporter, you would keep the story to yourself. This worked in his favor. But he still had to move quickly. He knew Angela was in L.A. and you were going to Vegas. I think he started in L.A., somehow grabbed Angela, and then killed her and set you up for it."

I sat back down.

"Yeah, that's obvious."

"He then focused his attention on you. He went to Vegas, probably driving through the night or flying out this morning, and tracked you to Ely. It would not have been hard to do. I think he was the man who followed you in the hallway at the hotel. He was going to make his move against you in your room. He stopped when he heard my voice and that has sort of puzzled me until now."

"Why?"

"Well, why did he abort the plan? Just because he heard you had company? This guy isn't shy about killing people. What would it matter to him if he had to kill you and the woman he heard in your room?"

"So then, why did he abort?"

"Because the plan wasn't to murder you and whoever you were with. The plan was for you to kill yourself."

"Come on."

"Think about it. It would be the best way for him to avoid detection. If you end up murdered in a hotel room in Ely, there is going to be an investigation that would lead to all of this unraveling. But if you were a suicide in a hotel room in Ely, then the investigation would go in a completely different direction."

I thought about this for a few moments and saw where she was going with it.

"Reporter gets laid off, has the indignity of having to train his own replacement, and has few prospects for another job," I said, reciting a litany of true facts. "He gets depressed and suicidal. Concocts a story about a serial killer running around two states as cover, then abducts and murders his young replacement. He then gives all his money to charity, cancels his credit cards and runs off to the middle of nowhere, where he kills himself in a hotel room."

She was nodding the whole time I was running it down.

"What's missing?" I asked. "How was he going to kill me and make it look like suicide?"

"You'd been drinking, right? You came into the room with two bottles of beer. I remember that."

"Yeah, I'd only had two before that."

"But it would help sell the scene. Empty bottles strewn around the hotel room. Cluttered room, cluttered mind, that sort of thing."

"But beer wouldn't kill me. How was he going to do it?"

"You already gave the answer earlier, Jack. You said you had a gun."

Bang. It all came together. I stood up and headed toward my bedroom. I'd bought a .45 caliber Colt Government Series 70 twelve years earlier, after my encounter with the Poet. He was still out there at the time and I wanted some protection in case he came calling on me. I kept the weapon in a drawer next to my bed and only took it out once a year to go to the range.

Rachel followed me into the bedroom and watched me slide open the drawer. The gun was gone.

I turned back to Rachel.

"You saved my life, you know that? No doubt about that now."

"I'm glad."

"How would he know I owned a gun?"

"Is it registered?"

"Yes, but what, now you're saying he can hack into the ATF computers? This is getting far-fetched, don't you think?"

"Actually, no. If he tapped the prison computer, I don't see why he couldn't get into the gun registry. And that may be only one place where he could have gotten it. Back during the period when you bought it, you were interviewed by everybody from Larry King to the *National Enquirer*. Did you ever put it out there that you owned a gun?"

I shook my head.

"Unbelievable. I did. I said it in a few interviews. I was hoping the word would get out and it would deter a surprise visit from the Poet."

"There you go."

"But for the record, I never did an interview with the *Enquirer*. They did a story on me and the Poet without my cooperation."

"Sorry."

"Anyway, this guy now isn't as smart as we think. There was one big flaw in his plan."

"What was that?"

"I flew to Vegas. All baggage is screened. I never would have gotten the gun there."

She nodded.

"Maybe not. But I think it is a widely accepted fact that the scanning process is not one hundred percent perfect. It would probably bother the investigators in Ely but not enough to make them change their conclusion. There are always loose ends in any investigation."

"Can we go back out to the living room?"

Rachel headed out of the room and I followed, taking a glance back at the bed as I went through the door. In the living room, I dropped down on the couch. A lot had happened in the last thirty-six hours. I was getting fatigued but knew there would be no rest for the weary for a long time.

"I thought of something else. Schifino."

"The lawyer in Vegas? What about him?"

"I went to him first and he knew everything. He could put the lie to my suicide."

Rachel considered this for a moment and then nodded.

"That could've put him in danger. Maybe the plan was to kill you and then double back to Vegas and take him out, too. Then, when the chance was missed with you, there was no reason to hit Schifino. I'll have the field office in Vegas make contact, anyway, and see about protection."

"Are you going to have them go up to Ely and pull the video from the casino where I sat with this guy?"

"I'll do that, too."

Rachel's phone rang and she answered immediately.

"It's just me and the homeowner," she said. "Jack McEvoy. He's a reporter for the *Times*. The victim here was a reporter as well."

She listened for a moment and said, "We're coming out now."

She closed the phone and told me the police were out front.

"They'll feel more comfortable if we come out to meet them."

We walked to the front door and Rachel opened it.

"Keep your hands in sight," Rachel said to me.

She walked out, holding her credentials high. There were two patrol cars and a detective cruiser in the street out front. Four uniformed officers and two detectives were waiting on the driveway. The uniformed officers pointed their flashlights at us.

When we got closer I recognized the two detectives from Hollywood Division. They held their guns down at their sides and looked ready to use them if I gave them the right reason.

I didn't.

didn't get to the *Times* until shortly before noon on Thursday. The place was bustling with activity. A lot of reporters and editors were moving about the newsroom like bees in a hive. I knew it was all because of Angela and what had happened. It's not every day that you come to work and find out your colleague has been brutally murdered.

And that another colleague is somehow involved.

Dorothy Fowler, the city editor, was the first to spot me as I came in from the stairwell. She jumped from her desk at the raft and came directly toward me.

"Jack, my office, please."

She changed directions and headed to the wall of glass. I followed, knowing every eye in the newsroom was on me once again. No longer because I was the one that got pink-slipped by the axman. They watched me now because I was the one who might have gotten Angela Cook killed.

We entered her small office and she told me to close the door. I did as instructed and then took the seat directly across the desk from her.

"What happened with the police?" she asked.

No howyadoin', are you all right or sorry about Angela. Right down to business and I liked it that way.

"Well, let's see," I said. "I spent about eight hours being questioned. First by the LAPD and the FBI, then the Santa Monica detectives joined in. They gave me a break for about an hour and then I had to tell the whole story again to the Las Vegas police, who flew in just to talk to me. After that, they let me go but wouldn't let me go back to my house because it's still an active crime scene. So I had them take me to the Kyoto Grand, where I checked into a room—and put it on the *Times*' tab, since I don't have a working credit card—took a shower and then walked over here."

The Kyoto was a block away and the *Times* used it to put up out-of-town reporters, new hires and job candidates when needed.

"That's fine," Fowler said. "What did you tell the police?"

"Basically, I told them what I tried to tell Prendo yesterday. I uncovered a killer out there who murdered Denise Babbit and a woman in Las Vegas named Sharon Oglevy. Somehow, either Angela or I hit a trip wire somewhere and alerted this guy that we were onto him. He then took steps to eliminate the threat. That included killing Angela first and going to Nevada to try to get me. But I was lucky. While I was unable to convince Prendo yesterday, I *had* convinced an FBI agent that all of this was legit, and she met me in Nevada to talk about it. Her presence kept the killer away from me. If she hadn't believed me and met with me, you'd be putting together stories about how I killed Angela and went off to the desert to kill myself. That's what the Unsub's plan was."

"Unsub?"

"Unknown subject. That's what the bureau is calling him."

Fowler shook her head in stunned disbelief.

"This is an amazing story. Do the police agree with it?"

"You mean, do they believe me? They let me go, didn't they?"

Her face colored in embarrassment.

"It's just hard for me to get my head around it, Jack. Nothing like this has ever happened in this newsroom."

"Actually, the cops probably wouldn't have believed it if it had just come from me. But I was with that FBI agent most of yesterday. We think we actually saw the guy in Nevada. And she was with me when I got home. She found Angela's body when we were searching the house. She backed me up on everything with the cops. And that's probably why I'm not talking to you through Plexiglas."

Mention of Angela's body brought a morbid pause to the conversation.

"It's just horrible," Fowler said.

"Yes. She was a sweet kid. I don't even want to think about what her last hours were like."

"How was she killed, Jack? Like the girl in the trunk?"

"Pretty much. It looked that way to me but I guess they won't know everything till the autopsy."

Fowler nodded somberly.

"How are they handling the investigation now, do you know?"

"They were putting together a task force with L.A., Las Vegas and Santa Monica contributing detectives and the FBI taking part as well. I think they are going to run it out of Parker Center."

"Can we get that confirmed so we can put it in one of the stories?"

"Yeah, I'll confirm it. I'm probably the only reporter they'll take a call from. How many inches are you giving me for the story?"

"Uh, Jack, that was one of the things I wanted to talk to you about."

I felt the bottom drop out of my stomach.

"I'm writing the main story, right?"

"We're going to go big with this. Main and sidebar on the front going to a double-truck inside. For once, we have a lot of space."

Double-truck meant two full inside pages. It was a lot of space but it took one of the paper's own reporters getting murdered to get it.

Dorothy continued the plan.

"Jerry Spencer is already on the ground in Las Vegas and Jill Meyerson is on her way up to Ely State Prison to try to talk to Brian Oglevy. In L.A., we've got GoGo Gonzmart writing the sidebar, which will be on Angela, and Teri Sparks down in South L.A. working on a piece on the kid charged with the Babbit murder. We have art on Angela and are looking for more."

"Is Alonzo Winslow getting out of juvy jail today?"

"We're not sure yet. Hopefully, it will take another day and we'll have that to run with tomorrow."

Even without Winslow getting out, they were going big. Sending Metro reporters out across the west and putting multiple writers on it locally was something I had not seen done by the *Times* since the fires ravaged the state the year before. It was exciting to be part of it, but not so exciting when considering what caused it.

"All right," I said. "I have stuff to contribute to almost all of those stories and I'll still pull together and write the main."

Dorothy nodded, hesitated and then dropped the bomb.

"Larry Bernard is writing the main, Jack."

I reacted swiftly and loudly.

"What the fuck are you talking about? This is my story, Dorothy! Actually, me and *Angela's* story."

Dorothy looked up over my shoulder and out to the newsroom. I suspected that my outburst had been heard through the glass. I didn't care.

"Jack, calm down and watch your language. I'm not going to let you talk to me the way you talked to Prendo yesterday."

I tried to pace my breathing and speak calmly.

"Okay, I apologize for the language. To you and Prendo. But you can't take this story away from me. It's *my* story. I started it, I'm writing it."

"Jack, you can't write it and you know it. You *are* the story. I need to get you with Larry so he can interview *you* and then write the story. The switchboard's taken more than thirty messages from reporters wanting to interview you, including the *New York Times,* Katie Couric, even Craig Ferguson from the *Late Late Show.*"

"Ferguson's not a reporter."

"Doesn't matter. The point is, you are the story, Jack. That's a fact. Now, we certainly need your help and your knowledge of everything related, but we can't let the subject of a major breaking story also write it. You were in police custody for eight hours today. What you told them is the basis of their investigation. How are you going to write about that? Are you going to interview yourself? Write it in first person?"

She paused to let me answer but I didn't.

"That's right," she continued. "Not going to happen. You can't do this, and I know you understand that."

I leaned forward and put my face in my hands. I knew she was right. I'd known it before I even entered the newsroom.

"This was supposed to be my big exit. Get that kid out of jail and go out in a blaze of glory. Put the big three-oh on my career."

"You're still going to get credit. There is no way the story can be anything but about you. Katie Couric, the *Late Late Show*—I'd say that's going out in a blaze of glory."

"I wanted to write it, not tell it to somebody else."

"Look, let's get this done today and then we can talk about doing a first-person piece when the dust settles. I promise you, you will get to write something about all of this at some point."

I finally sat back up and looked at her. For the first

time I noticed the photo taped to the wall behind her. It was a still shot from *The Wizard of Oz* that showed Dorothy skipping down the yellow brick road with the Tin Man, the Lion and the Scarecrow. Beneath the characters someone had printed in Magic Marker:

YOU'RE NOT IN KANSAS ANYMORE, DOROTHY

I had forgotten that Dorothy Fowler had come to the paper from the *Wichita Eagle*.

"All right, if you promise me that story."

"I promise, Jack."

"Okay. I'll tell Larry what I know."

I still felt defeated.

"Before you do, I need to make sure of one last thing," Dorothy said. "Are you comfortable going on the record with another reporter? Do you want to consult a lawyer first or anything like that?"

"What are you talking about?"

"Jack, I want to make sure you're protected. It's an ongoing investigation. I don't want something you say in the paper to be possibly used by the police to hurt you later."

I stood up but maintained composure and control.

"In other words, you don't believe any of this. You believe what he was hoping you would believe. That I killed her in some sort of psychotic breakdown over getting fired."

"No, Jack. I believe you. I just want you protected. And who is he that you're talking about?"

I pointed out the glass toward the newsroom.

"Who do you think? The guy! The Unsub! The killer who took Angela and the others."

"Okay, okay. I understand. I'm sorry I brought up the legal aspects of this. Let me get you with Larry in the conference room so you can have some privacy, okay?"

She stood up and rushed by me to leave the office and look for Larry Bernard. I stepped out and surveyed the newsroom. My eyes eventually came to Angela's empty cubicle. I walked over and saw that someone had placed a bouquet of flowers wrapped in cellophane diagonally across her desk. Immediately I was struck by the clear plastic wrapping around the flowers and it reminded me of the bag that had been used to suffocate her. Once again I saw Angela's face disappearing into the darkness beneath the bed.

"Excuse me, Jack?"

I almost jumped. I turned and saw it was Emily Gomez-Gonzmart. She was one of the best reporters on the Metro staff. Always hustling, always going after a story.

"Hey, GoGo."

"I'm sorry to interrupt but I'm putting together the story on Angela and wondered if I could get a little help from you. And maybe a quote I could use."

She was holding a pen and reporter's notebook. I went with the quote first.

"Uh, yeah, but I didn't really know her," I said. "I was just getting to know her, but from what I saw I could tell she was going to be a great reporter. She had the right mix of curiosity and drive and determination that a good reporter needs. She is going to be missed. Who knows what stories she would have written and what people she could have helped with those stories?"

I gave GoGo a moment to finish writing.

"How's that?"

"Good, Jack, thanks. Anybody you can suggest I talk to over in the cop shop?"

I shook my head.

"I don't know. She had just started and I don't think she had made an impression on anybody yet. I heard she had a blog. Have you looked at that?"

"Yeah, I've got the blog and it's got some contacts on it. I talked to a Professor Foley back at the University of Florida and a few others. I should be fine there. I was just looking for somebody local and outside the paper who might have something to say about her more recently."

"Well, she wrote a story on Monday about the cold case squad popping somebody for a twenty-year-old murder. Maybe somebody over there could say something. Try Rick Jackson or Tim Marcia. Those are the guys she spoke to. Also, Richard Bengston. Try him."

She wrote the names down.

"Thanks, I'll check it out."

"Good luck. I'll be around if you need me."

She left me then and I turned back to Angela's desk and looked again at the flowers. The glorification of Angela Cook was in high gear now and I was part of it with that quote I had just given GoGo.

Call me Mr. Cynical, but I couldn't help wondering if the bouquet of carnations and daisies was somebody's legitimate show of mourning, or if the whole thing had been staged for a photo that would be put in the next morning's edition.

An hour later I was sitting with Larry Bernard in the conference room normally reserved for news meetings. We had my files spread across the big table and were going step by step through the moves I had made on the story. Bernard had brought his A game. He was diligent about understanding my decisions and acute in his questions. I could tell he was excited about being the lead writer on a story that would go out across the country, if not around the world. Larry and I went back a long ways—we had worked together at the *Rocky* in Denver. If anybody got to run with my story, I was begrudgingly glad it was him.

It was important to Larry to get official confirmation from the police or FBI on the things I was telling him. So to his side he had a legal pad on which he wrote a series of questions he would later take to the authorities before writing his story. Because of that need to get to the task force before writing, Bernard was all business with me. There was very little small talk and I liked that. I didn't have any small talk left.

My throwaway phone buzzed in my pocket for the second time in fifteen minutes. The first time, I hadn't bothered to pull it out and I let it go to message. Larry and I had been in the middle of a key point of discussion and I didn't want the intrusion. But whoever called hadn't left a message, because I didn't get a follow-up voice-mail buzz.

Now the phone was buzzing again and this time I pulled it out to check the caller ID. The screen showed only a number but I readily recognized it because I had called it a few times in the past couple of days. It was Angela Cook's cell number. The number I had called after hearing that she was missing.

"Larry, I'll be right back."

I got up from the table and left the conference room while clicking on to the call. I headed toward my cubicle.

"Hello?"

"Is this Jack?"

"Yes, who is this?"

"This is your friend, Jack. From Ely."

I knew exactly who it was. There was that same empty-desert twang in his voice. Sideburns. I sat down at my desk and leaned forward to help insulate the conversation from any nearby ears.

"What do you want?" I asked.

"To see how you're doing," he said.

"Yeah, well, I'm doing fine, no thanks to you. In the hallway at the Nevada, why'd you stop? Instead of sticking with the plan, you just walked on by."

I thought I heard a low chuckle on the line.

"You had company and I wasn't expecting that, Jack. Who was she, your girlfriend?"

"Something like that. And she messed up your plan, right? You wanted to make it look like suicide."

Another chuckle.

"I can see you are very smart," he said. "Or are you just telling me what they've told you?"

"They?"

"Don't be silly, Jack. I know what's going on. The cat's out of the bag. There are a lot of stories being written for tomorrow's paper. But none of them with your name on it, Jack. What's up with that?"

That told me he was still floating around inside the *Times'* data system. I wondered if it would help the task force run him down.

"You there, Jack?"

"Yeah, I'm here."

"And it looks like you have no name for me yet, either."

"What do you mean?"

"Aren't you all going to give me a name? We all get names, you know. The Yorkshire Ripper. The Hillside Strangler. The Poet. You know about that one, right?"

"Yeah, we're giving you a name. We're calling you the Iron Maiden. How do you like that?"

This time I heard no chuckle in the silence that followed.

"Are you still there, Iron Maiden?"

"You should be careful, Jack. I could always try again, you know."

I laughed at him.

"Hey, I'm not hiding. I'm right here. Try again, if you've got the balls."

He was silent, so I laid it on thicker.

"Killing these defenseless women, that takes a lot of balls, doesn't it?"

The chuckle was back.

"You're very transparent, Jack. Are you working off a script?"

"I don't need a script."

"Well, I know what you're doing. Talking with a lot of bluster and bravado to bait the trap. Hoping I'll come to L.A. and go for you. Meantime, you have the FBI and the LAPD watching and ready to jump in and catch the monster just in the nick of time. Is that it, Jack?"

"If that's what you think."

"Well, it won't work that way. I'm a patient man, Jack. Time will pass, maybe even years will go by, and then I promise we'll meet again face-to-face. No disguise. I'll return your gun then."

His low chuckle came again and I got the impression that wherever he was calling from, he was trying to keep his voice and laugh down and not draw attention. I didn't know if it was an office or a public space but he was keeping himself contained. I was sure of it.

"Speaking of the gun, how was that going to be explained? You know, that I flew to Vegas but then somehow had my gun and killed myself with it? Seems like a flaw in the plan, doesn't it?"

He outright laughed this time.

"Jack, you are not in possession of all the facts yet, are you? When you are, then you will understand how flawless the plan was. My one mistake was the girl in the room. I didn't see that coming."

Neither did I but I wasn't saying so.

"Then I guess it wasn't so flawless, was it?"

"I can make up for it."

"Look, I'm having a busy day here. Why are you calling me?"

"I told you, to see how you are. To make your acquaintance. We're now going to be linked forever, aren't we?"

"Well, while I've got you on the line, can I ask you a few questions for the story we're putting together?"

"I don't think so, Jack. This is between you and me, not your readers."

"You know, you're right. The truth is, I wouldn't give you the space. You think I'm going to let you try to explain your sick fucking world in my newspaper?"

A dark silence followed.

"*You*," he finally said, his voice tight with anger. "You should respect me."

Now I laughed.

"Respect you? How about, Fuck you. You took a young girl who had nothing but—"

He interrupted me by making a noise like a muffled cough.

"Did you hear that, Jack? Do you know what that was?"

I didn't respond and then he made the sound again. Muffled, one syllable, quick. Then he did it a third time.

"Okay, I give up," I said.

"That was her, saying your name through plastic when there was no air left."

He laughed. I said nothing.

"You know what I tell them, Jack? I say, 'Breathe deep and it will all be over a lot faster.' "

He laughed again, long and hard, and made sure I heard it all before abruptly hanging up. I sat there for a long time with the phone still pressed against my ear.

"Sssst."

I looked up. It was Larry Bernard looking over the sound wall of my cubicle. He thought I was still on the line.

"How much longer?" he whispered.

I took the phone from my ear and covered the mouth-piece with my palm.

"A few more minutes. I'll come right back in."

"Okay. I'm going to go take a leak."

He left me then and I immediately called Rachel. The call was answered after four rings.

"Jack, I can't talk," she said by way of a greeting.

"You would've won the bet."

"What bet?"

"He just called me. The Unsub. He has Angela's cell phone."

"What did he say?"

"Not a lot. I think he was trying to find out who you are."

"What do you mean? How would he know about me?"

"He doesn't. He was trying to find out who the woman in the room back in Ely was. You spoiled everything by being there and he's curious."

"Look, Jack, whatever he said, you can't quote him in the paper. That sort of thing feeds the fire. If he gets hooked on headlines, then he's going to speed up his cycle. He could start killing for headlines."

"Don't worry. Nobody here knows he called me and I'm not writing the story, so he's not going in it. I'll save it for when I do write the story. I'll save it for the book."

It was the first time I had mentioned the possibility of getting a book out of this. But now it seemed entirely plausible. One way or another I was going to write this story.

"Did you record it?" Rachel asked.

"No, because I wasn't expecting it."

"We need to get your phone. We'll be able to ping the call and get the originating tower. It will get us close to where he's at. At least where he was when he made the call."

"It sounded like he was someplace where he had to speak quietly or it would attract attention. Like an office or something. He also made one slip."

"What was that?"

"I tried to bait him, to get him mad, and—"

"Jack, are you crazy? What are you doing?"

"I didn't want to be intimidated by him. So I went after him, only he thought I was working off a script given to me by you guys. He thought I was intentionally baiting him into coming after me. That's when he slipped. He said I was baiting him into *coming* to L.A. That's how he said it. Coming to L.A. So he's somewhere outside of L.A."

"That's good, Jack. But he could have been playing you. Intentionally saying that because he actually is in L.A. That's why I wish it was taped. So we could have it analyzed."

I hadn't thought of the reverse play.

"Well, sorry, no tape. There's one other thing, too."

"What is it?"

She seemed so short and to the point, I wondered if our conversation was being listened to.

"He's either still hacking into the computer system over here or he left some kind of spy program on it."

"At the *Times*? Why do you say that?"

"He knew about the story budget for tomorrow. He knew I wasn't writing any of the stories."

"That sounds like something we might be able to trace," she said excitedly.

"Yeah, well, good luck getting the *Times* to cooperate. And besides, if this guy's as smart as you're saying, he knows what he just told me and he knows the bug he planted is either untraceable or he'll just shut it down and zip it up."

"It's still worth a try. I will get somebody in our media office to make an approach to the *Times*. It's worth the shot."

I nodded.

"You never know. It could usher in a whole new era of media and law enforcement cooperation. Sort of like you and me, Rachel, but bigger."

I smiled and hoped she was smiling too.

"You are such an optimist, Jack. Speaking of cooperation, can I send somebody over for your phone now?"

"Yes, but what about sending yourself?"

"I can't. I'm in the middle of something here. I told you."

I didn't know how to read that.

"Are you in trouble, Rachel?"

"I don't know yet, but I have to go."

"Well, are you on the task force? Are they letting you work the case?"

"For now, yes."

"Okay, well, that's good."

"Yes."

We made arrangements for me to meet the agent she would send for the phone outside the door of the globe lobby in a half hour. It was then time for both of us to go back to work.

"Hang in there, Rachel," I said.

She was silent for a moment and then said, "You too, Jack."

We hung up then. And somehow, with all that had transpired in the last thirty-six hours, with what had happened to Angela and my having just been threatened by a serial killer, a part of me felt happy and hopeful.

I had a feeling, though, that it wasn't going to last.

SEVEN: The Farm

Carver intently watched the security screens. The two men at the front counter showed badges to Geneva. He couldn't tell what law enforcement agency they were from. By the time he had zoomed in, the badges had already been put away.

He watched Geneva pick up the phone and punch in three numbers. He knew she would be calling McGinnis's office. She spoke briefly, then hung up and signaled the two men with badges to one of the couches to wait.

Carver tried to keep his anxiety in check. The fight-or-flight impulse was firing in his brain as he reviewed his recent moves and tried to see where, if anywhere, he could have made a mistake. It was safe, he told himself. He was safe. The plan was good. Freddy Stone was the only issue of concern—the only aspect that could be considered a weak link—and Carver would have to take steps to make that potential problem go away.

On the screen he watched as Yolanda Chavez, McGinnis's second in command, entered the reception lobby and shook hands with the two men. They quickly showed badges again but then one took a folded document from the inside pocket of his suit coat and presented it to her. She studied it for a moment and then handed it back. She signaled for the two men to follow her and they went through the door into the interior of the building. By switching security screens Carver was able to follow them to the administration suite.

He got up and closed the door to his office. Back at his desk, he picked up his phone and punched in the extension for reception.

"Geneva, it's Mr. Carver. I happen to be watching the cameras and am curious about those two men who just entered. I saw them show badges. Who are they?"

"They're FBI agents."

The words froze his heart but he held himself steady and remained calm. After a moment, Geneva continued.

"They said they have a search warrant. I didn't see it but they showed it to Yolanda."

"A search warrant for what?"

"I'm not sure, Mr. Carver."

"Who did they ask to see?"

"No one. They just asked to see somebody in charge. I called Mr. McGinnis, and Yolanda came out to get them."

"Okay, thank you, Geneva."

He hung up the phone and refocused on his screen. He typed in a command that opened a new set of camera angles, a multiplex screen that showed the four private offices of the top administrators. These cameras were hidden in ceiling-mounted smoke detectors and the occupants of the offices knew nothing about them. The camera views came with audio feeds as well.

Carver saw the two FBI agents enter Declan McGinnis's office. He clicked his mouse on that camera and the image filled the entire screen. It was an angled over-head view of the room from a convex lens. The agents sat down with their backs to the camera and Yolanda took a seat on the right. Carver had a full view of McGinnis when the company CEO sat back down after shaking hands with the agents. One was black and one was white. They identified themselves as Bantam and Richmond.

"So I am told you have a search warrant of some sort?" McGinnis asked.

"Yes, sir, we do," Bantam said.

He pulled the document out of his suit again and passed it across the table.

"You are hosting a website called trunk murder dot com and we need to know every piece of information you have about it."

McGinnis didn't respond. He was reading the document. Carver reached up and ran his hands through his hair. He needed to know what was in that warrant and how close they were. He tried to calm down, reminding himself that he was prepared for this. He even expected this. He knew more about the FBI than the FBI knew about him. He could start right there.

He killed the feed and then the screen. He opened a desk drawer and pulled out the stack of monthly server volume reports his staff had prepared earlier in the week. Usually he filed them away until McGinnis asked for them and then he sent them up with one of his server engineers on his way out for a smoke. This time he would make the delivery himself. He tapped the stack on the desk and made the corners sharp, then he left and locked his office.

In the control room he told Mizzou and Kurt, the two engineers on duty, where he was going and then went out through the mantrap. Thankfully, Freddy Stone was not on shift until the evening, because he could never come back to Western Data. Carver knew how the FBI worked. They would take every name of every employee and run it through their computers. They would learn that Freddy Stone was not Freddy Stone and they would come back for him.

Carver wasn't going to allow that. He had other plans for Freddy.

He took the elevator up and entered the administration suite with his head down, reading the top page of the stack of reports. He nonchalantly looked up as he came in and saw through the open door of McGinnis's office that he had company. He pivoted and went to his secretary's desk.

"Give these to Declan when he's free," he said. "But no hurry."

He turned to leave the suite, hoping the motion of his pivot move had drawn the attention of McGinnis through the doorway. But he got all the way to the main door without being called.

He put his hand on the knob.

"Wesley?"

It was McGinnis, calling from his office. Carver turned around and glanced back. McGinnis was behind his desk, waving him into the office.

Carver entered. He nodded to the two men and completely ignored Chavez, whom he considered a worthless diversity hire. There was no place for Carver to sit but that was all right. Being the only one standing would give him a command presence.

"Wesley Carver, meet Agents Bantam and Richmond from the FBI's Phoenix office. I was just about to call down to the bunker for you."

Carver shook hands with the men and repeated his name politely each time.

"Wesley wears a number of hats around here," McGinnis said. "He's our chief technology officer and the one who designed most of this place. He's also our chief threat officer. What I like to call our—"

"Do we have a problem?" Carver cut in.

"We may," McGinnis said. "The agents have been telling me that we're hosting a website here that is of interest to them and they've got a warrant that allows them to see all documentation and records pertaining to its setup and operation."

"Terrorism?"

"They say they can't tell us."

"Should I go get Danny?"

"No, they don't want to talk to anybody in design and hosting just yet."

Carver put his hands into the pockets of his white lab coat because he knew it gave him the posture of a deep-thinking man. He then addressed the agents.

"Danny O'Connor is our chief of design and hosting," he said. "He should be brought in on this. You're not thinking he's a terrorist or something, are you?"

He smiled at the absurdity of what he had just suggested. Agent Bantam, the larger of the two agents, responded.

"No, we're not thinking that at all. We're on a fishing expedition here, and the fewer people brought into it, the better. Especially from the hosting side of your business."

Carver nodded and his eyes flicked momentarily in the direction of Chavez. But the agents didn't pick up on it. She remained in the meeting.

"What is the website?" Carver asked.

"Trunk murder dot com," McGinnis answered. "I just checked and it's part of a larger bundle. An account out of Seattle."

Carver nodded and kept a calm demeanor. He had a plan for this. He was better than them because he always had a plan.

He pointed to the screen on McGinnis's desk.

"Can we take a look at it or would that comp—"

"We would prefer not to at this point," Bantam said. "We think it could tip off the target. It is not a developed site. There's nothing to see. But it's a capture site, we believe."

"And we don't want to be captured," Carver said.

"Exactly."

"May I see the warrant?"

"Sure."

The document had been returned to Bantam while Carver was coming up from the bunker. The agent took it out again and handed it to Carver, who unfolded it and scanned it, hoping he was not giving anything away with his face. He checked himself to make sure he wasn't humming.

The search warrant was notable for what information it did not contain rather than for what it did. The bureau had a very cooperative federal judge in their corner, that seemed for sure. In very general terms the warrant described an investigation of an unknown subject using the Internet and crossing state lines to conduct a criminal conspiracy involving data theft and fraud. The word *murder* was nowhere in the warrant. The warrant sought complete access to the website and all information and records relating to its origin, operation and financing.

Carver knew the bureau would be unhappily surprised by what they got. He nodded as he scanned it.

"Well, we can get you all of this," he said. "What is the account in Seattle?"

"See Jane Run," Chavez said.

Carver turned to look at her, as if noticing her for the first time. She picked up on his vibe.

"Mr. McGinnis just asked me to check it," she explained. "That's the name of the company."

Well, he thought, at least she was good for something besides giving tours of the plant while the boss was away. He turned to the agents, making sure his back was to her and physically cutting her out of the discussion.

"Okay, we'll get this done," he said.

"How long are we talking about?" Bantam asked.

"Why don't you go to our wonderful cafeteria and get yourselves a cup of coffee. I'll be back with you before it's cool enough to drink."

McGinnis chuckled.

"He means that we don't have a cafeteria. We have machines that overheat the coffee."

"Well," Bantam said, "we appreciate the offer but we need to witness the execution of the warrant."

Carver nodded.

"Then stick with me and we'll go get the information you need. But there is still going to be an issue."

"What issue?" Bantam asked.

"You want all information pertaining to this website but you don't want to involve D and H. That's not going to work. I can vouch for Danny O'Connor. He's not a terrorist. I think we need to bring him in if we want to be thorough and get you everything you need."

Bantam nodded and took the suggestion under advisement.

"Let's move one step at a time. We'll bring Mr. O'Connor in when we need to."

Carver was silent as he acted like he was expecting more, then he nodded.

"Suit yourself, Agent Bantam."

"Thank you."

"Should we head down to the bunker, then?"

"Absolutely."

The two agents stood up, as did Chavez.

"Good luck, gentlemen," McGinnis offered. "I hope you catch the bad guys. We're willing to help in any way we can."

"Thank you, sir," Agent Richmond said.

As they left administration, Carver noticed that Chavez

was tagging along behind the agents. Carver was holding the door but when it was her turn to go through, he cut her off.

"We'll take it from here, thank you," he said.

He stepped through the doorway in front of her and pulled the door closed behind him.

EIGHT: Home Sweet Home

On Saturday morning I was in my room at the Kyoto reading Larry Bernard's front-page story about the release of Alonzo Winslow from juvenile custody when one of the detectives from Hollywood Division called me. Her name was Bynum. She told me my house had been cleared as a crime scene and returned to my custody.

"I can just go back?"

"That's right. You can go home now."

"Does that mean the investigation is complete? I mean, pending the arrest of the guy, of course."

"No, we still have a few loose ends we're trying to figure out."

"Loose ends?"

"I can't discuss the case with you."

"Well, can I ask you about Angela?"

"What about her?"

"I was wondering if she had been...you know, tortured or anything."

There was a pause while the detective decided how much to tell me.

"I'm sorry but the answer is yes. There was evidence of rape with a foreign object and the same pattern of slow suffocation as in the other cases. Multiple ligature marks on the neck. He repeatedly choked her out and revived her. Whether this was a means of getting her to talk about the story you two were working on, or just his way of getting off, is unclear at this time. I guess we will have to ask the man himself when we get him."

I was silent as I thought about the horror Angela had faced.

"Anything else, Jack? It's Saturday. I'm hoping to salvage half a day off with my daughter."

"Uh, no, sorry."

"Well, you can go home now. Have a nice day."

Bynum hung up and I sat there, thinking. Calling it "home" seemed wrong. I wasn't sure I wanted the house back, because I wasn't sure it was home any longer. My sleep—what little there was of it—had been invaded the last two nights by images of Angela Cook's face in the darkness under the bed and the muffled coughing sound so expertly implanted in my mind by her killer. Only in my dream, everything was underwater. Her wrists were not bound and she reached up to me as she sank. Her last cry for help came out in a bubble and when it broke with the sound the Unsub had made, I came awake.

To now live and try to sleep in the same place seemed impossible to me. I spread the curtains and looked out the single window of my small room. I had a view of the civic center. The beautiful and ageless City Hall rose in front of me. Next to it was the criminal courts building, as ugly as the prison most of its customers were headed to. The sidewalks and green lawns were empty. It was

Saturday and nobody came downtown on the weekend. I pulled the curtains closed.

I decided I would keep the room as long as the paper was paying. I would go to the house but only to get fresh clothes and other things I needed. In the afternoon I would call a Realtor and see about getting rid of the place. If I could. For Sale: Nicely kept and restored Hollywood bungalow where serial killer struck. Bring all offers.

My cell phone rang, jarring me out of the reverie. My real cell phone. I had finally gotten it turned back on with full function the day before. The caller ID said PRIVATE NUMBER and I had learned not to let those go unanswered.

It was Rachel.

"Hey," I said.

"You sound down. What's wrong?"

What a profiler. She had read me with one word. I decided not to bring up what Detective Bynum had said about Angela's torturous end.

"Nothing. I'm just…nothing. What's going on with you? Are you working?"

"Yeah."

"Want to take a break and get some coffee or something? I'm downtown."

"No, I can't."

I had not seen her since we had been split apart by the detectives after we'd found and reported Angela's body. As with everything else, the separation, though only forty-eight hours, was not going well for me. I stood up and started pacing in the small confines of the room.

"Well, when will I get to see you?" I asked.

"I don't know, Jack. Have some patience with me. I'm under the gun here."

I felt embarrassed and changed the subject.

"Speaking of under the gun, I could use an armed escort."

"For what?"

"The LAPD says I have access to my house again. They said I could go home but I don't think I can stay there. I just want to get some clothes but it's going to be sort of creepy being in there by myself."

"I'm sorry, Jack, I can't take you. If you are truly worried, though, I can make a call."

I was beginning to get the picture. This had happened to me with her once before. I had to resign myself to the fact that Rachel was like a feral cat. She was intrigued by what could be and hovered close to the touch of another, but ultimately she jumped back and away from it. If you pushed it, her claws came out.

"Never mind, Rachel, I was just trying to get you to come out."

"I am really sorry, Jack, but I can't do it."

"Why did you call?"

There was a silence before she answered.

"To check in and to update you on a few things. If you wanted to hear them."

"Down to business. Sure, go ahead."

I sat back down on the bed and opened a notebook to write in.

"Yesterday they confirmed that the trunk murder

website Angela visited was indeed the trip wire she stepped on," Rachel said. "But so far it's a dead end."

"A dead end? I thought everything can be traced on the Internet."

"The physical location of the site is a web-hosting facility in Mesa, Arizona, called Western Data Consultants. Agents went there with a warrant and were able to pull the details about the site setup and operation. It was registered through a company in Seattle called See Jane Run, which registers, designs and maintains numerous sites through Western Data. It's kind of a go-between company. It doesn't have the physical plant where websites are hosted on servers. That's what Western Data does. See Jane Run builds and maintains websites for clients and pays a company like Western Data to host them. Kind of a middle man."

"So did they go to Seattle?"

"Agents from the Seattle field office are handling it."

"And?"

"The trunk murder site was set up and paid for entirely over the Internet. No one at See Jane Run ever met the man who paid for it. The physical address given two years ago when the sites were set up was a mail drop near SeaTac that is no longer valid. We're trying to trace that but that will be a dead end, too. This guy is good."

"You just said 'sites'—plural. Were there more than one?"

"You noticed that. Yes, two sites. Trunk murder dot com was the first site and the second is called Denslow Data. That was the name he used in setting these up. Bill

Denslow. Both sites are on a five-year plan that he paid for in advance. He used a money order—untraceable except back to the point of purchase. Another dead end."

I took a couple moments to write some notes down.

"Okay," I finally said. "So is Denslow the Unsub?"

"The man posing as Denslow is the Unsub but we're not dumb enough to think he would put his real name on a website."

"Then what does it mean? D-E-N-slow. Is it like half an acronym or something?"

"It could be. We're working on it. So far we haven't found the connection. We're working on the possible acronym and the name itself. But we haven't come up with a Bill Denslow with any sort of criminal record that would approach this."

"Maybe it's just a guy the Unsub hated, growing up. Like a neighbor or a teacher."

"Could be."

"So why the two websites?"

"One was the capture site and one was the OP site."

"OP?"

"Observation point."

"You're completely losing me."

"Okay, the trunk murder site was set up to collect the IP—the computer address—of anybody who visited the site. This is what happened with Angela. You understand?"

"Right. She did a search and it brought her to the site."

"Right. The site collected IPs but was built so that those addresses were automatically forwarded to another dot com site. This one was called Denslow Data. This is a common practice. You go to a site and your ID is captured and sent on for marketing use elsewhere. It's essentially the origin of spam."

"Okay. So now Denslow Data has Angela's ID. What happened to it there?"

"Nothing. It stayed there."

"Then how did—"

"Look, here's the trick. Denslow Data was built with a function that was completely the opposite of the trunk murder site. It captures no data of visitors. You see what I'm getting at?"

"Nope."

"Okay, look at it from the Unsub's point of view. He has set up trunk murder dot com to capture the computer ID of anybody who might be onto him and looking for him. The only problem with that is if he went to the site to check it, then his own ID would be captured. And sure he could use somebody else's computer to run the check, but it would still help fix location. He could be tracked to a high degree through his own site."

I nodded as I finally understood the setup.

"I see," I said. "So he has the captured IP address forwarded to another site where there is no capture mechanism and he can check it without fear of being tracked."

"Exactly."

"So after Angela hit on the trunk murder site he went to the Denslow site and got her IP. He traced it back to the *Times* and figured this might be more than a morbid curiosity about trunk murders. He breaches the *Times* system and that leads him to me and Angela and our stories. He reads my e-mails and he knows that we are onto something. That I'm onto something and heading to Vegas."

"That's right. So he concocted the scheme to take you both out in a murder-suicide."

I was silent for a moment as I spun it once more. It added up, even though I didn't like the total.

"It was my e-mail that got her killed."

"No, Jack. You can't look at it that way. If anything, her fate was sealed when she checked out trunk murder dot com. You can't blame yourself for an e-mail you sent to an editor."

I didn't respond. I tried to put the question of guilt out of my head for a while and to concentrate on the Unsub.

"Jack, you there?"

"I'm just thinking. So this is all completely untraceable?"

"From this angle. Once we get this guy and grab his computer, we'll be able to tear it apart and trace his visits to Denslow. That will be solid evidence."

"You mean if he used his own computer."

"Yes."

"Seems unlikely, given the skill he's already shown."

"Maybe. It will depend on how often he checked his trap. It appears he was onto Angela less than twenty-four hours after her visit to the trunk murder site. That would indicate a routine, a daily trap check, and that might indicate he was using his own computer or one in close proximity."

I thought about all of this for a moment and leaned back on the pillow, closing my eyes. What I knew about the world was depressing.

"There's something else I want to tell you," Rachel said.

"What?"

I opened my eyes.

"We figured out how he drew Angela to your house."

"How?"

"You did it."

"What are you talking about? I was—"

"I know, I know. I am just saying that is how it was meant to look. We found her laptop in her apartment. In her e-mail account is an e-mail from you. It was sent Tuesday night. You said you had picked up some interesting information on the Winslow case. The Unsub, as you, said it was very important and invited her over to show it to her."

"Jesus!"

"She returned the e-mail, saying she was on her way. She came to your house and he was waiting for her. It was after you'd left for Vegas."

"He must've been watching my house. He watched me leave."

"You leave, he gets in and uses your home computer to send the message. Then he waits for her. And once he is through with her, he follows you out to Vegas to complete the setup by killing you and making it look like a suicide."

"But what about my gun? He gets in the house and

finds it easily enough. He could then drive it to Vegas to follow me. But it still doesn't explain how I supposedly got it there. I flew and I didn't check a bag. That's a big hole, isn't it?"

"We think we've got that filled in, too."

I squeezed my eyes shut again.

"Tell me."

"After he baited Angela he used your computer to print out a GO! cargo shipping form."

"Go? I've never heard of Go."

"It's a small competitor to FedEx and the others. G-O with an exclamation mark. Stands for Guaranteed Overnight. It's airport-to-airport shipping. A growing business now that airlines limit luggage and charge for it. You can download shipping forms off the Internet, and someone did just that on your computer. It was for a package sent first overnight to yourself. It was held for pickup at the cargo facility at McCarran International. No signature required. Just show your copy of the shipping form. You can drop packages off at LAX as late as eleven o'clock."

I could only shake my head.

"This is how we think he did it," Rachel said. "He baits Angela and then goes to work on the shipment. Angela shows up and he does his thing with her. He leaves her—whether she is dead or not at this point we don't know. He then goes to the airport and drops the package with the gun. They don't X-ray domestic packages at GO! He then either drives to Vegas or flies, quite possibly even on the same plane as you. Either way, once he's there, he picks up the package and has the gun. He then follows you to Ely to complete the plan."

"It seems so tight. Are you sure he could have pulled this off?"

"It is tight and we're not sure, but the scenario works."

"What about Schifino?"

"He's been briefed but doesn't feel he's in danger now, if he ever was. He declined protection but we're watching him anyway."

I wondered if the Las Vegas lawyer would ever realize how close he may have been to being the worst kind of victim. Rachel continued.

"I take it you would have called me by now if there had been any further contact from the Unsub."

"No, no contact. Besides, you have the phone. Has he tried calling it again?"

"No."

"What happened with the trace?"

"We traced his call to you to a cell tower at McCarran. The US Airways terminal. Within two hours of the call to you, there were flights from that terminal to twenty-four different American cities. He could have been going just about anywhere with connections from those twenty-four."

"What about Seattle?"

"It wasn't a direct flight but he could have flown to a connection city and gone from there. We are executing a search warrant today that will give us the passenger manifests from all the flights. We'll run the names through the computer and see what we get. This is our guy's first mistake and, hopefully, we'll make him pay for it."

"A mistake? How so?"

"He should never have called you. He should never have made contact. He gave us information and a location. It's very unlike what we've seen before from him."

"But you were the one who wanted to bet me that he would make contact. Why is it so shocking? You were right."

"Yes, but I said that before I knew all I know now. I think, based on what we now have in the profile of this man, that it was out of character for him to call you."

I thought about all of that for a few moments before asking the next question.

"What else is the bureau doing?"

"Well, we're profiling Babbit and Oglevy. We know they fit into his program and we need to figure out where they intersect and where he came across them. We're also still looking for his signature."

I sat up and wrote *signature* down in the notebook and then underlined it.

"The signature is different from his program."

"Yes, Jack. The program is what he does with the victim. The signature is something he leaves behind to mark his turf. It's the difference between a painting and the artist's signature marking it as his work. You can tell a van Gogh just by looking at it. But he also signed his work. Only with these killers the signature is not so obvious. Most times we don't see it until after. But if we could decipher the signature now, it might help lead us to him."

"Is that what they have you doing? Working on that?"

"Yes."

But she had hesitated before answering.

"Using your notes off my files?"

"That's right."

Now I hesitated, but not too long.

"That's a lie, Rachel. What is going on?"

"What are you talking about?"

"Because I have your notes right here, Rachel. When they finally cut me loose Thursday, I demanded that they give me all of my files and notes back. They gave me your notes, thinking they were mine. On your legal pad. I have them, Rachel, so why are you lying to me?"

"Jack, I am not lying. So what if you have my notes, you think I can't—"

"Where are you? Right now. Where exactly are you? Tell me the truth."

She hesitated.

"I'm in Washington."

"Shit, you're zeroing in on See Jane Run, right? I'm coming up there."

"Not that Washington, Jack."

This totally puzzled me and then my internal computer spit out a new scenario. Rachel had parlayed uncovering the Unsub into a return to the job she wanted and was best suited for.

"Are you working for Behavioral?"

"I wish. I'm at Washington Headquarters for an OPR hearing Monday morning."

I knew that the OPR was the Office of Professional Responsibility, the bureau's version of Internal Affairs.

"You told them about us? They're going after you for it?"

"No, Jack, I didn't tell them anything about that. It's about the jet I took to Nellis on Wednesday. After you called me."

I jumped off the bed and started pacing again.

"You have to be kidding me. What are they going to do?"

"I don't know."

"Doesn't it matter that you saved at least one life— mine—and in the process brought this killer to law enforcement attention? Do they know that they released a sixteen-year-old kid falsely accused of murder from jail yesterday because of you? Do they know an innocent man who has spent a year in a Nevada prison will get out soon? They should be giving you a medal, not a hearing."

There was silence and then she spoke.

"And they should be giving you a raise instead of laying you off, Jack. Look, I appreciate what you are saying, but the reality is, I made some bad judgments and they seem more concerned about that and the money it cost than anything else."

"Jesus Christ! If they do one thing to you, Rachel, it's going to be all over the front page. I will burn—"

"Jack, I can take care of myself. You have to worry about yourself right now, okay?"

"No, it's not okay. What time is the hearing Monday?"

"It's at nine."

I was going to alert Keisha, my ex-wife. I knew they wouldn't let her into a closed-door personnel hearing, but if they knew a *Times* reporter was hovering outside, waiting on the results, they might think twice about what they did inside.

"Jack, look, I know what you're thinking. But I want you to just cool your jets and let me deal with this. It's my job and my hearing. Okay?"

"I don't know. It's hard to just sit back when they are fucking with somebody...somebody I care about."

"Thank you, Jack, but if that is how you really feel about me, then I need you to stand down on this one. I'll let you know what happens as soon as I know."

"You promise?"

"I promise."

I yanked open the curtain again and a blast of sunlight entered the room.

"Okay."

"Thank you. Are you going to your house? If you really want it, I can get somebody to meet you there."

"Nah, I'll be all right. I was just making a play for you. I want to see you. But if you're not even in town... When did you get there, anyway?"

"This morning on a red-eye. I tried to delay it so I could stay on the case. But that's not the way the bureau works."

"Right."

"So I'm here and I'm meeting with my defense rep

to go over everything. In fact, he's going to be here any minute and I need to put some stuff together."

"Fine. I'll let you go. Where are you going to be staying?"

"The Hotel Monaco on F Street."

We ended the call after that. I stood at the window, looking out but not seeing what was there. I was thinking about Rachel fighting for her job and the one thing that seemed to keep her tethered to the world.

I realized she wasn't that much different from me.

NINE: The Dark of Dreams

Carver watched the home in Scottsdale from the darkness of his car. It was too early to make his move. He would wait and watch until he was sure it was safe. This didn't bother him. He enjoyed being alone and in the dark. It was his place. He had his music on the iPod and the Lizard King had kept him company his whole life.

I'm a changeling, see me change. I'm a changeling, see me change.

It had always been his anthem, a song to set his life by. He turned the volume up and closed his eyes. He reached his hand down to the side of the seat and pushed the button that reclined him farther.

The music transported him back. Past all the memories and nightmares. Back to the dressing room with Alma. She was supposed to be watching him but she had her hands full with the thread and needlework. She couldn't watch him all the time and it wasn't fair to expect it. There were house rules about mothers and children. The mother was ultimately responsible, even while onstage.

Young Wesley made his move, slipping through the

beaded curtains as quiet as a mouse. He was so small he only disturbed five or six strands. He then went down the hall past the foul-smelling bathroom to where the flashing lights emanated from.

He made the turn and there was Mr. Grable in his tuxedo, sitting on a stool. He was holding the microphone, waiting for the song to end.

The music was loud at this end of the hall, but not so loud that Wesley didn't hear the cheers—and some of the jeers. He crept up behind Mr. Grable and looked out between the legs of the stool. The stage was splashed with harsh white light. He saw her then. Naked in front of all the men. The music pulsing through him.

Girl, you gotta love your man...

She moved perfectly with the music. As if it had been written and recorded just for her. He watched and felt entranced. He didn't want the music to stop. It was perfect. She was perfect and he—

He was suddenly grabbed from behind by the back of his T-shirt's collar and yanked backward down the hall. He managed to look up and see it was Alma.

"You are a very bad little boy!" she scolded.

"No," he cried. "I wanna see my—"

"Not now, you don't!"

She dragged him back through the beads and into the dressing room. She pushed him down onto the pile of feather boas and silk scarves.

"You are in big troub—What is that?"

She was pointing at him, finger aimed low. At the place where he felt strange feelings begin from.

"I'm a good boy," he said.

"Not with that, you aren't," Alma said. "Let's see what you've got there."

She reached down and put her hand under his belt. She started to pull his pants down.

"You little pervert," Alma said. "I'm going to show you what we do with perverts around here."

Wesley was frozen in terror. That word she called him. He didn't know what it meant. He didn't know what to do.

The sharp knock of metal on glass cut through the music and the dream. Carver jumped up in his seat. Momentarily disoriented, he looked around, realized where he was, and pulled the buds out of his ears.

He looked out the window, and there was McGinnis, standing in the street. He was holding a leash that led down to the collar on a little pip-squeak dog. Carver saw the fat Notre Dame ring on his finger. He must have hit the window with it to get his attention.

Carver lowered the window. At the same time, he used his foot to make sure the gun he'd placed on the floor was out of sight.

"Wesley, what are you doing here?"

The dog started yapping before Carver could answer, and McGinnis shushed it.

"I wanted to talk to you," Carver said.

"Then, why didn't you come up to the house?"

"Because I also have to show you something."

"What are you talking about?"

"Get in and I'll take you."

"Take me where? It's almost midnight. I don't under—"

"It has to do with that visit from the FBI the other day. I think I know who they're looking for."

McGinnis took a step forward to look in closely at Carver.

"Wesley, what's going on? What do you mean 'who they're looking for'?"

"Just get in and I'll explain it on the way."

"What about my dog?"

"You can bring it. We won't be long."

McGinnis shook his head like he was annoyed with the whole thing but then walked around to get into the car. Carver leaned forward and quickly grabbed the gun off the floor and put it into the rear waistband of his pants. He'd have to live with the discomfort.

McGinnis put the dog in the backseat and then got into the front.

"It's a she," he said.

"What?" Carver asked.

"The dog's a she, not an it."

"Whatever. *She* won't pee in my car, will she?"

"Don't worry. She just went."

"Good."

Carver started driving out of the neighborhood.

"Is your house locked?" he asked.

"Yes, I lock up when we go on walks. You never know with the neighborhood kids. They all know I live alone."

"That's smart."

"Where are we going?"

"To where Freddy Stone lives."

"Okay, so now tell me what is going on and what it has to do with the FBI."

"I told you. I have to show you."

"Then tell me what you're going to show me. Have you talked to Stone? Did you ask him where the hell he's been?"

Carver shook his head.

"No, I haven't talked to him. That's why I went to his place tonight, to try to catch him. He wasn't there but I found something else. The website the FBI was asking about. He's the guy behind it."

"So as soon as he hears that the FBI came by with a warrant, he takes a hike."

"It looks that way."

"We need to call the FBI, Wesley. We can't look like we were protecting this guy, no matter what he was into."

"But it could hurt the business if it blows up in the media. It could bring us down."

McGinnis shook his head.

"We'll just have to take our lumps," he said emphatically. "Covering it up will never work."

"All right. We go to his place first and then we call the FBI. Do you remember the names of those two agents?"

"I have their cards at the office. One was named Bantam. I remember it because he was a big guy but his name was Bantam, like the bantamweight class in boxing, which is the small guys."

"Right. Now I remember."

The lights of the tall buildings in downtown Phoenix spread out before them on both sides of the freeway. Carver stopped talking and McGinnis did likewise. The dog was sleeping on the backseat of the car.

Carver's mind wandered back to the memory the music had conjured earlier. He wondered what had made him go down the hallway to look. He knew the answer was tangled down deep in his darkest roots. In a place no one could go.

TEN: Live at Five

never left my hotel room Saturday, even when some of the reporters on the weekend shift called and invited me over to the Red Wind for cocktails after work. They were celebrating another day on the front page with the story. The latest report being on Alonzo Winslow's first day of freedom and an update on the growing search for the trunk murder suspect. I didn't feel much like celebrating a story that was no longer mine. I also didn't go to the Red Wind anymore. They used to put the front pages of the A section, Metro and Sports over the urinals in the men's restroom. Now they had flat-screen plasma TVs tuned to Fox and CNN and Bloomberg. Each screen adding insult to injury, a reminder that our business was dying.

Instead I stayed in Saturday night and started working my way through the files, using Rachel's notes as a blueprint. With her in Washington and off the case, I felt uncomfortable leaving the profiling to nameless, faceless agents on the task force or as far away as Quantico. This was my story and I was going to keep out in front on it.

I worked late into the night, pulling together the details of two dead women's lives, looking for the commonality Rachel was sure was there. They were women from two different hometowns who had migrated to two different cities in two different states. As far as I could tell, they had never crossed paths, except on the outside chance that Denise Babbit had gone to Las Vegas and happened to catch the Femmes Fatales show at the Cleopatra.

Could that be the connection between their murders? It seemed far-fetched.

I finally exhausted that pursuit and decided to approach things from a completely different angle. The killer's angle. On a fresh sheet of Rachel's notebook paper, I started listing all the things the Unsub would have needed to know in order to accomplish each murder in terms of method, timing and location. This proved to be a daunting task and by midnight I was spent. I fell asleep in my clothes on top of the bedspread, the files and my notes all around me.

The four A.M. call from the front desk was jarring, but it saved me from my recurring dream of Angela.

"Hello," I croaked into the phone.

"Mr. McEvoy, your limo is here."

"My limo?"

"He said he was from CNN."

I had totally forgotten. It had been set up by the *Times'* media relations office on Friday. I was supposed to go live to the nation on a weekend show that ran from eight to ten on Sunday mornings. The problem with that was, it was eight to ten East Coast time, five to seven West Coast time. On Friday the show's producer had been unclear where in the show they would go to me. So I had to be ready to go live at five.

"Tell him I'll be down in ten minutes."

I actually took fifteen, dragging myself into the shower, shaving and getting dressed in the last unwrinkled shirt I had in the room. The driver didn't seem concerned and drove at a leisurely pace toward Hollywood. There was no traffic and we were making good time.

The car wasn't actually a limo. It was a Lincoln Town Car sedan. A year earlier I had written a series of stories about a lawyer who worked out of the back of a Lincoln Town Car while a client who was working off his fees drove him around. Sitting in the backseat now on the way to CNN, I got to like it. It was a good way to see L.A.

The CNN building was on Sunset Boulevard not far from the Hollywood police station. After passing through a security checkpoint in the lobby I went up to the studio where I was slated to be remotely interviewed from Atlanta for the weekend edition of a show called CNN Newsroom. I was led by a young person to the greenroom, and I found Wanda Sessums and Alonzo Winslow already there. For some reason I was shocked by the idea that they could have gotten up so early and beaten me—the professional journalist—to the studio.

Wanda looked at me like I was a stranger. Alonzo barely had his eyes open.

"Wanda, you remember me? I'm Jack McEvoy, the reporter? I came to see you last Monday."

She nodded and clicked an ill-fitting pair of dentures in her mouth. She had not worn them when I visited her at home.

"That's right. You the one who put all the lies in the paper about my Zo."

This statement perked Alonzo up.

"Well, he's out now, right?" I said quickly.

I stepped over and offered my hand to her grandson. He hesitantly took it and we shook but he seemed confused by who I was.

"Glad to meet you finally, Alonzo, and glad you're out. I'm Jack. I'm the reporter who talked to your grandmother and started the investigation that led to your release."

"My grandmother? Motherfucker, what you talking about?"

"He don't know what he talkin'," Wanda said quickly.

I suddenly understood the error of my ways. Wanda was his grandmother but had been playing his mother—Moms—because his real mother was on the street. He probably thought his real mother was his sister, if he knew her at all.

"Sorry, I got confused," I said. "Anyway, I think we are being interviewed together."

"Why the fuck you bein' interviewed?" Alonzo asked. "I'm the one spent the motherfuckin' time in jail."

"I think it's because I'm the one who got you out."

"Yeah, that funny. Mr. Meyer say he the one that got me out."

"Our lawyer got him out," Wanda chimed in.

"Then how come your lawyer isn't here and going on CNN?"

"He coming."

I nodded. This was news to me. When I left work Friday it was going to be just Alonzo and me on the show. Now we had Moms and Meyer aboard. I decided this was not going to go well on live broadcast. Too many people and at least one of them the broadcast censors would have issues with. I went over to a table where there was a coffee urn and poured a cup. I took it black. I then reached into a box of Krispy Kreme doughnuts and chose an Original Glazed. I tried to keep to myself and watch the overhead television, which was tuned to CNN and would soon be broadcasting the newsmagazine show we were scheduled to appear on. After a while a technician came in and wired us for sound, clipping a microphone to our collars and putting an audio feed earpiece into our ears and hiding all wires under our shirts.

"Can I speak to a producer?" I said quietly. "Alone?"

"Sure, I'll tell him."

I sat back down and waited and after four minutes I heard my name spoken by a male voice.

"Mr. McEvoy?"

I looked around and then realized the voice had come in over the earpiece.

"Yes, I'm here."

"This is Christian DuChateau in Atlanta. I'm producing today's show and I want to thank you for getting up so early to be on. We'll go over everything when we get you into the studio in a few minutes. But did you need to speak with me before that?"

"Yes, just hold on a second."

I walked out of the greenroom and into the hallway, closing the door behind me.

"I just wanted to make sure you've got somebody good on the beeper," I said in a low voice.

"I don't understand," DuChateau said. "What do you mean by 'beeper'?"

"I don't know what exactly it's called, but you should know that Alonzo Winslow may only be sixteen years old but he pretty much uses the word *motherfucker* about as often as you use the word *the*."

There was silence in response but not for too long.

"I understand," DuChateau said. "Thank you for the heads-up. We try to conduct pre-interviews with our guests but sometimes there isn't time. Is his lawyer there yet?"

"No."

"We can't seem to locate him and he isn't answering his cell. I was hoping he might be able to, uh, control his client."

"Well, at the moment, he isn't here. And you have to understand something, Christian. This kid didn't commit that murder but that doesn't mean he's this innocent young child, if you know what I mean. He's a gangbanger. He's a Crip and right now he's turning the greenroom blue. He's got his blue jeans, his blue plaid shirt, and at the moment he's wearing a blue do-rag."

There was no hesitation on the phone this time.

"Okay, I'll take care of this," the producer said. "If things fall out, are you willing to go on alone? The segment is eight minutes with a video report on the case in the middle. After you subtract the video and your intro, it's about four and a half to five minutes of airtime with our show host here in Atlanta. I don't think you'll be asked anything you haven't already been asked about the case."

"Whatever you need. I'm good to go."

"Okay, I'll get back to you."

DuChateau clicked off and I went back to the green-room. I sat on a sofa against the wall opposite Alonzo and his mother/grandmother. I engaged him in no conversation but eventually he tried to engage me.

"You say you started this whole thing up?"

I nodded.

"Yes, after your—after Wanda called me and told me you didn't do it."

"How come? No white man ever give a motherfucking shit about me 'fore this."

I shrugged.

"It was just part of my job. Wanda said the police had it wrong and so I looked into it. I found the other case like yours and put it all together."

Alonzo nodded thoughtfully.

"You gonna make a million dollahs?"

"What?"

"They pay you to be here? They ain't pay me. I ask for a few dollars for my time but they don't gimme a motherfuckin' cent, no."

"Yeah, well, it's the news. They don't usually pay."

"They makin' money off him," Wanda chimed in. "Why not pay the boy?"

I shrugged again.

"Well, you could ask them again, I guess," I offered.

"A'ight, I think I'm gonna ask 'em when we doin' the interview on live TV. What the muthafucka gonna say then, huh?"

I just nodded. I don't think Alonzo realized his mike was on and somebody down the hall or in Atlanta was probably listening to what he was saying. A minute after he voiced his plan the door opened and the technician came back into the greenroom and fetched me. As we walked out, Alonzo called after us.

"Hey, where you goin', now? When I get on the TV?"

The tech didn't answer. As we walked down the hall I looked at him. He looked worried.

"You the one who has to tell him he's not going on?"

He nodded.

"And all I can say is that I'm glad they put him through the metal detector in the lobby—and, don't worry, I did check to make sure."

I smiled and said good luck.

ELEVEN: The Cold, Hard Earth

t was almost sunrise. Carver could see the jagged line of light just beginning to etch the silhouette of the mountain chain. It was beautiful. He sat on a large rock and watched the light show as Stone labored in front of him. His young acolyte was working hard with the shovel and was down to the cold, hard earth that lies beneath the soft top of loose soil and sand.

"Freddy," Carver said calmly. "I want you to tell me again."

"I've already told you!"

"Then tell me again. I need to know exactly what was said because I need to know exactly the extent of the damage."

"There is no damage. Nothing!"

"Tell me again."

"Jesus!"

He drove the point of the shovel angrily down into the hole, the impact on rock and sand producing a sharp sound that echoed across the empty landscape. Carver looked around again to make sure they were alone. In the distance to the west, the lights of Mesa and Scottsdale looked like a brush fire spreading out of control. He reached behind his back and gripped the gun. He thought about it, then decided to wait. Freddy could still be useful. Carver would just teach him a lesson this time instead.

"Tell me again," Carver repeated.

"I just told him that he was lucky, all right?" Stone said. "That's all. And I tried to find out who the bitch was that was waiting for him in his room. The one that fucked the whole thing up."

"What else?"

"That was it. I told him that someday I would get his gun back to him, that I would personally deliver it."

Carver nodded. So far Stone had said the same thing each time he had recounted the conversation with McEvoy.

"Okay, and what did he say to you?"

"I told you, he didn't say much of anything. I think he was scared shitless."

"I don't believe you, Freddy."

"Well, that's the—oh, there is one thing he said."

Carver tried to remain calm.

"What?"

"He knows about our thing."

"What thing?"

"About the irons. That thing."

Carver tried to keep the urgency out of his voice.

"How does he know? You told him?"

"No, I didn't tell him shit. He knew. He just knew somehow."

"What did he know?"

"He said the name he was going to give us was the—"

"He said 'us'? He knows there are two of us?"

"No, no, I don't mean that. He never said that. He doesn't know that. He said the name he was going to put in the paper for me, because he thought it was only me, was Iron Maiden. That was what they were going to call us—I mean, me. He was just trying to get me mad, I think."

Carver thought for a moment. McEvoy knew more than he should know. He must have had help. It was more than access to information. He had insight and knowledge, and that made Carver think about the woman who had been in the room, waiting. The woman who saved McEvoy's life. Carver now thought he might know who she was.

"Is this deep enough or not?" Stone said.

Carver put his thoughts aside and got up. He stepped over to the grave and pointed his flashlight down.

"Yes, Freddy, that will be fine. Put the dog in first."

Carver turned his back while Stone reached over to pick up the little dog's body.

"Gently, Freddy."

He hated having to kill the dog. She had done nothing wrong. She was just collateral damage.

"Okay."

Carver turned. The dog was in the hole.

"Now him."

McGinnis's body was on the ground by the end of the grave. Stone reached forward and grabbed the ankles and started backing up in the grave, pulling the body into it. The shovel was leaning against the far wall of the excavation. Carver grabbed the handle and pulled it out as Stone moved back.

Stone walked the body in. McGinnis's shoulders and head dropped down the three feet with a dull thud. While Stone was still stooped forward holding the ankles, Carver swung the shovel and slammed the heel of it down between the younger man's shoulder blades.

The air blasted out of Stone's lungs and he fell forward in the grave, landing face-to-face with McGinnis. Carver quickly straddled the grave and pushed the point of the tool into the back of Stone's neck.

"Take a good look, Freddy," he said. "I had you dig this one deeper so I could put you in it on top of him."

"Please..."

"You broke the rules. I did *not* tell you to call McEvoy. I did *not* tell you to engage him in conversation. I *told* you to follow my instructions."

"I know, I know, I'm sorry. It'll never happen again. Please."

"I could make sure it doesn't happen again right now."

"No, please. I'll make up for it. I won't—"

"Shut up."

"Okay, but I—"

"I said shut up and listen!"

"Okay."

"Are you listening?"

Stone nodded, his face just inches from the lifeless eyes of Declan McGinnis.

"Do you remember where you were when I found you?"

Stone dutifully nodded.

"You were going to that dark place to face endless days of torment. But I saved you. I gave you a new name, I gave you a new life. I gave you the opportunity to escape from that and to join me in embracing the desires we share. I taught you the way and I only asked one thing in return. Do you remember what that was?"

"You said it was a partnership but not an equal partnership. I was the student and you were the teacher. I must do as you say."

Carver pushed the steel point deeper into Stone's neck.

"And yet here we are. And you have failed me."

"I won't let it happen again. Please."

Carver looked up from the grave and at the ridgeline. The jagged lines were cut more sharply now as the sky drew orange light. They had to finish up here quickly.

"Freddy, you have that wrong. *I* won't let it happen again."

"Let me do something. Let me make it up."

"You'll get that chance."

He pulled the shovel back and stepped off the grave.

"Bury them now."

Stone turned and looked up tentatively, fear still in his eyes. Carver held the shovel out to him. Stone got up and took it.

Carver reached behind his back and pulled out the gun. With great delight he watched Stone's eyes go wide. But then he pulled the handkerchief from his front pocket and started wiping the weapon clean of all fingerprints. When he was finished he dropped it into the grave by McGinnis's feet. He wasn't worried about Stone making a grab for it. Freddy was totally under his command and control.

"I am sorry, Freddy, but whatever we do about McEvoy, we won't be returning his gun to him. It's too risky to keep it around."

"Whatever you say."

Exactly, Carver thought.

"Hurry now," he said. "We're losing the dark."

Stone quickly started shoveling dirt and sand back into the hole.

TWELVE: Coast to Coast

As I should have expected, my segment on the morning show did not come up until the second hour. For forty-five minutes I sat in a small, dark studio and waited while watching the first half of the show on the camera monitor. It included a feature on Eric Clapton and Crossroads, the addiction recovery center he created in the Caribbean. The segment ended with concert footage of Clapton performing a bluesy, soulful version of "Somewhere over the Rainbow" that was wonderfully moving and hopeful in relation to the piece but truncated by a cut to a commercial.

During the break I got the one-minute warning and soon I was on live coast-to-coast and beyond. The show host in Atlanta threw me softball questions that I answered with an enthusiasm that falsely suggested I had never heard them before and that the story had not been playing for three days already in the *Times*. When I was finished and the program moved on to the next story, Christian DuChateau told me over the earpiece that I was free to go and that he owed me a favor for saving the show from the near disaster that was Alonzo Winslow. He told me that the limo would take me wherever I needed to go.

"Christian, would you mind if I used him to make one stop along the way? It won't take long."

"Not at all. I have somebody else taking Alonzo home, so you can use the car the rest of the morning if you need it. Like I said, I owe you one."

That worked for me. I made a quick stop in the green-room to grab another cup of coffee and found Alonzo and Wanda still there. They seemed to still be waiting for someone to take them to the studio to be interviewed. No one had told them yet that they had been canceled and they seemed too naive to realize it.

I decided not to be the bearer of bad news. I told them good-bye and gave them each a card with my cell phone number on it.

"Hey, I see you on the TV," Alonzo said, nodding to the flat-screen on the wall. "You cool, muthafucka. I get my turn now."

"Thanks, Alonzo. You take care."

"I'll take care as soon as somebody give me a million dollahs."

I nodded, grabbed another doughnut to go with my coffee and headed out of the room, leaving Alonzo waiting for a million dollars that wasn't going to come.

Once in the car, I told the driver about the stop I needed to make and he said he had already been told to go where I directed. We pulled into my driveway at twenty minutes after seven. I sat in the car, looking at the house for almost a minute before getting the courage to get out and go in.

I unlocked the front door and entered, stepping on

three days of mail that had been pushed through the slot. Neither rain nor snow nor yellow crime scene tape had stopped my mailman from his appointed rounds. I looked quickly through all the envelopes and found that two of my new credit cards had come in. I put these envelopes in my back pocket and left the rest on the floor.

Crime scene debris was littered throughout the house. Black fingerprint dust seemed to be on every surface. There were also empty tape dispensers and discarded rubber gloves all over the floor. It didn't appear that the investigators and technicians gave one thought to who would be returning to the house after they were gone.

I hesitated only briefly and then walked down the hallway and entered my bedroom. There was a musty smell here that was puzzling because it seemed stronger than the day we had found Angela's body. The box spring, mattress and bed frame were gone and I assumed they were being held for analysis and as evidence.

Pausing for a moment, I studied the spot where the bed had been. I wish I could say that at that moment my heart filled with sadness for Angela Cook. But somehow I was already past that point, or my mind was protecting itself and not allowing me to dwell on such things. If I thought about anything, I thought about how hard it was going to be to sell the place. If I felt anything, I felt the need to get out of there as soon as I could.

I walked quickly to the closet, remembering a story I had once written for the *Times* about a private company that offered a cleanup service at homes where murders and suicides had taken place. It was a thriving business.

I decided I would have to dig that story out of archives and give them a call. Maybe they'd give me a discount.

I pulled my big suitcase off the shelf in the closet. I put it down on the floor and a breath of stale air released as I flipped it open. I hadn't used it since I had moved into the house more than a decade earlier. I quickly started filling it with clothes that were on my usual rotation. When it was maxed out, I brought down my more-often-used duffel bag and filled it with shoes and belts and ties—even though I would soon have no use for ties. Lastly, I went into the bathroom and emptied everything on the sink and in the medicine cabinet into the plastic bag that lined the trash can.

"Need some help?"

I almost jumped through the shower curtain. I turned around and saw that it was the driver I had left at the car ten minutes earlier after telling him I would only be five minutes.

"You scared me, man."

"I just wanted to see if you needed—What happened here?"

He was staring at the rubber gloves strewn on the floor and at the big empty spot where the bed used to be.

"It's a long story. If you could get that big suitcase out to the car, I'll get the rest. I need to check something on my computer before we leave."

I grabbed my racquetball racquet off a hook on the bedroom door and then followed him out with the bag and the duffel. I dumped it all in the trunk next to the big suitcase and then headed back toward the house. I noticed the neighbor across the street was at the bottom of her driveway, watching me. She was holding her home-delivered *Times* in her hand. I waved but she didn't return the gesture and I realized that she wasn't going to be friendly or neighborly to me anymore. I had brought darkness and death to our fair neighborhood.

Back inside the house I went directly to the office. But when I entered, I immediately saw that my desktop computer was not on my desktop. It was gone and I realized that the police or the FBI had taken it. Somehow, knowing that a bunch of strange men were looking through all my work and personal files, including my ill-fated novel, made me feel exposed in a whole new way. I was not the killer out there on the loose but the FBI had my computer. When Rachel got back from Washington, I was going to ask her to get it back for me.

My shoulders sagged a little and I could feel that the hard exterior I had put on to help me get through the return to my house was slipping. I had to get out or the horrors of what had happened to Angela would creep back into my thoughts and paralyze me. I had to keep moving.

My last stop in the house was the kitchen. I checked the refrigerator and took all the outdated or close-to-outdated items out and dumped them in the trash can. I dropped in the bananas from the fruit bowl and a half loaf of bread from one of the cabinets. I then went out the back door and put the bag in the bigger can next to the garage. I went inside again, locked up and went out the front door to the waiting car.

"Back to the Kyoto," I told the driver.

I had almost a full day still ahead and it was time to get to work.

As we drove away I saw that my neighbor had gone back inside her safe little home. I was drawn to turn and look through the rear window at my house. It was the only place I had ever owned and I had never contemplated not living there. I realized that one killer had given it to me and another had taken it away.

We made the turn onto Sunset and I lost sight of it.

THIRTEEN: Together Again

Carver worked his hunch on the computer while Stone gathered the things he wanted to take with him. Between searches Carver shredded the pages in Stone's recycle box. He wanted to leave the FBI something that would keep its agents busy.

He stopped everything when the photo and story appeared on the screen. He scanned it quickly, then looked across the warehouse at Stone. He was throwing clothing into a black trash bag. He had no suitcase. Carver could tell he was working gingerly and was still in some pain.

"I was right," Carver said. "She's in L.A."

Stone dropped the bag he was filling and crossed the concrete floor. He looked over Carver's shoulder at the middle screen. Carver double-clicked the photo to make it larger.

"Is that her?" he asked.

"I told you, all I got was a quick glance when I went by the room. I didn't really even see her face. She was in a chair sort of to the side. I didn't have the angle on her face. It could be her, but maybe not."

"I think it was her. She was with Jack. Rachel and Jack, together again."

"Wait a minute. Rachel?"

"Yes, Special Agent Rachel Walling."

"I think...I think he said that name."

"Who?"

"McEvoy. When he opened the door and went in the room. When I was coming up behind him. I heard her. She said, 'Hello, Jack.' And then he said something and I think he said her name. I think he said something like 'Rachel, what are you doing?' "

"Are you sure? You didn't say anything about a name before."

"I know, but you saying that brought it back. I am sure he said that name."

Carver got excited by the prospect of McEvoy and Walling being on his trail. It raised the stakes considerably to have two such opponents.

"What's that story about?" Stone asked.

"It's about her and an L.A. cop getting the guy they called the Bagman. He cut up women and put them in trash bags. This picture was taken at the press conference they had. Two and a half years ago in L.A. They killed the Bagman."

Carver could hear Stone breathing through his mouth.

"Finish gathering your things now, Freddy."

"What are we going to do? Go after her now?"

"No, I don't think so. I think we sit back and wait."

"For what?"

"For her. She'll come to us, and when she does, she'll be a prize."

Carver waited to see if Stone would say anything,

whether he would object or offer his opinion. But Stone said nothing, showing he had apparently retained something from the morning's lesson.

"How's your back?" Carver asked.

"It hurts but it's fine."

"Are you sure?"

"I'm fine."

"Good."

Carver cut the Internet link and stood up. He reached down behind the computer tower and detached the keyboard cable. He knew that the bureau could gather DNA from the microscopic bits of skin that fell between the letters on a keyboard. He would not leave this board behind.

"Let's hurry up and finish now," he said. "After that, we'll go get you a massage and take care of that back."

"I don't need a massage. I'm fine."

"I don't want you hurting. I'm going to need you at full strength when Agent Walling shows up."

"Don't worry. I'll be ready."

FOURTEEN: One False Move

On Monday morning I went on eastern daylight time. I wanted to be ready to react when Rachel called from Washington, so I got up early and cruised into the newsroom at six A.M. to continue my work with the files.

The place was completely dead, not a reporter or editor in sight, and I got a stark feeling for what the future held. At one time the newsroom was the best place in the world to work. A bustling place of camaraderie, competition, gossip, cynical wit and humor, it was at the crossroads of ideas and debate. It produced stories and pages that were vibrant and intelligent, that set the agenda for what was discussed and considered important in a city as diverse and exciting as Los Angeles. Now thousands of pages of editorial content were being cut each year and soon the paper would be like the newsroom, an intellectual ghost town. In many ways I was relieved that I would not be around to see it.

I sat down in my cubicle and checked e-mail first. My account had been reopened by the newsroom techs with a new password the Friday before. Over the weekend I had accumulated almost forty e-mails, most from strangers in reaction to the stories about the trunk murders. I read and deleted each, not willing to take the time to respond. Two were from people who said they were serial killers themselves and had put me on their list of targets. These I kept to show Rachel but I wasn't too worried about them. One of the writers had spelled it *cereal* and I took this as a hint that I was dealing with either a prankster or someone of deficient intelligence.

I also got an angry e-mail from the photographer Sonny Lester, who said I had double-crossed him by not putting him on the story as I had agreed. I fired back an equally angry e-mail asking him which story he was talking about, since none of the stories on the case carried my byline. I said I had been left out to a greater extent than him and invited him to take all complaints to Dorothy Fowler, the city editor.

After that I unpacked the files and my laptop from my backpack and got down to work. The night before, I had made a lot of headway. I had completed my study of the records relating to the murder of Denise Babbit and had composed a profile of the murder along with a comprehensive list of the things about the victim that the killer would have had to know in order to commit the crime in the manner in which it was carried out. I was halfway through my study of Sharon Oglevy's murder and was still compiling the same sort of information.

I set to work and was undisturbed as the newsroom slowly came to life, editors and reporters trudging in, coffee cups in hand, to start another week of work. At eight o'clock I broke for coffee and a doughnut and then made a round of calls at the cop shop, seeing if there was anything interesting on the overnight sheets, anything that might take me away from the task at hand.

Satisfied that all was quiet for the time being, I went back to the murder files and was just completing my profile of the Oglevy case when my first e-mail of the day chimed on my computer. I looked up. The e-mail was from the axman, Richard Kramer. The missive was short on content but long on intrigue.

From: Richard Kramer <RichardKramer@LATimes.com>
Subject: Re: today
Date: May 18, 2009 9:11 AM PDT
To: JackMcEvoy@LATimes.com

Jack, swing on by when you get a chance.

RK

I looked over the edge of my cubicle wall and at the line of glass offices. I didn't see Kramer in his but from my angle I couldn't see his desk. He was probably in there, waiting to give me the word on who would be taking Angela Cook's place on the cop beat. Once more I would be squiring a young replacement around Parker Center, introducing this new reporter to the same people I had introduced Angela to just a week before.

I decided to get it over with. I stood up and made my

way to the glass wall. Kramer was in there, typing out an e-mail to another hapless recipient. The door was open but I knocked on it before entering. Kramer turned from his screen and beckoned me in.

"Jack, have a seat. How are we doing this morning?"

I took one of the two chairs in front of his desk and sat down.

"I don't know about you but I'm doing okay, I guess. Considering."

Kramer nodded thoughtfully.

"Yes, it's been an amazing ten days since you last sat in that chair."

I had actually been sitting in the other chair when he had told me I was downsized but it wasn't worth the correction. I remained silent, waiting for whatever it was he was going to say to me—or to us, if he was going to continue to refer to both of us.

"I've got some good news for you here," he said.

He smiled and moved a thick document from the side of his desk to front and center. He looked down at it as he spoke.

"You see, Jack, we think this trunk murder case is going to have legs. Whether they catch this guy soon or not, it's a story we're going to ride with for a while. And so, we're thinking we're going to need you, Jack. Plain and simple, we want you to stick around."

I looked at him blankly.

"You mean I'm not being laid off?"

Kramer continued as if I had not asked a question, as if he had not heard me make a sound at all.

"What we're offering here is a six-month contract extension that would commence upon signing," he said.

"You mean, then, I'm still laid off, but not for six months."

Kramer turned the document around and slid it across the desk to me so I could read it.

"It's a standard extension we will be using a lot around here, Jack."

"I don't have a contract. How can it be extended when I don't have a contract in the first place?"

"They call it that because you are currently an employee and there is an implied contract. So any change in status that *is* contracturally agreed to is called an extension. It's just legal mumbojumbo, Jack."

I didn't tell him that *contracturally* was not a word. I was speed-reading the front page of the document until I bottomed out on a big fat speed bump.

"This pays me thirty thousand dollars for six months," I said.

"Yes, that is the standard extension rate."

I did the quick, rough math.

"Let's see, that would be about eighteen thousand less than I make for six months now. So you want me to take less to help you stay out front with this story. And let me guess..."

I picked up the document and started flipping through it.

"...I'm betting I no longer get any medical, dental or pension benefits under this contract. Is that right?"

I couldn't find it and I guessed that there wasn't a clause on benefits because they simply did not exist.

"Jack," Kramer said in a calming tone. "There is some negotiation I can do financially, but you would have to pick up the benefits yourself. It's the way we're going with this now. It's simply the wave of the future."

I dropped the contract back on his desk and looked up at him.

"Wait till it's your turn," I said.

"Excuse me?"

"You think it ends with us? The reporters and the copy editors? You think if you're a good soldier and do their bidding that you'll be safe in the end?"

"Jack, I don't think my situation is what we're discuss—"

"I don't care if it is or it isn't. I'm not signing this. I'd rather take my chances on unemployment. And I will. But someday they're going to come for you and ask you to sign one of these things and then you'll have to wonder how you'll pay for your kids' teeth and their doctors and their school and everything else. And I hope it's okay with you because it's simply the wave of the future."

"Jack, you don't even have kids. And threatening me because I do is—"

"I'm not threatening you and that's not the point, *Crammer*. The point I'm trying to make is..."

I stared at him for a long moment.

"Never mind."

I got up and walked out of the office and straight back to my pod. Along the way I looked at my watch and then pulled out my cell phone to see whether I had somehow missed a call. I hadn't. It was nearing one P.M.

in Washington, D.C., and I had heard nothing yet from Rachel.

Back at the cubicle I checked the phone and the e-mail and I had no messages there either.

I had been silent and had avoided intruding on her till now. But I needed to know what was happening. I called her cell and it went right to voice mail without a ring. I told her to call me as soon as she could and clicked off. On the slim chance her phone was dead or she had forgotten to turn it back on after the hearing, I called the Hotel Monaco and asked for her room. But I was told she had checked out that morning.

My desk phone buzzed as soon as I hung up. It was Larry Bernard from two pods away.

"What did Kramer want, to hire your sorry ass back?"

"Yeah."

"What? Really?"

"At a reduced rate, of course. I told him to cram it."

"Are you kidding, man? They've got you by the balls. Where else are you going to go?"

"Well, for one thing I'm not going to work here on a contract that pays me way less and takes away all my benefits. And that's what I told him. Anyway, I've got to go. Are you making the checks on the story today?"

"Yeah, I'm on it."

"Anything new?"

"Not that they're telling me. It's too early, anyway. Hey, I TiVoed you on CNN yesterday. You were good. But I thought they were supposed to have Winslow on. That's why I put it on. They were promoting it at first and then he wasn't on."

"He showed but then they decided they couldn't put him on the air."

"How come?"

"His penchant for using the word *motherfucker* in every sentence he speaks."

"Oh, yeah. When we talked to him Friday I picked up on that."

"Hard not to. I'll talk to you later."

"Wait, where are you going?"

"Hunting."

"What?"

I put the phone down on his question, shoved my laptop and files into my backpack and headed out of the newsroom to the stairwell. The newsroom might have at one time been the best place in the world to work. But it wasn't now. People like the axman and the unseen forces behind him had made it forbidding and claustrophobic. I had to get away. I felt like I was a man without home or office to go to. But I still had a car, and in L.A. the car was king.

headed west, jumping onto the 10 Freeway and taking it toward the beach. I was going against the grain
of traffic and moved smoothly toward the clean ocean
air. I didn't know exactly where I was going but I drove
with subconscious purpose, as though the hands on the
wheel and the foot on the pedal knew what my brain
didn't.

In Santa Monica I exited on Fourth Street and then
took Pico down to the beach. I pulled into the parking
lot where Denise Babbit's car had been abandoned by
Alonzo Winslow. The lot was almost empty and I parked
in the same row and maybe even the same space where
she had been left.

The sun had not burned off the marine layer yet and
the sky was overcast. The Ferris wheel on the pier was
shrouded in the mist.

Now what? I thought to myself. I checked my phone
again. No messages. I watched a group of surfers coming
in from their morning sets. They went to their cars and
trucks, stripped off their wet suits and showered with
gallon jugs of water, then wrapped towels around their
bodies, pulled off their board shorts and changed into
dry clothes underneath. It was the time-honored way of

the pre-work surfer. One of them had a bumper sticker on his Subaru that made me smile.

CAN'T WE ALL GET A LONGBOARD?

I opened my backpack and pulled out Rachel's legal pad. I had filled in several pages with my own notes from the survey of the files. I flipped to the last page and studied what I had put down.

WHAT HE NEEDED TO KNOW

Denise Babbit
1. Details of prior arrest
2. Car—trunk space
3. Work location
4. Work schedule—abducted after work
5. Visual—body type—giraffe, legs

Sharon Oglevy
1. Husband's threat
2. His car—trunk space
3. Work location
4. Work schedule—abducted after work
5. Visual—body type—giraffe, legs
6. Husband's home location

The two lists were short and almost identical and I felt sure that they held the connection between the two women and their killer. From the killer's angle, these were all things that he would seemingly need to know before he made his move.

I lowered the car's windows to let the damp sea air in. I thought about the Unsub and how he had come to choose these two women from these two different places.

The simple answer was that he had seen them. They both displayed their bodies publicly. If he was looking for a specific set of physical attributes, he could have seen both Denise Babbit and Sharon Oglevy onstage.

Or on computer. The night before, while composing the lists, I had checked and found that both the Femmes Fatales exotic revue and Club Snake Pit had websites that featured photographs of their dancers. There were numerous photos of each dancer, including full-length shots that showed their legs and feet. On www.femmes fatalesatthecleo.com, there were chorus-line shots that showed the dancers high-kicking at the camera. If the Unsub's paraphilia included leg braces and the need for a giraffe body type, as Rachel had suggested, then the website would have allowed him to research his prey.

Once a victim was chosen, the killer would need to go to work identifying the woman and filling in the other details on the lists. It could be done that way but I had a hunch that it wasn't. I felt sure that there was something else in play here, that the victims were connected in some other way.

I zeroed in on the first item on both lists. It seemed clear to me that at some point the killer had acquainted himself with the details of each of his victims' legal affairs.

With Denise Babbit, he had to have known of her arrest last year for buying drugs and that the arrest took place outside the Rodia Gardens housing project. This information inspired the idea of leaving her body in the trunk of her car nearby, knowing that the car might be stolen and moved but ultimately traced back to that location. The obvious explanation would be that she had gone there again to buy drugs. A smooth deflection away from the true facts.

With Sharon Oglevy, the killer had to have known the details of her divorce. In particular, he had to have known of her husband's alleged threat to kill her and bury her out in the desert. From that knowledge would spring the idea of putting her body in the trunk of his car.

In both cases the legal details could have been obtained by the killer because they were contained in court documents that were open to the public. There was nothing in any of the records I had that indicated that the Oglevy divorce records had been sealed. And as far as Denise Babbit went, criminal prosecutions were part of the public record.

Then it hit me. The thing I had missed. Denise Babbit had been arrested a year before her death but at the time of her murder the prosecution was ongoing. She was on what defense lawyers called "pee and see" status. Her attorney had gotten her into a pretrial intervention program. As part of her outpatient drug-abuse treatment, her urine was tested once a month for indications of drug use and the courts were ostensibly waiting to see if she straightened out her life. If she did, the charges against her would go away. If her attorney was good, he'd even get the arrest expunged from her record.

All of that was just legal detail but now I saw something in it I had overlooked before. If her case was still active, it would not yet have been entered into the public record. And if it was not part of the public record, available to any citizen by computer or visit to the courthouse, then how did the Unsub get the details he needed to set up her murder?

I thought for a few moments about how I could answer that question and decided that the only way would be to get the information from Denise Babbit herself, or from someone else directly associated with her case—the prosecutor or the defense attorney. I leafed through the documents in the Babbit file until I found the name of her attorney and then I made the call.

"Daly and Mills, this is Newanna speaking. How can I help you?"

"May I speak to Tom Fox?"

"Mr. Fox is in court this morning. Can I take a message?"

"Will he be back at lunchtime?"

I checked my watch. It was almost eleven. Noting the time gave me another stab of anxiety over still not hearing anything from Rachel.

"He usually comes back at lunch but there is no guarantee of that."

I gave her my name and number and told her I was a reporter with the *Times* and to tell Fox that the call was important.

After closing the phone I booted up my laptop and put the Internet slot card in place. I decided I would test my theory and see if I could access Denise Babbit's court records online.

I spent twenty minutes on the project but could glean very little information about Babbit's arrest and prosecution from the state's publicly accessed legal data services or the private legal search engine the *Times* subscribed to. I did, however, pick up a reference to her attorney's e-mail address and composed a quick message in hopes that he received e-mail on his cell phone and would return my request for a phone call sooner rather than later.

From: Jack McEvoy <JackMcEvoy@LATimes.com>
Subject: Denise Babbit
Date: May 18, 2009 10:57 AM PDT
To: TFox@dalyandmills.com

Mr. Fox, I am a reporter with the Los Angeles Times working on the ongoing story about Denise Babbit's murder. You may have already spoken to one of my colleagues about your representation of Denise, but I need to speak with you as soon as possible about a new angle of investigation I am following. Please call or e-mail as soon as possible. Thank you.

Jack McEvoy

I sent the message and knew that all I could do was wait. I checked the time on the corner of the computer screen and realized it was now after two P.M. in Washington, D.C. There seemed no way that Rachel's hearing could have lasted this long.

My computer dinged and I looked down and saw I had already gotten a return e-mail from Fox.

From: Tom Fox <TFox@dalyandmills.com>
Subject: RE: Denise Babbit
Date: May 18, 2009 11:01 AM PDT
To: JackMcEvoy@LATimes.com

Hi, I cannot respond to your e-mail in a timely manner because I am in trial this week. You will hear from me or my assistant, Madison, as soon as possible. Thank you.

Tom Fox
Senior Partner, Daly & Mills, Counselors at Law
www.dalyandmills.com

It was an automatically generated response, which meant Fox had not yet seen my message. I got the feeling I would not be hearing from him until lunchtime—if I was lucky.

I noticed the law firm's website listed at the bottom of the message and clicked on the link. It brought me to a site that boldly trumpeted the services the firm provided its prospective clients. The firm's attorneys specialized in both criminal and civil law and there was a window marked DO YOU HAVE A CASE? in which the site visitor could submit the particulars of their situation for a free review and opinion from one of the firm's legal experts.

At the bottom of the page was a listing of the firm's partners by name. I was about to click on Tom Fox's name to see if I could pull up a bio when I saw the line and link that ran along the very bottom of the page.

Site Design and Optimization
by *Western Data Consultants*

It felt to me like atoms crashing together and creating a new and priceless substance. All in a moment I knew I had the connection. The law firm's website was hosted in the same location as the Unsub's trip-wire sites. That was too coincidental to be coincidence. The internal portals opened up wide, and adrenaline dumped into my bloodstream. I quickly clicked on the link and I was taken to the homepage of Western Data Consultants.

The website offered a guided tour of the facility in Mesa, Arizona, which provided state-of-the-art security and service in the areas of data storage, managed hosting and web-based grid solutions—whatever that meant.

I clicked on an icon that said SEE THE BUNKER and was taken to a page with photos and descriptions of an underground server farm. It was a colocation center where data from client corporations and businesses was stored and accessible to those clients twenty-four hours a day through high-speed fiber-optic connections and backbone Internet providers. Forty server towers stood in perfect rows. The room was concrete lined, infrared monitored and hermetically sealed. It was twenty feet belowground.

The website heavily sold the security of Western Data. *What comes in doesn't go out unless you ask for it.* The company offered businesses big and small an economical means of storing and securing data through instant or interval backup. Every keystroke made on a computer at a law firm in Los Angeles could be instantly recorded and stored in Mesa.

I went back to my files and pulled out the documents William Schifino had given me in Las Vegas. Included in these was the Oglevy divorce file. I put the name of Brian Oglevy's divorce lawyer into my search engine and got an address and contact number but no website. I put the name of Sharon Oglevy's attorney into the search window next and this time got an address, phone number and website.

I went to the website for Allmand, Bradshaw and Ward and scrolled to the bottom of the homepage. There it was.

Site Design and Optimization
by *Western Data Consultants*

I had confirmed the connection but not the specifics. The two law firms used Western Data to design and host their websites. I needed to know if the firms were also storing their case files on Western Data servers. I thought about a plan for a few moments and then opened my phone to call the firm.

"Allmand, Bradshaw and Ward, can I help you?"

"Yes, can I speak to the managing partner?"

"I will put you through to his office."

I waited, rehearsing my lines, hoping this would work.

"Mr. Kenney's office, can I help you?"

"Yes, my name is Jack McEvoy. I'm working with William Schifino and Associates and I'm in the process of setting up a website and data storage system for the firm. I've been talking to Western Data down in Arizona about their services and they mentioned Allmand, Bradshaw and Ward as one of their clients here in Vegas. I was wondering if I could talk to Mr. Kenney about how it has been working with Western Data."

"Mr. Kenney is not in today."

"Hmmm. Do you know if there's anybody else I could talk to there? We were thinking about pulling the trigger on this today."

"Mr. Kenney is in charge of our firm's web presence and data colocation. You would need to speak to him."

"Then you do use Western Data for colocation? I wasn't sure if it was just for the website or not."

"Yes, we do, but you will have to speak to Mr. Kenney about it."

"Thank you. I will call back in the morning."

I closed the phone. I had what I needed from Allmand, Bradshaw and Ward. I next called Daly & Mills back and went through the same ruse, getting the same backhand confirmation from an assistant to the managing partner.

I felt that I had nailed the connection. Both of the law firms that had represented the Unsub's two victims stored their case files at Western Data Consultants in Mesa. That had to be the place where Denise Babbit and Sharon Oglevy crossed paths. That was where the Unsub had found and chosen them.

I shoved all the files back into my backpack and started the car.

On the way to the airport I called Southwest Airlines and bought a round-trip ticket that left LAX at one o'clock and would get me into Phoenix an hour later. I next booked a rental car and was contemplating the call I would need to make to my ace, when my phone started buzzing.

The screen said PRIVATE CALLER and I knew it was Rachel finally calling me back.

"Hello?"

"Jack, it's me."

"Rachel, it's about time. Where are you?"

"At the airport. I'm coming back."

"Switch your flight. Meet me in Phoenix."

"What?"

"I found the connection. It's Western Data. I'm going there now."

"Jack, what are you talking about?"

"I'll tell you when I see you. Will you come?"

There was a long delay.

"Rachel, will you come?"

"Yes, Jack, I'll come."

"Good. I have a car booked. Make the switch and then call me back with your arrival time. I'll pick you up at Sky Harbor."

"Okay."

"How did the OPR hearing go? It seemed like it went really long."

Again, a hesitation. I heard an airport announcement in the background.

"Rachel?"

"I quit, Jack. I'm not an agent anymore."

When Rachel came through the terminal exit at Sky Harbor International, she was pulling a roller bag with one hand and carrying a laptop briefcase with the other. I was standing with all the limo drivers holding signs with their arriving passengers' names on them and I saw Rachel before she saw me. She was looking back and forth for me but not paying attention to what or who was directly in front of her.

I stepped into her path and she almost walked into me. Then she stopped and relaxed her arms a little bit without letting go of her bags. It was an obvious invitation. I stepped up and pulled her into a tight hug. I didn't kiss her, I just held her. She bowed her head into the crook of my neck and we said nothing for possibly as long as a minute.

"Hi," I finally said.

"Hi," she said back.

"Long day, huh?"

"The longest."

"You okay?"

"I will be."

I reached down and took the handle of the roller bag

out of her grasp. Then I turned her toward the exit to the parking garage.

"This way. I already got the car and the hotel."

"Great."

We walked silently and I kept my arm around her. Rachel had not told me a lot on the phone, only that she had been forced to quit to avoid prosecution for misuse of government funds—the FBI jet she had taken to Nellis in order to save me. I wasn't going to push her for more information but eventually I wanted to know the details. And the names. The bottom line was that she had lost her job coming to save me. The only way I was going to be able to live with that was if I somehow tried to set it straight. The only way I knew how to do that was to write about it.

"The hotel's pretty nice," I said. "But I only got one room. I didn't know if you wanted—"

"One room is perfect. I don't have to worry about things like that anymore."

I nodded and assumed she meant that she no longer had to worry about sleeping with someone who was part of an investigation. It seemed that no matter what I said or asked, I was going to trigger thoughts about the job and career she had just lost. I tried a new direction.

"So are you hungry? Do you want to get something to eat or go right to the hotel or what?"

"What about Western Data?"

"I called and set up an appointment. They said it had to be tomorrow because the CEO is out today."

I checked my watch and it was almost six.

"They're probably closed now, anyway. So tomorrow at ten we go in. We ask for a guy named McGinnis. He apparently runs the place."

"And they fell for the charade you told me you were going to pull?"

"It's not a charade. I have the letter from Schifino and that makes me legit."

"You can convince yourself of anything, can't you? Doesn't your paper have some kind of code of ethics that prevents you from misrepresenting yourself?"

"Yeah, we've got a code but there are always gray areas. I'm going undercover to get information that cannot be gathered any other way."

I shrugged as if to say, no big deal. We got to my rental car and I loaded her bag in the trunk.

"Jack, I want to go there now," Rachel said as we got in the car.

"Where?"

"Western Data."

"You can't get in without an appointment and our appointment's tomorrow."

"Fine, we don't go in. But we can still case the joint. I just want to see it."

"Why?"

"Because I need something to take my mind off what happened today in Washington. Okay?"

"Got it. We're going."

I looked up Western Data's address in my notebook and plugged it into the car's GPS. Soon we were on a freeway heading east from the airport. Traffic moved smoothly and we were to Mesa after two freeway changes and twenty minutes of driving.

Western Data Consultants loomed small on the horizon on McKellips Road on the east side of Mesa. It was in a sparsely developed area of warehouses and small businesses surrounded by scrub brush and Sonora cacti. It was a one-story, sand-colored building of block construction with only two windows located on either side of the front door. The address number was painted on the top right corner of the building but there was no other sign on the facade or anywhere else on the fenced property.

"Are you sure that's it?" Rachel asked as I drove by the first time.

"Yeah, the woman I made the appointment with said they had no signs on the property. It's part of the security—not advertising exactly what they do here."

"It's smaller than I thought it would be."

"You have to remember, most of it is underground."

"Right, right."

A few blocks past the target, there was a coffee shop called Hightower Grounds. I pulled in to turn around and then we took another pass at Western Data. This time the property was on Rachel's side and she turned all the way in her seat to view it.

"They've got cameras all over the place," she said. "I count one, two, three...six cameras on the outside."

"Cameras inside and out, according to the website," I responded. "That's what they sell. Security."

"Either the real thing or the appearance of it."

I looked over at her.

"What do you mean by that?"

She shrugged.

"Nothing, really. It's just that all those cameras look impressive. But if nobody is on the other end looking through them, then what do you have?"

I nodded.

"Do you want me to turn around and go by again?"

"No, I've seen enough. I'm hungry now, Jack."

"Okay. Where do you want to go? We passed a barbecue place when we got off the freeway. Otherwise, that coffee shop back there is the only—"

"I want to go to the hotel. Let's get room service and raid the minibar."

I looked over at her and thought I detected a smile on her face.

"That sounds like a plan to me."

I had already set the address for the Mesa Verde Inn into the car's GPS device and it took us only ten minutes to get there. I parked in the garage behind the hotel and we went in.

Once we got to the room, we both kicked off our shoes and drank Pyrat rum out of water glasses while sitting side by side and propped against the bed's multiple pillows.

Finally, Rachel let out a long, loud sigh, which seemed to expel many of the frustrations of the day. She held her almost empty glass up.

"This stuff is good," she said.

I nodded in agreement.

"I've had it before. It comes from the island of Anguilla in the British West Indies. I went there on my honeymoon—a place called Cap Juluca. They had a bottle of this stuff in the room. A whole bottle, not these little minibar servings. We motored through that whole thing in one night. Drinking it straight, just like this."

"I don't want to hear about your honeymoon, you know?"

"Sorry. It was more like a vacation, anyway. It was more than a year after we actually got married."

That killed the conversation for a while and I watched Rachel in the mirror on the wall across from the bed. After a few minutes she shook her head as a bad thought crept in.

"You know what, Rachel? Fuck 'em. It's the nature of any bureaucracy to eliminate the freethinkers and doers, the people they actually need the most."

"I don't really care about the nature of any bureaucracy. I was a goddamn FBI agent! What am I going to do now? What are we going to do now?"

I liked that she had thrown the *we* in there at the end.

"We'll think of something. Who knows, maybe we pool our skills and become private eyes. I can see it now. Walling and McEvoy, Discreet Investigations."

She shook her head again but this time she finally smiled.

"Well, thanks for putting my name first on the door."

"Oh, don't worry, you're the CEO. We'll use your picture on the billboards, too. That'll really bring in the business."

Now she actually laughed. I didn't know if it was the rum or my words but something was cheering her. I put my glass down on the bed table and turned to her. Our eyes were only inches apart.

"I'll always put you first, Rachel. Always."

This time she placed her hand on the back of my neck and pulled me into the kiss.

After we made love, Rachel seemed invigorated while I felt completely spent. She jumped up from the bed naked and went to her roller bag. She opened it up and started looking through her belongings.

"Don't get dressed," I said. "Can't we just stay in bed for a little while?"

"No, I'm not getting dressed. I got you a present and I know it's in here some—Here it is."

She came back to the bed and handed me a little black felt pouch I knew came from a jewelry store. I opened it up and out came a silver neck chain with a pendant. The pendant was a silver-plated bullet.

"A silver bullet? What, are we going after a werewolf or something?"

"No, a *single* bullet. Remember what I told you about the single-bullet theory?"

"Oh...yeah."

I felt embarrassed by my inappropriate attempt at humor. This was something important to her and I had trampled on the moment with the stupid werewolf line.

"Where'd you get this?"

"I had a lot of time to kill yesterday, so I was walking around the District and went into this jewelry store near

FBI headquarters. I guess they know their neighborhood clientele because they were selling bullets as jewelry."

I nodded as I turned the bullet in my fingers.

"There's no name on it. You said the theory was that everybody's got a bullet out there with someone's name on it."

Rachel shrugged.

"It was a Sunday and I guess the engraver was off. They said I'd have to come back today if I wanted to put anything on it. I obviously didn't get the chance."

I opened the clasp and reached up to put it around her neck. She lifted a hand to stop me.

"No, it's yours. I got it for you."

"I know. But why don't you give it to me when it's got your name on it?"

She thought about that for a moment and then dropped her hand away. I put the chain around her neck and clasped it. She looked at me with a smile.

"You know what?" she asked.

"What?"

"I'm really starving now."

I almost laughed at the abrupt change in direction.

"Okay, then let's order room service."

"I want a steak. And more rum."

We ordered and both of us were able to get showers in before the food arrived. We ate in our hotel bathrobes while sitting across from each other at the table the room service waiter had rolled into the room. I could see the silver chain on Rachel's neck but the bullet had been tucked inside her thick, white robe. Her hair was wet and completely uncombed and she looked good enough to eat for dessert.

"This guy who told you about the single-bullet theory, he was a cop or an agent, right?"

"A cop."

"Do I know him?"

"Know him? I'm not sure anybody really knows him, including me. But I've seen his name in a few of your stories in the last couple years. Why do you care?"

I ignored her question and asked my own.

"So did you show him the door or was it the other way around?"

"I think it was me. I knew it wasn't right."

"Great, so this guy you dumped is out there and he carries a gun and now you're with me."

She smiled and shook her head.

"This is so not an issue. Can we just change the subject?"

"Fine. What do you want to talk about, then? You want to finally tell me about what happened in D.C. today?"

She finished a bite of steak before answering.

"There is nothing really to talk about," she said. "They had me. I had misled my supervisor about the interview at Ely, and he authorized the flight. They did their little investigation and did the math and said I used about fourteen thousand dollars' worth of Jet A fuel and that constitutes misuse of government funds on a felony level. They had a prosecutor out in the hallway and ready to go with it if I wanted to push it. I would've been booked right there and then."

"That's incredible."

"The thing is, I was planning to do the interview at Ely and that would have made everything fine. But things changed when you told me about Angela being missing. I never got to Ely."

"This is bureaucracy at its worst. I have to write about this."

"You can't, Jack. That was part of the deal. I signed a confidentiality agreement, which I've already violated by telling you what I just told you. But if it makes its way into print, they will probably end up charging me after all."

"Not if the story is so embarrassing to them that the only out is to drop the whole thing and restore your status as an agent."

She poured another round of rum into one of the snifters that had been delivered with the bottle. With her fingers she transferred a single cube of ice from her water glass to the snifter, then rolled the glass in her hand a few times before drinking from it.

"That's easy for you to say. You're not the one betting that they will see the light instead of seeing a way to put you in jail."

I shook my head.

"Rachel, your actions, no matter how ill-advised or even illegal, saved my life for sure and probably a bunch of others'. You've got William Schifino and all the victims this Unsub will never get to now that he is known to authorities. Doesn't that count for anything?"

"Jack, don't you understand? They didn't like me at the bureau. Not for a long time. They thought they had me out of sight and out of mind but then I forced them to move me out of South Dakota. I got a piece of leverage and I used it, but they didn't like that and they didn't forget it. It's just like anything else in life. One false move and you are vulnerable. They waited until I made the mistake that made me vulnerable, and they moved in. It doesn't matter how many people I may have saved. There's no hard evidence of anything. But the fuel bill on that jet? That's evidence."

I gave up. She couldn't be consoled. I watched her take down her whole snifter of rum and then spit the ice cube back into the bottom of the glass. She then poured herself another shot.

"You better have some of this before I drink it all," she said.

I held my snifter across the table and she poured in a sizable shot. I clicked my glass off hers and took a long pull. It went down smooth as honey.

"Better be careful," I said. "This stuff is easy to get blasted on."

"I want to get blasted."

"Yeah, well, we'll have to leave here by about nine-thirty tomorrow morning if you want to make our appointment on time."

She put her glass down heavily and drunkenly on the table.

"Yeah, what about that? What exactly are we doing tomorrow, Jack? You know I have no badge anymore. I don't even have a gun and you want to just waltz into this place?"

"I want to see it. I want to figure out if he's in there. After that, we can call in the bureau or the police or whoever you want. But it's my lead and I want to get in there first."

"And then write about it in the paper."

"Maybe, if they let me. But one way or another I'm going to write about this whole thing. So I want to be there first."

"Just make sure you change my name in your book, to protect the guilty."

"Sure. What do you want to be called?"

She tilted her head and tightened her lips as she thought about it. She raised her glass again and took a small sip, then answered.

"How about Agent Misty Monroe?"

"Sounds like a porn star."

"Good."

She put her glass down again and her face turned serious.

"So...enough fun and games. We go in there and we what, just ask which one of them is the serial killer?"

"No, we go in there and act like prospective clients. We take a tour of the place and meet as many people as we can. We ask questions about security and who has access to the sensitive legal files our firm will be backing up in storage. Things like that."

"And?"

"And we hope that somebody gives themselves away or maybe I see the guy from Ely with the sideburns."

"Would you even recognize him without his disguise?"

"Probably not, but he doesn't know that. He might see me and make a run for it and then—*ta da!*—we have our guy."

I raised my hands palms-out like a magician who has completed a difficult trick.

"This doesn't sound like a plan, Jack. It sounds like you're making it up as you go along."

"Maybe I am and maybe that's why I need you to be there."

"I have no idea what you mean by that."

I got up and came around to her side and got down on one knee. She was about to raise her glass for another drink when I put my hand on her forearm.

"Look, I don't need your gun or your badge, Rachel. I want you there because if somebody in that place makes a false move, even a small one, you're going to read it and then we've got him."

She pushed my hand off her arm.

"Look, you're exaggerating. If you think I'm some sort of mind reader who can—"

"Not a mind reader, Rachel, but you've got instincts. You do this work the way Magic Johnson used to play basketball. With a knowledge and sense of the full court. After just a five-minute phone conversation with me you stole an FBI plane and flew to Nevada because you knew. You *knew*, Rachel. And it saved my life. That's instinct, and that's why I want you there tomorrow."

She looked at me for a long moment and then nodded so slightly I almost didn't see it.

"Okay, Jack," she said. "Then I'll be there."

The rich rum didn't do us any favors in the morning. Rachel and I were both moving pretty slowly but still managed to get out of the hotel with more than enough time to make our appointment. We stopped at Hightower Grounds first to get some caffeine moving in our veins, then doubled back to Western Data.

The front gate of the complex was open and I pulled into the parking space closest to the front door. Before turning the car off, I took a final drag on my coffee and then asked Rachel a question.

"When the agents from the Phoenix office went in here last week, did they tell them what it was about?"

"No, they said as little about the investigation as possible."

"Standard procedure. What about the search warrant? Didn't it lay it all out?"

She shook her head.

"The warrant was issued by a grand jury that has a blanket mandate to investigate Internet fraud. The use of the trunk murder site fits under that. It gave us camouflage."

"Good."

"We did our part, Jack. You guys didn't do yours."

"What are you talking about?"

I noted her use of the word *we*.

"You're asking if the Unsub, who may or may not be in this place, is aware that Western Data might fall into a greater focus. The answer is yes, but not because of anything the bureau did. Your newspaper, Jack, in its account of Angela Cook's death, mentioned that investigators were checking the possible connection to a website she had visited. You didn't name the site but that only leaves your competitors and readers out of the loop. The Unsub certainly knows the site and knows that if we are onto it, then it may only be a matter of time until we put it together and show up here again."

"We?"

"Them. The bureau."

I nodded. She was right. The story in the *Times* had blown it.

"Then, I guess we better go in before *them* shows up."

We got out and I grabbed my sport coat out of the backseat and put it on while on my way to the door. I was wearing the new shirt I had bought the day before at an airport shop while waiting for Rachel to land. I wore the same tie for a second day. Rachel was wearing her usual agent outfit—a navy suit with a dark blouse— and she looked impressive, even if she wasn't an agent anymore.

We had to push a button at the door and identify ourselves through a speaker before being buzzed in. There was a small entrance area and a woman sitting behind a reception counter. I assumed she was the person who had just talked to us through the speaker.

"We're a little early," I said. "We have a ten o'clock appointment with Mr. McGinnis."

"Yes, Ms. Chavez will be showing you the plant," the receptionist said cheerfully. "Let's see if she's ready to go a few minutes early."

I shook my head.

"No, our appointment was with Mr. McGinnis, the company CEO. We came down from Las Vegas to see him."

"I'm sorry, but that's not going to be possible. Mr. McGinnis has unexpectedly been detained. He is not on the premises at the moment."

"Well, where is he? I thought your company wanted our business, and we wanted to talk with him about our particular needs."

"Let me see if I can get Ms. Chavez. I'm sure she will be able to speak to your needs."

The receptionist picked up the phone and punched in three digits. I looked at Rachel, who raised an eyebrow. She was getting the same vibe I was getting. Something was off about this.

The receptionist spoke quietly and quickly into the phone and then hung up. She looked up and smiled at us.

"Ms. Chavez will be right out."

"Right out" took ten minutes. A door finally opened behind the reception counter and a young woman with dark hair and dark features stepped out. She came around the counter and held her hand out to me.

"Mr. McEvoy, I'm Yolanda Chavez, Mr. McGinnis's executive assistant. I hope you don't mind my taking you around today."

I shook her hand and introduced Rachel.

"Our appointment was with Declan McGinnis," Rachel said. "We were led to believe that a firm of our size and business would merit the attention of the CEO."

"Yes, I assure you that we are very interested in your business. But Mr. McGinnis is home ill today. I hope you understand."

I looked at Rachel and shrugged.

"Well," I said. "If we could still get the tour, we could then talk to Mr. McGinnis when he's feeling better."

"Of course," Chavez said. "And I can assure you that I've conducted the plant tour several times. If you can give me about ten minutes, I will show you around."

"Perfect."

Chavez nodded, then leaned over the reception counter and reached down for two clipboards. She handed them to us.

"We first have to get a security clearance," she said. "If each of you could sign this waiver, I will go make copies of your driver's licenses. And the letter of introduction you said you had."

"You really need our licenses?" I asked in mild protest.

My concern was that our California licenses might raise a security flag since we had said we were from Las Vegas.

"I'm afraid that is our security protocol. It's required of anyone taking the facility tour. There are no exceptions."

"Good to hear. I was just making sure."

I smiled. She didn't. Rachel and I handed over our licenses and Chavez studied them for indications they were counterfeit.

"You're both from California? I thought you—"

"We're both new hires. I'm doing mostly investigative work and Rachel will be the firm's IT person—once we reconfigure our IT."

I smiled again. Chavez looked at me, adjusted her horn-rimmed glasses and asked for the letter from my new employer. I pulled it out of the inside pocket of my jacket and handed it over. Chavez said she would be back to collect us for the tour in ten minutes.

Rachel and I sat down on the couch beneath one of the windows and read the waiver form attached to the clipboards. It was a fairly straightforward waiver with check boxes stating that the signer was not an employee of a competitor, would take no photographs during the tour of the facility and would not reveal or copy any of the trade practices, procedures or secrets revealed during the tour.

"They're pretty serious," I said.

"It's a competitive business," Rachel said.

I scribbled my signature on the line and dated it. Rachel did the same.

"What do you think?" I whispered, my eyes on the receptionist.

"About what?" Rachel asked.

"About McGinnis not being here and the lack of a solid explanation why. First he's 'unexpectedly detained,' next he's 'home sick.' I mean, which is it?"

The receptionist looked up from her computer screen and right at me. I didn't know if she had heard me. I smiled at her and she quickly looked down at her screen again.

"I think we should talk about it after," Rachel whispered.

"Roger that," I whispered back.

We sat silently until Chavez returned to the reception area. She handed us our driver's licenses and we gave her the clipboards. She studied the signatures on each.

"I spoke to Mr. Schifino," she said matter-of-factly.

"You did?" I said a little too un-matter-of-factly.

"Yes, to verify everything. He wants you to call him as soon as possible."

I nodded vigorously. Schifino had been blindsided by the call but must have come through.

"We will as soon as we finish the tour," I said.

"He's just anxious to make a decision and to get things going," Rachel added.

"Well, if you follow me, we'll get the show on the road and I'm sure you will make the right decision," Chavez said.

Chavez used a key card to open the door between the reception area and the rest of the facility. I noticed that it had her photo on it. We stepped into a hallway and she turned to face us.

"Before we go into the graphic design and web hosting

labs, let me tell you a little bit about our history and what we do here," she said.

I pulled a reporter's notebook out of my back pocket and prepared to take notes. It was the wrong move. Chavez immediately pointed to the notebook.

"Mr. McEvoy, remember the document you just signed," she said. "General notes are fine but no specifics or proprietary details of our facility should be recorded in any manner, including written notes."

"Sorry. Forgot."

I put the notebook away and signaled our host to continue the presentation.

"We opened for operation just four years ago. Keying on the growing demand for high-volume, secure data management and storage, Declan McGinnis, our CEO and founding partner, created Western Data. He brought together some of the best and brightest in the industry to design this state-of-the-art facility. We have almost one thousand clients, ranging from small law firms to major corporations. Our facility can service the needs of any size company located anywhere in the world.

"You may find it interesting that the American law firm has become our most common client. We are strategically designed to provide a full raft of services specifically aimed at satisfying the needs of the law firm of any size in any location. From web hosting to colocation, we are the one-stop shop for your firm."

She made a full turn with her arms outstretched, as if to take in the whole building, although we were still standing in a hallway.

"After receiving funding from various investment blocs, Mr. McGinnis zeroed in on Mesa as the place to build Western Data after a yearlong search determined that the area best met the critical location criteria. He was looking for a place where there were low risks of natural disaster and terrorist attack as well as a ready supply of power that would allow the company to guarantee twenty-four/seven uptime. In addition and just as important, he was looking for a location with direct-access bridges to major networks with massive volumes of reliable bandwidth and dark fiber."

"Dark fiber?" I asked and then immediately regretted having revealed that I did not know something I possibly should have known in the position I was supposed to be in. But Rachel stepped in and saved me.

"Unused fiber optics," she said. "In place in existing networks but untapped and available."

"Exactly," Chavez said.

She pushed through the double doors.

"Added to these site-specific demands, Mr. McGinnis would design and build a facility with the highest level of security in order to meet compliance demands for hosting HIPAA, SOX and S-A-S seventy."

I'd learned my lesson. This time I just nodded as if I knew exactly what she was talking about.

"Just a few details about plant security and integrity," Chavez said. "We operate in a hardened structure able to withstand a seven-point-oh earthquake. There are no distinguishing exterior features connecting it to data storage. All visitors are subject to security clearance and recorded while on site twenty-four/seven with the camera recordings archived for forty-five days."

She pointed to the casino-style camera ball located on the ceiling above. I looked up, smiled and waved. Rachel threw me a look that told me to stop behaving like a child. Chavez never noticed. She was too busy continuing the rundown.

"All secure areas of the facility are protected by key cards and biometric hand scanners. Security and monitoring is done from the network operations center, which is located in the underground bunker adjacent to the colocation center, or 'farm,' as we like to call it."

She went on to describe the plant's cooling, power and network systems and their backup and redundant subsystems, but I was losing interest. We had moved into a vast lab where more than a dozen techs were building and operating websites for Western Data's massive client base. As we walked through, I saw screens on the various desks and noted the repeated legal motifs—the scales of justice, the judge's gavel—that indicated they were law firm clients.

Chavez introduced us to a graphic designer named Danny O'Connor, who was a supervisor in the lab, and he gave us a five-minute rap about the personalized, 24/7 service we would receive if our firm signed up with Western Data. He was quick to mention that recent surveys had shown that increasingly consumers were turning to the Internet for all their needs, including identifying and contacting law firms for legal representation of any kind. I studied him as he spoke, looking for any sign that he was stressed or maybe preoccupied by something other than the potential clients in front of him. But he seemed normal and fully plugged into the sales pitch. I also decided he was too chunky to have been Sideburns. That's one thing you can't do when you are wearing a disguise: decrease your body mass.

I looked past him at the many techs working in cubicles, hoping to see somebody giving us the suspicious eye or maybe ducking behind their screen. Half of them were women and easy to dismiss. With the men, I saw nobody I thought might have been the man who had gone to Ely to kill me.

"It used to be you wanted the ad on the back of the Yellow Pages," Danny told us. "Nowadays you'll get more business with a bang-up website through which the potential client can make immediate connection and contact."

I nodded and wished I could tell Danny that I was well versed in how the Internet had changed the world. I was one of the people it had run over.

"That's why we're here," I said instead.

While Chavez made a call on her cell, we spent another ten minutes with O'Connor and looked at a variety of websites for law firms that the facility designed and hosted. They ranged from the basic homepage model containing all contact information to multilevel sites with photos and bios of every attorney in the firm, histories and press releases on high-profile cases, and interactive media and video graphics of lawyers telling viewers they were the best.

After we were finished in the design lab, Chavez took

us through a door with her key card and into another hallway, which led to an elevator alcove. She needed her key card again to summon the elevator.

"I am going to take you down now to what we call the 'bunker,'" she said. "Our knock room is there, along with the main plant facilities and the server farm dedicated to colocation services."

Once again I couldn't help myself.

"Knock room?" I asked.

"Network Operations Center," Chavez said. "It's the heart of our enterprise, really."

As we entered the elevator, Chavez explained that we were going down only one level structurally but that it totaled a twenty-foot descent beneath the surface. The desert had been deeply excavated in order to help make the bunker impenetrable by both man and nature. The elevator took nearly thirty seconds to make the drop and I wondered if it moved so slowly in order to make prospective clients think they were journeying to the center of the earth.

"Are there stairs?" I asked.

"Yes, there are stairs," Chavez said.

Once we reached the bottom, the elevator opened on a space Chavez called the octagon. It was an eight-walled waiting room with four doors in addition to the elevator. Chavez pointed to each one.

"Our knock room, our core network equipment room, plant facilities and our colocation control room, which leads to the server farm. We'll take a peek in the network operations center and the colocation center, but only employees with full-access clearance can enter the 'core,' as they call it."

"Why is that?"

"The equipment is too vital and much of it is of proprietary design. We don't show it to anyone, not even our oldest clients."

Chavez slid her key card through the locking device of the NOC door and we entered a narrow room just barely big enough for the three of us.

"Each of the locations in the bunker is entered through a mantrap. When I carded the outside door I set off a tone inside. The techs in there now have the opportunity to view us and hit an emergency stop if we are determined to be intruders."

She waved to an overhead camera and then slid her card through the lock on the next door. We entered the network operations center, which was slightly underwhelming. I was expecting a NASA launch center but we got two rows of computer stations with three technicians monitoring multiple computer screens showing both digital and video feeds. Chavez explained that the techs were monitoring power, temperature, bandwidth and every other measurable aspect of Western Data's operations, as well as the two hundred cameras located throughout the facility.

Nothing struck me as sinister or relating to the Unsub. I saw no one here that I thought could be Sideburns. No one did a double take when they looked up and saw me. They all looked rather bored with the routine of potential clients coming through on tour.

I asked no questions and waited impatiently while Chavez continued her sales pitch, primarily making eye contact with Rachel, the law firm's IT chief. Looking at the techs studiously avoiding acknowledgment of our presence, I got the feeling that it was so routine that it was almost an act, that when Chavez's card set off the intruder alert, the techs wiped the solitaire off their screens, closed the comic books and snapped to attention before we came through the second door. Maybe when there were no visitors in the building, the mantrap doors were simply propped open.

"Should we head over to the farm now?" Chavez finally asked.

"Sure," I said.

"I'm going to turn you over to our CTO, who runs the data center. I need to step out and make another quick phone call, but then I will be back to collect you. You'll be in good hands with Mr. Carver. He's also our CTE."

My face must have shown I was confused and about to ask the question.

"Chief threat engineer," Rachel answered before I could ask it.

"Yes," Chavez said. "He's our scarecrow."

We went through another mantrap and then entered the data center. We stepped into a dimly lit room set up similarly to the NOC room with three workstations and multiple computer screens at each. Two young men sat at side-by-side stations, while the other was empty. To the left of this line of stations was an open door revealing a small private office that appeared empty. The workstations faced two large windows and a glass door that looked out on a large space where there were several rows of server towers under bright overhead lighting. I had seen this room on the website. The farm.

The two men swiveled in their chairs to look up at us when we came through the door but then almost immediately turned back to their work. It was just another dog and pony show to them. They wore shirts and ties but with their scruffy hair and cheeks they looked like they should be in T-shirts and blue jeans.

"Kurt, I thought Mr. Carver was in the center," Chavez said.

One of the men turned back to us. He was a pimply-faced kid of no more than twenty-five. There was a pathetic attempt at a beard on his chin. He was about as suspicious as flowers at a wedding.

"He went into the farm to check server seventy-seven. We got a capacity light on it that doesn't make sense."

Chavez stepped up to the unused workstation and raised a microphone that was built into the desk. She clicked a button on the stem and spoke.

"Mr. Carver, can you break away for a few minutes to tell our guests about the data center?"

There was no reply for several seconds and then she tried again.

"Mr. Carver, are you out there?"

More time went by and then a scratchy voice finally came through an overhead speaker.

"Yes, on my way."

Chavez turned to Rachel and me and then looked at her watch.

"Okay, then. He will handle this part of your journey and I will collect you in about twenty minutes. After that, the tour will be completed unless you have specific questions about the facility or operation."

She turned to leave and I saw her eyes hold for a moment on a cardboard box sitting on the chair in front of the empty desk.

"Are these Fred's things?" she asked without looking at the two techs.

"Yup," Kurt said. "He didn't get a chance to get it all. We boxed it up and were thinking about taking it to him. We forgot yesterday."

Chavez frowned for only a moment, then turned toward the door without responding. Rachel and I were left standing and waiting. Eventually through the glass I saw a man in a white lab coat walking down one of the aisles created by the rows of server towers. He was tall and thin and at least fifteen years older than Sideburns. I knew you could make yourself older with a disguise. But making yourself shorter was tough. Rachel turned and subtly gave me a questioning look anyway. I surreptitiously shook my head. Not him.

"Here comes our scarecrow," Kurt said.

I looked at the kid.

"Why do you call him that? Because he's skinny?"

"'Cause he's in charge of keepin' all the dirty, nasty birds off the crops."

I was about to ask what he meant by that, when Rachel once again filled in the blanks.

"Hackers, trolls, virus carriers," she said. "He's in charge of security on the data farm."

I nodded. The man in the lab coat made his way to the glass door and reached for an unseen locking mechanism to his right. I heard a metallic click and then he slid the door open. He entered and pulled the door closed behind him, testing to make sure it had properly locked. I felt cool air from the server room wash over me. I noticed that right next to the door was an electronic hand reader—it took more than a simple key card to access the actual farm. Mounted above the reader was a case with a glass door that contained what looked like a pair of gas masks.

"Hello, I'm Wesley Carver, chief technology officer here at Western Data. How do you do?"

He extended his hand first to Rachel, who shook it

and told him her name. He then turned to me and I did the same.

"Yolanda left you with me, then?" he asked.

"She said she'd come back for us in twenty minutes," I said.

"Well, I'll do my best to keep you entertained. Have you met the crew? This is Kurt and Mizzou, our server support engineers on shift today. They keep things running while I get to putter around on the farm and chase down the people who think they can have a go at the palace walls."

"The hackers?" Rachel asked.

"Yes, well, you see, places like this are a bit of a challenge to the people out there with nothing better to do. We have to constantly be aware and alert. So far, so good, you know? As long as we're better than they are we'll do fine."

"That's good to hear," I said.

"But not really what you came to hear. Since Yolanda handed the baton to me, let me tell you a little bit about what we've got in here, yeah?"

Rachel nodded and signaled with her hand for him to proceed.

"Please."

Carver turned so he was facing the windows and looking into the server room.

"Well, this is really the heart and brains of the beast down here," he said. "As I'm sure Yolanda has told you, data storage, colocation, dry-docking, whatever you want to call it, is the main service we provide here at Western Data. O'Connor and his boys up on the design and hosting floor might talk a good game, but this down here is what we have that nobody else has."

I noticed Kurt and Mizzou nod to each other and give each other a fist bump.

"No other aspect of the digital business world has grown so exponentially fast as this segment," Carver said. "Safe, clean storage and access to vital company records and archives. Advanced and dependable connectivity. This is what we offer. We eliminate the need to build this network infrastructure privately. We offer the advantage of our own direct, high-speed, redundant Internet backbone. Why build it in the back room of your law firm when you can have it here and have the same sort of access without the overhead costs or the stress of managing and maintaining it?"

"We're already sold on that, Mr. Carver," Rachel said. "That's why we're here and why we've been looking at other facilities as well. So can you tell us a little bit about your plant and your personnel? Because this is where we'll make our choice. We don't need to be convinced of the product. We need to be convinced of the people we are entrusting our data to."

I liked how she was moving it away from technology and in the direction of people. Carver held up a finger as if to make a point.

"Exactly," he said. "It always comes down to people, doesn't it?"

"Usually," Rachel said.

"Then let me give you a quick overview of what we have here and then perhaps we could retire to my office and discuss personnel issues."

He walked around the line of workstations so that he was standing directly in front of the big windows that looked into the server room. We followed him around and he continued the tour.

"Okay, then. I designed the data center to be state of the art in terms of technology and security. What you see before you here is our server room. The farm. These big, long towers hold approximately one thousand managed, dedicated servers on direct line with our clients. What that means is that if you sign on with Western Data, your firm will have its own server or servers in this room. Your data is not commingled on a server with any other firm's data. You get your own managed server with one-hundred-megabit service. That gives you instant access from wherever you are located to the information you store here. It allows you interval backup or immediate backup. If needed, every keystroke made on your computers in—Where are you located?"

"Las Vegas," I said.

"Las Vegas, then. And what is the business?"

"A law firm."

"Ah, another law firm. So then, if needed, every keystroke made on a computer in your law firm could be instantaneously backed up and stored here. In other words, you would never lose anything. Not a digit. That computer in Las Vegas could be struck by lightning and the last word typed on it would be safe and sound right here."

"Well, let's hope it doesn't come to that," Rachel said, smiling.

"Of course not," Carver said quickly and humorlessly. "But I am just telling you the parameters of the service we provide here. Now, security. What good is it to back everything up here if it is not safe?"

"Exactly," Rachel said.

She took a step closer to the window and in doing so moved in front of me. I could clearly see that she wanted to make the lead connection to Carver, and that was fine with me. I stepped back and left them standing side by side at the window.

"Well, we're talking about two different things here," Carver said. "Plant security and data security. Let's talk about the facility first."

Carver covered a lot of the ground Chavez had already covered but Rachel didn't interrupt him. Eventually, he homed in on the data center and offered some new information.

"This room is completely impregnable. First off, all the walls, floor and ceiling are two-foot-thick concrete with double rebar and rubber membrane to protect it from water sources. These windows are level-eight glass laminates that are impact resistant and ballistic proof. You could hit it with both barrels of a shotgun and you'd probably only hurt yourself with the ricochet. And this door is the only means of entry and exit and is controlled by biometric hand scan."

He pointed to the device next to the glass door.

"Access to the server room is limited to server engineers and key personnel only. The biometric scanner unlocks the door after reading and confirming three distinct hand groups: palm print, vein pattern and hand geometry. It also checks for a pulse. So nobody can get away with chopping my hand off and using it to get into the server farm."

Carver smiled but Rachel and I didn't join in.

"What about if there's an emergency?" I asked. "Could people be stuck in there?"

"No, of course not. From the inside you simply push a release button that opens the lock and then slide open the door. The system is designed to keep intruders out, not keep people in."

He looked at me to see if I understood. I nodded.

Carver leaned back and pointed to the three digital temperature gauges located above the main window on the server room.

"We keep the farm cooled to sixty-two degrees and have plenty of redundant power as well as a backup cooling system. As far as fire protection goes, we employ a three-stage protection scheme. We have a standard VESDA system with a—"

"Vesda?" I asked.

"Very Early Smoke Detection Alarm, which relies on laser-based smoke detectors. In the event of a fire the VESDA will activate a series of alarms followed by the waterless fire-suppression system."

Carver pointed to a row of red pressure tanks lined on the back wall.

"There you see our CO_2 tanks, which are part of this

system. If there is a fire, carbon dioxide floods the room, extinguishing fire without harming any of the electronics or the client data."

"What about people?" I asked.

Carver leaned back again so he could see around Rachel to look at me.

"Very good question, Mr. McEvoy. The three-stage alarm allows sixty seconds for any personnel in the server room to escape. Additionally, our server room protocol requires anyone entering the server room to carry a respirator on their person as a WCS redundancy."

From the pocket of his lab coat he withdrew a breathing mask similar to the two hanging in the case by the door.

"WCS?" I asked.

"Worst-Case Scenario," Rachel said.

Carver put the mask back in his pocket.

"Let's see, what else can I tell you? We custom-build our own server racks in a shop attached to the equipment room down here in the bunker. We have multiple servers and attendant electronics in stock and we can hit the ground running to provide for all our clients' needs. We can replace any piece of equipment on the farm within an hour of malfunction. What you are looking at here is a reliable and secure national network infrastructure. Does either of you have any questions about this aspect of our facility?"

I had nothing because I was pretty much at sea on the technology. But Rachel nodded like she understood everything that had been said.

"So again, it's about people," she said. "No matter how well you build the mousetrap, it always comes down to the people who operate it."

Carver brought his hand to his chin and nodded. He was looking out into the server room but I could see his face reflected in the thick glass.

"Why don't we step into my office so we can discuss that aspect of our operation."

We followed him around the workstations to his office. Along the way I looked down into the cardboard box that was on the chair of the empty station. It looked like it was mostly full of personal belongings. Magazines, a William Gibson novel, a box of American Spirit cigarettes, a *Star Trek* coffee mug full of pens, pencils and disposable lighters. I also saw a variety of flash drives, a set of keys and an iPod.

Carver held the door to his office and then closed it after we entered. We took the two seats in front of the glass table he used as a desk. He had a twenty-inch computer screen on a pivoting arm, which he pushed out of the way so he could see us. There was a second, smaller screen beneath the glass of his desk. On it was a video image of the server room. I noticed that Mizzou had just entered the farm and was walking down one of the aisles created by the rows of server towers.

"Where are you staying?" Carver asked as he moved behind his worktable.

"The Mesa Verde," I said.

"Nice place. They have a great brunch on Sundays."

Carver sat down.

"Now, then, you want to talk about people," he said, looking directly at Rachel.

"Yes, we do. We appreciate the tour of the facility but, frankly, that's not why we are here. Everything that you and Ms. Chavez have shown us is on your website. We really came to get a feel for the people we would work with and entrust our data to. We're disappointed we were unable to meet Declan McGinnis and, frankly, a little put off by it. We haven't received a credible explanation for why he stood us up."

Carver raised his hands in a gesture of surrender.

"Yolanda is not at liberty to discuss personnel matters."

"Well, I hope you can understand our position," Rachel said. "We came to establish a relationship and the man who was supposed to be here is not here."

"Completely understandable," Carver said. "But as a director of the company I can assure you that Declan's situation in no way affects our operation here. He simply took a few days off."

"Well, that is troubling, because that's the third different explanation we've gotten. It doesn't leave us with a good impression."

Carver nodded and exhaled heavily.

"If I could tell you more I would," he said. "But you have to realize that what we sell here is confidentiality and security. And that starts with our own personnel. If that explanation is not acceptable, then we might not be the firm you are looking for."

He had drawn a line. Rachel capitulated.

"Very well, Mr. Carver. Then tell us about the people who work for you. The information we would store in this facility is of a highly sensitive nature. How do you ensure the integrity of the facility? I look at your two— what are they called, server engineers? I look at them and I have to say they look to me like the type of people you are protecting this facility from."

Carver smiled broadly and nodded.

"To be honest, Rachel—can I call you Rachel?"

"That's my name."

"To be honest, when Declan is here and I know a prospective client is coming in on tour, I usually send those two out back for a smoke break. But the reality of this facility and the reality of the world is that those young men are the best and the brightest when it comes to this work. I'm being straight with you. Yes, there is no doubt that some of our employees have done their share of hacking and mischief before coming to work here. And that's because sometimes it takes a sly fox to catch a sly fox or at least to know how he thinks. But every employee here is thoroughly vetted for criminal records and tendencies, as well as the content of their character and psychological makeup.

"We have never had an employee break company protocols or make an unauthorized intrusion into client data, if that's what your concern is. Not only do we qualify each individual for employment, but we closely watch them after. You could say that we are our own best clients. Every keystroke made on a keyboard in this building is backed up. We can look at what an employee is doing in real time or has done at any time prior. We randomly exercise both of those options routinely."

Rachel and I nodded in unison. But we knew something Carver either didn't know or was expertly covering up. Someone here *had* dipped into client data. A killer had stalked his prey in the digital fields of the farm.

"What happened to the guy who worked out there?" I asked, jerking a thumb in the direction of the outer room. "I think they said his name was Fred. It looks like he's gone and his stuff is in a box. Why did he leave without taking his personal things?"

Carver hesitated before answering. I could tell he was being cautious.

"Yes, Mr. McEvoy. He has not picked up his belongings yet. But he will and that is why we placed them in a box for him."

I noticed that I was still Mr. McEvoy with him, while Rachel had moved on to being on a first-name basis.

"Well, was he fired? What did he do?"

"No, he was not fired. He quit for unknown reasons. He failed to show up for his shift Friday night and instead sent me an e-mail saying he resigned to pursue other things. That is all there is to it. These young kids, they are in high demand. I'm assuming Freddy was lured away by a competitor. We pay well here but somebody else can always pay better."

I nodded as if I agreed completely but I was thinking about the contents of the box out there and putting other things with it. The FBI visits and asks questions about the trunk murder website on Friday and Freddy splits without so much as coming back in for his iPod.

And what about McGinnis? I was about to ask if his disappearance could be related to Freddy's abrupt departure but was interrupted by the mantrap buzzer. The screen beneath Carver's glass desk automatically switched to the camera in the mantrap and I saw Yolanda Chavez coming back in to collect us. Rachel leaned forward, inadvertently putting an urgent spin on her question.

"What is Freddy's last name?"

As if they had a prescribed length of buffer space between them, Carver leaned back a distance equal to Rachel's forward movement. She was still acting like an agent, asking direct questions and expecting answers because of the juice the bureau carried.

"Why would you want his name? He no longer works here."

"I don't know. I just…"

Rachel was cornered. There was no good answer to the question, at least from Carver's point of view. The question alone threw suspicion on our motives. But we got lucky when Chavez poked her head in through the door.

"So how are we doing in here?" she asked.

Carver kept his eyes on Rachel.

"We're doing fine," he said. "Are there any other questions I can answer?"

Still backpedaling, Rachel looked at me and I shook my head.

"I think I've seen all I need to see," I said. "I appreciate the information and the tour."

"Yes, thank you," Rachel said. "Your facility is very impressive."

"Then I'll take you back up to the surface now and let you sit down with an account representative if you wish."

Rachel got up and turned toward the door. I pushed back my chair and stood up. I thanked Carver again and reached across the table to shake his hand.

"Nice to meet you, Jack," he said. "I hope to see you again."

I nodded. I had made it to the first-name list.

"Me, too."

The car was as hot as an oven when we got back into it. I quickly turned the key, cranked the air-conditioning to high and lowered my window until the car started to cool.

"What do you think?" I asked Rachel.

"Let's get out of here first," she replied.

"Okay."

The steering wheel burned my hands. Using just the heel of my left palm I backed out of the space. But I didn't drive immediately to the exit. Instead I drove to the far corner of the lot and made a U-turn at the back of the Western Data building.

"What are you doing?" Rachel asked.

"I just wanted to see what was back here. We're allowed. We're prospective clients, remember?"

As we made the turn and headed toward the exit, I caught a passing glimpse of the rear of the building. More cameras. And there was an exit door and a bench beneath a small awning. On either side was a sand jar ashtray, and there, sitting on a bench, was the server engineer named Mizzou. He was smoking a cigarette.

"The smokers' porch," Rachel asked. "Satisfied?"

I waved to Mizzou through the open window and he nodded back. We headed toward the gate.

"I thought he was working in the server room. I saw him on Carver's screen."

"Well, when addiction calls..."

"But can you imagine having to come out here in the thick of the summer just to smoke? You'd get fried, even with that awning."

"I guess that's what they make SPF ninety for."

I closed my window after I turned back out onto the main road. When we were no longer in view of Western Data I thought it was finally safe to ask my question again.

"So what do you think?"

"I think I almost blew it. Maybe I did."

"You mean at the end? I think we're fine. We were saved by Chavez. You just have to remember you no longer carry that badge that opens all doors and makes people quiver and answer your questions."

"Thanks, Jack. I'll remember that."

I realized how callous I must have sounded.

"Sorry, Rachel. I didn't mean—"

"It's okay. I know what you meant. I'm just touchy because you're right and I know it. I'm not what I was twenty-four hours ago. I guess I have to relearn my finesse. My days of bowling people over with the power and the might are gone."

She looked out her window, so I couldn't see her face.

"Look, right now, I don't care about your finesse.

What about your vibe back there? What do you think of Carver and everybody else? What do we do now?"

She turned back to me.

"I'm more interested in who I didn't see than who I did see."

"You mean Freddy?"

"And McGinnis. I think we have to find out who this Freddy who quit is and what the deal is with McGinnis."

I nodded. We were on the same page.

"You think they're connected, Freddy quitting and McGinnis not showing up?"

"We won't know until we talk to them both."

"Yeah, how do we find them? We don't even know Freddy's last name."

She hesitated before answering.

"I could try to make some calls, see if anybody is still talking to me. I am sure that when they went in there last week with a warrant, they got a list of names of all employees. That would have been standard procedure."

I thought that was wishful thinking on her part. In law enforcement bureaucracies, once you were out, you were out. And that was probably more so with the FBI than anywhere else. The ranks in the bureau were so tight, even legitimate, badge-carrying cops couldn't get through. I thought Rachel was in for a rude awakening if she thought her old comrades were going to take her calls, run down names and share information. She was going to quickly find out that she was on the outside looking in—through six-inch glass.

"What if that doesn't work?"

"Then I don't know," she said curtly. "I guess we do it the old-fashioned way. We go back and sit on that place and wait for Freddy's slacker buddies to punch out and go home. They'll either lead us right to him or we can *finesse* it out of them."

She said it with full sarcasm but I liked the plan and thought it could work to find out who Freddy was and where he lived. I just wasn't sure we were going to find Freddy himself. I had a feeling Freddy was in the wind.

"I think it's a good plan, but my vibe is that Freddy's long gone. He didn't just quit. He split town."

"Why?"

"Did you look in that box?"

"No, I was too busy keeping Carver busy. You were supposed to look in the box."

That was news to me but I smiled. It was the first sign I registered that she viewed us as partners on this case.

"Really? That's what you were doing?"

"Absolutely. What was in the box?"

"Stuff you wouldn't leave behind if you're just quitting your job. Cigarettes, flash drives and an iPod. Kids that age, their iPod is indispensable. Plus, the timing of it. The FBI shows up one day and he's gone the same night. I don't think we're going to find him here in Mesa, Arizona."

Rachel didn't respond. I glanced over and saw her furrowed brow.

"What are you thinking?"

"That you're probably right. And it makes me think we have to call in the pros. Like I said, they probably already have his name and they can run him down quickly. We're just spinning our wheels out here and kicking sand in the air."

"Not yet, Rachel. Let's at least see what we can find out today."

"I don't like it. We should call them."

"Not yet."

"Look, you made the connection. No matter what happens it will be because you made the break. You'll get the credit."

"I'm not worried about the credit."

"Then, why are you doing this? Don't tell me it's still about the story. Aren't you over that yet?"

"Are you over being an agent yet?"

She didn't answer and looked out the window again.

"Same as me," I said. "This is my last story and it's important. Besides, this could be your ticket back inside. You identify the Unsub and they're going to give you back your badge."

She shook her head.

"Jack, you don't know anything about the bureau. There are no second acts. I resigned under threat of prosecution. Don't you get it? I could find Osama bin Laden hiding in a cave in Griffith Park and they wouldn't take me back."

"Okay, okay. Sorry."

We drove in silence after that and soon I saw a barbecue

restaurant called Rosie's come up on the right. It was early for lunch but the intensity of posing as someone I was not for the past hour had left me famished. I pulled in.

"Let's get something to eat, make some calls and then go back and wait for Kurt and Mizzou to punch out," I said.

"You got it, partner," Rachel said.

FIFTEEN: The Farm

C arver sat in his office, studying the camera angles. Over one hundred views of the building and its surroundings. All at his command. At the moment, he was manipulating the exterior camera located on one of the top corners at the front of the building. By raising and turning the lens, and adjusting the focus, he could see up and down McKellips Road.

It didn't take long to spot them. He knew they'd come back. He knew about thought processes.

McEvoy and Walling were parked next to the wall outside the Public Storage center. They were watching Western Data at the same time he was watching them. Only he wasn't as obvious about it.

Carver toyed with the idea of letting them bake out there. Waiting longer to give them what they wanted. But then he decided to get things moving. He picked up his phone and punched in three numbers.

"Mizzou, come in here, please. It's unlocked."

He put the phone down and waited. Mizzou opened the door without a knock and stepped in.

"Close the door," Carver said.

The young computer genius did as instructed and then approached Carver's worktable.

"What's up, boss?"

"I want you to take that box of Freddy's belongings and deliver them to him."

"I thought you said he blew town."

Carver looked up at him. He thought that someday he would hire somebody who didn't take issue with everything he said.

"I said he probably did. But that's beside the point. Those people that were in here earlier today saw that box on his damn chair and realized we either had to fire somebody or we have a turnover problem. Either way, it doesn't instill confidence in the prospective customer."

"I understand."

"Good. Then, take that box, strap it to the back of your motorcycle and take it to his warehouse. You know where that is, don't you?"

"Yeah, I've been there."

"Good, then go."

"But Kurt and me were in the middle of breaking down thirty-seven to see where the heat buildup's coming from. We got a flash on it."

"Good, I am sure he can handle it from here. I want you to make that delivery."

"And then come all the way back?"

Carver looked at his watch. He knew Mizzou was angling for the rest of the day off. Little did he know that Carver already knew that he wouldn't be returning—not on this day, at least.

"Fine," he said as though he were frustrated about

being cornered. "Take the rest of the day. Just go. Now, before I change my mind."

Mizzou left the office, closing the door behind him. Carver watched anxiously on the cameras, waiting to track him once he got on his beloved motorcycle in the parking lot. He seemed to be taking forever to get out there. Carver started humming. He went to his old standby, the song that had pervaded all corners of his life for as long as he could remember. Soon he quietly sang his two favorite lines and found himself repeating them faster and faster instead of continuing the lyrics of the song.

> There's a killer on the road; his brain is squirming like a toad
> There's a killer on the road; his brain is squirming like a toad
> There's a killer on the road; his brain is squirming like a toad
> There's a killer on the road; his brain is squirming like a toad...
> If you give this man a ride...

Finally, Mizzou entered the camera frame and started securing the cardboard box to the small cargo rack behind the seat. He was smoking a cigarette and Carver saw it was almost burned down to the filter. This explained the delay. Mizzou had taken the time to go to the bench at the back of the plant and maybe visit with his fellow smokers.

Finally, the box was secured on the motorcycle. Mizzou flicked away the butt of his cigarette and put on his helmet. He straddled the bike, started the engine and rode out through the open front gate.

Carver tracked him out the whole way and then turned the camera toward the Public Storage center down the street. He saw that McEvoy and Walling had seen the box and taken the bait. McEvoy was pulling out to follow.

SIXTEEN: Dark Fiber

We had found a shaded spot next to the front wall of a Public Storage center and had just settled in for what might be a long, hot and fruitless wait, when we got lucky. A motorcyclist pulled out of the Western Data entrance and headed west on McKellips Road. It was impossible to tell who was on the bike because the rider wore a full-mask helmet, but Rachel and I both recognized the cardboard box that was lashed to a rear rack with bungee cords.

"Follow the box," Rachel said.

I restarted the car and quickly pulled onto McKellips. Following a motorcycle in a tin can rental car wasn't my idea of a good plan but there was no alternative. I pinned the accelerator and quickly pulled within a hundred yards of the box.

"Don't get too close!" Rachel said excitedly.

"I'm not. I'm just trying to catch up."

She leaned forward nervously and put her hands on the dashboard.

"This is not good. Following a motorcycle with four cars trading off the lead is difficult; this is going to be a nightmare with just us."

It was true. Motorcycles were able to slip through

traffic with ease. Most riders seemed to have a general disdain for the concept of marked lanes of travel.

"You want me to pull over and you drive?"

"No, just do the best you can."

I managed to stay with the box for the next ten minutes through stop-and-go traffic and then we got lucky. The motorcycle cut into a freeway entrance and got up on the 202 heading toward Phoenix. I had no problem keeping pace here. The motorcycle stayed a steady ten miles over the speed limit and I hummed along two lanes over and a hundred yards back. For fifteen minutes we followed him in clear traffic as he transitioned onto I-10 and then North I-17 through the heart of Phoenix.

Rachel began to breathe easier and even leaned back in her seat. She thought we had disguised our tail well enough that she told me to pull up in our lane so she could get a better look at the man on the motorcycle.

"That's Mizzou," she said. "I can tell by his clothes."

I glanced over but couldn't tell. I had not committed to memory the details of what I had seen in the bunker. Rachel had and that was one of the things that made her so good at what she did.

"If you say so. What do you think he's doing, anyway?"

I started falling back again to avoid being spotted by Mizzou.

"Taking Freddy his box."

"I know that. But I mean, why now?"

"Maybe it's his lunch break or maybe he's finished work for the day. Could be a lot of reasons."

Something about that explanation bothered me but I

didn't have a lot of time to think about it. The motorcycle started gliding across four lanes of interstate in front of me and heading toward the next exit. I made the same maneuvers and fell in behind him on the exit with a car between us. We caught the light on green and headed west on Thomas Road. Pretty soon we were in a warehouse district where small businesses and art galleries were trying to stake a claim in an area that looked like it had been deserted by manufacturers long ago.

Mizzou stopped in front of a one-story brick building and dismounted. I pulled to the curb a half block away. There was little traffic and few cars were parked in the area. We stood out like, well, cops on an obvious surveillance. But Mizzou never checked his surroundings for a tail. He took off his helmet, confirming Rachel's identification, and put it over the headlight. He then unhooked the bungee cords and took the box off the bike rack. He carried it toward a large sliding door at the side of the building.

Hanging on a chain was a round free weight like the kind used on barbells. Mizzou grabbed it and pounded it on the door, making a banging sound I could hear a half block away with the windows up. He waited and we waited but nobody came and opened the door. Mizzou pounded again and got the same negative result. He then walked over to a large window that was so dirty there was no need for blinds on the inside. He used his hand to rub away some of the grime and looked in. I couldn't tell whether he saw anyone or not. He went back to the door and pounded one more time. Then for the hell of it he grabbed the door handle and tried to slide it open. To his surprise and ours, the door easily moved on its rollers. It was unlocked.

Mizzou hesitated and for the first time looked around. His eyes didn't hold on my car. They quickly returned to the open door. It looked like he called out, and then after a few seconds he went in and slid the door closed behind him.

"What do you think?" I asked.

"I think we need to get in there," Rachel said. "Freddy's obviously not there, and who knows if Mizzou is going to lock that place up or decide to take something of value to the investigation. It's an uncontrolled situation and we should be in there."

I dropped the car into gear and drove the remaining half block to the building. Rachel was out and moving toward the sliding door before I had it back in park. I jumped out and followed.

Rachel pulled the door open just enough for us to slip in. It was dark inside and it took a few moments for my eyes to adjust. When they finally did, I saw Rachel was twenty feet in front of me, walking toward the middle of the warehouse. The place was wide open with steel roof supports going up every twenty feet. Drywall partitions had been erected to divide it into living, working and exercise space. I saw the barbell rack and bench the door knocker had come from. There was also a basketball rim and at least a half court of space in which to play. Farther down was a dresser and an unmade bed. Against one of the partitions was a refrigerator and a table with a microwave, but there was no sink or stove or anything else resembling a kitchen. I saw the box Mizzou had carried on the table next to the microwave but I saw no sign of Mizzou.

I caught up to Rachel as we passed a partition and I saw a workstation set up against the wall. There were three screens on shelves above a desk and a PC underneath it. The keyboard, however, was missing. The shelves were crowded with code books, software boxes and other electronic equipment. But still no sign of Mizzou.

"Where'd he go?" I whispered.

Rachel raised her hand to silence me and walked toward the workstation. She seemed to study the spot where the keyboard should have been.

"He took the keyboard," she whispered. "He knows what we can—"

She stopped at the sound of a toilet flushing. It came from the far corner of the warehouse and was followed by the sound of another door being slid open. Rachel reached up to one of the shelves and grabbed a cable tie used for bunching computer wires, then grabbed me by the elbow and pulled me around a wall to the sleeping area. We stood, backs against the wall, and waited for Mizzou to pass. I could hear his approaching steps on the concrete floor. Rachel moved past me to the edge of the partition. Just at the moment Mizzou passed the edge, she sprang forward, grabbing him by the wrist and neck and spinning him onto the bed before he knew what was happening. She planted him face-first and hard on the mattress and in one fluid move jumped on his back.

"Don't move!" she yelled.

"Wait! What is—"

"Stop struggling! I said, don't move!"

She yanked his hands behind his back and used the cable tie to quickly bind them.

"What is this? What did I do?"

"What are you doing here?"

He tried to look up but Rachel smashed his face back into the mattress.

"I said, what are you doing here?"

"I came to drop off Freddy's shit and just decided to use the can."

"Breaking and entering is a felony."

"I didn't break in. And I didn't steal shit. Freddy never minds it. You can ask him."

"Where is Freddy?"

"I don't know. Who are you, anyway?"

"Never mind who I am. Who is Freddy?"

"What? He lives here."

"Who is he?"

"I don't know. Freddy Stone. I work with him. I mean, I used—Hey, you! You're that lady that was on the tour today. What are you doing, man?"

Rachel climbed backward off of him, since hiding her identity no longer mattered. Mizzou turned around on the bed and propped himself up. Wide-eyed, he looked from Rachel to me and back to Rachel.

"Where is Freddy?" Rachel demanded.

"I don't know," Mizzou said. "Nobody's seen him."

"Since when?"

"When do you think? Since he quit. What is going on here? First the FBI and now you two. Who are you, anyway?"

"Don't worry about it. Where would Freddy go?"

"I don't know. How would I know?"

Mizzou suddenly stood up as if he were simply going to walk out and ride away with his hands bound behind his back. Rachel roughly slammed him back onto the bed.

"You can't do this! I don't even think you're cops. I want a lawyer."

Rachel took a threatening step closer to the bed. She spoke in a low, calm voice.

"If we're not cops, what makes you think we would get you a lawyer?"

Mizzou's eyes became scared then as he realized he had stumbled into something he might not be able to stumble out of.

"Look," he said. "I'll tell you everything I know. Just let me go."

I was still leaning against the partition wall, trying to act like it was just another day at the office and that sometimes people ended up as collateral damage when things were getting done.

"Where can I find Freddy?" Rachel asked.

"I told you!" Mizzou yelped. "I don't know. I would tell you if I knew but I don't know!"

"Is Freddy a hacker?"

She gestured toward the wall. The workstation was on the other side.

"More like a troller. He likes fucking with people, doin' pranks and shit."

"What about you? Did you do some of that with him? Don't lie."

"One time. But I didn't like it, messing people up for no good reason."

"What's your name?"

"Matthew Mardsen."

"Okay, Matthew Mardsen, what about Declan Mc-Ginnis?"

"What about him?"

"Where is he?"

"I don't know. I heard he e-mailed that he was home sick."

"Do you believe that?"

He shrugged.

"I don't know. I guess."

"Did anybody talk to him?"

"I don't know. That kind of stuff is above my pay grade."

"And that's it?"

"That's all I know!"

"Then, stand up."

"What?"

"Stand up and turn around."

"What are you going to do?"

"I said, stand up and turn around. Never mind what I'm going to do."

He reluctantly did what he was told. If he could have turned his head a hundred eighty degrees to keep his eyes on Rachel, he would have. As it was, he must have been close to one-twenty.

"I told you everything I know," he offered desperately.

Rachel came up close behind him and spoke directly into his ear.

"If I find out differently, I'm going to come back for you," she said.

Holding him by the cable tie she pulled him around the wall into the workstation. She took a pair of scissors off the shelf and cut the binding from his wrists.

"Get out of here and don't tell anybody what happened," she said. "If you do, we'll know."

"I won't. I promise I won't."

"Go!"

He almost slipped on the polished concrete when he turned to head toward the door. It was a long walk and his pride deserted him when he was ten feet from freedom. He ran those final steps, slid the door open and slammed it home behind him. Within five seconds we heard the motorcycle kick to life.

"I liked that move, throwing him down on the bed like that," I said. "I think I've seen that before."

Rachel offered a very thin smile in return and then got down to business.

"I don't know if he's going to go running to the cops or not, but let's not take too much more time here."

"Let's get the hell out now."

"No, not yet. Look around, see what you can find out

about this guy. Ten minutes and then we're out of here. Don't leave your fingerprints."

"Great. How do I do that?"

"You're a newspaper reporter. You have your trusty pen?"

"Sure."

"Use that. Ten minutes."

But we didn't need ten minutes. It quickly became clear that the place had been stripped of anything remotely personal about Freddy Stone. Using my pen to open cabinets and drawers, I found them empty or containing only generic kitchen tools and food packages. The refrigerator was almost empty. The freezer contained a couple of frozen pizzas and an empty ice tray. I checked in and under the dresser. Empty. I looked under the bed and between the mattress and box spring. There was nothing. Even the trash cans were empty.

"Let's go," Rachel said.

I looked up from checking under the bed and saw she was already to the door. Under her arm she was carrying the box that Mizzou had just dropped off. I remembered seeing the flash drives in there. Maybe the drives would hold information we needed. I hurried after her, but when I went through the open door, she was not at the car. I turned and caught a glimpse of her rounding the corner of the building and entering the alley.

"Hey!"

I trotted over to the alley and made the turn. She was walking with purpose down the center of the alley.

"Rachel, where are you going?"

"There were three trash cans in there," she called back over her shoulder. "All of them were empty."

It was then that I realized she was heading toward the first of two industrial-size Dumpsters that were pushed into alcoves on opposite sides of the alley. Just as I caught up with her she handed me Freddy Stone's box.

"Hold this."

She flung the heavy steel lid up and it banged loudly against the wall behind it. I glanced down into Freddy's box and saw that somebody, probably Mizzou, had taken his cigarettes. I doubted he would miss them.

"You checked the kitchen cabinets, right?" Rachel asked.

"Yeah."

"Were there any trash can liners?"

It took me a moment to understand.

"Uh, yeah, yeah, a box under the sink."

"Black or white?"

"Uh..."

I closed my eyes to try to visualize what I had seen in the cabinet under the sink.

"...black. Black with the red drawstring."

"Good. That narrows it down."

She was reaching into the Dumpster, moving things around. It was half full and smelled awful. Most of the detritus was not in bags but had been dumped in directly from waste containers. Most of it was construction debris from a repair or renovation project. The rest was rotting garbage.

"Let's try the other."

We crossed the alley to the other alcove. I put the box down on the ground and threw open the heavy lid of the Dumpster. The odor was even more stunning and at first I thought we had found Freddy Stone. I stepped back and turned away, blowing air through my mouth and nose to keep the stench away.

"Don't worry, it's not him," Rachel said.

"How do you know?"

"Because I know what a rotting body smells like, and it's worse."

I moved back to the Dumpster. There were several plastic trash bags in this container, many of them black and many of them torn and spilling putrid garbage.

"Your arms are longer," Rachel said. "Pull out the black bags."

"I just bought this shirt," I said in protest as I reached in.

I pulled out every black bag that wasn't already torn and revealing its contents and dropped them on the ground. Rachel started opening them by tearing the plastic in such a way that the contents stayed in place inside. Like performing an autopsy on a garbage bag.

"Do it like this and don't mix contents from different bags," she said.

"Got it. What are we looking for? We don't even know if this stuff is from Stone's place."

"I know but we have to look. Maybe something will make sense."

The first bag I opened mostly contained the confetti of shredded documents.

"I've got shreddings here."

Rachel looked over.

"That could be his. There was a shredder by the work-station. Put that one aside."

I did as I was told and opened the next bag. This one contained what looked like basic household trash. I immediately recognized one of the empty food boxes.

"This is him. He had the same brand of microwave pizza in the freezer."

Rachel looked over.

"Good. Look for anything of a personal nature."

She didn't have to tell me that but I didn't object. I carefully moved my hands through the refuse in the torn bag. I could tell it had all come from the kitchen area. Food boxes, cans, rotting banana peels and apple cores. I realized it wasn't as bad as it could have been. There was only a microwave in the warehouse loft. It made the choices narrow and the food came in nice clean containers that could be hermetically sealed before being tossed.

At the bottom of the bag was a newspaper. I carefully pulled it out, thinking the date of the edition might help us narrow down when the bag had been tossed into the Dumpster. It was folded into quarters in the way a traveler might carry it. It was the previous Wednesday's edition of the *Las Vegas Review-Journal*. That was the day I had been in Vegas.

I unfolded it and noticed the face of a man in a photograph on the front page had been doodled on in black marker. Someone had awarded the man sunglasses and a set of devil's horns and the requisite pointy beard. There was also a coffee ring on the photo. The ring partially obscured a name written with the same marker.

"I've got a Vegas paper with a name written here."

Rachel looked up immediately from the bag she had her hands in.

"What name?"

"It's blurred by a coffee ring. It's Georgette something. Begins with a B and ends M-A-N."

I held the paper up and angled it so she could see the front page. She studied it for a second and I saw recognition fire in her eyes. She stood up.

"This is it. You found it."

"Found what?"

"He's our guy. Remember, I told you about the e-mail to the prison in Ely that got Oglevy put in lockdown? It was from the warden's secretary to the warden."

"Yeah."

"Her name is Georgette Brockman."

Still crouched on my haunches next to the open bag, I stared up at Rachel as I put it all together. There was only one reason Freddy Stone would have that name written on a Las Vegas newspaper in his warehouse. He had trailed me to Vegas and knew I was going up to Ely to talk to Oglevy. He was the one who wanted to isolate me in the middle of nowhere. He was Sideburns. He was the Unsub.

Rachel took the newspaper from me. Her conclusions were the same as mine.

"He was in Nevada trailing you. He got her name and wrote it down while he was hacking the prison system's database. This is the link, Jack. You did it!"

I got up and approached her.

"*We* did it, Rachel. But what do we do now?"

She lowered the paper to her side and I saw a sad realization play on her face.

"I don't think we should be touching anything else here. We need to back off and call in the bureau. They have to take it from here."

Equipmentwise, the FBI always seemed ready for anything. Within an hour of Rachel's calling the local field office, we were placed in separate interrogation rooms in a nondescript vehicle the size of a bus. It was parked outside the warehouse where Freddy Stone had lived. We were being questioned by agents inside while other agents on the outside were in the warehouse and the nearby alley, looking for further signs of Stone's involvement in the trunk murders as well as his current whereabouts.

Of course, the FBI didn't call them interrogation rooms and would have objected to my calling the converted mobile home the *Guantánamo Express*. They called it a mobile witness interview unit.

My room was a windowless cube about ten feet by ten feet and my interrogator was an agent named John Bantam. This was a misnomer because Bantam was so big he seemed to fill the whole room. He paced back and forth in front of me, regularly slapping his leg with the legal pad he carried in a way I think was designed to make me think that my head could be its next destination.

Bantam grilled me for an hour about how I had made the connection to Western Data and all the moves Rachel and I had made after that. All the way, I took the advice Rachel gave me right before the federal troops showed up:

Do not lie. Lying to a federal agent is a crime. Once you commit it, they have you. Do not lie about anything.

So I told the truth, but not the whole truth. I answered only the questions put to me and offered no detail that was not specifically asked for. Bantam seemed frustrated the whole time, annoyed with not being able to ask the right question. A sheen of sweat was forming on his black skin. I thought maybe he was the embodiment of the whole bureau's frustration with the fact that a newspaper reporter had made a connection they had missed. Either way, he was not happy with me. The session went from a cordial interview to a tense interrogation and it seemed to go on and on.

Finally, I hit my limit and stood up from the folding chair I had been seated in. Even with me standing, Bantam still had six inches on me.

"Look, I told you all I know. I have a story to go write."

"Sit down. We're not finished."

"This was a voluntary interview. You don't tell me when it's finished. I've answered every one of your questions and now you're just repeating yourself, trying to see if I get crossed up. It's not going to happen because I only told you the truth. Now, can I go or not?"

"I could arrest you right now for breaking and entering and impersonating a federal agent."

"Well, if you are going to make things up, I guess you could arrest me for all kinds of things. But I didn't break and enter. I followed someone into the warehouse when we saw him enter and thought he might be committing a crime. And I did not impersonate a federal agent. That kid might have thought we were agents but neither of us said or did anything that even remotely indicated that."

"Sit down. We're not done."

"I think we are."

Bantam slapped the pad against his leg and turned his back to me. He walked to the door and then turned back.

"We need you to hold your story," he said.

I nodded. Now we were finally down to it.

"This is what this was all about? The interrogation? The intimidation?"

"It wasn't an interrogation. Believe me, you'd know it if it were."

"Whatever. I can't hold the story. It's a major break in a major case. Besides, splashing Stone's face across the media might help you catch him."

Bantam shook his head.

"Not yet. We need twenty-four hours to assess what we've got here and at the other locations. We want to do that before he knows we're onto him. Splashing his face across the media will be fine after that."

I sat back down on the folding chair as I thought about the possibilities. I was supposed to discuss any deal not to publish with my editors but I was beyond all of that now. This was my last story and I was going to call my own shots.

Bantam took a chair that was leaning on the wall,

unfolded it and sat down for the first time during the session. He positioned himself directly in front of me.

I looked at my watch. It was almost four o'clock. The editors in Los Angeles were about to go into the daily meeting and set the next day's front page.

"This is what I am willing to do," I said. "Today is Tuesday. I hold the story and write it tomorrow for Thursday's paper. We keep it off the website so it won't get picked up by the wire services until early Thursday morning and won't start making waves on TV until after that."

I looked at my watch again.

"That would give you a solid thirty-six hours, at least." Bantam nodded.

"Okay. I think that will work."

He made a move to get up.

"Wait a minute, that's not all. *And*, this is what I want in return. I obviously want exclusivity. I made this break and so the story is mine. No leaks and no press conferences until after my story hits the front of the *Times*."

"That's no problem. We'll—"

"I'm not finished. There's more. I want access. I want to be in the loop. I want to know what is going on. I want to be embedded."

He smirked and shook his head.

"We don't do embedded. You want to be embedded, then go to Iraq. We don't take citizens, especially reporters, inside investigations. It could be dangerous and it complicates things. And, legally, it could compromise a prosecution."

"Then, we don't have a deal and I need to call my editor right now."

I reached into my pocket for my cell phone. It was a dramatic move I hoped would force the issue.

"All right, wait," Bantam said. "I can't make this call. Sit tight and I'll get back to you."

He stood up and left the room, closing the door. I got up and checked the knob. As I had guessed, the door was locked. I pulled my phone and checked the screen. It said NO SERVICE. The soundproofing of the cube probably knocked down service, and Bantam had probably known it all along.

I spent another hour sitting on the hard folding chair, occasionally getting up to knock loudly on the door or to pace in the tiny room the way Bantam had. The abandonment started to work on me. I kept checking my watch or opening my phone, even though I knew there was no service and that wasn't going to change. At one point I decided to test my paranoid theory that I was being watched and listened to the whole time I was in the room. I opened my phone and walked the corners like a man reading a Geiger counter. In the third corner I acted like I had found service and started through the motions of making a call and talking excitedly to my editor, telling him I was ready to dictate a major breaking story on the identity of the trunk killer.

But Bantam didn't come rushing in and it only proved one of two possibilities. That the room wasn't wired for sight and sound, or that the agents outside watching me knew my cell service was blocked and I couldn't possibly have made the call I had just pretended to make.

Finally, at 5:15 the door opened. But it wasn't Bantam who entered. It was Rachel. I stood up. My eyes probably showed my surprise but my tongue held in check.

"Sit down, Jack," Rachel said.

I hesitated but then sat back down.

Rachel took the other seat and sat down in front of me. I looked at her and pointed to the ceiling, raising my eyebrows in question.

"Yes, we're being recorded," Rachel said. "Audio and visual. But you can speak freely, Jack."

I shrugged.

"Well, something tells me you've put on weight since I last saw you. Like maybe a badge and a gun?"

She nodded.

"I actually don't have the badge or gun yet but they're on their way."

"Don't tell me, you found Osama bin Laden in Griffith Park?"

"Not exactly."

"But you were reinstated."

"Technically, my resignation had not been signed off on yet. The slow pace of bureaucracy, you know? I got lucky. I was allowed to withdraw it."

I leaned forward and whispered.

"What about the jet?"

"You don't have to whisper. The jet is no longer an issue."

"I hope you got it in writing."

"I got what I needed."

I nodded. I knew the score. She had used what leverage she had to make a deal.

"So let me guess, they want it to read that an agent identified Freddy Stone as the Unsub, not someone they had just run out of the bureau."

She nodded.

"Something like that. I am now assigned to dealing with you. They're not going to let you inside the tape, Jack. It's a recipe for disaster. You remember what happened with the Poet."

"That was then and this is now."

"It's still not going to happen."

"Look, can we get out of this cube? Can we just take a walk where there are no hidden cameras or microphones?"

"Sure, let's walk."

She stood up and went to the door. She knocked with a two-and-one pattern and the door was opened immediately. As we stepped into the narrow hallway that led to the front of the bus and the exit, I noticed Bantam was behind the door. I knocked the two-and-one pattern on it.

"If only I had known the combo," I said. "I could've been out of here an hour ago."

He found no humor in my comment. I turned away and followed Rachel out of the bus. Outside I could see that the warehouse and the alley were still nests of bureau activity. Several agents and technicians were moving about, collecting evidence, taking measurements and photos, writing notes on clipboards.

"All these people, have they found anything we didn't find?"

She smiled slyly.

"Not so far."

"Bantam said the bureau was swarming other locations—plural. What other locations?"

"Look, Jack, before we talk we need to be straight on something. This isn't a ride-along and you're not embedded. I am your contact, your source, as long as you hold the story for a day the way you offered."

"The offer was based on full access."

"Come on, Jack, that's not going to happen. But you have me and you can trust me. You go back to L.A. and you write your story tomorrow. I'll tell you everything I can tell you."

I moved away from her down the sidewalk toward the alley.

"See, that's what I'm worried about. You will tell me everything that you can tell me. Who decides what you can tell me?"

"I will tell you everything I know."

"But will you know everything?"

"Jack, come on. Stop with the semantics. Do you trust me? Isn't that what you said when you called me up out of the blue last week from the middle of the desert?"

I looked in her eyes for a moment and then back to the alley.

"Of course I trust you."

"Then that's all you need. Go back to L.A. Tomorrow you can call me every hour on the hour if you want and I will tell you what we've got. You will be up to speed until the moment you put the story in the paper. It will be your story and nobody else's. I promise you that."

I didn't say anything. I stared into the alley, where there were several agents and techs dissecting the black trash bags we had found. They were documenting each piece of garbage and debris like archaeologists at a dig in Egypt.

Rachel grew impatient.

"Then do we have a deal, Jack?"

I looked at her.

"Yes, we have a deal."

"My one request is that when you write it, you identify me as an agent. You don't mention my resignation or its withdrawal."

"Is that your request or the bureau's?"

"Does it matter? Will you do it or not?"

I nodded.

"Yes, Rachel, I'll do it. Your secret is safe with me."

"Thank you."

I turned away from the alley to face her.

"So what's happening right now? What about the other locations Bantam mentioned?"

"We also have agents at Western Data and at the home of Declan McGinnis in Scottsdale."

"And what's McGinnis have to say for himself?"

"Nothing so far. We haven't found him."

"He's missing?"

She shrugged.

"We're not sure whether he's voluntarily or involuntarily missing, but he's gone. And so is his dog. It's possible that he did some investigating on his own after the agents visited Friday. He might have gotten too close to Stone, and Stone reacted. There's another possibility, too."

"That they were in it together?"

She nodded.

"Yes, a team. McGinnis and Stone. And wherever they are, they're together."

I thought about it and knew it was not without precedent. The Hillside Strangler turned out to be two cousins. And there were other serial killer teams before and after. Bittaker and Norris came to mind. Two of the most heinous sex killers to ever walk the planet somehow found each other and became a team in California. They tape-recorded their torture sessions. A cop once gave me a copy of one such session that took place in the back of a van. After the first scream of panic and pain, I turned the thing off.

"You see, Jack? This is why we need time before the media firestorm. Both men had laptops and they took those with them. But they also had computers at Western Data and we have them. We've got an EER team coming in from Quantico. They'll be on the ground by—"

"Ear?"

"E-E-R. Electronic Evidence Retrieval team. They're in the air now. We'll put them on the system at Western Data and see what we can learn. And remember what we already learned today. That place is wired for sight and sound. The archived recordings should be able to help us as well."

I nodded. I was still thinking about McGinnis and Stone working together as a tag team of murderers.

"What do you think?" I asked Rachel. "You think it's one Unsub or two?"

"I'm not ready to say for sure yet. But I think we're talking about a team here."

"Why?"

"You know the scenario we spun the other night? Where the Unsub comes to L.A., lures Angela to your house, then kills her and flies to Vegas to follow you?"

"Yeah."

"Well, the bureau checked every airline flying out of LAX and Burbank to Vegas that night. Only four passengers on the late flights bought tickets that night. Everybody else had reservations. Agents tracked and interviewed three of them and they were cleared. The fourth, of course, was you."

"Okay, then he could have driven."

She shook her head.

"He could have driven but why send the GO! package overnight if you were driving to Vegas. You see? Sending the package overnight only works if he was flying over and was going to pick it up, or if he was sending it to somebody."

"His partner."

I nodded and started pacing in a circle as I riffed on this new scenario. It all seemed to make sense.

"So Angela goes to the trap site and alerts them. They

read her e-mail. They read my e-mail. And their response is that one goes to L.A. to take care of her and one goes to Vegas to take care of me."

"That's how I'm seeing it."

"Wait. What about her phone? You said the bureau traced the call the killer made to me on her phone to the airport in Vegas. How did the phone get to—"

"The GO! package. He sent your gun *and* her phone. They knew it would be a way of further tying you to her murder. After your suicide, the cops would find her phone in your room. Then when it didn't work out as planned, Stone called you from the airport. Maybe he just wanted to chat, or maybe he knew it would help set the idea that there was one killer out there who had gone from L.A. to Vegas."

"Stone? So you're saying McGinnis went to L.A. for Angela, and Stone went to Vegas for me."

She nodded.

"You said the man with sideburns was no older than thirty. Stone is twenty-six and McGinnis is forty-six. You can disguise appearance but one of the hardest things to do without being obvious about it is to disguise age. And it's much harder to go younger than older. I'm betting your man with the sideburns was Stone."

It made sense to me.

"There's another thing that indicates we're dealing with a team here," Rachel said. "It was right in front of us the whole time."

"What's that?"

"A loose end from the Denise Babbit killing. She was

put in the trunk of her own car and it was abandoned in South L.A., where Alonzo Winslow happened upon it."

"Yeah, so?"

"So if the killer worked alone, how did he get out of South L.A. after he dropped off the car? We're talking late at night in a predominantly black neighborhood. Did he take a bus or call a cab and wait on the curb? Rodia Gardens is about a mile from the nearest Metro stop. Did he just walk it, a white man in a black neighborhood in the middle of the night? I don't think so. You don't end a murder as well planned as this with that kind of getaway. None of those scenarios makes much sense."

"So whoever dropped her car off had a ride out of there."

"You got it."

I nodded and went silent for a long moment while I thought of all the new information. Rachel finally interrupted.

"I'm going to have to get to work, Jack," she said. "And you need to get on a plane."

"What is your assignment? I mean, besides me."

"I'm going to work with the EER team at Western Data. I need to get over there now to get things ready."

"Did they shut that place down?"

"More or less. They sent everybody home except for a skeleton crew to keep systems operating and to help with the EER team. I think Carver in the bunker and O'Connor on the surface, maybe a few others."

"This is going to put them out of business."

"We can't help that. Besides, if the CEO of that company and his young cohort were dipping into stored data to find victims for their shared kill dreams, then I think their customers are entitled to know that. What happens after that happens."

I nodded.

"I guess so."

"Jack, you gotta go. I told Bantam I could handle this. I wish I could hug you but now's not the time. But I want you to be very careful. Get back to L.A. and be safe. Call me for anything and, obviously, call me if you hear from one of these men again."

I nodded.

"I'm going back to the hotel to get my stuff. You want me to leave the room for you?"

"No, the bureau's paying my way now. When you check out, can you just leave my bag with the front desk? I'll check back in there later."

"Okay, Rachel. And you be careful yourself."

As I turned to head to my car, I slyly reached out and squeezed her wrist. I hoped the message was felt loud and clear; we were in this together.

Ten minutes later the warehouse was in my rearview mirror and I was on the way back to the Mesa Verde Inn. I was on hold with Southwest Airlines, waiting to book a flight back to L.A., but I could not concentrate on anything other than the idea that the Unsub was actually two killers acting in unison.

To me, the idea of two people meeting and acting on the

same wavelength of sexual sadism and murder more than doubled the sense of dread such dark things conjured. I thought of the term Yolanda Chavez had used during the tour of Western Data. *Dark fiber.* Could there be anything as deep and dark in the fiber of one's being as the desire to share such things as what had happened to Denise Babbit and the other victims? I didn't think so and the thought of it chilled me to the center of my soul.

SEVENTEEN: The Farm

The three agents comprising the FBI Electronic Evidence Retrieval team had commandeered the three workstations in the control room. Carver was left pacing behind them and occasionally looking over their shoulders at their screens. He wasn't worried because he knew they would find only what he wanted them to find. But he had to act like he was worried. After all, what was happening here was threatening the reputation of Western Data and its business across the country.

"Mr. Carver, you really need to relax," Agent Torres said. "It's going to be a long night and your pacing back and forth like that will only make it longer—for you and us."

"Sorry," Carver said. "I'm just worried about what this is all going to mean, you know?"

"Yes, sir, we understand," Torres said. "Why don't you—"

The agent was interrupted by the sound of "Riders on the Storm" coming from the pocket of Carver's lab coat.

"Excuse me," Carver said.

He pulled the cell phone out of his pocket and answered it.

"It's me," Freddy Stone said.

"Hi, there," Carver said cheerily for the benefit of the agents.

"Have they found it yet?"

"Not yet. I'm still here and it's going to be a while."

"I go ahead with the plan then?"

"You'll just have to play without me."

"This is my test, isn't it? I have to prove myself to you."

He said it with a slight note of indignation.

"After what happened last week, I'm happy to sit this one out."

There was a pause and then Stone changed directions.

"Do those agents know who I am yet?"

"I don't know but there's nothing I can do about it right now. Work comes first. I'm sure I'll be available next week and you can take my money again then."

Carver hoped his lines fell within the bounds of poker talk for the listening agents.

"I'll meet you later at the place?" Stone asked.

"Yes, my place. You bring the chips and beer. See you then. I gotta go."

He ended the call and dropped the phone back into his pocket. Stone's hedging and indignation were beginning to concern Carver. A few days ago he was begging for his life; today he didn't like being told what to do. Carver began to second-guess himself. He probably should have ended it in the desert and put Stone in the hole with McGinnis and the dog. End of story. End of threat.

He could still do it. Later tonight maybe. Another two-for-one opportunity. It would be the end of the line for Stone and a lot of other things. Western Data would not be able to withstand the scandal. It would close and Carver would move on. By himself. Like before. He would take the lessons he had learned and begin again somewhere else. He was the Changeling. He knew he could do it.

I'm a changeling, see me change. I'm a changeling, see me change.

Torres turned from his screen and looked at Carver. Carver checked himself. Had he been humming?

"Poker night?" Torres asked.

"Yeah. Sorry for the intrusion."

"Sorry you're missing your game."

"That's okay. You guys are probably saving me fifty bucks."

"The bureau is always happy to help out."

Torres smiled and the other agent, the woman named Mowry, smiled, too.

Carver tried to smile but it felt phony and he stopped. The truth was, he had nothing to smile about.

EIGHTEEN: A Call to Action

stayed in my hotel room the whole evening, writing most of the next day's story and repeatedly calling Rachel. The story was easy to put together. I first talked to my ace, Prendergast, about it and wrote up a budget line. I sent that in and then started constructing the story. Though it was not going to run until the next news cycle, I already had the main components well in hand. Beginning the following morning I would gather the latest details and just stick them in.

That is, if I was given any new details. What had been a mild dose of paranoia bloomed into something larger when my hourly calls to Rachel's cell went unanswered and the messages unreturned. My plans for the evening—and the future—hit the rocks of doubt.

Finally, just before eleven o'clock, my cell phone rang. The caller ID said Mesa Verde Inn. It was Rachel.

"How's L.A.?" she asked.

"L.A.'s fine," I said. "I've been trying to call you. Didn't you get my messages?"

"I'm sorry. My phone died. I was on it so much earlier. I'm back at the hotel now and just checked in. Thank you for leaving my bag with the desk."

The dead phone explanation sounded plausible. I started to relax.

"No problem," I said. "What room did they put you in?"

"Seven seventeen. What about you, did you go back to your house after all?"

"No, I'm still at the hotel."

"Really? I just called the Kyoto and they put me through to your room but I got no answer."

"Oh. It must have been when I went down the hall to get ice."

I stared at the bottle of Grand Embrace Cabernet I had gotten from room service.

"So," I said, to change the subject, "are you in for the night, then?"

"Jeez, I hope so. I just ordered room service. I suppose I'll get called back out if they find something at Western Data."

"What do you mean, there are still people in there?"

"The EER team is still there. They're guzzling Red Bull like it's water and working on into the night. Carver's with them. But I couldn't go the distance. I had to get some food and sleep."

"And Carver's just going to let them work through the night?"

"Turns out the scarecrow is a night owl. He takes several midnight shifts every week. Says he gets his best work done then, so he's cool with staying."

"What'd you order to eat?"

"Good old comfort food. A cheeseburger and fries."

I smiled.

"I had the same thing, but skipped the cheese. No Pyrat rum or wine?"

"Nope, now that I'm back on the bureau per diem, no alcohol allowed. Not that I couldn't use it."

I smiled but decided to get down to business first.

"So what's the latest update on McGinnis and Stone?"

There was a hesitation in her response.

"Jack, I'm tired. It's been a long day and I've been in that bunker for the last four hours. I was hoping I could eat my dinner, take a hot bath and we could just leave business for tomorrow."

"Look, I'm tired, too, Rachel, but remember I let you push me out of the way on the promise you would keep me informed. I haven't heard from you since I left the warehouse and now you're telling me you're too tired to talk."

Another hesitation.

"Okay, okay, you're right. So let's get this over with. The update is that there is good and bad news. The good news is that we know who Freddy Stone really is and he's not Freddy Stone. Knowing his real identity will hopefully help us run him down."

"Freddy Stone's an alias? How'd he get by the supposedly vaunted security screening at Western Data? Didn't they check his prints?"

"The thing is, company records show Declan McGinnis signed off on hiring him. So he could have greased it."

I nodded. McGinnis could have gotten his partner in murder into the company, no sweat.

"Okay, so who is he?"

I opened my backpack on the bed and took out a note-book and pen.

"His real name is Marc Courier. That's Marc with a *c*. Same age, twenty-six, with two felony arrests in Illinois for fraud. He skipped three years ago before trial. They were identity theft cases. He got credit cards, opened bank accounts, the whole nine yards. His history indicates he's a gifted hacker and vicious troll with a long history of digital breaches and assaults. He's a bad guy and he was right there in the bunker."

"When did he come to work for Western Data?"

"Also three years ago. It looks like he split Chicago and almost immediately ended up in Mesa with the new name."

"So McGinnis already knew him?"

"We think he recruited him. You know, it always used to be an amazing thing when two like-minded killers would hook up. You would think, What are the chances? But the Internet is a whole new ball game. It's the great intersection, for things good and bad. With chat rooms and websites devoted to any fetish and paraphilia imaginable, we have people with similar interests hooking up every minute of the day. We are going to see more and more of this, Jack. Where they take it out of fantasy and cyberspace and into the real world. Meeting people with shared beliefs helps justify those beliefs. It emboldens. Sometimes it's a call to action."

"Did the name Freddy Stone belong to somebody else?"

"No, it looks like it was fabricated."

"Any history of violence or sex offenses back in Chicago?"

"When he was arrested three years ago in Chicago, his computer was seized and they found a lot of porn. I am told it included a few Bangkok torture films but he wasn't charged with anything. It's too hard to make a case because the films carry disclaimers that they're all actors and nothing is real, even though it most likely is real torture and pain."

"What about stuff with leg braces, that sort of thing?"

"Nothing like that on the record but we'll look into all of that, believe me. If the link between Courier and McGinnis is abasiophilia, we will find it. If they met in an iron maiden chat room we will find it."

"How'd you make Courier's ID?"

"The handprint stored on the biometric reader on the entrance to the server farm."

I finished writing and checked my notes, looking for my next question.

"Will I be able to get a mug shot of Courier?"

"Check your e-mail. I sent one before I left. I want you to see if he looks familiar."

I pulled my laptop across the bed and logged on to my e-mail. Her message was on top of the pile. I opened the photo and stared at a mug shot of Marc Courier from his arrest three years before. He had long dark hair and a scraggly goatee and mustache. He looked like he would fit in seamlessly with Kurt and Mizzou in the bunker at Western Data.

"Could it be the man from the hotel in Ely?" Rachel asked.

I studied the photo without answering.

"Jack?"

"I don't know. It could be. I wish I had seen his eyes."

I studied the photo for a few more seconds and then moved on.

"So you said you had good and bad news. What's the bad news?"

"Before he split, Courier planted replicating viruses in his own computer in the lab at Western Data and in the company archives. It chewed through almost everything by the time it was discovered tonight. The camera archives are gone. So is a lot of the company data."

"What's that mean?"

"It means we're not going to be able to track his movements as easily as we had hoped. You know, when he was there, when he wasn't, any sort of connections or meetings with McGinnis, that sort of thing. E-mails back and forth. It would have been good to have."

"How did that go unnoticed by Carver and all the safeguards they supposedly have in place there?"

"The easiest thing in the world to pull off is an inside job. Courier knew the defense systems. He built a virus that navigated around them."

"What about McGinnis and his computer?"

"Better luck there, I am told. But they started on that late tonight, so I won't know more until tomorrow when I go in. A search team was at his house all night as well.

He lives alone, no family. I heard they found some interesting stuff but the search is ongoing."

"How interesting?"

"Well, I don't know if you want to hear this, Jack, but they found a copy of your book on the Poet on his bookshelf. I told you we'd find it."

I didn't reply. I felt a sudden heat on my face and neck and was silent while I considered the idea that I had written a book that might have in some way been a primer for another killer. It was by no means a how-to book but it certainly outlined how profiling and serial killer investigations were carried out by the FBI.

I needed to change the subject.

"What else did they find?"

"I haven't seen this yet but I am told they found a complete set of ankle-to-thigh leg braces designed for a woman. There was also pornography dealing with the subject."

"Man, this is one sick son of a bitch."

I wrote a few notes about the findings, then flipped back through the pages to see if anything prompted another question. Between what I knew and had seen and what Rachel was telling me, I would have a hell of a story for the next day.

"So Western Data is completely closed down, right?"

"Pretty much. I mean, the websites that are hosted at the company are still operating. We froze the colocation center, though. No data is going in or out until the EER team completes its assessment."

"Some of the clients, like the big law firms, are going to go ape shit when they find out the FBI has custody of their stored files, aren't they?"

"Probably, but we're not opening any stored files. At least not yet. We are just maintaining the system as is for the time being. Nothing in or out. We worked with Carver on a message that went out to all clients to keep them informed. It said that the situation is temporary and that Carver, as a representative of the company, was observing the FBI investigation and ensuring the integrity of the files, yada, yada, yada. That's the best we can do. If they go ape shit, then I guess they go ape shit."

"What about Carver? You checked him out, right?"

"Yes, he's clean, all the way back to MIT. We need to trust somebody inside and I guess it's him."

I was silent as I wrote a few final notes. I had more than enough to write the story the next day. Even if I couldn't get through to Rachel, I was sure my story would lead the paper and draw national attention. Two serial killers for the price of one.

"Jack, you there?"

"Yeah, I'm just writing. Anything else?"

"That's about it."

"You're being careful?"

"Of course. My gun and badge are being overnighted to me. I'll be locked and loaded tomorrow morning."

"Then you'll be all set."

"I will. Can we finally talk about us now?"

I was suddenly speared through the chest with anxiety. She wanted to get the work-related discussion out of the way so she could get to what she really wanted to say about our relationship. After all the unanswered phone calls, I didn't think it was going to be good news.

"Uh, sure," I said. "What about us?"

I got up off the bed, ready to take the news standing up. I walked over to the bottle of wine and picked it up. I was staring at it when she spoke.

"Well, you know, I didn't want this to be all business."

I felt a little better. I put the bottle down again and started to loosen the spear.

"Me, too."

"In fact, I was thinking...I know this is going to sound crazy."

"What is?"

"Well, when they offered me my job back today, I felt so...I don't know, elated, I guess. Vindicated in some way. But then when I got back here by myself tonight, I started thinking about that thing you said when you were joking around."

I couldn't remember what she meant so I played along.

"And?"

She sort of laughed before answering.

"And, well, I think it really could be kind of fun if we tried it."

I was racking my brain, wondering if this had something to do with the single-bullet theory. *What was it I had said?*

"You really think so?"

"Well, I don't know anything about business or how we would get clients, but I think I'd like working with you on investigations. It would be fun. It's already been fun."

Now I remembered. Walling and McEvoy, Discreet Investigations. I smiled. I pulled the spear out of my chest and slammed it point-first into the hard ground, staking a claim like that astronaut who put the flag on the moon.

"Yeah, Rachel, it's been nice," I said, hoping my cool bravado masked my inner relief. "But I don't know. You were pretty upset when you were facing life without a badge."

"I know. Maybe I'm kidding myself. We'd probably end up doing divorce work and that's gotta kill the soul over time."

"Yeah."

"Well, it's something to think about."

"Hey, I've got nothing lined up. So you won't hear me objecting. I just want to make sure you don't make a mistake. I mean, is everything suddenly forgiven there with the bureau? They just gave you your job back and that's that?"

"Probably not. They'll lie in wait for me. They always do."

I heard the knock on her door and the muffled voice of someone calling out, "Room service."

"My dinner's here," Rachel said. "I gotta go."

"Okay. I'll see you later, Rachel."

"Okay, Jack. Good night."

I smiled as I disconnected the call. Later would be sooner than she thought.

After brushing my teeth and checking myself in the mirror, I grabbed the bottle of Grand Embrace and slipped the folding corkscrew that room service had provided into my pocket. I made sure I had my key card and left the room.

The stairwell was right outside my door, and Rachel was only one floor up and a few doors down, so I decided not to waste any time. I hit the door and started up the concrete stairs two at a time, taking a quick look over the railing and down the center shaft to the ground. I got a quick dose of vertigo and pulled back and continued up. I made the turn on the middle landing, thinking about what her first words were going to be when she answered her door and saw me. I was smiling when I crested the next flight. And that's when I saw a man lying flat on his back next to the door to the seventh-floor hallway. He was wearing black pants and a white shirt with a bow tie.

All in a moment I realized he was the room service waiter who had earlier brought me my dinner and the bottle of wine I was now holding. As I got to the top step, I saw blood on the concrete, leaking from beneath him. I dropped to my knees next to him and put the bottle down.

"Hey!"

I pushed his shoulder to see if I could get a response. There was nothing and I thought he was dead. I saw the ID tag clipped to his belt, confirming my recognition. EDWARD HOOVER, KITCHEN STAFF.

I made another quick leap.

Rachel!

I jumped up and yanked the door open. As I entered the seventh-floor hallway, I pulled my phone and punched in 911. The hotel was designed in a wide *U* pattern and I was on the upper right branch. I started moving down the hallway, checking the numbers on the doors. 722, 721, 720 . . . I got to Rachel's room and saw the door was ajar. I pushed through without knocking.

"Rachel?"

The room was empty but there were obvious signs of a struggle. Plates, silverware and French fries from a room service table were strewn across the floor. The bedcovers were gone and there was a pillow smeared with blood on the floor.

I realized I was holding my phone down at my side and there was a tinny voice calling to me. I headed back out into the hall as I raised the phone.

"Hello?"

"Nine-one-one, what is your emergency?"

I started running down the hall, panic engulfing me as I yelled into the phone.

"I need help! Mesa Verde Inn, seventh floor! Now!"

I made the turn into the central hallway and caught a split-second glimpse of a man with bleached-blond hair and wearing a red waiter's jacket. He was pushing a large laundry cart through a pair of double doors on the far side of the guest elevators. Though it had been only a quick view, the picture didn't add up.

"Hey!"

I increased my speed, covered the ground quickly and hit the double doors just seconds after I saw them close. I came into a small housekeeping vestibule and saw the door of a service elevator closing. I lunged for the door, reaching my hand out, but I was too late. It was gone. I backed away and looked up. There were no numbers or arrows above the door that would tell me which way he was going. I smashed back through the double doors and ran to the guest elevators. The stairwells, at either end of the hallway, were too far to consider.

I quickly pushed the down button, thinking it was the obvious choice to make. It led to the exit. It led to escape. I thought about the laundry cart and the forward-leaning angle of the man who was pushing it. There was something heavier than laundry in it, I was sure. He had Rachel.

There were four guest elevators and I got lucky. As soon as I hit the button the door chimed and an elevator opened. I leaped through the opening door and saw that the lobby button was already lit. I machine-gunned the close-door button and waited interminably long as the door slowly, gently closed.

"Easy, buddy. We'll get there."

I turned and saw there was a man already on the elevator. He was wearing a conventioneer's name tag with a blue ribbon hanging from it. I was about to tell him it was an emergency, when I remembered the phone in my hand.

"Hello? Are you still there?"

There was static on the line but I still had a connection. I could feel the elevator start to drop quickly.

"Yes, sir. I've dispatched the police. Can you tell me—"

"Listen to me, there's a guy dressed like a waiter and he's trying to abduct a federal agent. Call the FBI. Send every—Hello? Are you there?"

Nothing. I'd lost the call. I felt the elevator come to a hard stop as we reached the lobby. The conventioneer pushed back into the corner and tried to disappear. I stepped up to the doors and moved through them before they had barely opened.

I stepped into an alcove off the lobby. Adjusting my bearings in relation to where the service elevator would be located, I took a left and then another left through a door marked EMPLOYEES ONLY and entered a rear hallway. I heard kitchen noises and smelled food. There were stainless-steel shelves lined with commercial-size cans of food and other products. I saw the service elevator but no sign of the man in the red jacket or the laundry cart.

Had I beaten the service elevator down? Or had he gone up?

I pushed the elevator call button.

"Hey, you're not supposed to be back here."

I turned quickly to see a man in kitchen whites and a dirty apron walking toward me in the hall.

"Did you see a guy pushing a laundry cart?" I asked quickly.

"Not in the kitchen, I didn't."

"Is there a basement?"

The man took an unlit cigarette out of his mouth to answer.

"There ain't no basement."

He gestured with the hand holding the cigarette. I realized he was going outside for a smoke break. There was an exit somewhere close.

"Is there a way out from here to the parking garage?"

He pointed past me.

"The loading dock is—Hey, look out!"

I started to turn back to the elevator just as the laundry cart came crashing into me. It hit me thigh high and my upper body pivoted over the edge. I put my hands out to break my fall into the pile of linens and the bedspread in it. I could feel something soft but solid under the covers and knew it was Rachel. I pushed my weight backward and slid back onto my feet.

I looked up and saw the elevator closing again as the man in the red jacket held his hand on the door-close button. I looked at his face and recognized it from the mug shot I had seen earlier that night. He was cleaned up and blond now, but I was sure it was Marc Courier. I looked back at the elevator control panel and saw a floor light glowing from the top. Courier was going back up.

I reached into the cart and yanked back the bedspread.

There was Rachel. She was still wearing the clothes she'd had on earlier in the day. She was facedown with her arms and legs hog-tied behind her back. A terry cloth belt from a hotel room bathrobe had been tied as a gag across her mouth. Her nose and mouth were bleeding profusely. Her eyes were glassy and distant.

"*Rachel!*"

I reached down and pulled the gag down off her mouth.

"*Rachel? Are you all right? Can you hear me?*"

She didn't respond. The kitchen man stepped over and looked down into the cart.

"What the hell is going on?"

She was bound with plastic cable ties. I pulled the folding corkscrew out of my pocket and used the small blade designed for cap cutting to slice through the plastic.

"Help me get her out!"

We carefully lifted her out of the cart and put her on the floor. I dropped down next to her and made sure the blood had not closed off her airways. Her nostrils were caked with it but her mouth was clear. She had been beaten and her face was beginning to swell.

I looked up at the kitchen man.

"Go call security. And nine-one-one. Now! *GO!*"

He started running down the hall for a phone. I looked back down at Rachel and saw she was becoming alert.

"Jack?"

"It's all right, Rachel. You're safe."

Her eyes looked scared and hurt. I felt a rage building inside me.

From down the hallway I heard the kitchen man yell.

"They're coming! Paramedics and police!"

I didn't look up at him. I kept my eyes on Rachel.

"There, you hear that? Help is on the way."

She nodded and I saw more life returning to her eyes. She coughed and tried to sit up. I helped her and then pulled her into a hug. I rubbed the back of her neck.

She whispered something I couldn't hear and I pulled back to look at her and asked her to say it again.

"I thought you were in L.A."

I smiled and shook my head.

"I was too paranoid about going away from the story. And from you. I was going to surprise you with a good bottle of wine. That's when I saw him. It was Courier."

She made a slight nodding motion.

"You saved me, Jack. I didn't recognize him through the peephole. When I opened the door, it was too late. He hit me. I tried to fight but he had a knife."

I shushed her. No explanation was necessary.

"Listen, was he by himself? Was McGinnis there?"

She shook her head.

"I only saw Courier. I recognized him too late."

"Don't worry about it."

The kitchen man was standing back down the hall, now with other men dressed in kitchen clothes. I signaled them to come forward and they didn't move at first. Then one reluctantly stepped forward and the others followed.

"Push that elevator button for me," I said.

"You sure?" one asked.

"Just do it."

I leaned down and put my face into the crook of Rachel's neck. I hugged her tightly, breathed in her scent and whispered in her ear.

"He went up. I'm going to go get him."

"No, Jack, you wait here. Stay with me."

I pulled up and looked into her eyes. I said nothing until I heard the elevator open. I then looked up at the kitchen man I had originally spoken to. On his white shirt the name *Hank* was embroidered.

"Where's security?"

"They should be here," he said. "They're coming."

"Okay, I want you men to wait here with her. Don't leave her. When security gets here, you tell them there's another victim on the seventh-floor stairwell and that I went up to the top to look for the guy. Tell security to cover all the exits and elevators. This guy went up, but he's gonna have to try to come down."

Rachel started to get up.

"I'm going with you," she said.

"No, you're not. You're hurt. You stay here and I'll be right back. I promise."

I left her there and stepped onto the elevator. I pushed the 12 button and looked back at Rachel. As the door closed I noticed that Hank the kitchen man was nervously lighting his cigarette.

It was a damn-the-rules moment for both of us.

The service elevator moved slowly upward and I came to realize that so much of Rachel's rescue had relied on pure luck—a slow elevator, my staying in Mesa to surprise her, my taking the stairs with the bottle of wine. But I didn't want to dwell on what could have been. I concentrated on the moment and when the elevator finally reached the top of the building, I stood ready with the one-inch corkscrew blade as the door opened. I realized I should have grabbed a better weapon from the kitchen, but it was too late now.

The housekeeping vestibule on twelve was empty except for the red waiter's jacket I saw dropped on the floor. I pushed through the swinging doors and into the central hallway. I could hear sirens coming from outside the building now. A lot of them.

Looking both ways I saw nothing and I started to realize that a one-man search of a twelve-story hotel nearly as wide as it was tall was going to be a waste of time. Between elevators and stairwells, Courier had his choice of multiple escape routes.

I decided to go back down to Rachel and leave the search for hotel security and the arriving police.

But I knew that on the way down I could cover at least

one of those exit routes. Maybe my luck would hold. I chose the north stairwell because it was closest to the hotel's parking garage. And it was the stairwell Courier had used earlier to hide the body of the room service waiter.

I went down the hallway, rounded the corner and then pushed through the exit door. I first looked over the railing and down the shaft. I saw nothing and heard only the echo of the sirens. I was just about to head down the steps, when I noticed that even though I was on the top floor of the hotel, the stairs continued up.

If there was access to the roof, I needed to check it. I headed up.

The stairwell was dimly lit by a sconce on each landing. Each floor was broken into two sets of stairs and landings in the routine back-and-forth design. When I reached the midlevel and turned to take the next set of stairs to what would be the thirteenth floor, I saw the upper and final landing was crowded with stored hotel room furnishings. I came all the way up to where the stairs ended in a large storage area. There were bed tables stacked on top of one another and mattresses leaning four deep against one of the walls. There were stacks of chairs and mini-refrigerators and pre–flat-screen-era television cabinets. I was reminded of the filing cabinets I had seen in the Public Defender's Office hallway. There had to be multiple code violations here, but who was looking? Who ever came up here? Who cared?

I worked my way around a grouping of standing stainless-steel lamps and toward a door with a small square window at face height. The word ROOF had been painted on it with a stencil. But when I got to it, I found the door was locked. I pushed hard on the release bar but it wouldn't move. Something had jammed or locked the mechanism and the door wouldn't budge. I looked through the window and saw a flat gravel roof running behind the barrel-tiled parapets of the hotel. Across a forty-yard expanse of gravel I could see the structure that housed the building's elevator equipment. Beyond that was another door to the stairwell on the other side of the hotel.

I shifted to my left and leaned in closer to the window so I could get a wider view of the roof. Courier could be out there.

Just as I did this, I saw a blurred reflection of movement in the glass.

Someone was behind me.

Instinctively, I jumped sideways and turned at the same time. Courier's arm swung down with a knife and barely missed me as he crashed into the door.

I planted my feet and then drove my body into his, bringing my arm up and stabbing my own blade into his side.

But my weapon was too short. I scored a direct hit but didn't do enough damage to bring down the target. Courier yelped and brought his forearm down on my wrist, knocking my blade to the floor. He then took an enraged, roundhouse swing at me with his own. I managed to duck underneath it but got a good look at his blade. It was at least four inches long and I knew if he connected with it, it would be a one-and-done proposition for me.

Courier made another jab and this time I parried to the right and caught his wrist. The only advantage I had was my size. I was older and slower than Courier, but I had forty pounds on him. While holding his knife hand away, I threw my body into him again, knocking him back through the forest of stand-up lamps and onto the concrete floor.

He broke free during the fall and then scrabbled to his feet with the knife ready. I grabbed one of the lamps, holding its round base out and ready to spar at him and deflect the next assault.

For a moment nothing happened. He held the knife at the ready and we seemed to be taking each other's measure, waiting for the other to make the next move. I then made a charge with the lamp base but he sidestepped it easily. We then squared off again. He had a desperate sort of smile on his face and was breathing heavily.

"Where are you going to go, Courier? You hear all those sirens? They're here, man. There's going to be cops and FBI all over this place in two minutes. Where're you going to go then?"

He didn't say anything and I took another poke at him with the lamp. He grabbed the base and we momentarily struggled for control of it, but I pushed him back into a stack of mini-refrigerators and they crashed to the floor.

I had no experience in the area of knife fighting, but my instincts told me to keep talking. If I distracted Courier, then I would lessen the threat from the knife and possibly get an open shot at him. So I kept throwing the questions at him, waiting for my moment.

"Where's your partner? Where's McGinnis? What did he do, send you to do the dirty work by yourself? Just like Nevada, huh? You missed your chance again."

Courier grinned at me but didn't take the bait.

"Does he just tell you what to do? Like your mentor on murder or something? Man, the master's not going to be very happy with you tonight. You're zero for two, man."

This time he couldn't control it.

"McGinnis is dead, you dumb fuck! I buried him in the desert. Just like I was going to bury your bitch after I was through with her."

I feigned another jab at him with the lamp and tried to keep him talking.

"I don't get it, Courier. If he's dead, why didn't you just run? Why risk everything to go for her?"

At the same moment he opened his mouth to reply, I faked a jab at his chest with the lamp and then brought the base up into his face, catching him flush on the jaw. Courier staggered backward momentarily and I quickly moved in, hurling the lamp at him first and then going for the knife with both hands. We smashed into a television cabinet and fell to the floor, me on top of him and grappling for control of the knife.

He shifted his weight beneath me and we rolled three times, with him ending up on top. I kept both hands on his wrist and he pushed his free hand into my face, trying to break my grip by stiff-arming me away. I finally managed to bend his wrist at a painful angle. He cried out and the knife came free and clattered to the concrete. With an elbow I shoved it toward the stairwell shaft but it stopped just shy of the mark, balancing on the edge below the blue guardrail. It was six feet away.

I went after him like an animal then, punching and kicking and fueled by a primal rage I had never felt before. I grabbed an ear and tried to rip it off. I swung an elbow into his teeth. But the energy of youth gradually gave him the upper hand. I was tiring quickly and he managed to pull back and get distance. He then brought a knee up into my crotch and the air exploded out of my lungs. Paralyzing pain shot through me and weakened my hold. He broke completely free and got up to go for the knife.

Calling on my last reserve of strength, I half crawled, half lunged after him as I struggled to my feet. I was hurt and spent but I knew that if he got to the knife, I would be dead.

I threw my weight into him from behind. He lurched forward into the railing, his upper body pivoting over it. Without thinking, I reached down, grabbed one of his legs and flipped him all the way over the rail. He tried to grab the steel piping but his grip slipped and he fell.

His scream lasted only two seconds. His head hit either a railing or the concrete siding of the shaft, and after that, he fell silently, his body caroming from side to side on its way down thirteen floors.

I watched him all the way. Until the final, loud impact echoed all the way back up to me.

I wish I could say I felt guilt or even a sense of remorse. But I felt like cheering every moment of his fall.

The next morning I went back to Los Angeles for real, leaning against the plane's window and sleeping the whole way. I had spent most of the night in the now familiar surroundings of the FBI. Agent Bantam and I faced off again in the mobile interview room for several hours, during which I told and retold the story of what I had done the evening before and how Courier came to fall thirteen floors to his death. I told him what Courier had said about McGinnis and the desert and the plan for Rachel Walling.

During the interview Bantam never dropped the mask of detached federal agent. He never said thank you for saving the life of his fellow agent. He just asked questions, sometimes five or six different times and ways. And when it was finally over, he informed me that the details regarding the death of Marc Courier would be submitted to a state grand jury to determine if a crime had been committed or if my actions constituted self-defense. It was only then that he broke the mold and spoke to me like a human being.

"I have mixed feelings about you, McEvoy. You no doubt saved Agent Walling's life but going up there after Courier was the wrong move. You should have waited. If you had, he might be alive right now and we might have some of the answers. As it is, if McGinnis is really dead, most of the secrets went down that shaft with Courier. It's a big desert out there, if you know what I mean."

"Yeah, well, I'm sorry about that, Agent Bantam. I kind of look at it like if I hadn't gone after him, he might have gotten away. And if that had happened, the chances are, you wouldn't get any answers either. You'd just get more bodies."

"Maybe. But we'll never know."

"So what happens now?"

"Like I said, we'll present it to the grand jury. I doubt you'll have any problems. The world's not exactly going to feel sorry for Marc Courier."

"I don't mean with me. I'm not worried about that. With the investigation, what happens now?"

He paused as if to consider whether he should tell me anything.

"We'll try to re-create the trail. That's all we can do. We're not done at Western Data. We'll continue there and we'll try to put together a picture of what these men did. And we'll keep looking for McGinnis. Dead or alive. We only have Courier's word that he's dead. Personally, I'm not sure I believe it."

I shrugged. I had accurately reported what Courier had said. I would leave it to the experts to determine if it was the truth. If they wanted to put a picture of McGinnis in every post office in the country, that was fine with me.

"Can I go back to L.A. now?"

"You're free to go. But if anything else comes to mind, you call us. Likewise, we'll call you."

"Got it."

He didn't shake my hand. He just opened the door. When I stepped out of the bus, Rachel was waiting for me. We were in the front parking lot of the Mesa Verde Inn. It was close to five in the morning but neither of us seemed very tired. The paramedics had checked her out. The swelling was already beginning to subside but she had a badly cut and bruised lip and a contusion below the corner of her left eye. She had refused a transport to a local hospital for further examination. The last thing she would do at this point would be leave the center of the investigation.

"How are you feeling?" I asked.

"I'm okay," she said. "How are you?"

"I'm fine. Bantam said I'm clear to take off. I think I'll catch the first flight back to L.A."

"You're not going to stay for the press conference?"

I shook my head.

"What are they going to say that I don't already know?"

"Nothing."

"How long do you think you'll be here?"

"I don't know. I guess until they wrap things up. Which won't happen until we know all there is to know."

I nodded and checked my watch. The first flight to L.A. probably wouldn't be for another two hours.

"You want to go get breakfast somewhere?" I asked.

She tried to crinkle her lips to show disdain for the idea but the pain foiled the effort.

"I'm not that hungry. I just wanted to say good-bye. I need to get back to Western Data. They found the mother lode."

"Which is what?"

"An unaccounted-for server that both McGinnis and Courier had been accessing. It's got archived videos, Jack. They filmed their crimes."

"And both of them are in the videos?"

"I haven't seen them but I am told they are not readily identifiable. They wear masks and shoot at angles that mostly show their victims, not them. I was told that in one of the videos, McGinnis is wearing an executioner's hood—like the one worn by the Zodiac."

"You're kid—Wait a minute, he'd have to be sixty-some years old to be the Zodiac."

"No, they're not suggesting that—you can buy the hood in cult stores in San Francisco. It's just a sign of who they are. It's like having your book on the bedside. They know history. And it shows how much fear plays a part in their program. Scaring their victims was part of the rush."

I didn't think you needed to be an FBI profiler to understand that. But it brought to mind how truly horrible the last moments of their victims' lives were.

I once again remembered the audiotape of the Bittaker and Norris torture session in the back of the van. I couldn't listen then. I almost didn't want the answer to the question I had now.

"Is Angela on film?"

"No, she was too recent. But there are others."

"You mean victims?"

Rachel glanced over my shoulder at the door to the FBI bus and then back at me. I guessed that she might be talking out of turn, no matter the deal I supposedly had.

"Yes. They haven't looked at everything yet but they have at least six different victims. McGinnis and Courier were doing this a long time."

Now I wasn't so sure I wanted to leave. The bottom line was that the bigger the body count, the bigger the story. Two killers, at least six victims . . . If it was possible for the story to get bigger than it already was, then it had just happened.

"What about the braces? Were you right about that?"

She nodded solemnly. It was one of those times that being right wasn't such a good thing.

"Yeah, they made the victims wear leg braces."

I shook my head as if to ward off the thought of it. I checked my pockets. I had no pen and my notebook was back up in my room.

"You have a pen?" I asked Rachel. "I need to write this down."

"No, Jack, I don't have a pen to give you. I told you more than I should have. At this point it's just raw data. Wait till I have a better handle on everything and then I'll call you. Your deadline isn't for another twelve hours, at least."

She was right. I had a full day to put the story together, and the information would develop through the day. Besides that, I knew that when I got back to the news-room, I would face the same issue as the week before. I was part of the story again. I had killed one of the two men the story was about. Conflict of interest dictated that I wouldn't be writing it. I was going to sit with Larry Bernard once again and feed him a front-page story that would echo around the world. It was frustrating but by now I was getting used to it.

"All right, Rachel. I guess I'll go up and pack my stuff, then head to the airport."

"Okay, Jack. I'll call you. I promise."

I liked that she promised before I had to ask. I looked at her for a moment, wanting to make a move to touch and hold her. She seemed to read me. She took the first step and pulled me into a tight embrace.

"You saved my life tonight, Jack. You think you're getting out of here with just a handshake?"

"I was sort of hoping there would be more than that."

I kissed her lightly on the cheek, avoiding her bruised lips. If Agent Bantam or anybody else behind the smoked black windows of the FBI mobile command center was watching, neither one of us cared.

It was almost a minute before Rachel and I separated. She looked into my eyes and nodded.

"Go write your story, Jack."

"I will...if they let me."

I turned and walked toward the hotel.

All eyes were on me as I walked through the news-room. It had spread as quickly as a Santa Ana wind through the newsroom that I had killed a man the night before. Many probably thought I had avenged Angela Cook. Others may have thought I was some sort of danger freak who put myself in harm's way for the thrill of it.

As I approached my cubicle the phone was buzzing and the message light was on. I put my backpack on the floor and decided I would deal with all the callers and messages later. It was almost eleven o'clock, so I walked over to the raft to see if Prendo was in yet. I wanted to get this part over with. If I was going to give my information to another reporter, I wanted to start giving it up now.

Prendo wasn't in but Dorothy Fowler was sitting at the head of the raft. She looked up from her computer screen, saw me and did a double take.

"Jack, how are you?"

I shrugged.

"Okay, I guess. When's Prendo coming in?"

"Probably not till one. Are you up to working today?"

"You mean, do I feel bad about the guy who fell down

the stairwell last night? No, Dorothy, I'm actually okay with that. I feel fine. As the cops say, NHI—no human involved. The guy was a killer who liked to torture women while he raped and suffocated them. I don't feel too bad about what happened to him. In fact, I sort of wish he had been conscious the whole way down."

"Okay. I think I understand that."

"The only thing I don't feel good about right now is that I'm guessing I don't get to write the story, right?"

She frowned and nodded.

"I'm afraid not, Jack."

"Déjà vu all over again."

She squinted her eyes at me like she was wondering if I realized the inanity of what I had just said.

"It's a saying. Yogi Berra? The baseball guy?"

She didn't get it. I could feel the eyes and ears of the newsroom on us.

"Never mind. Who do you want me to give my stuff to? The FBI has confirmed to me that there were two killers and they have found videos of them with several victims. At least six besides Angela. They'll be announcing all of this at a press conference but I have lots of stuff they won't be putting out. We'll kick ass with this."

"Just what I want to hear. I'm going to put you with Larry Bernard again for continuity. You have your notes? Are you ready to go?"

"Ready when he is."

"Okay, let me call and book the conference room again so you guys can go to work."

I spent the next two hours giving Larry Bernard

everything I had, turning over my notes and filling him in off the top of my head with regard to my own actions. Larry then interviewed me for a sidebar story on my hand-to-hand battle with the serial killer.

"Too bad you didn't let him answer that last question," he said.

"What are you talking about?"

"At the end, when you asked him why he didn't just take off instead of going after Walling, that's the essential question, isn't it? Why didn't he run? He went after her and it didn't make a lot of sense. He was responding to you but you said you hit him with the lamp before he answered that one."

I didn't like the question. It was as if he was suspicious of my veracity or what I had done.

"Look, it was a knife fight and I didn't have a knife. I wasn't interviewing the guy. I was trying to distract him. If he was thinking about my questions, then he wasn't thinking about putting the knife in my throat. It worked. When I saw my chance I took it. I got the upper hand and that's why I'm alive and he's not."

Larry leaned forward and checked his tape recorder to make sure it was still operating.

"That's a good quote," he said.

I'd been a reporter for twenty-plus years and I had just been baited by my own friend and colleague.

"I want to take a break. How much more do you need?"

"I actually think I'm good," Larry said, his manner completely unapologetic. It was just business. "Let's take a break and I'll go through my notes and make sure.

Why don't you call Agent Walling and see if anything's come up in the last few hours."

"She would have called me."

"You sure?"

I stood up.

"Yes, I'm sure. Stop trying to work me, Larry. I know how it's done."

He raised his hands in surrender. But he was smiling.

"Okay, okay. Go take your break. I have to write up a couple budget lines anyway."

I left the conference room and went back to my cubicle. I picked up the phone and checked messages. I had nine of them, most from other news outlets wanting me to comment for their own reports. The CNN producer I had saved from the wrath of the censors by heading off Alonzo Winslow's interview left a message that he wanted me back on for the report on the latest turn of events.

I would deal with all such requests the next day, after the story had run exclusively in the *Times*. I was being loyal to the end, even though I didn't know why I should be.

The last message was from my long-lost literary agent. I hadn't heard from him in more than a year, and then it was only to tell me he had been unable to sell my latest book proposal—a year in the life of a cold case detective. His message informed me that he was already fielding offers for a book about the trunk murders case. He asked if the killer had been given a name by the media yet. He said a catchy name would make the book easier to package, market and sell. He wanted me to be thinking about that, he said, and to sit tight while he wheeled and dealed.

My agent was behind the curve, not realizing yet that there were two killers, not one. But the message made any frustration I was feeling about not getting to write the day's story go away. I was tempted to call the agent back but decided to wait until I heard from him with significant news. I then hatched a scheme in which I would tell him I would only take a deal from a publisher who would promise to publish my first novel as well. If they wanted the nonfiction story badly enough, they would take the deal.

After hanging up the phone, I went to my screen and looked into the city basket to see if Larry Bernard's stories were on the daily budget. As expected, the top of the budget was weighted with a three-story package on the case.

SERIAL—A man suspected of being a serial killer who took part in the killings of at least seven women, including a *Times* reporter, died Tuesday night in Mesa, AZ, after a confrontation with another reporter for the newspaper led to his falling thirteen floors down a hotel stairwell shaft. Marc Courier, 26, a Chicago native, was identified as one of two men suspected in a string of sexually motivated abductions and murders of women in at least two states. The other suspect was identified by the FBI as Declan McGinnis, 46, also of Mesa. Agents said McGinnis was the chief executive officer of a data storage facility from which victims were chosen from stored law firm files. Courier worked for McGinnis at Western Data Consultants and had direct access to the files in question. Though Courier claimed to a *Times* reporter that he had killed McGinnis, the FBI has listed his whereabouts as unknown. 45 inches w/mug shot of Courier. BERNARD

SERIAL SIDE—In a life-or-death struggle, *Times* reporter Jack McEvoy grappled with the knife-wielding Marc Courier on the top floor of the Mesa Verde Inn before distracting him with the tools of his trade: words. When the suspected serial killer dropped his guard, McEvoy got the upper hand and Courier fell down a stairwell shaft to his death. Authorities say the suspect left behind more questions than answers. 18 inches w/art BERNARD

DATA—They call them bunkers and farms. They sit in pastures and deserts. They are as nondescript as the nameless warehouses that line industrial streets in every city in the country. Data storage centers are billed as economical, dependable and secure. They store vital digital files that remain just a fingertip away no matter where your business is located. But this week's investigation into how two men used stored files to choose, stalk and prey on women is raising questions about the industry that has seen explosive growth in recent years. Authorities say the bottom-line question is not where or how you should store your digital information. The question is, who is minding it? The *Times* learns that many storage facilities hire the best and the brightest to safeguard their data. The problem is, sometimes the best and the brightest are former criminals. Suspect Marc Courier is a case in point. 25 inches w/art GOMEZ-GONZMART

They were going all-out again. The story package would lead the paper and be the authoritative report on the case. All other media outlets would have to credit the *Times* or scramble to match it. It would be a good day for the *Times*. The editors could already smell a Pulitzer.

I closed the screen and thought about the sidebar story Larry was going to write. He was right. There were more questions than answers.

I opened a new document on the screen and wrote my best recollection of the exact exchange I'd had with Courier. It took me only five minutes because the truth was that not a lot was said.

ME: Where's McGinnis? Did he send you to do the dirty work? Just like in Nevada?

HIM: No response.

ME: Does he tell you what to do? He's your mentor on murder and tonight the master won't be happy with the student. You went zero for two.

HIM: McGinnis is dead, you dumb fuck! I buried him in the desert. Just like I was going to bury your bitch when I was through with her.

ME: Why didn't you just run? Why risk everything to go for her?

HIM: No answer.

When I was finished I read it a couple of times and made a few fixes and additions. Larry was right. It came down to that last question. Courier had been about to respond but I'd used the distraction to catch him off guard. I didn't regret that. The distraction may have saved my life. But I sure wished I had an answer to the question I had asked.

The next morning the *Times* basked in the glow of national news exposure and I was along for the ride. I had written none of the stories causing the nationwide media stir but I was the subject of two of them. My phone never stopped buzzing and my e-mail box overflowed early.

But I didn't answer my calls or e-mails. I wasn't basking. I was brooding. I had spent the night with the unanswered question I had posed to Marc Courier, and no matter which way I considered it, things didn't add up. What was Courier doing there? What was the great reward for such a large risk? Was it Rachel? The abduction and murder of a federal agent would certainly place McGinnis and Courier in the upper pantheon of killers whose deadly lore made them household names. But was that what they wanted? There had been no indication that these two were interested in harnessing public attention. They had carefully planned and camouflaged their murders. The attempt to abduct Rachel did not fit with the history leading up to it. And so there had to be another reason.

I started to look at it from another angle. I thought about what would have happened if I had gone to Los

Angeles and Courier had been successful in grabbing Rachel and getting her out of the hotel.

It seemed likely to me that the abduction would have been discovered shortly after it occurred, when the room service waiter did not report back to the kitchen. I estimated that within an hour the hotel would have been a hive of activity. The FBI would have swarmed the hotel and the area, knocked on every door and turned over every rock in an attempt to find and rescue one of their own. But by then Courier would have been long gone.

It was clear the abduction would have drawn the bureau in and caused a massive distraction from its investigation of McGinnis and Courier. But it was also clear that this would be only a temporary shift. My guess was that before noon the next day, agents would be coming in by the planeload in a federal show of might and determination. This would allow them to overcome any distraction and put even more pressure on the investigation, all the while maintaining a suffocating effort to find Rachel.

The more I thought about it, the more I wished I'd given Courier the chance to answer that last question: Why didn't you run?

I didn't have the answer and it was too late to get it directly from the source. So I kept working it around in my head until it was all there was to think about.

"Jack?"

I looked over the wall of my cubicle and saw Molly Robards, the secretary to the assistant managing editor.

"Yes?"

"You're not answering your phone and your e-mail box is full."

"Yeah, I'm getting too many—is that a problem?"

"Mr. Kramer would like to see you."

"Oh, okay."

I didn't make a move but neither did she. It was clear she had been sent to retrieve me. I finally pushed my chair back and got up.

Kramer was waiting for me with a big, phony smile on his face. I had a feeling that whatever he was about to tell me was not his idea. I took this as a good sign, since his ideas were seldom good ones.

"Jack, sit down."

I did. He straightened things up on his desk before proceeding.

"Well, I've got some good news for you."

He gave me the smile again. The same one he'd had on when he told me I was out.

"Really?"

"We've decided to withdraw your termination plan."

"What's that mean? I'm not laid off?"

"Exactly."

"What about my pay and benefits?"

"Nothing's changed. Same old same old."

It was just like Rachel getting her badge back. I felt a trill of excitement but then reality hit home.

"So what's that mean, you lay somebody else off instead of me?"

Kramer cleared his throat.

"Jack, I'm not going to lie to you. Our objective was

to drop one hundred slots in editorial by June first. You were number ninety-nine—it was that close."

"So I keep my job and somebody else gets the ax."

"Angela Cook will be the ninety-ninth slot. We won't be replacing her."

"That's convenient. Who is the big one hundred?"

I swiveled in the chair and looked out through the glass at the newsroom.

"Bernard? GoGo? Collins—"

Kramer cut me off.

"Jack, I can't discuss that with you."

I turned back to him.

"But somebody else is about to get the hook because I got to stay. What happens after this story winds down? Will you call me back in here and can me all over again?"

"We're not expecting another involuntary reduction in force. The new owner has made it—"

"What about the next new owner? And the one after that?"

"Look, I didn't bring you in here so you could preach to me. The news business is undergoing serious changes. It's a life-and-death struggle. The question is, do you want to keep your job or not? I'm offering it to you."

I swiveled all the way around so my back was to him and I was looking out at the newsroom. I wouldn't miss the place. I would only miss some of the people. Without turning back to Kramer I gave him my answer.

"This morning my literary agent in New York woke me up at six. He said he had gotten me an offer for a two-book deal. A quarter million dollars. It would take me almost three years to make that here. And on top of that, I got a job offer from the Velvet Coffin. Don Goodwin is starting an investigations page on his website. To sort of pick up the slack where the *Times* drops the ball. Doesn't pay a lot but it pays. And I can work from home—wherever that may be."

I stood up and turned back to Kramer.

"I told him yes. So thanks for the offer but you can put me down as number one hundred on your thirty list. After tomorrow, I'm gone."

"You took a job with a competitor?" Kramer said indignantly.

"What did you expect? You laid me off, remember?"

"But I'm rescinding that," he sputtered. "We already made our quota."

"Who? Who'd you fire?"

Kramer looked down at his desk and whispered the latest victim's name.

"Michael Warren."

I shook my head.

"It figures. The one guy in the newsroom I wouldn't give the time of day and now I'm saving his job. You can hire'm back, because I don't want your job anymore."

"Then I want you to clear your desk out right now. I'll call security and have you escorted out."

I smiled down at him as he picked up the phone.

"Fine by me."

I found an empty cardboard box in the copy shop and ten minutes later was filling it with the things I wanted to keep from my desk. The first to go in was the worn red dictionary my mother had given me. After that, there wasn't much else worth keeping. A Montblanc desk clock which somehow had never been stolen, a red stapler and a few files containing call sheets and source contacts. That was it.

A guy from security watched over me as I packed and I got the feeling it wasn't the first time he had been placed in such an awkward position. I took mercy on him and didn't blame him for just doing his job. But having him standing at my desk was like waving a flag. Soon Larry Bernard came over.

"What's going on? You have till tomorrow."

"Not anymore. Crammer told me to hit the road."

"How come? What did you do?"

"He tried to give me my job back but I told him he could keep it."

"*What?* You turned—"

"I got a new job, Larry. Two of them, actually."

My box was as full as it was going to get. It looked pitiful. Not much for seven years on the job. I stood up, slung my backpack over my shoulder and picked up the box, ready to go.

"What about the story?" Larry asked.

"It's your story. You've got a handle on it."

"Yeah, through you. Who am I going to get to give me the inside stuff?"

"You're a reporter. You'll figure it out."

"Can I call you?"

"No, you can't call me."

Larry frowned, but I didn't let him swing too long.

"But you can take me to lunch on the *Times* expense account. Then I'll talk to you."

"You're the man."

"See you around, Larry."

I headed for the elevator alcove, the security man trailing behind me. I took a wide look around the newsroom but made sure my eyes never caught on anybody else's. I didn't want any good-byes. I walked along the row of glass offices and didn't bother to look in at any of the editors I had worked for. I just wanted to get out of there.

"Jack?"

I stopped and turned around. Dorothy Fowler had stepped out of the glass office I had just passed. She beckoned me back.

"Can you come in for a minute before you go?"

I hesitated and shrugged. Then handed the box to the security man.

"Be right back."

I stepped into the city editor's office and slipped off my backpack as I sat down in front of her desk. She had a sly smile on her face. She spoke in a low voice, as if she was worried that what she said might be heard in the next office down.

"I told Richard he was kidding himself. That you wouldn't take the job back. They think people are like puppets and they can play with the strings."

"You shouldn't have been so sure. I almost took it."

"I doubt that, Jack. Very much."

I thought that was a compliment. I nodded and looked behind her at the wall covered with photos and cards and newspaper clips. She had a classic headline from one of the New York tabs on the wall: "Headless Body in Topless Bar." You couldn't beat that one.

"What will you do now?"

I gave her a more expansive version of what I had told Kramer. I would write a book about my part in the Courier-McGinnis story, then I would get a long-awaited shot at publishing a novel. All the while, I would be on the masthead at velvetcoffin.com and free to tackle the investigative projects of my choosing. It wouldn't pay much but it would be journalism. I was just making the jump to the digital world.

"That all sounds great," she said. "We're really going to miss you around here. You are one of the best."

I don't take compliments like that well. I'm cynical and look for the angle. If I was that good, why did I get put on the thirty list in the first place? The answer had to be that I was good but not good enough and she was just blowing smoke. I looked away from her, as I do when someone is lying to my face, and back at the images taped to the wall.

That's when I saw it. Something that had eluded me before. But not this time. I bent forward so I could see it better and then I stood up and leaned across her desk.

"Jack, what?"

I pointed to the wall.

"Can I see that? The photo from *The Wizard of Oz*."

Fowler reached up and pulled it off the wall and handed it to me.

"It's a joke from a friend," she said. "I'm from Kansas."

"I get that," I said.

I studied the photo, zeroing in on the Scarecrow. The photo was too small for me to be completely sure.

"Can I run a search on your computer real quick?" I asked.

I was coming around her desk before she answered.

"Uh, sure, what is it that—"

"I'm not sure yet."

She got up and got out of the way. I took her seat, looked at her screen and opened up Google. The machine was running slowly.

"Come on, come on, come on."

"Jack, what is it?"

"Let me just..."

The search window finally came up and I clicked over to Google Images. I typed *Scarecrow* into the search block and let it fly.

My screen soon filled with sixteen small images of scarecrows. There were photos of the lovable character from *The Wizard of Oz* movie and color sketches from Batman comic books of a villain called the Scarecrow. There were several other photos and drawings of scarecrows from books and movies and Halloween costume catalogs. They ranged from the benign and friendly to the horrible and menacing. Some had cheerful eyes and smiles and some had their eyes and mouths stitched closed.

I spent two minutes clicking on each photo and enlarging it. I studied them and, sixteen for sixteen, they all had one thing in common. Each scarecrow's construction included a burlap bag pulled over the head to form a face. Each bag was cinched around the neck with a cord. Sometimes it was a thick rope and sometimes it was basic household clothesline. But it didn't matter. The image was consistent and it matched what I had seen in the files I had accumulated as well as the lasting image I had of Angela Cook.

I could see now that in the murders a clear plastic bag had been used to create the face of the scarecrow. No burlap, but this inconsistency with the established imagery didn't matter. The construction was the same. A bag over the head and a rope around the neck were used to create the same image.

I clicked to the next screen of images. Again the same construction. This time the images were older, going back through a century to the original illustrations in the book *The Wonderful Wizard of Oz*. And then I saw it. The illustrations were credited to William Wallace Denslow. William Denslow as in Bill Denslow, as in Denslow Data.

I felt no doubt that I had just found the signature. The secret signature that Rachel had told me would be there.

I killed the screen and stood up.

"I have to go."

I went around her desk and grabbed my backpack off the floor.

"Jack?" Fowler asked.

I headed toward the door.

"It was nice working with you, Dorothy."

The plane landed hard on the tarmac at Sky Harbor but I barely noticed. I had gotten so used to flying in the last two weeks that I didn't even bother to look out the window anymore to psychically nurse the plane to a safe touchdown.

I had not called Rachel yet. I wanted to get to Arizona first so that whatever happened with my information included my involvement. Technically, I was no longer a reporter, but I was still protecting my story.

The delay also allowed me to think more about what I had and to work out an approach. After picking up a rental and getting to Mesa, I pulled into the lot of a convenience store and went in to buy a throwaway phone. I knew Rachel was working in the bunker at Western Data. When I called her, I didn't want her seeing my name on the ID screen and then answering with it in front of Carver.

Finally ready and back in the car, I made the call and she answered after five rings.

"Hello, this is Agent Walling."

"It's me. Don't say my name."

There was a pause before she continued.

"How can I help you?"

"Are you with Carver?"

"Yes."

"Okay, I'm in Mesa and about ten minutes away. I need to meet you without anybody else in there knowing."

"I'm sorry, that's not going to be possible. What is this about?"

At least she was playing along.

"I can't tell you. I have to show you. Did you eat lunch yet?"

"Yes."

"Okay, tell them you need a latte or something you can't get out of one of their machines. Meet me at Hightower Grounds in ten minutes. Take their latte orders if you have to. Sell it and get out of there and meet me. I don't want to come near Western Data because of the cameras all over that place."

"And you can't give me any idea what this is all about?"

"It's about Carver, so don't ask questions like that. Just make the excuse and meet me. Don't tell anyone that I'm here or what you're really doing."

She didn't respond and I grew impatient.

"Rachel, will you be there or not?"

"That will be fine," she finally said. "I'll talk to you then."

She clicked off the call.

In another five minutes I was at Hightower Grounds. The place had obviously been named for the old desert observation tower that rose behind it. It looked like the tower was closed now but it was festooned on top with cell repeaters and antennas.

I went in and found the place almost empty. A couple of customers who looked like college students sat by themselves with laptops open in front of them. I went to the counter and ordered two cups of coffee and then set my computer up on a table in a corner away from the other customers.

After I picked up the two cups I had ordered, I doused mine liberally with sugar and milk and returned to my table. Through the window I checked the parking lot and saw no sign of Rachel. I sat down and took a sip of steaming coffee and connected to the Internet through the coffee shop's free WiFi.

Fifteen minutes went by. I checked messages and thought about what I would say to Rachel—if she showed up. I got the page of scarecrow images up on my screen and was ready to go. I was down to reading the receipt that had come with the coffee.

Free WiFi with every purchase!
Check us out on the net
www.hightowergrounds.com

I crumpled it and threw it toward a trash can and missed. After getting up and putting in the rebound, I opened my throwaway and was about to call Rachel again, when I finally saw her pull into the lot and park. She came in, saw me and diverted directly to my table. She was holding a piece of paper with coffee orders written down on it.

"The last time I went out for coffee I was a rookie

agent at a hostage negotiation in Baltimore," she said. "I don't do this, Jack, so this better be good."

"Don't worry, it is. I think. Why don't you just sit down?"

She did and I pushed the cup of black coffee across the table to her. She didn't touch it. She was wearing sunglasses but I could see the deep line of purple under her left eye. The swelling of her jaw was completely gone now and the split in her lip was hidden beneath her lip gloss. You had to look for it to see it. I had been wondering if it would be proper to lean over and try to hug or kiss her but took the hint from her all-business demeanor and kept my distance.

"Okay, Jack, I'm here. What are you doing here?"

"I think I found the signature. If I'm right, McGinnis was just a cover. A fall guy. The other killer is the Scarecrow. It's got to be Carver."

She stared at me for a long moment, her eyes revealing nothing through the shades. Finally, she spoke.

"So you jumped on a plane, frequent flier that you are, to come over here and tell me the man I'm working beside is also the killer I've been chasing."

"That's right."

"This better be good, Jack."

"Who's back in the bunker with Carver?"

"Two agents from the EER team, Torres and Mowry. But never mind them. Tell me what's going on."

I tried to set the stage for what I would show her on the laptop.

"First of all, I was bothered by a question. What was the plan in abducting you?"

"After seeing some of the video recovered in the bunker, I don't want to think about that."

"Sorry, wrong choice of words. I don't mean what was going to happen to you. What I mean is *why* you. Why take so big a risk to go after you? The easy answer is that it would create a large distraction from the central investigation. And that is true, but at best it would be a temporary diversion. Agents would start pouring into this place by the dozens. Pretty soon you wouldn't be able to run a stop sign without getting pulled over by the feds. Diversion over."

Rachel followed the logic and nodded in agreement.

"Okay, but what if there was another reason?" I asked. "You have two killers out there. A mentor and a student. The student tries to abduct you on his own. Why?"

"Because McGinnis was dead," Rachel said. "There was only the student."

"Okay, then if that is true, why even make the move? Why go after you? Why not get the hell out of Dodge instead? You see, it isn't adding up. At least with the way we've been looking at it. We think grabbing you was a diversionary move. But it really wasn't."

"Then what was it?"

"Well, what if McGinnis wasn't the mentor? What if he was meant to look like he was? What if he was just a fall guy and abducting you was part of a plan to secure the real mentor? To help him get away."

"What about the evidence we recovered?"

"You mean him having my book on his bookshelf and the leg braces and porno in the house? Isn't that kind of convenient?"

"That stuff wasn't left lying around the house. It was hidden and only found after an hours-long search. But never mind all of that. Yes, it could have been planted. I'm thinking more about the server in Western Data we found that was full of video evidence."

"First of all, you said he isn't identifiable on the videos. And who is to say he and Courier were the only ones with access to that server. Couldn't the evidence on there have been planted just like the stuff at the house?"

She didn't respond right away and I knew I had her thinking. Maybe she had thought all along that things were hanging too easily on McGinnis. But then she shook her head like this didn't add up either.

"It still doesn't make sense if you're claiming the mentor is Carver. He didn't try to get away. When Courier was trying to grab me, Carver was in the bunker with Torres and..."

She didn't finish. I did.

"Mowry. Yes, he was with two FBI agents."

I watched the realization come to her.

"He would have a perfect alibi because two agents would vouch for him," she finally said. "If I disappeared while he was with the EER team, he would have an alibi and the bureau would be almost certain that it was McGinnis and Courier who had grabbed me."

I nodded.

"It would not only put Carver above suspicion, it would keep him right in the middle of your investigation."

I waited only a second for her to respond. When she didn't, I pressed on.

"Think about it. How did Courier know what hotel you were in? We told Carver when he asked us during the tour. Remember? Then he told Courier. He *sent* Courier."

She shook her head.

"And last night I even said I was going back to the hotel to get room service and to go to sleep."

I spread my hands as if to say the conclusion was obvious.

"But this isn't enough, Jack. It doesn't add up to Carver being—"

"I know. But maybe this does."

I turned the computer so she could see the screen. I had the page of scarecrow images up on Google. She leaned over and looked at it first, then pulled the computer all the way over to her side of the table. She worked the keyboard and blew the images up, one by one. I didn't need to say anything.

"Denslow!" she suddenly said. "Did you see this? The original illustrator of *Wizard of Oz* was named William Denslow."

"Yeah, I saw that. That's why I'm here."

"It still doesn't connect directly to Carver."

"It doesn't matter. There's a lot of smoke here, Rachel. Carver connects to a lot of it. He had access to McGinnis and Freddy Stone. He had access to the servers. We also know he has the technical skills we've seen all through this."

Rachel was typing on my laptop while she responded.

"There is still no direct connection, Jack. This could just as easily be someone setting up Carver as it is—I just got another hit. I Googled the name Freddy Stone. Take a look at this."

She turned the laptop around so I could see the screen. On it was a Wikipedia biography of an early twentieth-century actor named Fred Stone. The bio said Stone was best known for first establishing the character of the Scarecrow in the 1902 Broadway version of *The Wizard of Oz.*

"See, it's got to be Carver. All the spokes in the wheel come to him in the center. He's making scarecrows out of the victims. It's his secret signature."

Rachel shook her head once.

"Look, we checked him out! He was clean. He's some sort of genius out of MIT."

"Clean how? You mean no arrest record? It wouldn't be the first time one of these guys operated completely beneath law enforcement radar. Ted Bundy worked at some sort of crisis hotline when he wasn't out killing women. It put him in constant contact with the police. Besides that, the geniuses are the ones you gotta watch out for, you ask me."

"But I have a vibe for these guys and I didn't pick up a thing. I had lunch with him today. He took me to McGinnis's favorite barbecue joint."

I could see self-doubt in her eyes. She hadn't seen this coming.

"Let's go get him," I said. "We confront him and make him talk. Most of these serials are proud of their work. My bet is he'll talk."

She looked up from the screen at me.

"Go get him? Jack, you're not an agent and you're not a cop. You're a reporter."

"Not anymore. I got walked out by security today with a cardboard box. I'm done as a reporter."

"What? Why?"

"It's a long story that I'll tell you later. What are we going to do about Carver?"

"I don't know, Jack."

"Well, you can't just go back there and bring him his latte."

I noticed one of the customers sitting a few tables behind Rachel turn from the screen of his laptop and look up toward the open-beamed ceiling and smile. He then raised a fist and offered up his middle finger. I followed his gaze to one of the crossbeams. There was a small black camera mounted on the beam, its lens trained on the sitting area of the coffee shop. The kid turned back and started typing on his computer.

I jumped up, leaving Rachel and moving toward him.

"Hey," I said, pointing up at the camera. "What is that? Where's it go?"

The kid crinkled his nose at my stupidity and shrugged.

"It's a live cam, man. It goes everywhere. I just got a shout from a buddy in Amsterdam who saw me."

It suddenly dawned on me. The receipt. *Free WiFi with every purchase. Check us out on the net.* I turned and looked at Rachel. The laptop, with a full-screen photo of a Scarecrow on it, was facing the camera. I turned back and looked up at the lens. Call it a premonition or call it certain knowledge, but I knew I was looking back at Carver.

"Rachel?" I said, not looking away. "Did you tell him where you were going to get coffee?"

"Yes," she said from behind me. "I said I was just going down the street."

That confirmed it. I turned and walked back to the table. I picked up the laptop and closed it.

"He's been watching us," I said. "We gotta go."

I headed out of the coffee shop and she came out right behind me.

"I'll drive," she said.

Rachel turned her rental car through the main gate and went charging up to the front door of Western Data. She was driving one-handed, working her phone with the other. She threw the car into park and we got out.

"Something's wrong," she said. "Neither of them is answering."

Rachel used a Western Data key card to unlock and enter the front door. The reception desk was empty and we quickly moved to the next door. As we entered the internal hallway, she pulled her gun out of a holster that was on her belt under her jacket.

"I don't know what's going on but he's still here," she said.

"Carver?" I asked. "How do you know that?"

"I rode with him to lunch. His car is still out there. The silver Lexus."

We took the stairs down to the octagon room and approached the mantrap leading to the bunker. Rachel hesitated before opening the door.

"What?" I whispered.

"He'll know we're coming in. Stay behind me."

She raised the gun and we squeezed in together, then

quickly moved to the second door. When we came through the other side, the control room was empty.

"This isn't right," Rachel said. "Where is everybody? And that's supposed to be open."

She pointed to the glass door that led to the server room. It was closed. I scanned the control room and saw the door to Carver's private office was ajar. I moved toward it and pushed it all the way open.

The room was empty. I stepped in and went to Carver's worktable. I put one finger down on the touch pad and the two screens came alive. On the main screen I was looking at an overhead view of the coffee shop where I had just made a case to Rachel that Carver was the Unsub.

"Rachel?"

She came in and I pointed at the screen.

"He was watching us."

She hurried back into the control room and I followed her. She moved to the center workstation, put her gun down on the desk and started working the keyboard and touch pad. The two monitors came alive and soon she had pulled up multiplex screens divided into thirty-two interior camera views of the facility. But all of the squares were black. She started flipping through several screens and found the same thing each time. All cameras were dark.

"He's killed all of the cameras," Rachel said. "What is—"

"Wait. There!"

I pointed to one camera angle surrounded by several black squares. Rachel manipulated the touch pad and brought the image up to full screen.

The camera view captured a passageway between two rows of server towers in the farm. Lying facedown on the floor were two bodies, their wrists cuffed behind their backs and their ankles bound with cable ties.

Rachel grabbed the stem microphone attached to the desk, depressed the button and almost shrieked into it.

"George! Sarah! Can you hear me?"

At the sound of Rachel's voice the figures on the screen stirred and the male raised his head. It looked like there was blood on his white shirt.

"Rachel?" he said, his voice sounding weak over an overhead speaker. "I can hear you."

"Where is he? Where's Carver, George?"

"I don't know. He was just here. He just brought us in here."

"What happened?"

"After you left he went into his office. He was in there for a little bit and when he came out, he got the drop on us. He grabbed my gun out of my briefcase. He herded us in here and put us on the floor. I tried to talk to him but he wouldn't talk."

"Sarah, where's your weapon?"

"He got that, too," Mowry called out. "I'm sorry, Rachel. We didn't see it coming."

"Not your fault. It's mine. We're going to get you out of there."

Rachel released the microphone and quickly came around the workstation, bringing her weapon with her. She went to the biometric reader and put her hand on the scanner.

"He could be in there, waiting," I warned.

"I know, but what am I going to do, leave them lying in there?"

The device completed the scan and she grabbed the handle to slide the door open. It didn't move. Her hand scan had been rejected.

Rachel looked back at the scanner.

"That makes no sense. My profile was put in yesterday."

She put her hand on the scanner and began the procedure again.

"Who put it in?" I asked.

She looked back at me and didn't need to answer for me to know it had been Carver.

"Who else can open that door?" I asked.

"Nobody who's on this side. It was me, Mowry and Torres."

"What about employees here?"

She stepped away from the scanner and tried the door again. It didn't budge.

"They're on a skeleton staff upstairs and there's nobody with authorization for the farm. We're screwed! We can't get—"

"Rachel!"

I pointed at the screen. Carver had suddenly stepped into the view of the one working camera in the server room. He stood in front of the two agents on the floor, hands in the pockets of his lab coat, and looking directly up at the camera.

Rachel quickly came around to see the screen.

"What's he doing?" she asked.

I didn't need to answer because it became clear that Carver was pulling a box of cigarettes and a throwaway lighter from his pockets. In one of those moments when the mind delivers useless information I realized they were probably the cigarettes missing from Freddy Stone's/Marc Courier's box of belongings. As we watched, Carver calmly drew a cigarette from the box and put it in his mouth.

Rachel quickly pulled over the microphone.

"Wesley? What's going on?"

Carver was raising the lighter to the end of the cigarette but stopped when he heard the question. He looked back up at the camera.

"You can dispense with the niceties, Agent Walling. We're at the end of the dance now."

"What are you doing?" she said more forcefully.

"You know what I'm doing," Carver said. "I'm ending it. I'd rather not spend the rest of my days chased like an animal and then put in a cage. Being put on display, trotted out for interviews with bureau shrinks and profilers hoping to learn all the dark secrets in the universe. I think I would find that to be a fate worse than death, Agent Walling."

He raised the lighter again.

"Don't, Wesley! At least let Agents Mowry and Torres go. They did nothing to hurt you."

"That's not the point, is it? The world hurt me, Rachel, and that's enough. I'm sure you've studied the psychology before."

Rachel took her hand off the transmit button and quickly turned to me.

"Get on the computer. Shut down the VESDA system."

"No, you do it! I don't know the first thing about—"

"Is Jack there with you?" Carver asked.

I hand-signaled Rachel to trade places with me. I moved to the microphone while she dropped into a seat and went to work on the computer. I depressed the button and spoke to the man who murdered Angela Cook.

"I'm here, Carver. This is not how this should end."

"No, Jack, it's the only end. You have slain another giant. You're the hero of the hour."

"No, not yet. I want to tell your story...Wesley. Let me explain it to the world."

On the screen, Carver shook his head.

"Some things can't be explained. Some stories are too dark to be told."

He flicked the lighter and the flame came up. He started to light the cigarette.

"Carver, no! Those are innocent people in there!"

Carver inhaled deeply, held it, and then tilted his head back and exhaled a stream of smoke toward the ceiling. I was sure he had positioned himself under one of the infrared smoke detectors.

"No one is innocent, Jack," he said. "You should know that."

He drew in more smoke and spoke almost casually, gesturing with the hand holding the cigarette, a small trail of blue smoke following it in the air.

"I know Agent Walling and you are trying to shut

down the system but that isn't going to work. I took the liberty of resetting it. Only I have access now. And the exhaust component that takes the carbon dioxide out of the room one minute after dispersal has been checked off for maintenance. I wanted to make sure there would be no mistakes. And no survivors."

Carver exhaled, sending another jet of smoke toward the ceiling. I looked over at Rachel. Her fingers were racing across the keyboard but she was shaking her head.

"I can't do it," she said. "He changed all the authorization codes. I can't get into—"

The blast of an alarm horn filled the control room. The system had been tripped. A red band two inches thick crossed every screen in the control room. An electronic voice, female and calm, read the words crossing on the band aloud.

"*Attention, the VESDA fire suppression system has been activated. All personnel must exit the server room. The VESDA fire suppression system will engage in one minute.*"

Rachel ran both hands through her hair and stared helplessly at the screen in front of her. Carver was blowing another round of smoke toward the ceiling. There was a look of calm resignation on his face.

"Rachel!" Mowry called from behind him. "Get us out of here!"

Carver looked back at his captives and shook his head.

"It's over," he said. "This is the end."

Just then I was jolted by a second blast of the warning horn.

"Attention, the VESDA fire suppression system has been activated. All personnel must exit the server room. The VESDA fire suppression system will engage in forty-five seconds."

Rachel stood up and grabbed her gun off the desk.

"Get down, Jack!"

"Rachel, no, it's bulletproof!"

"According to him."

She took aim with a two-handed grip and fired three quick rounds at the window directly in front of her. The explosions were deafening. But the bullets barely impacted the glass and ricocheted wildly in the control room.

"Rachel, no!"

"Stay down!"

She fired two more bullets into the glass door and got the same negative result. One of the ricocheting slugs took out one of the screens in front of me, the image of Carver disappearing as it went black.

Rachel slowly lowered her gun. As if to accentuate her defeat, the warning horn blasted again.

"Attention, the VESDA fire suppression system has been activated. All personnel must exit the server room. The VESDA fire suppression system will engage in thirty seconds."

I looked out through the windows into the server room. Black pipes ran along the ceiling in a grid pattern and then down the back wall to the row of red CO_2 canisters. The system was about to go. It would extinguish three lives but there was no fire in the server room.

"Rachel, there must be something we can do."

"What, Jack? I tried. There is nothing left!"

She slammed her gun down on a workstation and slid into the chair. I came over, put my hands on the desktop and leaned over her.

"You have to keep trying! There's got to be a back door to the system. These guys always put in back—"

I stopped and looked out into the server room as I realized something. And the horn blasted again, but this time I barely heard it.

"Attention, the VESDA fire suppression system has been activated. All personnel must exit the server room. The VESDA fire suppression system will engage in fifteen seconds."

Carver was nowhere to be seen through the windows. He had chosen an aisle between two rows of towers out of view from the control room. Was this because of the location of the smoke detector or for some other reason?

I looked over at the undamaged screen in front of Rachel. It showed a multiplex cut of thirty-two cameras that had been turned dark by Carver. I hadn't thought about why until now.

All in a moment the atoms smashed together again. Everything became clearer. Not just what I saw in front of me but what I had seen before—Mizzou out back smoking after I had seen him go into the server room. I had a new idea. The right idea.

"Rachel—"

The horn blast came loud and long this time. Rachel stood up and stared at the glass as the CO_2 system engaged. A white gas exploded out of the pipes crossing the ceiling of the server room. Within seconds the windows were fogged and useless. The high-velocity discharge created a high-pitched whistle that came loud and clear through the thick glass.

"Rachel!" I yelled. "Give me your key. I'm going after Carver."

She turned and looked at me.

"What are you talking about?"

"He's not killing himself! He's got that breather and there's got to be a back door!"

The whistling stopped and we both turned back to the windows. It was a complete whiteout in the server room but the CO_2 delivery had stopped.

"Give me the key, Rachel."

She looked at me.

"I should go."

"No, you need to call for backup and medical emergency. Then work the computer. Find the back door."

There wasn't time to think and consider things. People were dying. We both knew it. She pulled the key out of her pocket and gave it to me. I turned to go.

"Wait! Take this."

I turned back and she handed me her gun. I took it without hesitation, then headed into the mantrap.

Rachel's gun felt heavier in my hand than I remembered my own gun ever feeling. As I moved through the mantrap, I raised it, checked the action and sighted down its barrel. I was only a once-a-year-at-the-range type of shooter but I knew I would be ready to use the weapon if necessary. I went through the next door and entered the octagon with the muzzle up. There was no one there.

I quickly crossed the room to the door on the opposite side. I knew from the website tour that this led to the large rooms that housed the power and cooling systems for the facility. The workshop where Carver and his techs built the server towers was back here, too. My guess was that there would be a second stairwell also.

I moved into the plant facilities room first. It was a wide space with large equipment. An air-conditioning system the size of a Winnebago sat in the center of the room connected to numerous overhead ducts and cables. Past this were backup systems and generators. I ran to a door on the far left side and used Rachel's key card to open it.

I stepped into a long and narrow equipment room. There was a second door at the other end and my sense of the building's plan told me it would lead to the server room.

Moving quickly to it, I saw that there was another biometric hand scanner mounted to the left of the door. Above it was a case holding the emergency breathing devices. It had to be a back door to the server room.

There was no way to tell whether Carver had already made his escape. But I had no time to wait to see if he would come through. I turned and headed back. I quickly moved through the plant facilities room again until I reached a set of double doors on the far side.

Holding the gun up and ready, I opened one of the doors with the key card and stepped into the workshop. This was another large room with tool benches lining the right and left walls and a work space in the center, where one of the black server towers was in midconstruction. The framework and sidings were complete but the interior shelves for servers had not been installed.

Beyond the server tower I saw a circular stairway leading up to the surface. This had to be the way up to the back door and the smokers' bench.

I quickly moved around the tower and headed for the stairs.

"Hello, Jack."

Just as I heard my name, I felt the muzzle of the gun on the back of my neck. I hadn't even seen Carver. He had stepped out from behind the server tower as I had passed.

"A cynical reporter. I should've known that you wouldn't buy my suicide."

His free hand grabbed hold of my collar from the back and the gun remained pressed against my skin.

"You can drop the gun now."

I dropped the weapon and it made a loud clatter on the concrete floor.

"I take it that was Agent Walling's, yes? So why don't we go back and pay her a visit? And we'll end this thing right now. Or, who knows, maybe I'll just end it for you and take her with me. I think I'd like to spend some time with Agent—"

I heard an impact of heavy object on flesh and bone and Carver fell into my back and then dropped to the floor. I turned and there was Rachel, holding an industrial-size wrench she had taken off the workbench.

"Rachel! What are—"

"He left Mowry's key card on her workstation. I followed you out. Come on. Let's get him back to the control room."

"What are you talking about?"

"His hand. He can open the server room."

We bent down to Carver, who was moaning and moving slowly on the concrete floor. Rachel took her weapon and the one Carver was holding. I saw a second gun in his waistband and grabbed it. I secured it in my own waistband and then helped Rachel drag Carver to his feet.

"The back door is closer," I said. "And there are breathers there."

"Lead the way. Hurry!"

We quickly walked, half carried Carver through the

facilities room and into the narrow equipment room beyond. The whole way, he moaned and uttered words I couldn't understand. He was tall but thin and his weight was not overbearing.

"Jack, that was good, figuring out the back door. I just hope we're not too late."

I had no idea how much time had passed but was thinking in terms of its being seconds not minutes. I didn't respond to Rachel but believed we had a good chance to get to her fellow agents in time. When we reached the back door of the server room, I took on Carver's weight and started to turn him so Rachel would be able to put his hand up on the scanner.

At that moment, I felt Carver's body stiffen. He was ready for me. He grabbed my hand and pivoted, letting my momentum carry me off balance. My shoulder slammed into the door as Carver dropped one hand and went for the gun in my waistband. I grabbed at his wrist but was too late. His right hand closed around the gun. I was between him and Rachel and I suddenly realized that she couldn't see the gun and that Carver was going to kill us both.

"*Gun!*" I yelled.

There was a sudden sharp explosion next to my ear and Carver's hands fell away from me and he slumped to the floor. A spray of blood hit me as he fell.

I stepped back and doubled over, holding my ear. The ringing was as loud as a passing train. I turned and looked up to see Rachel still holding her gun up in firing position.

"Jack, you okay?"

"Yeah, fine!"

"Quick, grab him! Before we lose the pulse."

I moved behind Carver so I could get my arms underneath his shoulders and lift him up. Even with Rachel helping, it was a struggle. But we managed to get him upright and then I held him under the arms while she extended his right hand onto the reader.

There was a metal snap as the door's lock disengaged and Rachel pushed it open.

I dropped Carver on the threshold, keeping the door open to let air in. I opened the case and grabbed the breathers. There were only two.

"Here!"

I gave one to Rachel as we entered the farm. The mist in the server room was dissipating. Visibility was about six feet. Rachel and I put on the breathers and opened the airways, but Rachel kept pulling hers off her mouth in order to call out her fellow agents' names.

She got no responses. We moved down a central corridor between two lines of servers and were lucky as we came upon Torres and Mowry almost right away. Carver had put them near the back door so he would be able to escape quickly.

Rachel crouched down next to the agents and tried to shake them awake. Neither was responsive. She tore off her breather and put it into Torres's mouth. I took mine off and put it in Mowry's.

"You take him, I'll take her!" she yelled.

We each grabbed one of the agents under the arms

and dragged them back toward the door we had entered from. My guy was light and easy to move and I got a good lead on Rachel. But I started running out of steam halfway there. I needed oxygen myself.

The closer we got to the open door, the more air I began to get into my lungs. Finally I reached the door and dragged Torres over Carver's body and into the equipment room. The bumpy landing seemed to jump-start Torres. He started coughing and coming to even before I put him down.

Rachel came in behind me with Mowry.

"I don't think she's breathing!"

Rachel pulled the breather out of Mowry's mouth and started CPR procedures.

"Jack, how is he?" she asked without taking her focus off of Mowry.

"He's good. He's breathing."

I moved to Rachel's side as she conducted mouth-to-mouth. I wasn't sure how I could help but in a few moments Mowry convulsed and started coughing. She turned on her side and brought her legs up into the fetal position.

"It's okay, Sarah," Rachel said. "You're all right. You made it. You're safe."

She gently patted Mowry's shoulder and I heard the agent manage to cough out a thank-you and then ask about her partner.

"He'll be fine," Rachel said.

I moved to the nearby wall and sat with my back against it. I was spent. My eyes drifted to the body of

Carver sprawled on the floor near the door. I could see both entry and exit wounds. The bullet had strafed across his frontal lobes. He had not moved since he had fallen but after a while I thought I could see the slight tic of a pulse on his neck just below the ear.

Exhausted, Rachel moved over and slid down the wall next to me.

"Backup's coming. I should probably go up and wait for them so I can show them the way down here."

"Catch your breath first. Are you okay?"

She nodded yes but she was still breathing heavily. So was I. I watched her eyes and saw them focus on Carver.

"It's too bad, you know?"

"What is?"

"That with both Courier and Carver gone, the secrets died with them. Everybody's dead and we've got nothing, no clue to what made them do what they did."

I shook my head slowly.

"I got news for you. I think the Scarecrow's still alive."

NINETEEN: Bakersfield

t has been six weeks since the events that took place in Mesa. Still, those events remain vivid in my memory and imagination.

I am writing now. Every day. I usually find a crowded coffee shop in the afternoon in which to set up my laptop. I have learned that I cannot write in authorial silence. I must fight distraction and white noise. I must come as close as possible to the experience of writing in a crowded newsroom. I seem to need the din of background conversations, ringing phones and keyboards clacking to feel comfortable and at home. Of course, it is an artificial replacement for the real thing. There is no camaraderie in a coffee shop. No sense of "us against the world." These are things I am sure I will miss about the newsroom forever.

I reserve the mornings for research on my subject. Wesley John Carver remains largely an enigma but I am getting closer to who and what he is. As he lies in the twilight world of a coma in the hospital ward of the Metropolitan Correctional Center in Los Angeles, I close in on him.

Some of what I know has come from the FBI, which continues to work the case in Arizona, Nevada and

California. But most of it I have gotten on my own and from several sources.

Carver was a killer of high intelligence and clear-eyed self-understanding. He was clever and calculating, and able to manipulate people by tapping into their deepest and darkest desires. He lurked on websites and chat rooms, identified potential disciples and victims and then followed them home, tracing them through the labyrinthine portals of the digital world. He then made casual contact in the real world. He used them or killed them or both.

He had been doing it for years—well before Western Data and the trunk murders had caught anyone's eye. Marc Courier had only been the latest in a long line of followers.

Still, the record of grim deeds Carver committed cannot overshadow the motivations behind it. That is what my editor in New York tells me each time we talk. I must be able to tell more than what happened. I must tell why. It's breadth and depth again—the ol' B and D—and I am used to that.

What I have learned so far is this: Carver grew up an only child without ever knowing who his father was. His mother worked the strip club circuit, which kept the two of them on the road from Los Angeles to San Francisco to New York and back during his younger years. He was what they called a dressing-room baby, held backstage in the arms of housemothers, costumers and other dancers while his own mother worked in the spotlights out front. She was a featured act, performing under the stage name

"L.A. Woman" and dancing exclusively to the music of the signature Los Angeles rock band of the era, The Doors.

There are hints that Carver was abused sexually by more than one of the people he was left with in dressing rooms and that on many nights he slept in the same hotel room where his mother entertained men who had paid to be with her.

Most notable in all of this was that his mother had developed an unnamed but degenerative bone disease that threatened her livelihood. When not onstage, and away from the world in which she worked, she often wore leg braces prescribed to provide support for weakening ligaments and joints. Young Wesley was often called upon to help secure the leather straps around his mother's legs.

It is a dismal and depressing portrait, but not one that adds up to multiple murder. The secret ingredients of that carcinogen have not yet been revealed—by me or the FBI. What made the horrors of Carver's upbringing metastasize into the cancer of his adulthood remains to be learned. But Rachel often reminds me of her favorite line from a Coen brothers film: *Nobody knows anybody, not that well.* She tells me no one will ever know what sent Wesley Carver down the path he took.

I am in Bakersfield today. For the fourth day in a row I will spend the morning with Karen Carver and she will tell me her memories of her son. She has not seen or talked to him since the day he left as an eighteen-year-old for MIT, but her knowledge of his early life and her willingness to share it with me bring me closer to answering the question of why.

Tomorrow I will drive home, my conversations with the now wheelchair-bound mother of the killer completed for the time being. There is other research to complete and a looming deadline for my book. More important than all of that, it has been five days since I have seen Rachel and the separation has grown difficult to take. I've become a believer in the single-bullet theory and need to return home.

Meantime, the prognosis for Wesley Carver is not good. The physicians who tend to him believe he will never regain consciousness, that the damage from Rachel's bullet has left him in permanent darkness. He mumbles and sometimes hums in his prison bed but that is all there will ever be.

There are some who have called for his prosecution, conviction and execution in such a state. And others have called this idea barbaric, no matter how heinous the crimes he is accused of committing. At a recent rally outside the corrections center in downtown L.A., one crowd marched with signs that said PULL THE PLUG ON MURDER, while the signs of the competing group said ALL LIFE IS SACRED.

I wonder what Carver would think of such a thing. Would he be amused? Would he feel comforted?

All I know is that I can't erase the image of Angela Cook slipping into darkness, her eyes open and afraid. I believe that Wesley Carver has already been convicted in some sort of court of higher reason. And he is serving a life sentence without the possibility of parole.

TWENTY: The Scarecrow

Carver waited in darkness. His mind was a jumble of thoughts. So many he was not sure which were true memories and which were made up.

They filtered through his mind like smoke. Nothing that stayed. Nothing that he could grab on to.

He heard the voices on occasion but could not make them out clearly. They were like muffled conversations all around him. Nobody was talking to him. They were talking around him. When he asked questions, nobody answered.

He still had his music and it was the only thing that saved him. He heard it and tried to sing along but often he had no voice and had to just hum. He kept falling behind.

This is the end ... beautiful friend, the end ...

He believed it was his father's voice that sang to him. The father he never knew, coming to him in the grace of music.

Like in church.

He felt a terrible amount of pain. Like an ax embedded in the center of his forehead. Unrelenting pain. He waited for someone to stop it. To save him from it. But no one came. No one heard him.

He waited in darkness.

Acknowledgments

The author gratefully acknowledges the help of many in the research, writing and editing of this book. They include Asya Muchnick, Bill Massey, Daniel Daly, Dennis "Cisco" Wojciechowski, James Swain, Jane Davis, Jeff Pollack, Linda Connelly, Mary Mercer, Pamela Marshall, Pamela Wilson, Philip Spitzer, Roger Mills, Scott B. Anderson, Shannon Byrne, Sue Gissal and Terrell Lee Lankford.

Many thanks also to Gregory Hoblit, Greg Stout, Jeff Pollack, John Houghton, Mike Roche, Rick Jackson and Tim Marcia.

LAPD DETECTIVE
RENÉE BALLARD TEAMS
UP WITH HARRY BOSCH
IN THE NEW NOVEL
BY MICHAEL CONNELLY

PLEASE TURN THE PAGE FOR A
PREVIEW OF

DARK SACRED NIGHT

AVAILABLE OCTOBER 2018

BALLARD

1

The patrol officers had left the front door open. They thought they were doing her a favor, airing the place out. But that was a violation of crime scene protocol regarding evidence containment. Bugs could go in and out. There were extenuating circumstances, though. The report that Ballard had gotten from the watch lieutenant was that the body was two to three days old in a closed house with no air conditioning and, in his words, ripe as a bag of skunks.

There were two black-and-whites parked along the curb in front of Ballard. Three blue suits were standing between them, waiting for her. Ballard didn't really expect them to have stayed inside with the body.

Up above, an airship circled at three hundred feet, holding its beam on the street. It looked like a leash of light, tethering the circling craft, keeping it from flying away.

Ballard killed the engine but sat in her city ride for a moment. She had parked in front of the gap between two houses and could look out at the lights of the city spreading in a vast carpet below. Not many people realized that

Hollywood Boulevard wound up into the mountains, narrow and tight, to where it was strictly residential and far in all ways from the glitz and grime of the Hollywood Boulevard tourist mecca, where visitors posed with costumed superheroes and sidewalk stars. Up here it was money and power and Ballard knew that a murder in the hills always brought out the department's big guns. She was just babysitting. She would not have this case for long. It would go to West Bureau or possibly even Robbery-Homicide Division downtown.

She looked away from the view and tapped the overhead light so she could see her notebook. She had just come from her day's first call out, a routine break-in off Melrose, and had her notes for the report she would write once she got back to Hollywood Division. She flipped to a fresh page and wrote the time—1:47 a.m.—and the address. She then turned the light off and got out, leaving the blue flashers on. She went to the trunk, where she kept her crime scene kit.

It was a Tuesday morning, her third shift of a week running solo, and Ballard knew she would need to get at least one more wear out of her suit. That meant not fouling it with the stink of decomp. At the open trunk she slipped off her jacket, folded it carefully, and placed it in one of the empty cardboard evidence boxes. She then removed her crime scene overalls from a plastic bag and pulled them on over her boots, slacks, and blouse. She zipped them up to her chin and then, placing one boot and then the other up on the bumper, tightened the Velcro cuffs around her ankles. After she did the same around her wrists, her clothes were hermetically sealed.

She got gloves and a breathing mask out of the kit and, leaving the trunk open, walked up to join the three uniformed officers. As she approached, she recognized Sergeant Stan Dvorek, the area boss, and two officers whose longevity on the graveyard shift got them the cushy and slow Hollywood Hills beat.

Dvorek was leaning against one of the car's trunk with his arms folded in front of his chest. He was known as the Relic. Anybody who actually liked being on the midnight shift and lasted significant years on it ended up with a nickname. Dvorek was the current record holder, celebrating his tenth year on the late show just a month before. The officers with him, Anthony Anzelone and Dwight Doucette, were Caspar and Deuce. Ballard, with little more than two years on graveyard, had no nickname bestowed upon her yet. At least none that she knew about.

"Fellas," Ballard said.

"Whoa, Sally Ride," Dvorek said. "When's the shuttle taking off?"

Ballard spread her arms to display herself. She knew the overalls were baggy and looked like a space suit. She thought maybe she had just been christened with a nickname.

"That would be never," she said. "So whadda we got that chased you out of the house?"

"It's bad in there," said Anzelone.

"It's been cooking," Doucette added.

The Relic pushed off the trunk of his car and got serious.

"Female white, fifties, looks like blunt-force trauma and facial lacerations," he said. "Looks like somebody worked her over pretty good. Domicile in disarray. Could've been a break-in."

"Sexual assault?" Ballard asked.

"Her nightgown's pulled up. She's exposed."

"Okay, I'm going in. Which one of you brave lads wants to walk me through it?"

There were no immediate volunteers.

"Deuce, you're low man," Dvorek said.

"Shit," said Doucette.

He pulled a blue bandanna up from around his neck and over his mouth and nose.

"You look like a fucking Crip," Anzelone said.

"Why, because I'm black?" Doucette asked.

"Because you're wearing a fucking blue bandanna," Anzelone said. "If it was red, I'd say you look like a fucking Blood."

"Just show her," Dvorek said. "I really don't want to be here all night."

Doucette broke off the banter and headed toward the open door of the house. Ballard followed.

"How'd we get this thing so late, anyway?" she asked.

"Next-door neighbor got a call from the victim's niece back in New York," Doucette said. "Neighbor has a key and the niece asked him to check because the lady wasn't responding to social media or cell calls for a few days. The neighbor opens the door, gets hit with the funk, and calls us."

"At one o'clock in the morning?"

"No, much earlier. But see, he reported it as a suspicious odor but didn't go in and confirm the DB. So we are not talking about a hot shot. PM watch was cranking last night, so it got put on the back burner and then passed on to us. We got it in roll call and came by here as soon as we could."

Ballard nodded. The buck had been passed shift to shift because nobody wants to work a possible body case that has been cooking in a closed house.

"Where's the neighbor now?" Ballard asked.

"Back home," Doucette said. "Probably taking a shower and sticking Vicks Vapo up his nose. He's never going to be the same again."

"We gotta get his prints to exclude him, even if he says he didn't go in."

"Roger that. I'll get the print car up here."

Ballard followed Doucette over the threshold and into the house. The breathing mask was almost useless. The putrid odor of death hit her strongly, even though she was breathing through her mouth.

She looked around. The house was cantilevered out over the hillside, making the view through the floor-to-ceiling glass wall a stunning sheath of twinkling lights. Even at this hour the city seemed alive and pulsing with light and grand possibilities.

"What about lights?" Ballard asked.

"Nothing was on in here when we came in," said Doucette.

Ballard noted the answer. No lights on could mean that the intrusion occurred during the daytime or late at night, after the homeowner had shut things down for the night. She knew that most home invasions were night-time capers.

Doucette, who was also wearing gloves, hit a wall switch by the door and turned on a line of ceiling lights. The interior was an open-loft design, taking advantage of the view from any spot in the living room, dining room, kitchen. The staggering view was counterbalanced on the rear wall by three large paintings that were part of a series depicting a woman's red lips.

Ballard noticed broken glass on the floor near the kitchen island but she saw no shattered windows.

"Any sign of a break-in?" she asked.

"Not that we saw," Doucette said. "There's broken shit all over the place but no broken windows, no obvious point of entry that we found."

"Okay."

"The body's down here."

He moved into a hallway off the living room and held his hand over the bandanna and his mouth as a second brace of protection against the intensifying odor.

Ballard followed. The house was a single-level contemporary. She guessed it was built in the fifties, when one level was enough. Nowadays anything built in the hills was multilevel and built to the maximum extent of code.

They passed open doorways to a bedroom and a bathroom, then entered a master bedroom that was in disarray with a lamp on the floor, its shade dented and bulb shattered. Clothes were strewn haphazardly over the bed, and a long-stemmed glass that had contained what looked like red wine was snapped in two on the white rug, its contents spread in a splash stain.

"Here you go," Doucette said.

He pointed through the open door of the bathroom and then stepped back to allow Ballard in first.

Ballard stood in the doorway but did not enter the bathroom. The victim was faceup on the floor. She was a large woman with her arms and legs spread wide. Her eyes were open, her lower lip torn, and her upper right cheek gashed open, exposing grayish pink tissue. A halo of dried blood from an unseen scalp wound surrounded her head on the white tile squares.

A flannel nightgown with hummingbirds on it was pulled up over the hips and bunched above the abdomen and around the breasts. Her feet were bare and spread three feet apart. There was no visual injury to the genitalia.

Ballard could see herself in a floor-to-ceiling mirror on the opposite wall of the room. She squatted down in the doorway and kept her hands on her thighs. She studied the tiled floor for footprints, blood, and other evidence. Besides the blood that had pooled and dried around the dead woman's head, she noted an intermittent ribbon of small blood smears on the floor between the body and the bedroom.

"Deuce, go close the front door," she said.

"Uh, okay," Doucette said. "Any reason?"

"Just do it. Then check the kitchen."

"For what?"

"A water bowl on the floor. Go."

Doucette left and Ballard heard his heavy footsteps move back up the hallway. She stood and entered the room, came up close on the body, and squatted again. She leaned down, putting a hand on the floor for balance, in an attempt to see the scalp wound. The dead woman's hair was too thick and curly for her to locate it.

Ballard looked around the room. The bathtub was surrounded by a marble sill holding multiple jars of various bath salts and candles burned down to nothing. There was a folded towel on the sill as well. Ballard shifted so she could see into the tub. It was empty but the drain stopper was down. It was the kind with a rubber lip that creates a seal. Ballard reached over, turned on the cold water for a few seconds and then turned it off.

She stood up and stepped over to the edge of the tub. She had put in enough water to surround the drain. She waited and watched.

"There's a water bowl."

Ballard turned. Doucette was back.

"Did you close the front door?" she asked.

"It's closed," Doucette said.

"Okay, look around. I think it's a cat. Something small. You'll have to call animal control."

"What?"

Ballard pointed down at the dead woman.

"An animal did that. A hungry one. They start with the soft tissue."

"Are you fucking kidding me?"

Ballard looked back into the tub. Half of the water she had put into the tub was gone. The drain's rubber seal had a slow leak.

"There's no bleeding with the facial injuries," she said. "That happened postmortem. The head wound on the back of the head is what killed her."

Doucette nodded.

"Someone came up and cracked her head from behind," he said.

"No," Ballard said. "It's an accidental death."

"How?" Doucette asked.

Ballard pointed to the array of items on the bathtub sill.

"Based on decomp, I'd say it happened three nights ago," she said. "She turns out the lights in the house to get ready for bed. Probably that lamp on the floor in the bedroom was the one she left on. She comes in here, fills the tub, lights her candles, gets her towel ready. The hot water steams the tiles and she slips, maybe when she remembered she left her glass of wine on the bed table. Or when she started pulling up the nightgown so she could get in the tub."

"What about the lamp and the spilled wine?" Doucette asked.

"The cat."

"So, you just stood here and figured all this out?"

Ballard ignored the question.

"She was carrying a lot of weight," she said. "Maybe

a sudden redirection as she was getting undressed—'Oh, I forgot my wine'—causes her to slip and she cracks her skull on the lip of the tub. She's dead, the candles burn out, the water slowly leaks down the drain."

This explanation only brought silence from Doucette. Ballard looked down at the dead woman's ravaged face.

"The second day or so, the cat got hungry," Ballard concluded. "It went a little nuts, then it found her."

"Jesus," Doucette said.

"Get your partner in here, Deuce. Find the cat."

"But wait a minute. If she was about to take a bath, why's she already in a nightgown?"

Ballard gestured to the mirror.

"She was obese," Ballard said. "She probably didn't like looking at herself naked in the mirror. So she comes home from work or her day, gets into nightclothes, gets her wine, maybe watches TV, who knows? She stayed dressed until it was time to get in the tub."

Ballard turned to go past Doucette and step out of the room.

"Find the cat," she said.

2

By three a.m. Ballard had cleared the scene of the death investigation and was back at Hollywood Division, working in a cubicle in the detective bureau. That vast room, which housed the workstations of forty-eight detectives by day, was deserted after midnight and Ballard always had her pick of the place. She chose a desk in the far corner, away from spillover noise and radio chatter from the watch commander's office down the front hallway. At five-seven she could sit down and disappear behind the computer screen and the half walls of the workstation like a soldier in a foxhole. She could focus and get her report writing done.

She had already completed the report on the home break-in that she had rolled on earlier in the night and was now ready to type up the accidental death report on the bathtub case. She was working alone, her partner, John Jenkins, on bereavement leave. There were no replacements for detectives who worked the late show. Ballard was halfway through a Tuesday night of at least a week going solo. It all depended on when Jenkins came back. His wife had endured a long, painful death from cancer. It tore him up and Ballard told him to take all the time he needed.

She opened her notebook to the page containing the details she had written about the second investigation and then opened up a blank incident report on her screen. Before beginning she dipped her chin and pulled the collar of her blouse up to her nose. She thought she picked up the slight odor of decomposition and death but couldn't be sure if it had permeated her clothes or was simply an olfactory memory.

While her head was down, she heard the metal-on-metal bang of a file drawer being closed. She looked up over the workstation divider to the far side of the bureau, where four-drawer file cabinets ran the length of the room. Every pair of detectives was assigned a four-drawer stack for storage.

But the man Ballard saw now opening another drawer to check its contents was not a detective she recognized, and she knew them all from once-a-month squad meetings that drew her to the station during daylight hours. The man who was seemingly checking file drawers at random had gray hair and a mustache. Ballard instinctively knew he didn't belong. She scanned the entire squad room to see if there was anybody else. The rest of the place was deserted.

The man opened and closed yet another drawer. Ballard used the sound to cover getting up from her chair. She squatted down and used the row of work cubicles as a blind as she moved to the central aisle, which would allow her to come up behind the intruder without being seen.

She had left her suit jacket in the cardboard box in the trunk of her car. This gave her unfettered access to the Glock holstered on her hip. She put her hand on the grips of the weapon and came to a stop ten feet behind the man.

"Hey, what's up?" she asked.

The man froze. He slowly raised his hands out of the open file drawer he was looking through and held them so she could see them.

"That's good," Ballard said. "Now, you mind telling me who you are and what you're doing?"

"Name's Bosch," he said. "I came in to see somebody."

"What, somebody hiding in the files?"

"No, I used to work here. I know Money up front. He told me I could wait in the break room while they called the guy in. I sort of started wandering. My bad."

Ballard came down from high alert and took her hand off her gun. She knew the name Bosch, and the fact that he knew the watch commander's nickname gave her some ease as well. But she still was suspicious.

"You kept a key to your old cabinet?" she asked.

"No," Bosch said. "It was unlocked."

Ballard could see the push-in lock at the top of the cabinet was indeed extended in unlocked position. Most detectives kept their files locked.

"You got some ID?" she asked.

"Sure," Bosch said. "But just so you know, I'm a police

officer. I have a gun on my left hip and you're going to see it when I reach back for my ID. Okay?"

Ballard brought her hand back up to her hip.

"Thanks for the heads-up," she said. "Tell you what, forget the ID for now. Why don't we secure the weapon first? Then we'll—"

"There you are, Harry."

Ballard looked to her right and saw Lieutenant Munroe, the watch commander, entering the squad room. He saw Ballard and read her stance.

"Ballard, what's going on?" he asked.

"He came in here and was going through the files," Ballard said. "I didn't know who he was."

"You can stand down," Munroe said. "He's good people—used to work homicide here. Back when we had a homicide table."

Munroe turned his gaze to Bosch.

"Harry, what the hell were you doing?" he asked.

Bosch shrugged.

"Just checking my old drawers," he said. "Sort of got tired of waiting."

"Well, Dvorek's in the house and waiting in the writing room," Munroe said. "And I need you to talk to him now. I don't like taking him off the street. He's one of my best guys and I want him back out there."

"Got it," Bosch said.

Bosch followed Munroe to the front hallway, which led to the watch office and the report-writing room, where Dvorek was waiting. Bosch looked back at Ballard as he went and nodded. Ballard just watched him go.

After they were gone, Ballard stepped over to the file drawer Bosch had last been looking in. There was a business card taped to it. That's what everybody did to mark their drawers.

DETECTIVE CESAR RIVERA
HOLLYWOOD SEX CRIMES UNIT

She checked the contents of the drawer. It was only half full and the files had fallen forward, probably while Bosch was leafing through them. She pushed them back up so they were standing and looked at what Rivera had written on the tabs. They were mostly victim names and case numbers. Others were marked with the main streets in Hollywood Division, probably containing miscellaneous reports of suspicious activities or persons.

She closed the drawer and checked the two above it, remembering that she had initially heard Bosch open at least three drawers.

These drawers were like the first, containing case files primarily listed by victim name, specific sex crime, and case number. At the front of the top drawer she noticed a paper clip that had been bent and twisted. She studied the push-button lock on the top corner of the cabinet. It was a basic lock and she knew it could easily have been picked with a paper clip. Security of the files themselves were not a priority because they were contained in a high-security police station.

Ballard closed the drawers and locked the cabinet and went back to the desk she had been using. She remained intrigued by Bosch's middle-of-the-night visit. She knew he had used the paper clip to unlock the file cabinet and that indicated he had more than a casual interest in the contents of its drawers. His nostalgic story about checking out his old file drawers had been a lie.

She picked up the coffee cup on the desk and walked down the hall to the first-floor break room to replenish it. The room was empty as usual. She refilled and carried the cup down the hallway to the watch office. Lieutenant Munroe was at his desk, looking at a deployment screen that showed a map of the division and the GPS markers for the patrol units out there. He didn't hear Ballard until she came up behind him.

"Quiet?" she asked.

"For the moment," Munroe said.

Ballard pointed to a cluster of three GPS locators in the same spot.

"What's happening there?"

"That's the Mariscos Reyes truck. I've got three units ten-seven there."

It was a lunch break at a food truck at Sunset and Western. It made Ballard realize she had not taken a food break and was getting hungry. She wasn't sure she wanted seafood, however.

"So, what did Bosch want?"

"He wanted to talk to the Relic about a body he found nine years ago. I take it Bosch is looking into it."

"He said he's still a cop. Not for us, right?"

"Nah, he's a reserve up in the Valley for San Fernando PD."

"What's San Fernando got to do with a murder down here?"

"I don't know, Ballard. You shoulda asked him while he was here. He's gone now."

"That was quick."

"Because the Relic couldn't remember shit."

"Is Dvorek back out there?"

Munroe pointed to the three-car cluster on the screen.

"He's back out, but code seven at the moment."

"I was thinking about going over there, getting a couple shrimp tacos. You want me to bring you back something?"

"No, I'm good. Take a rover with you."

"Roger that."

On the way back to the D bureau she stopped in the break room and dumped the coffee in the sink, rinsed out the cup, and put it on the drying rack. She then pulled a rover out of the charging rack in the bureau and headed out the back door of the station to her city car. The middle-watch chill had set in and she got her suit jacket out of the trunk and put it on before driving out of the lot.

The Relic was still parked at the food truck when Ballard arrived. As a sergeant, Dvorek rode in a solo car, so he had a tendency to hang with other officers on break for the company.

"Sally Ride," he said, when he noticed Ballard studying the chalkboard menu.

"What's up, Sarge?" she said.

"Halfway through another night in paradise."

"Yeah."

Ballard ordered one shrimp taco and doused it liberally with one of the hot sauces from the condiment table. She took it over to Dvorek's black-and-white, where he was leaning against the front fender and finishing his own meal. Two other patrol officers were eating inside their car parked in front of his.

Ballard leaned against the fender next to him.

"Whatcha get?" Dvorek asked.

"Shrimp," Ballard said. "I only order off the blackboard. Means it's fresh, right? They don't know what they'll have until they buy it at the docks. Then they write it down."

"If you think so."

"I need to think so."

She took her first bite. It was good and there was no fishy taste. She inspected the shrimp inside the taco and it looked like it had been cleaned.

"Not bad," she said.

"I had the fish special," Dvorek said. "It's probably going to take me off the street as soon as it gets down into the lower track."

"TMI, Sergeant. But speaking of coming in off the street, what did that guy Bosch want with you?"

"You saw him?"

"I caught him snooping in the files in the D bureau."

"Yeah, he's kind of desperate. Looking for any angle on a case he's working."

"In Hollywood? I thought he worked for San Fernando PD these days."

"He does. But this is a private thing he's working. A girl who got killed here about nine years ago. I was the one who found the body, but damn if I could remember much that helped him."

Ballard took another bite and started nodding. She asked the next question with her mouth full of shrimp and tortilla.

"Who was the girl?" she asked.

"A runaway. Name was Daisy. She was fifteen and putting it out on the street. Sad case. One night she got in the wrong car. I found her body in an alley behind the Pantages. Came in on an anonymous call—I do remember that."

"Was that a street name?"

"No, the real thing. Daisy Clayton."

"Was Cesar Rivera working the sex table back then?"

"Cesar? I'm not sure. We're talking nine years ago. He coulda been on sex then."

"Well, did you remember Cesar having anything to do with the case back then? Bosch picked his file cabinet."

Dvorek shrugged.

"I found the body and called it in, Renée—that's it," he said. "I had no part in it after that. I remember they sent me down to the end of the alley to string tape and keep people out. I was a slick sleeve back then."

Uniformed cops got a hash mark on their sleeves for every five years of service. Back then, the Relic was a near-rookie. Ballard nodded and asked her last question.

"Did Bosch ask you anything I didn't just ask?"

"Yeah, but it wasn't about her. He asked about Daisy's

boyfriend and whether I ever saw him on the street again after the murder."

"Who was the boyfriend?"

"Just another runaway throwaway. I knew him as Speedy. Bosch said his name was Adam something. I forget. But the answer was no, I never saw that one after that."

"What was their relationship?"

"They ran in a group. You know, for protection. Girl like that, she needed a guy out there. Like a pimp. She worked the street, he watched out for her, and they split the profits. Except that night, he dropped the ball. Too bad for her."

Ballard nodded. She guessed that Bosch wanted to talk to Adam/Speedy as the person who would know the most about who Daisy Clayton knew and interacted with, and where she went on the last night of her life.

He could also have been a suspect.

"You know about Bosch, right?" Dvorek asked.

"Yeah," Ballard said. "He worked in the division way back when."

"You know the stars out on the front sidewalk?"

"'Course."

There were memorial stars on the sidewalk in front of Hollywood Station honoring officers from the division who were killed in the line of duty.

"Well, there's one out there," Dvorek said. "Lieutenant Harvey Pounds. The story on him was he was Bosch's L-T when he worked here, and he got abducted and died of a heart attack when he was being tortured on a case Bosch was working."

Ballard had never heard the story before.

"Anybody ever go down for it?" she asked.

"Depends on who you talk to," Dvorek said. "It's supposedly cleared-other, but it's another mystery in the big bad city. The word was that something Bosch did got the guy killed."

"Cleared-other" was a designation for a case that was officially closed but without an arrest or prosecution.

"Supposedly the file on it is sealed. High Jingo."

"High Jingo" was LAPD-speak for when a case involved department politics. The kind of case where a career could be diverted by a wrong move.

The information on Bosch was interesting but not on point. Before Ballard could think of a question that would steer Dvorek back toward the Daisy Clayton case, his rover squawked and he took a call from the watch office. Ballard listened as Lieutenant Munroe dispatched him to a Beachwood Canyon address to supervise a team responding to a domestic dispute.

"Gotta go," he said as he balled up the foil his tacos had come in. "Unless you want to ride along and back me up."

It was said in jest, Ballard knew. The Relic didn't need backup from the late show detective.

"I'll see you back at the barn," she said. "Unless that goes sideways and you need a detective."

"Roger that," he said.

3

D
ayside detectives were all about traffic patterns.
Most days the majority of daysiders got to the
bureau before six a.m. so they could split by midafternoon, missing the traffic swell both coming and
going. Ballard counted on this when she decided she was
going to ask Cesar Rivera about the Daisy Clayton case.
She spent the remainder of her shift waiting on his arrival
by pulling up and studying the electronic records available on the murder of Daisy Clayton.

The murder book, a blue binder full of printed reports
and photos, was still the bible of a homicide investigation
in the Los Angeles Police Department, but as the world
turned digital, so did the department. Using her detective
services password, Ballard was able to access many of the
reports and photos from the case that had been scanned
into the department's digital archives. Most important,
she was able to view the chronological record, which
was always the spine of the case, a narrative of all moves
made by investigators assigned to the case.

Ballard determined immediately that the nine-year-
old murder was officially classified as a cold case and

assigned to the Open-Unsolved Unit, which was part
of the elite Robbery-Homicide Division working out of
headquarters downtown. Ballard had once been assigned
to the RHD and knew many of the detectives and associated players. Included in that number was her former
lieutenant, who pushed her up against a wall and tried to
force himself on her in a bathroom at a squad Christmas
party three years earlier. Her rejection of him and sub-
sequent complaint and internal investigation was what
landed her on the night shift at Hollywood Division.
The complaint was determined to be unfounded because
her own partner at the time did not back her up, even
though he had witnessed the altercation. Department
administrators determined that it would be for the good
of all involved to separate Ballard and Lieutenant Robert
Olivas. He stayed put in RHD and Ballard was moved
out, the message to her clear. Olivas got by unscathed,
while she went from an elite unit to a posting no one
ever applied or volunteered for, a slot normally reserved
for the department's freaks and fuckups.

In recent months, the irony of this was not lost on Ballard as the country and the Hollywood entertainment
industry in particular were awash in scandals involving
sexual harassment and worse. The chief of police even
instituted a task force to handle all the claims pouring in
from Hollywood, many of them decades old. Of course,
the chief's task force was composed of RHD detectives,
and Olivas was one of its supervisors.

The history with Olivas was not far from Ballard's
mind as her curiosity about Bosch and the case he was

working sent her into the department's digital channels. She knew that her snooping around on the Daisy Clayton case could come to the attention of her nemesis and he might attempt to do something about it.

The threat was there but it wasn't enough to stop her. She wasn't afraid of Olivas when he followed her into the bathroom at the Christmas party three years ago; she shoved him back and he fell into a bathtub. She wasn't afraid of him now.

She scrolled to the end of the chrono first in order to see the latest moves on the case, if any. She quickly learned that outside of annual due diligence checks, the investigation had largely been dormant for eight years, until it was assigned six months earlier to a cold case detective named Lucia Soto. Ballard didn't know Soto but she knew of her. She was the youngest female detective ever assigned to RHD, beating the record Ballard had previously held by being eight months younger when appointed.

"Lucky Lucy," Ballard said out loud.

Ballard also knew that Soto was currently assigned to the Hollywood Sex Harassment task force because the powers that be in the department—mostly white men— knew that putting as many women on the task force as possible was a prudent move. Soto, who already had a media profile and nickname because of an act of heroism that led to her RHD posting, was often used as the face of the task force when it came to press conferences and other media interactions.

This knowledge now gave Ballard pause. She put

together a quick chronology. Six months earlier, Soto either requested or was assigned to the unsolved Daisy Clayton case. Shortly after, she was reassigned from the Open-Unsolved Unit to the harassment task force. Then Bosch shows up at Hollywood Station to ask questions about the case and attempt to get a look at the files of a sex crimes detective.

There was a connection there that Ballard didn't yet have. She quickly found it and started to understand things better when she conducted a new search of the department database and called up all cases in which Bosch was listed as having been a lead investigator. She zeroed in on the last case he handled before leaving the department. It was a multiple-victim murder involving an arson of an apartment building in which several victims, including children, died of smoke inhalation. On several of the reports associated with the case Bosch's partner was listed as Lucia Soto.

Ballard now had the connection—Soto took the Clayton case on and then somehow drew her former partner Bosch into it, even though he was no longer with the department. But Ballard didn't have the cause, meaning there was no explanation as to why Soto would go outside the department for help with the investigation, especially when she was moved out of Open-Unsolved for the task force.

Unable to answer that question for the moment, Ballard went back to the case files and started reviewing the investigation from the start. Daisy Clayton was deemed a chronic runaway who repeatedly left her own home as well as the temporary group homes and shelters she was placed in by the Department of Children and Family Services. Each time she ran, she ended up on the streets of Hollywood, joining other runaways and throwaways in homeless camps and squats in abandoned structures. She abused alcohol and drugs and sold herself on the streets.

The first record of a police interaction with Daisy was nineteen months before her death. It was the first of several arrests for drugs, loitering, and solicitation for prostitution. Because of her age, the early arrests only resulted in her being returned to her single mother, Elizabeth, or to DCF authorities. But nothing seemed to stop the cycle of her returning to the streets and of being under the influence of Adam Sands, a nineteen-year-old former runaway with his own history of drugs and crime.

Sands was interviewed at length by the original investigators on the case and was eliminated as a potential suspect through confirmation of an alibi. He was being held in the Hollywood Division jail at the time of Daisy Clayton's murder.

Cleared as a suspect, Sands was questioned extensively about the victim's routines and relationships. He claimed to have no information on who she had met with on the night of her murder. He revealed that her routine was to loiter near a shopping plaza on Hollywood Boulevard near Western Avenue that included a mini-market and a liquor store. She would solicit men as they were leaving the stores and then have sex with them in their cars after they drove into one of the many nearby alleys for privacy. Sands said he often stood lookout for her during the transactions but on the night in question he had been grabbed by police on a warrant for not appearing in court on a misdemeanor drug charge.

Daisy was left on her own at the shopping plaza and her body was found the next night in one of the alleys she used for her tricks. The body was found nude and had been cleaned with bleach. None of the victim's clothes were ever found. Detectives determined that as many as twenty hours passed between the time she was last seen at the shopping plaza soliciting johns and when police received an anonymous call about a body being seen in an alley and Officer Dvorek was dispatched to roll on the call. The missing hours were never accounted for but it was clear from the bleaching of the body that Daisy had been taken somewhere and then used and murdered, and her body was carefully cleaned of any evidence that might lead to her killer.

The one clue that the original detectives puzzled over throughout the investigation was a bruise on the body that they were convinced was a mark left by the killer. It was a circle two inches in diameter on the upper right hip of the body. Within the circle was a crossword with the letters A-S-P arranged horizontally and vertically with the S in common.

The circle around the crossword appeared to possibly be a snake eating itself but the blurring of the bruising in the tissue made this impossible to confirm. Detectives believed the mark might have come from some sort of stamp or weapon. Many hours of investigative work were expended on its meaning and application but no definitive conclusion was reached. The case was originally investigated by two homicide detectives assigned to the Hollywood Division and then reassigned to Wilshire Division when the regional homicide teams were consolidated and Hollywood lost its fabled murder unit. The investigators' names were King and Carswell, and Ballard knew neither of them.

Time of death was established during the autopsy at ten hours after the victim was last seen and ten hours before the body was found.

The coroner's report listed the cause of death as manual strangulation. It further defined this conclusion by stating that marks left on the victim's neck by the killer's hands indicated that she was strangled from behind, possibly while being sexually assaulted. Tissue damage in both the vagina and anus was listed as both pre- and postmortem. The victim's fingernails were also removed postmortem, a move by the killer viewed as an attempt to make sure no biological evidence was left behind.

The body also showed postmortem abrasions and scratches that investigators believed occurred during an effort to clean the victim with a stiff brush and bleach, which was found in all orifices as well as the mouth and throat and ear canals of the victim. This led the medical examiner to conclude that the body had been submerged in bleach during this cleaning process.

This finding coupled with the time of death led investigators to conclude that Daisy had been taken off the street and to a hotel room or other location by the killer where a bleach bath could be prepared for cleaning the body.

"He's a planner," Ballard said out loud.

The conclusions about the bleach led the original investigators to spend much of their time during the initial days of the investigation on a thorough canvass of every motel and hotel in the Hollywood area that offered direct access to rooms off the parking lot. Photos of Daisy were shown to employees on all shifts, housekeepers were quizzed with regard to any reports of a strong odor of bleach, trash dumpsters were searched for bleach containers. Nothing came of the effort. The location of the murder was never determined, and without a crime scene, the case was handicapped from the start. Six months into the investigation the case went cold with no new leads and no suspects.

Ballard saved the crime scene photos for last because she knew they would be difficult to view. She wasn't wrong. The victim's age, the marks on her body and neck showing the overwhelming strength of her killer, her final naked repose on a spread of trash on the dirty asphalt...it all drew a sense of horror in Ballard, a sad empathy for this girl and what she had been through. Ballard had never been a detective who could leave the work in a drawer at the end of shift. She carried it with her and it was her empathy that fueled her.

Before being assigned to the night beat, Ballard had been working toward a specialization in sexually motivated homicide at RHD. Her then-partner, Ken Chastain, was one of the premier investigators of sex killings in the department. Both had taken classes from and been mentored by Detective David Lambkin, long considered the department expert, until he pulled the pin and left the city for the Pacific Northwest.

That pursuit was largely sidelined by her transfer to the late show, but now as she reviewed the Clayton files, she saw a sexual predator hiding behind the words and reports, a predator unidentified for nine years now, and she felt a deep tug inside. It was the thing that went way back to her first thoughts of being a cop and a hunter of men who hurt women and leave them like trash in the alley. In her mind, she already gave this one a name—the Bleacher—and she wanted in on whatever it was that Harry Bosch was doing.

Ballard was pulled out of these thoughts when she heard voices. She looked up from the screen and over the workstation wall. She saw two detectives taking off their suit jackets and draping them over their chairs, readying for a new day of work.

One of them was Cesar Rivera.

4

Ballard packed up her things and left her borrowed workstation. She first went into the print room to gather the reports she had fed into the communal printer after she had typed them up earlier. The detective squad lieutenant was old school and still liked hard-copy reports from her in the morning, even though she also filed them digitally. She separated the reports on the death investigation and the earlier burglary call, stapled them, and then walked them to the in-box on the desk of the lieutenant's adjutant so they were ready for his arrival. She then sauntered over to the sex crimes section and came up behind Rivera as he was sitting at his station and preparing for the day by dumping an airline-size bottle of whiskey into a mug of coffee. She didn't let on that she had seen this when she spoke.

"Hail, Cesar."

Rivera jolted a bit in his seat, afraid his morning routine had been seen. He swiveled his chair around but relaxed when he saw it was Ballard. He knew she would not make any waves.

"Renée," he said. "What's up, girl? You got something for me?"

Ballard let the *girl* go. It was the least of the infractions that occurred around the department.

"No, nothing," she said. "Quiet night."

She came around and leaned an elbow on the cubicle partition.

"So what's up?" Rivera asked.

"About to leave," Ballard said. "I was wondering, though. You know a guy used to work out of here named Harry Bosch? He worked homicide."

She pointed to the corner of the room where the homicide squad was once located. It was now the Crimes Against Persons section.

"Before my time," Rivera said. "I mean, I know who he is—everybody does, I think. But no, I never dealt with the guy. Why?"

"He was in the station this morning," Ballard said.

"You mean on graveyard?"

"Yeah, he said he came in to talk to Dvorek about an old homicide. But I found him looking through your cabinets."

She pointed toward the long row of file cabinets running along the wall. Rivera shook his head in confusion.

"My cabinets?" Rivera said. "What the fuck?"

"How long have you been at Hollywood Division, Cesar?" Ballard asked.

"Seven years, what's that got to—"

"You know the name Daisy Clayton? She was murdered in '09. Classified as sexually motivated."

Rivera shook his head.

"That was before my time here," he said. "I was at Hollenbeck then."

He got up and walked over to the row of file cabinets. He pulled a set of keys out of his pocket and opened the top drawer of his four-drawer stack.

"Locked now," he said. "Was locked when I left last night."

"I locked it after he left," Ballard said.

She said nothing about finding the bent paper clip in the drawer.

"Isn't Bosch retired?" Rivera said. "How'd he get in here?"

"He used his friendship with Lieutenant Munroe to get in and waited for Dvorek to come in off patrol," Ballard said. "He wandered, and that's when I saw him looking in the files. I was working over in the corner and he didn't see me."

"He's the one who mentioned the Daisy case?"

"Daisy Clayton. No, actually I talked to Dvorek about what Bosch wanted to talk to him about and he told me about Clayton. Dvorek was first officer on scene with her. Bosch wanted to talk about the case."

"I take it it's still open."

"Yes. Hollywood had it initially, now it's assigned to Open-Unsolved downtown."

Rivera walked back to his desk but stayed standing while he grabbed his coffee cup and took a long drink out of it. He then abruptly pulled the cup away from his mouth.

"Shit, I know what he was doing," he said.

"What?" Ballard asked.

There was a sense of urgency in her voice.

"I got here just as they were reorganizing and moving homicide over to Wilshire Division," Rivera said. "The sex table was expanding and they brought me in. Me and Sandoval were add-ons, not replacements. We both came from Hollenbeck, see."

"Okay," Ballard said.

"So the lieutenant assigned me that cabinet, all four drawers, and gave me the key. But when I opened the top drawer to put stuff in there, it was full. All four drawers were full. Same with Sandoval—his four were filled up as well."

"Filled with what? You mean with files?"

"No, every drawer was filled with shake cards. Stacks and stacks of them crammed in there. The homicide guys and the other detectives had decided to keep the old cards after the department went digital. They stuck them in the file drawers."

Ballard knew that Rivera was talking about what were officially called field interview cards. They were 3 x 5 cards that were filled out by officers when they encountered people on the streets and while they were on patrol. The front of each card was a form with specific identifiers regarding the person interviewed, such as name, date of birth, address, gang affiliation, tattoos, and known associates. The back of each card was blank and that was where the officer could write any ancillary information about the person being interviewed.

Officers carried stacks of blank FI cards on their person or in their patrol cars—Ballard had always kept hers under the sun visor in her car when she had worked patrol in Pacific Division. At the end of shift, the cards were turned in to the divisional watch commander and the information on them was entered by clerical staff into a searchable database. Should a name that was run through the database produce a match, the inquiring officer or detective would have a ready set of facts, addresses, and known associates to start with.

The American Civil Liberties Union had long protested the department's use of the cards and the collection of information from citizens who had not committed crimes, calling the practice unlawful search and seizure and routinely referring to the unwarranted Q&As as shakedowns. The department had fended off all legal attempts to stop the practice, and many of the rank and file referred to the 3 x 5 cards as shake cards, a not-so-subtle dig at the ACLU.

"Why were they keeping them?" Ballard asked. "Everything was put into the database and would be easier to find there."

"I don't know," Rivera said. "They didn't do it that way at Hollenbeck."

"So, what did you do, clear them out?"

"Yeah, me and Sandy emptied the drawers."

"You threw them all out?"

"No, if I've learned anything in this department, it's not to be the guy who fucks up. We boxed them and took them to storage, let it be somebody else's problem."

"What storage?"

"Across the lot."

Ballard nodded. She knew he meant the structure at the south end of the station's parking lot. It was a single-level building that had once been a city utilities office but had been turned over to the station when more space was needed. The building was largely unused now. A gym for officers' use and a padded martial arts room had been set up in two of the larger rooms but the smaller offices were empty or used for nonevidentiary storage.

"So, this was seven years ago?" she asked.

"More or less," Rivera said. "We didn't move it all at once. I cleared one drawer out and when it got filled and I had to go down to the next, I'd clear that one. It went like that. Took about a year."

"So, what makes you think that Bosch was looking for shake cards last night?"

Rivera shrugged.

"There would have been shake cards in there from the time of the murder you're talking about, right?"

"But the info on the shake cards is in the database?"

"Supposedly. But what do you put in the search window? See what I mean? There's a flaw. If he wanted to see who was hanging around Hollywood at the time of the murder, how do you search the database for that?"

Ballard nodded in agreement but knew that there were many ways to search the database to pull up info on field interviews by geography and time frame. She thought Rivera was wrong about that but probably right about

Bosch. He was looking for the shake cards but he probably had a different purpose in mind.

"Well," she said. "I'm out of here. Have a good one. Stay safe."

"Yeah, you too, Ballard," Rivera said.

Ballard left the detective bureau and went up to the women's locker room on the second floor. She changed out of her suit and into her sweats. Her plan was to head out to Venice, pick up her dog, and then carry her tent and a paddleboard out to the beach. In the afternoon, after she had rested and considered her approach, she'd deal with Bosch.

The morning sun blistered her eyes as she crossed the parking lot behind the station. She walked past her van and continued on to the old utilities building. She entered and found a couple other denizens of the late show working out before heading home after the morning rush hour.

She threw a mock salute at them and went down a hallway that led to former city offices now used for indiscriminate storage. The first room she checked contained items recovered in one of her own cases. The year before, she had taken down a burglar who had filled a motel room with property either stolen from the homes he broke into or bought with the money and credit cards he had stolen. Now a year later, much of it had still not been claimed and would remain in storage until the division organized an open house for victims as a last chance for them to claim their property.

The next room down was stacked with cardboard boxes containing old case files that for various reasons had to be kept. Ballard looked around here and moved several boxes in order to get to others. Soon enough, she opened a dusty box that was filled with FI cards. She had hit pay dirt.

Twenty minutes later she had culled twelve boxes of FI cards and lined them along the wall in the hallway. By individually sampling cards from each of the boxes she was able to determine that the cards spanned the years from 2006, when the digitizing initiative began, to 2010, when the homicide section was moved out of Hollywood Division. With the homicide detectives gone, there was no one in the bureau who felt the need to keep the original cards.

Ballard estimated that each of the boxes held up to a thousand cards. It would take several hours to comb through them all thoroughly. She wondered if that was what Bosch was expecting to do, or if he was planning a more precise search for one card or one night in particular. Perhaps the night Daisy Clayton was taken off the street.

Ballard knew she wouldn't know the answer until she asked Bosch.

She left a note on the row of boxes in the hallway, saying that the boxes were on hold for her. She returned to the parking lot and got into her van after checking the straps holding her boards to the roof racks. Shortly after she had been assigned to Hollywood Division and word leaked that she was involved in an internal harassment investigation, there were some in the division who attempted to retaliate against her. Sometimes it was basic bullying, sometimes it went deeper. One morning at the end of her shift, when she stopped her van at the station lot's electric gate, her paddleboard slid forward off the roof and crashed against the gate, splintering the nose's fiberglass. She repaired the board herself and started checking the rack straps every morning after her shift.

She took La Brea down to the 10 freeway and headed west toward the beach. She waited until a few minutes after eight o'clock to call the number for RHD that she still had programmed in her phone. A clerk answered and Ballard asked for Lucy Soto. She said the name with a clipped familiarity that imparted the idea that this was a cop-to-cop call. The transfer was made without question.

"This is Detective Soto."

"This is Detective Ballard, Hollywood Division."

There was a pause before Soto responded.

"I know who you are," she said. "How can I help you, Detective Ballard?"

Ballard was used to detectives she didn't know personally knowing about her. With female detectives, there was always an awkward moment. They either admired Ballard for her perseverance in the department or believed her actions had made their own jobs more difficult. Ballard always had to find out which it was, and Soto's opener gave no hint as to which camp she was in.

Her repeating Ballard's name out loud might have been a move to let someone like a partner or supervisor on the task force know who she was talking to.

Not being able to read Soto yet, Ballard just pressed on.

"I work the late show here," she said. "Some nights it keeps me running, some nights not so much. My L-T likes me to have a hobby case to kind of keep me busy."

"I don't understand," Soto said. "What's this have to do with me? I'm sort of in the middle of—"

"Yeah, I know you're busy. You're on the harassment task force. That's why I'm calling. One of your cold cases—that you're not working because of the task force—I was wondering if I could take a whack at it."

"Which case, Ballard?"

"Daisy Clayton. Fifteen-year-old murdered up here in—"

"I know the case. What makes you so interested?"

"It was a big case here at the time. I heard some blue suiters talking about it, pulled up what I could on the box, and got interested. It looked like with this task force thing you weren't doing much with it at the moment."

"And you want to give it a shot."

"I make no promises but, yeah, I'd like to do some work on it. I would keep you fully in the loop. It's still your case. I'd just do some street work."

Ballard was on the freeway but not moving. Her weeding through the boxes in the storage room had pushed her into the heart of rush hour. She knew the morning breeze would also be in full effect on the coast and she'd be paddling against it and the chop it would kick up. She was missing her window.

"It's nine years later," Soto said. "I'm not sure the street's going to produce anything. Especially on grave-yard. You'll be spinning your wheels."

"Well, maybe," Ballard said. "But they're my wheels to spin. You okay with this or not?"

There was another long pause. Enough time for Ballard to move the van about five feet.

"There's something you should know," Soto said. "There's somebody else looking into it. Somebody outside the department."

"Oh, yeah?" Ballard said. "Who's that?"

"My old partner. His name's Harry Bosch. He's retired now but he...he needs the work."

"Okay. Anything else I should know? Was this one of his cases?"

"No. But he knows the victim's mother. He's doing it for her."

"Good to know."

Ballard was now getting a better sense of the lay of the land. It was the true purpose of her call. Permission to work the case was the least of her concerns.

It was now time to end the call.

"If I come up with anything, I'll feed it to you," Ballard said. "And I'll let you get back to the reckoning."

Ballard thought she heard a muffled laugh.

"Hey, Ballard?" Soto then added quietly. "I said I knew who you were. I also know who Olivas is. I mean,

I work with him. I want you to know I appreciate what you did and I know you paid a price. I just wanted to say that."

Ballard nodded to herself.

"That's good to know," she said. "I'll be in touch."

BOSCH

5

From the San Fernando Courthouse it was only a block's walk back to the old jail where Bosch did his file work. He covered the distance quickly, a spring in his step caused by the search warrant in his hand. Judge Atticus Finch Landry had read it and signed it while Bosch had waited outside his chambers in the courtroom. Bosch now had forty-eight hours to execute the warrant and hopefully find the bullet that would lead to a match that would lead to an arrest and the closing of another case.

He took the shortcut through the city's Public Works yard to the back door of the old jail. He pulled the key to the padlock as he moved toward the former drunk tank, where the open-case files were kept on steel shelves. He found that he had left the lock open and silently chastised himself. It was a breach of his own as well as departmental protocol. The files were to be kept locked up at all times. And Bosch liked to keep the matters on his desk secure at all times too, even during a forty-minute search-warrant run to the courthouse next door.

He moved behind his makeshift desk—an old wooden door set across two stacks of file boxes—and sat down.

Immediately, he saw the twisted paper clip sitting there on top of his closed laptop.

He stared at it. He had not put it there.

"You forgot that."

Bosch looked up. The woman—the detective—from the night before at Hollywood Station was straddling the old bench that ran between the freestanding shelves full of case files. He could not have seen her coming into the cell. He looked over at the open door where the padlock dangled from its chain.

"Ballard, right?" he said. "Good to know I'm not going crazy—I thought I had locked up."

"I let myself in," Ballard said. "Lock picking one-oh-one."

"It's a good skill to have. Meantime, I'm kind of busy here. Just got a search warrant I need to figure out how to execute without my suspect finding out. What do you want, Detective Ballard?"

"I want in."

"In?"

"Daisy Clayton."

Bosch considered her for a moment. She was attractive, maybe midthirties, and was wearing off-duty clothes. The night before, she was in a sharp-cut suit that made her seem more formidable—a must in the LAPD, where Bosch knew female detectives were often treated like office secretaries.

Ballard also had a deep tan, which to Bosch was at odds with the idea that someone who worked graveyard would need to sleep during the day and avoid the sun. But most of all he was impressed that it had been only twelve hours since she had surprised him at the file cabinets in the Hollywood detective bureau and she already appeared to have caught up to him and what he was doing.

"I talked to your old partner, Lucy," Ballard said. "She gave me her blessing. It is a Hollywood case, after all."

"Was—till RHD took it," Bosch said. "They have standing now, not Hollywood."

"And what's your standing? You're out of the LAPD. Doesn't seem to be any link to the town of San Fernando that I could see in the book."

In his capacity as an SFPD reserve officer for the past three years, Bosch had largely been working on a backlog on cold cases of all kinds—murders, rapes, assaults. But the work was part time.

"They give me a lot of freedom up here," Bosch said. "I work these cases and I also work my own. Daisy Clayton's one of my own. You could say I have a vested interest. That's my standing."

"And I have twelve boxes of shake cards at Hollywood Station," Ballard said.

Bosch nodded. He was even more impressed. She had somehow figured out exactly what he had gone to Hollywood for. As he studied her, he decided it wasn't all tan. She had a mix of races in her skin. He guessed that she was probably Polynesian.

"I figure between the two of us, we could get through them in a couple nights," Ballard said.

There was the offer. She wanted in and would give Bosch what he was looking for in trade.

"The shake cards are a long shot," he said. "Truth is, I've run the string out on the case. I was hoping there might be something there."

"That's surprising," Ballard said. "I heard you're the kind of guy who never lets the string run out."

Bosch didn't know what to say to that. He shrugged.

Ballard got up and walked toward him down the aisle between the shelves.

"Sometimes it's slow, sometimes it isn't," she said. "I'm going to start looking through the cards tonight. Between calls. Anything in particular I should look for?"

Bosch paused but knew he needed to make a decision. Trust her or keep her on the outside.

"Vans," he said. "Look for work vans, guys who carry chemicals maybe."

"For transporting her," she said.

"For the whole thing."

"It said in the book the guy took her home or to a motel. Some place with a bathtub. For the bleaching."

Bosch shook his head.

"No, he didn't use a bathtub," he said.

She stared at him, waiting, not asking the obvious question of how he knew there was no bathtub used.

"All right, come with me," he finally said.

He got up and led her out of the cell and back to the door to the Public Works yard.

"You looked at the book and the photos, right?" he said.

"Yes," she said. "Everything that was digitized."

They walked into the yard, which was a large open-air

square surrounded by walls. There were four bays, where equipment was stored and repaired. Bosch led Ballard into one of these.

"You saw the mark on the body?"

"The A-S-P?"

"Right. But they got the meaning of it wrong. The original detectives. They went down a spiral with it and it was all wrong."

He went to a workbench and reached up to a large translucent plastic tub with a blue snap on top. He brought it down and held it out to her.

"Twenty-five-gallon container," Bosch said. "Daisy was five-two, a hundred and five pounds. Small. He put her in one of these, then put in the bleach as needed. He didn't use a bathtub."

Ballard studied the container. Bosch's explanation was plausible but not conclusive.

"That's a theory," she said.

"No theory," he said.

He put the container down on the floor so he could unsnap the top. He then lifted the tub up and angled it so she could see into it. He reached inside and pointed to a manufacturer's seal stamped into the plastic at the bottom. It was a two-inch circle with the A-S-P reading horizontally and vertically in the center.

"A-S-P," he said. "American Storage Products or American Soft Plastics. Same company, two names. The killer put her in one of these. He didn't need a bathtub or a motel. One of these and a van."

Ballard reached into the container and ran a finger

over the manufacturer's seal. Bosch knew she was drawing the same conclusion he had. The logo was stamped into the plastic on the underside of the tub, creating a ridged impression on the inside. If Daisy's skin was pressed against the ridges, the logo would have left its mark.

Ballard pulled her arm out and looked up from the tub to Bosch.

"How'd you figure this out?" she asked.

"I thought like he did," Bosch said.

"Let me guess, these are untraceable."

"They make them in Gardena, ship them everywhere, sell them online. No trace possible."

"That would be too easy."

"Yeah."

Bosch snapped the top back on the tub and was about to put it back up on the high shelf.

"Can I take it?" Ballard asked.

Bosch turned to her. He knew he could replace it and knew she could easily get her own. He guessed it was a move to draw him further into a partnership. If he gave her something, then it meant they were working together.

He handed the tub over.

"It's yours," he said.

"Thank you," she said.

She looked at the open gate to the Public Works yard.

"Okay, so I start tonight on shakes," she said.

Bosch nodded.

"Where were they?" he asked.

"In storage," Ballard said. "Nobody wanted to throw them out."

"I figured. It was smart."

"Right. Well, I'm gonna go. Might even go in early to get started."

"Happy hunting. If I can get by, I will. But I have this search warrant and forty-eight hours to execute."

"Right."

"Otherwise, call me if you find something."

He reached into a pocket and produced a business card with his cell number on it.

"Copy that," she said.

Ballard walked off, carrying the container in front of her by holding it by indented grips on either side. As Bosch watched, she made a smooth U-turn and came back to him.

"Lucy Soto said you know Daisy's mother," she said. "Is that the standing you said you had?"

"I guess you could say that," Bosch said. "When did you talk to Soto?"

Ballard realized that she had made a mistake revealing her conversation with Soto. She quickly tried to cover.

"Oh, I just called her to get permission to pull files on the case," she said. "Where's the mother—if I want to talk to her?"

"My house. I can arrange it."

"You live with her?"

"She's staying with me. It's temporary."

"Okay. Got it."

Ballard turned again and walked off. Bosch watched her go. She made no further U-turns.

Real Men or
Real Teachers?